CHARTER
FOR
MURDER

A medieval monastic murder mystery
set in a Chaucerian world

by

Edward Fennell

The First in the 'Gentil Knight' series

INSERTS PUBLISHING

20 Egbert Road, Winchester
Hampshire SO23 7EB

Copyright © Edward Fennell 2021

Fennell, Edward, Charter for Murder,
The First in the 'Gentil Knight' series Kindle Edition.
Cover design © Edward Fennell 2021
Cover photography ©Edward Fennell

ISBN: 978-1-9196161-1-7
Print version: 2021-06-29

*Cover illustration: A corbel from Hyde Abbey now in
St. Bartholomew Church, Winchester – Image by the author*

For ALYS

In Memory of Geoffrey Chaucer and also his
contemporaries now buried in the 'Unnamed Grave' in the
Church of St. Bartholomew, Hyde, Winchester within the
historic precincts of Hyde Abbey

Edward Fennell is a journalist and writer specialising in legal and business affairs. For over thirty years he contributed to The Times law pages and has written a number of law firms' and chambers' histories. He lives in Winchester and conceived *Hyde900*, a community organisation dedicated to telling the story of Hyde Abbey. He was significantly involved in the BBC 2 TV documentary *The Search for Alfred the Great*.

AUTHOR'S FOREWORD

The setting for *Charter for Murder* is principally Hyde Abbey, the final resting place of King Alfred the Great and for over four hundred years a large and important monastery just outside Winchester. It was razed to the ground during the dissolution of the monasteries. The remains of King Alfred and his family were shattered and scattered across the site in the late 18th century.

The date of *Charter for Murder* is the Spring of 1381 – the year of the Peasants' Revolt – and the story features characters inspired by the Prologue to Geoffrey Chaucer's *Canterbury Tales*, written a short time later.

Aside from the chapter titles there is no use of 'Chaucerian language'. A number of historical people, places and events are referenced. For more see the Historical Notes at the back of this book and visit the website **The World of the Gentil Knight www.gentilknight.co.uk**

With thanks to friends and colleagues in Hyde900, the University of Winchester, the English Project, Winchester College, and all those who have helped to assemble this text and ideas for publication and launch including particularly David Eno, Peter Todd, Tony Hill, Joe Low, Nigel Bradshaw, Rose Burns and Professor Christopher Mulvey.

Edward Fennell
Winchester
Summer 2021
Email: edward.fennell@yahoo.co.uk

CHARTER FOR MURDER: THE COMPAIGNYE

Characters in **bold** feature in the Prologue to the Canterbury Tales by Geoffrey Chaucer. Those in *italics* and **bold** are historical figures.

THE 'GENTIL KNIGHT'S PARTY

Sir Matthew de Somborne – a returned crusader, the **Gentil Knight**

Damian – Sir Matthew's son and **Squire**,

Osric – Sir Mathew's **Yeoman** (a rural factotum, 'with a brown visage')

IN WINCHESTER

Father Compton – the acting abbot of Hyde Abbey

Brother Thomas – his assistant, on attachment from Winchester Cathedral

Father Eynesham – **a Monk**, the cellarer of Hyde Abbey

Brother Peter – librarian and in charge of the scriptorium at Hyde Abbey

Brother Walter – the infirmarian at Hyde Abbey

Brother Michael – the porter on the abbey's Outer Court gate

Brother Timothy – his assistant, on attachment from Winchester Cathedral

Dr Aloysious Nafis – consultant **Doctor of Physic** to all Winchester's monasteries and convents

Prior Hugh – the senior figure at Winchester Cathedral and advisor to

William of Wykeham, the Bishop of Winchester

THE PILGRIMS AND THEIR FRIENDS AND ASSOCIATES

John Twyford – **The Clerk of Oxenford**

Madame Eglentyne – **Prioress** of Wintney Priory

Rector Lydezorde, Confessor to the Prioress and a **Nun's Priest**

Father Gregory – the **Nun's Priest**

Sister Avelina – a **Nun** at Wintney, assistant to Madame Eglentyne

Mistress Alison – A **'Wife of Bath'**, a businesswoman trading in textiles

Sergeant Henry – A **Sergeant of the Law**, a lawyer from St.Paul's in London

Sir Roger Odiham – A **Franklin**, a landowner and supporter of John of Gaunt,

Mildrede – a popular young lady in Hyde

Harry Bailey – the **Host** of the Tabard Inn, Southwark

William Gascoigne – a distinguished lawyer of the Temple, later Chief Justice of England

John of Gaunt, Duke of Lancaster, Uncle to King Richard II and a rival for power to William of Wykeham.

CHARTER FOR MURDER
CONTENTS

DAY FOUR: WINCHESTER/BASYNG/WINTNEY

DAY FIVE: GUILDFORD/LONDON

DAY SIX: THE TABARD & THE TEMPLE

CHAPTER 1
'De loved chivalRie'

I was home from the wars but too full of warfare to be at peace with my spirit or the world. I needed to resurrect my life and my family. My reputation was high but rested uncomfortably on my shoulders. I knew myself too well to be deceived by what others said about me.

By now I had not seen my wife, Matilda, nor son Damian, for almost five years. My engagement as a crusader had taken me from the north of Africa, to the eastern edge of the Mediterranean and then on to the boundaries of Prussia. But after one particularly bloody yet inconsequential battle in a remote part of Lithuania I resolved to come home. I made my apologies to the Emperor and he rewarded me well because I had done sterling service.

Sending ahead of my return and shipping out of Barfleur, I had proposed to Matilda and Damian that they should meet me in Southampton one month hence in March of the year of Our Lord 1381.

I knew from my compatriot brothers-in-arms who came and went like flotsam and jetsam in this endless war that England was not in a happy state.

Memories of the pestilence were still vivid. The young king, Richard, was hardly in control. The country folk were ground down and indignant at new taxes. My own estate, I suspected, would have to be put on a new footing. But all of those concerns were forgotten at the joy of seeing Damian, now twenty years old, in company with Osric, our seasoned yeoman, at the Bear Inn in Blue Anchor Lane near the Southampton dockside.

"But where is your mama, Damian," I asked having hugged the lad. "At home preparing festivities?"

Already he and Osric, alike, were in tears.

"I am sorry to say, my lord, that mistress has gone to the Lord," said Osric. "It was a month ago. An accident. Riding in the forest. Already she was with the Virgin Mother when we found her. Right was done by her. There was a large funeral in the Priory at Mottisfont.

1

It was shortly after that we heard of your coming home. I am so, so sorry."

What could I say or feel? So many times I had seen the deaths – massacres - of others. I had played my part and I was now sick of it. So now the finger of death was pointing at my own family. Grief and numbness, both together, flooded through me. I hugged Damian tighter. I had been a young father to him; Matilda an even younger mother. But I had been distracted by the allure of war and the glory of crusade. And maybe my love for his mother had gone stale. But I had resolved to make recompense for both. And now destiny was laughing at my vanity and arrogance.

I will say no more about this raw start to my return except that it confirmed my deepest fear. Divine justice was beginning to repay me for my own sins. I might have fought under the Cross but I could not claim that I fought for its compassion. All I could now hope for was its forgiveness.

I realised then that to start my life anew I must atone for my crimes and misdeeds. No court on earth would ever arraign me or call me to account. On the contrary I would be lauded and acclaimed for my triumphs in battle and skill in the lists. Kings in foreign courts had toasted me at their high tables. And I had brought men to justice to pay the penalty for their crimes. But the judgement of heaven hereafter awaited my appearance. For that I must now begin to prepare and if I could not erase my memories at least I could do penance for them.

So I resolved to do like so many others when change is necessary. I would go on pilgrimage to the tomb of St Thomas at Canterbury and take Damian and Osric with me.

"Will you come, Damian? I need to know you again. And you, me. And gradually, in your own time you can recall your mother so I might do justice to her memory."

"Certainly, father. Willingly."

Damian was a handsome, fine lad. The sorrow of his mother's death still lay heavy but after the third week at home my presence

2

began to work on him even in the sadness. For years he had had a mother but no father. Now his mother was gone but father had returned. He had already gained some brief military experience himself away in France with the forces of the Duke of Lancaster. But now, with me by his side, a new life was on hand.

"And what about you, Osric? You seem to have filled in some of the gaps which I left in my negligence. Will you join us in this adventure?"

"Indeed, master. It's time I did some travelling on the roads. I have immersed myself in the greenwood too long. It would be good to see something new – and, of course," he added, "pay homage to the good saint."

And so it was agreed and a little over a month after I had arrived back in England, in early April, the three of us set off from my estate near King's Somborne for Winchester, just ten miles away. With so much to organise and so many people to see both for celebration and grieving I had not even time to have my clothing properly washed – my fustian was in a particularly poorly state. But I had no woman in my life to correct it. And I had quietly resolved not to wash it until my conscience felt clean. So only my horse was new, but even he was soberly fitted out. I was not intending going on pilgrimage in any finery.

Staying overnight at the Black Swan near the cathedral in Winchester we were shrived early the following morning and then spent several hours in prayer and reflection on our knees before the shrine of St. Swithun, the starting point for the long route to Canterbury. In the early afternoon we left Winchester from the north gate on the road to London but made just the very short journey to the abbey of Hyde in the city's outskirts, as old as the cathedral itself and the burial place of kings from ages past. I planned to spend our first night there and reacquaint myself with the abbot who I had forewarned of our coming.

But our arrival at the outer gate of this fine large abbey was not what I had expected. We had heard the commotion from a hundred paces away. The ordinary folk, many pilgrims like ourselves, were crammed, agitated, into the Forecourt. Standing in my stirrups I waved at the doorkeeper – a familiar figure from years past. "Brother Michael! Michael! It's me Sir Matthew – back from crusade. What's going on?"

Michael, the porter, was attempting to calm the crowd but glancing towards me a gratifying look of recognition crossed his face. "Sir Matthew! Welcome, welcome. I was told you were coming - but what a time to choose!"

We pushed our horses through the mass of people attracting looks of both respect and hostility. "Come through Sir Matthew – and your companions. The abbot – or rather Father Compton - will be pleased to see you. For this afternoon the most terrible thing has happened."

"What, Michael? – tell us," I demanded.

"Murder, sir. Dreadful murder. Our librarian, Brother Peter. Murdered this afternoon – and all is in dismay for no-one knows who did it. The murderer is still loose."

Moving through to the calmer atmosphere of the Outer Close we tied up the horses and went towards the Almoner's Hall. But suddenly a sound of clamour erupted and as we entered we could see a gang of abbey servants scurrying around as if chasing a rat. A monk whom I recognised as having been the cellarer, Father Eynesham, was shouting directions. "I think we've got him here," cried one of the men. "Yes, here we are – got you, you villain!"

A small, thin young man, heavily hooded, was hauled out from behind the curtain.

"Murderer! Murderer!" screamed a monk dressed as a cook.

"No! No! Not me!" shouted the young man.

"I'll take charge now," said the cellarer, asserting his authority and backing it up with the help of two of the burly brothers who grabbed the young man by his arms. "But let's take a look at you."

Pulling back the hood, the cellarer gasped.

"John! JOHN! What in heaven's name are you doing here? You're supposed to be at Oxford!"

CHAPTER 2
'For crewely the game is well begonne'

Dinner that evening in the abbot's dining room was a strained affair. As was the custom, a select group of the more distinguished visitors to the monastery had been invited to the private chamber for supper. But there was no abbot to greet us. I learned that my old acquaintance Abbot Pechy had recently died – chillingly on the same day as Matilda.

As yet no replacement had been found so instead it was the Prior, Father Compton, who was in charge for the time being. He was elderly and clearly having difficulty in finding his feet. I had made his acquaintance briefly before I had left for the crusades. He had struck me then as being without great capacity so it was a surprise to see him now selected to this significant responsibility even temporarily. The events of the afternoon had clearly disturbed him greatly. He was at a loss how to handle it. Even when he was expressing condolences to me about the loss of dear Matilda he was almost incoherent and that embarrassed rather then comforted me. Death and disorder it seemed were everywhere.

After saying grace and before the serving of our first course he indicated that he wished to speak. My eyes had already been drawn to the startlingly vibrant and beautiful glass in the window behind him but there was a contrast between that and the slight and nervous-looking figure who now stood up.

"Dear Guests, words cannot express my sadness that we are dining in such terrible circumstances. I know that some of you - Madame Eglentyne, Sir Matthew and Sergeant Henry - are old friends of the abbey and you know our ways." He nodded in my direction and towards a man who had a legal cast of features. He then almost bowed towards a finely dressed nun who gave a tight, uncomfortable smile in reply.

"As to our other guests - dear Mistress Alison and you Sir

5

Roger, friend of Sergeant Henry - this could not be a worse introduction to our beautiful but troubled abbey."

Mistress Alison was dressed vividly in red, slightly overweight but shapely nonetheless. Sir Roger, meanwhile, looked as if he might need to go on a diet. Neither, however, appeared to be looking forward to this particular meal.

"I confess that I am at a loss," continued Father Compton. "The death of dear brother Peter is just the latest tragedy which has beset us since, dreadful to admit, the passing of Abbot Pechy. Even he, it must be said, experienced difficulties during his last years. And now we have this. It truly has been a most troubling time. And as the acting abbot I feel it all very deeply."

He stopped to look round the table, appealing almost for sympathy before resuming in a defensive tone of voice. "But let me be clear, dear guests, I did not take on this role willingly – quite the opposite – but even you Father Eynesham declined."

Father Compton looked across at the cellarer who had this afternoon apprehended the apparent murderer, now confined, as we had been told, in the abbey's secure store rooms.

"Oh, Father Compton!" the cellarer responded almost laughingly, unperplexed it seemed by the afternoon's tragic events.

"You were eminently better qualified than I am for so important a position. Of course, we all support you. For as long as it is necessary for you to be in that chair you can count on our devotion."

The cellarer spoke smoothly, confidently and with a hint of condescension. "But I have to agree with you," he continued in a more serious tone. "Dear guests, our abbey has suffered – and I use the word 'suffered' deliberately – in the last year or so. And the question now has to be addressed immediately as to what to do about this young man, John Twyford, whom I managed to catch as he tried to escape, in a very cowardly way, from the murder of dear Brother Peter. We must not let this matter be delayed for too long. The cathedral would not like it."

He looked almost menacingly at the abbot.

Looking miserable Father Compton paused, only to say. "It's all so terrible – John, of all people!"

The obvious question hung in the air.

"Perhaps you could enlighten us, Father Compton," I said, "as to who this man, John, is?"

"Let me answer that, if you don't mind Father Compton," broke in the cellarer again. "John Twyford is a very intelligent but also a very silly young man. He had some education here in the abbey when a boy and that was when I first came across him. He was a bright lad and we recognised that, frankly, he deserved a slightly higher level of schooling than we could offer. And so he became attached to the bishop instead. And at the cathedral he did very well apparently."

He paused for this message to sink in. The Bishop of Winchester, William of Wykeham, was not only the greatest cleric in the south of England but under the old king, Edward, he had been the most important subject in the kingdom. Even now under the new young king, he still had influence. His reputation ran throughout the church and state alike.

"So, John went to Oxford almost two years ago to be at this new college of the Bishop's," continued the cellarer. "To me it seems a waste of time and money but there we are. And, as they say, he has 'fallen in love with learning."

Father Eynesham gave mocking emphasis to the word 'love' as if trying to squeeze out of it as many meanings as it could carry.

"But I doubt if he has any plans for a career. All John does, it seems is read, read, read. So he has maintained some small contact with us to use the monastery's library when he is back in Winchester. But I cannot say that I am fond of the boy. I think that he is too clever by half and he's sly. And what he was doing here today I have no idea! He had certainly not introduced himself to me. So you can imagine my shock when I pulled off the hood of the murderer as I saw it – and it was him! And after all that Brother Peter had done for that boy!"

"So you are convinced that he is the murderer of Brother

Peter are you, Father Eynesham?" asked Madame Eglentyne. "Did you actually see it?"

"Let me put it this way," said Eynesham. "It looked that way to me at the time. And after all, who else could it possibly have been? I saw no-one else!"

He looked around the table, rather preening himself as if this had been a splendid account.

"Hmm, I am not sure that this is the time or place to go into the details of this dreadful affair..." said Father Compton as an awkward silence descended. Then after a few seconds he turned to the legal-looking gentleman. "Sergeant Henry can we have the benefit of your advice?"

The lawyer smiled as if used to being consulted on difficult matters. If he was worried about being caught up in a murder scene he did not show it. Instead, he pulled himself up in his chair and looked around the table as if he was at a formal meeting and spoke briskly.

"Madame Eglentyne, Father Compton, Father Eynesham – you know me. And I am delighted to make the acquaintance of my other fellow-guests," he said, acknowledging the rest of us. "Now, of course, it grieves me bitterly to be here in the abbey on such a difficult occasion. This was surely not intended to happen. But my work in the law is, for the most part on matters of land and business at St. Paul's in London. Murder is a little way out of my parish, as one might say. However, as far as I can make out this abbey has jurisdiction over its own affairs on such a matter – especially as John, the suspect, is a student. So my advice, such as it is, Father Compton is that you must hold your own investigation and then come to your own conclusion – ideally in consultation with other senior monks and maybe other experts who might be available to offer advice. Of course if you decide that this young man, John, is the culprit then you might want to involve the civil authorities. But I think the jurisdiction is yours – and you should probably keep it that way."

"Sadly I think there can be no doubt about his guilt," said

Cellarer Eynesham once more, glancing at his neighbours as if challenging them to contradict him.

"Really?" I said, feeling that the time had come to introduce myself to the discussion. "The boy looked petrified and, frankly, rather weak-willed to me. Not your obvious killer. Perhaps you could explain why you are so confident?"

"Well, I saw him – or at least I saw a hooded figure who turned out to be him – coming out of the library just before I went in. There was Brother Peter stretched out, dead, and the hooded figure was by this time running away. What else is there to be said? I gave chase. And we caught him!"

Father Compton coughed. "My brothers and sisters in Christ. This matter is at the front of all our minds but I take note of what Sergeant Henry has said – we the abbey have now to investigate and come to our own conclusions. So as several of you around this table are likely to be involved in this investigation I should prefer us not to discuss it any further now but to defer until tomorrow morning in a more ordered way. As Sergeant Henry has indicated matters of this kind are not his special business. So..."

The abbot turned towards me with a pained look. "Sir Matthew, I know it is a very large request, especially to a man in your sad circumstances, but I wonder whether you might look into this terrible affair for us? As I understand it you have had some experience of this kind of matter before?"

My reputation, it seemed, had gone before me and not just as a warrior. It was true that when I had been in Prussia there had been a number of murders amongst the crusaders themselves. We were a mixed and motley bunch – Germans, Italians, French and even one or two Spaniards. Some were effectively little better than mercenaries and there was sometimes as much violence off the battlefield as on it. The Teutonic Order asked me to take charge and get to the bottom of what was happening and then bring the culprits to justice. I had done so with some success. But that was in very different circumstances – drunken brawls between battle-hardened fighters often over women and in front of many witnesses. This struck me as being rather more complicated.

"I was rather hoping to put all that behind me when I came home, Father Compton," I replied, "As you know, my son and I are just about to make pilgrimage to Canterbury. I suspect that many of you are too," I said, gesturing around the table and receiving nods in reply.

The abbot's face dropped as if preparing for a rebuff. But my conscience pricked me. Maybe this was one of the ways that I could begin to redeem myself. If this could mark my first small step towards bringing a little justice to the world then I would be at fault to avoid it. So I added, "But of course, if there is anything that I can do to help the abbey then I shall, naturally, be content to comply."

"Excellent! I am so grateful!" the abbot responded with enthusiasm. At last he had found someone else to whom he could pass on the responsibility. "I am happy to place the initial investigation entirely in your hands, Sir Matthew. Please see me after compline tomorrow and then do what you think best. And in the light of your agreement may I suggest, ladies and gentlemen, that those of you planning to set out for Canterbury tomorrow delay your departure for, say, two days so that you and dear Sir Matthew can travel together? It is only a fair reward for him to have some congenial company en route – and indeed gain the benefit of your experience and advice too. It would be unreasonable to put the whole weight on Sir Matthew's shoulders."

There were only half-hearted indications of agreement from around the table. And Sergeant Henry and his friend the Franklin, Sir Roger Odiham, looked particularly uncertain.

"We have been away from town already for several days," said the Sergeant. "Both Roger and I have some urgent matters to be getting on with."

"That's right," agreed Roger in a sonorous voice. "Matters of court and at court...important matters"

Father Compton sensed that he needed to offer a modest

10

incentive.

"Of course, I understand. Well, think on it overnight if you would and as a gesture of my – indeed our house's - appreciation you are all invited to stay at no expense at the abbey's inn in Southwark when you make your break in London. You might have heard of it – the Tabard? Now, let's eat. Oh – and more wine please, steward."

The atmosphere relaxed a little and dinner commenced.

CHAPTER 3
'Ꝥutten hym in worshipful servyse'

When I got back to our lodging in the abbey's guest rooms I found that Damian and Osric had just returned from what sounded like a riotous evening. After a simple meal in the almoner's hall they had not, as I had hoped, composed themselves modestly for the spiritual journey to come, but had strolled back into Winchester to sample the night life.

"I hope that you've not been leading my son astray, Osric, and him so young and innocent?" I said only half jokingly.

The two of them looked at each other and burst out laughing,

"You can rest assured my lord, I am in no position to lead your worthy son astray – he can perfectly do that for himself! He has been in France, you know!"

At this they started to punch each other playfully with Damian giggling for all his worth. Already it seemed the grief caused by his mother's death was starting to wear off. He had his life ahead of him and was intent on enjoying it. I was only forty but I felt my life was already entering its final chapters.

"Hmm, well, I probably don't need to hear any more," I said with as much suspicious disapproval as I could muster. But the obvious thoughts ran through my mind. What would I have done at Damian's age? And as for Osric, I concluded that with his rustic worldly wisdom he would have to be left to his own devices.

"So, I've had a surprising evening," I said, moving the conversation on. "You might not believe it but the acting abbot, Father Compton, has just asked me to investigate Brother Peter's murder. He is clearly out of his depth – after all, he is only the fill-in abbot while they try to get a better candidate. But what happens next to this young man, John, the Oxford student and the prime suspect, depends on Father Compton's judgement. And, frankly, I don't think he trusts his own judgement. That's why he's asked me to take it on instead."

13

"So you are going to turn 'Inquisitor', are you father?" asked Damian looking impressed.

"I'd prefer not to put it that way," I said firmly, having seen enough of Grand Inquisitors down in Spain. "But Father Compton had heard something of my little adventures in Prussia and turned for me to help."

"You've not told me anything about these 'little adventures', father," said Damian.

"All in good time," I replied, "all in good time. There'll be plenty of opportunity as we make our way to Canterbury. But right now, I've got two days to get to the bottom of this murder. Or at least to work out whether this boy, John, did it or not. I hope that I can rely on you and Osric to help me out – to get to the bottom of things?"

Damian and Osric looked at each other. "Of course we will, father!" said Damian. And then the pair of them burst out laughing again. I was not pleased.

"Look boys, if you're going to help me then you've got to take it seriously – there are two peoples' lives involved – one dead, one living."

That seemed to sober them up somewhat.

"Sorry, lord," said Osric apologetically. "I understand."

"And I hope you do, Damian?"

"Yes, I do, father – it's just the surprise of it, that's all."

"Well, we'll see how it goes," I said implying that they were both on probation. "So, as a start, did you come across anything interesting in the course of the evening? Hear anything about the murder in any of the dens of iniquity I suspect that you've been visiting?"

"Everyone in the town is right shook up about it," replied Osric. "But it was odd, they didn't seem that surprised," he continued. "They were shocked but they were not surprised – that's the best way to put it."

"And the people here in the abbey? Did you talk to anyone in the almoner's hall?"

14

"The pilgrims were all horrified and almost terrified," said Damian. "But then they've just arrived and they know nothing much about the place. I tried to speak to one of the monks about it but he stayed silent."

"So are you thinking that they know something but are keeping it to themselves?" I asked. "After all monks are obliged by their vows to remains silent."

"To be honest, I suspect a lot of them here forgot their vows a long time ago, lord," Osric replied boldly. "It was more that this murder was part of a pattern, as if bad things keep on happening. It's like they were almost accustomed to it – they just want to shrug their shoulders, keep their heads down and get on with it – although, I don't suppose that they have murders every day."

"My impression from the people in town," broke in Damian, "is that this abbey is suffering some kind of blight. As Osric says, accidents keep on happening in the buildings, small fires and that kind of thing. And the monks have a poor reputation for how they conduct themselves – even worse than most monks. There's a feeling that the place is going to rack and ruin."

"And does that upset people – I mean the locals? How do they feel about the monks?"

"Father, this town is full of monks and friars and nuns of all description from the various convents and monasteries. We saw lots of them this evening in this brilliant inn – Le Taverne de Paradyse, it was called. Lots of different people. Some foreign. And plenty of these so-called religious. But my impression is that the monks from Hyde carry a particularly bad smell about them. Why? I don't know. But I seem to remember that the monks over at Mottisfont at mama's funeral made odd remarks about this place. When we ..." he stopped, looked upset for a moment or two but then pulled himself together. "When we buried mother there was one monk we met who has just come back from Winchester. We overheard him talking about this place as if things weren't right here."

"Oh dear!" I said feeling genuinely saddened. "It wasn't like

15

this five years ago before I went away."

"But, father, lots of things have changed in the past five years – you know that yourself," said Damian, with a slight edge to his voice.

I grunted.

"What about you, Osric - anything to add?" I asked.

"I'm not a monk, thank God, but I do know a bit about nature – including human nature," he replied, affecting some worldly wisdom. "And as Damian says, there are lots of people wandering around this town in clerical dress of all kinds – including another lot of monks over at the Cathedral. And for me that suggests rivalry between them. There might even be ganging up against this lot here. Because they're outsiders, aren't they? I mean they're outside the walls. Why's that then?"

"Yes, well there's probably some straightforward historical reason for it, I suppose," I said a bit doubtfully. "Anyway, it's given me lots to think about. The place has certainly changed."

I was right but I could not have imagined by how much nor, more importantly, exactly why.

16

CHAPTER 4
'In derknesse and horrible and strong prisoun'

After a modest breakfast the following morning we returned to our room and a plan was agreed. Damian and I would go together to meet Father Compton while Osric would make himself known among the lay servants of the monastery to pick up more of the gossip.

I knew from past experience that it was often the least of people who knew most of what was going on. Osric would also mingle with the constant flow of pilgrims and other folk passing through the Forecourt of the abbey. If there was further talk in the town about scandal in the abbey then he should try to follow it up.

Father Compton had just returned from the abbey's chapel and seemed reluctant to be drawn back into the grim affairs of the previous day. He had delegated the job to me and wanted to leave it there. Nonetheless he smiled politely enough when I introduced Damian and explained that together, father and son, we would do our very best to help him and the abbey in this most perplexing of situations.

"Now, Father Compton, the immediate thing I must do is talk to this boy, John. I understand he's under lock and key?"

"Yes, that's right. Father Eynesham, our cellarer whom you met last night, has him confined in one of our secure store rooms in the Outer Court. There is a Brother down there now keeping an eye on him and – out of compassion - we are treating him as one of our own community. Indeed he once was – as a boy, that is. He faces the most serious accusations but, for the time being, nothing has been proved against him. That's in your hands. Nonetheless as Sergeant Henry said last night, the obligation is on us, the abbey, to administer justice. So we welcome your guidance on that."

He looked at me expectantly.

"Well, I am gratified by your trust in me, Father. I must warn you though that this matter is quite unlike anything I had to deal with in Prussia. There it was just thugs mauling each other to death. Here it is…well, that remains to be seen. So Damian and I will do the elementary things first. We will question John on what he has to say for himself and then we'll see where it leads. But, as I said, I am not a professional investigator."

"But, Sir Matthew, you are a soldier and a man of worldly experience – attributes which are entirely absent in this community – so we are very grateful to you for all you will do for us," came the reply. Once again I felt the acting abbot was relieved that, somehow, the matter had been passed on elsewhere.

"So, I'll take you both down to see John now," he said. "And then, if you will excuse me, I have other things I must deal with."

"Of course, I entirely understand," I replied. And that seemed to be it. He was almost washing his hands of it. But as we walked around the abbey's cloisters he stopped abruptly as if a thought had suddenly occurred to him.

"Look, I know what Father Eynesham said to you about John last night – and some of it is true. He was a bright but irritating boy. But, even so, it's difficult to believe he could be capable of murder. It might be possible that something very scandalous happened yesterday to provoke John. But my advice is to trust your own judgement. Don't be too swayed by Father Eynesham. You do not have to find John guilty merely on his instruction."

I was somewhat taken aback by this remark. Maybe there was more spark in this acting abbot than I had previously judged. But what did he mean by 'very scandalous'? He gave me no opportunity to ask. He resumed walking briskly and led us to the store.

"How's our prisoner faring?" he asked the monk standing outside the locked door. "Not well – not well at all," was the stony reply.

Having thanked Father Compton and entered the cell-like room Damian and I could see what the monk meant. John was dishevelled and curled up in a corner with his back to the world. Small and thin though he already was, he looked as if he had shrunk still further. He was a pathetic sight.

"Good morning, John," I said bending over and tapping him on the shoulder. "Could you turn round please so we can speak to you."

Slowly he responded, putting his back against the wall and looking up at us.

"My name, John, is Sir Matthew de Somborne and this is my son Damian. Father Compton has asked us to talk to you to find out exactly what happened yesterday. Do you understand?"

"I didn't do it, I didn't do it," said John quickly in an educated but frightened voice. "I thought something strange was happening – but not that."

I looked at John for a moment or two trying to get the measure of him.

"When you say 'that', what do you you mean exactly?"

"The death of Peter."

"So you knew Peter did you?"

"Yes."

"You knew him well?"

"Quite well," John responded cautiously before adding. "You could say very well."

"And how did you know him? I understand that you are studying at Oxford."

"I am," he said. "But I often come back to Winchester and I use the library here at the abbey. I'm well-known to the monks. I was schooled here for a few years when I was a boy. They allow me to."

"Yes, so we were told. So Peter helped you use the library did he?"

"In his own way he did."

"By which you mean?"

"He allowed me to browse around and read the books and manuscripts that interested me."

19

"But he did not get involved very much in what you were doing," I queried.

"Peter did not get very much involved in anything in this library," he said, slightly derisively. "At least not lately."

"That's a strange thing to say."

"Peter was a strange sort of man," said John emphasizing hard on 'strange'.

"You better tell me a bit more about what you mean by that."

John looked irritated as if he had already had quite enough of talking to me. Perhaps he did not quite appreciate that his life might hang on what he said.

"The library here is full of many special books," he said. "Many valuable books. Many important books. It should be the job of the librarian to know his books, to be familiar with them and to know how they are organised. He should be like a shepherd to his flock. But Peter did not do any of those things. Or very few of them. It was chaotic."

"So has it always been like this?" I asked.

"No, just recently," he replied. "But maybe in the last year or so it's got really bad and Brother Peter was useless. Even though I came here only, perhaps, six times a year I knew better than he did where things were. But there was no order to it. It was annoying – it took ages to find whatever you wanted."

"So that was his strangeness was it – being disorganised?"

"He was strange in other ways too."

"Do you want to tell me about his strangeness?"

"Not particularly."

"Are you sure? It might help me. It might help you too."

"I don't want to talk about it!"

"Alright, well I am not going to push you – yet. But, tell me, do you think his strangeness played any part in his death?"

"I have no idea at all!" responded John sharply. "In fact, I know no more about how or why he died than you do – I just happened to have had the bad luck to be still there in the library when it happened and be the person to have discovered his body. It's stupid that its been suggested that I was responsible. But that's typical of Father Eynesham."

In his own, whining way he sounded genuine. But if Brother Peter was strange than John too came across as odd, at least to me from my soldier's perspective.

"Thank you, John, I understand. So now..." I paused to give emphasis to the next question. "Tell us exactly what happened yesterday."

He sighed heavily and looked at both Damian and me with a mix of wariness and resentment. He took a breath and then started.

"I arrived in the library and it was much the same as usual. Everything looking untidy and there was no-one there. It was empty. I was looking around for the things I was after and I was still there when Peter came in. He looked a bit unsteady on his feet. Worse than I'd seen him before because – as you might have heard – Peter had a reputation for being fond of his wine. I said hello but he barely responded. Just slumped down in his chair in that little out-of-the way office area and then seemed to fall asleep instantly."

"I see. So what happened then?"

"The library as you know is L-shaped. It turns a corner. I thought the things that I needed might be around the other side although, of course, you could never quite tell given the state of disorder of everything. So after Peter arrived I moved there and stayed for some time. Anyway, I could not find the things at first and was picking up items here and there trying to sort out the ones I wanted. And then I heard some voices around the other side followed by a cry of some sort. But I was too concentrated on my own search to pay much attention."

"So you didn't go and see what was going on?"

"No, it was a little later that I returned to the front of the library and there was Peter on the floor looking, well, dead. I was shocked and shouted out, tried to lift him up but he collapsed back on the floor. And that completely shook me up. I staggered across to the door. And I ran out shouting 'No, NO No' – or something like that. I wanted to get downstairs into the open. And then I was aware that someone was following me and thought that they might want to injure me too. And that was when I ran across to the almoner's hall. And you know what happened after that. They arrested me. For no reason at all."

As I listened to his account I realised that I did not know that the library was L-shaped. I felt foolish that I had not been to the site of the murder. And I already felt rather inadequate to this task. But I could hardly stop now.

"And that person following you turned out to be the cellarer did it? Father Eynesham?" I continued.

"I suppose it must have been. It was certainly him who was shouting out and had me lifted up and taken over here. It was all just mad."

"So to be clear. You are saying that you were innocently in the library and while you were there something happened. We don't yet quite know what happened but whatever it was, you were not involved in any violence towards Brother Peter."

"That's absolutely right. I didn't do it."

"Didn't do what exactly?" I said, keen to understand how much John knew of the injuries.

"Why, kill him! Isn't that what we're talking about," he replied with some impatience.

"But how was he killed? Did you see? What exactly was it that killed him?"

John hesitated. Then looked puzzled.

"Well I'm not sure. I suppose I assumed that he had been strangled. Or maybe hit very hard. I didn't really examine him. All I was aware of was that deadness in his eyes. I had no doubt in my mind at all that life had gone out of him. And then it struck me that maybe I was now also at risk."

"Why at risk?"

"Well, I didn't know for sure that the people who'd come into the library – and I suppose had murdered him - had yet

22

gone. They could have been waiting for their next victim for all I knew."

"It was more than one person was it?"

"I think so but I'm not sure"

"And you didn't recognise their voices?"

"No, it was too muffled and I was really concentrating on looking at the shelves."

"And the person who then followed you – whom we now know to be Father Eynesham – is there any chance that he could have been one of them – the murderers, I mean?" A bit of a risky question, maybe, but worth asking, I thought.

"That's pretty unlikely I should imagine," he asserted.

"But you would have recognised his voice, wouldn't you, I suppose?"

"As I said, I couldn't hear the voices clearly."

"And so where do you think Father Eynesham came from when he started to chase you?"

"He must have come out of the library after he'd seen the body."

"So you think it possible that he might have been actually in the library at the time you discovered Brother Peter."

"You've seen the place – it's not likely but it's not impossible. But I certainly didn't see him. I think he probably came into the library straight after I had left it, seen the body and drawn his own – quite wrong – conclusions. "

Again I was annoyed with myself for not having visited the library before seeing John. If I was going to do my best with this investigation then I needed to think things through properly in advance.

"Thank you very much, John. That's been very helpful."

"You do believe me, don't you? I can assure you that I'm telling the truth."

"It's been very informative," I said deliberately. "And now, have you had anything to eat or drink?"

"No, nothing since yesterday when it all happened. I've not

really felt hungry – but I am thirsty – very thirsty."

"All right, well we'll do something about that. I need to go and talk to other people. But Damian will go and get some food and water for you and then I hope we can get things sorted out as quickly as possible. But you'll have to stay here for the time being. Damian, come with me and we'll go to the kitchens. John, I am sure I'll see you again soon."

When we had got back into the Outer Court I asked Damian what he made of it.

"Well, I don't know what to make of it but I don't make much of him."

Although the two young men were not far apart in age – John, I reckoned, was about a year older - they could not have been more different in personality. And yet there was, curiously, some strange similarity between them – maybe both being Hampshire born and bred had something to do with it. But John clearly loved books while my Damian had little use for them aside, that is, from glancing over troubadour love songs. Instead his interest was in swordplay, horse-riding and jousting. But maybe talking to John would widen his horizons somewhat.

"Right Damian, this is what I want you to do," I said to him. "Take John some nice bread and beer from the kitchens. Give it to him, be friendly, and encourage him to get stuck into it. But then ask him more about Peter. Was he always drunk and disorderly or had something changed him? Presumably he must have had some talents to be appointed librarian in the first place. Did he have any enemies? Had he made himself unpopular? And that 'strangeness' which John referred to. Try and find out more about that. I can have a guess at what he was referring to. You probably can as well. That could explain a lot. But take your time."

"So," paused Damian. "You think by strangeness we're talking about liking pretty young boys a bit too much?"

"Well, I can't deny it's the first thing that dropped into my head. I don't know too much about St. Benedict's rule but I've got a feeling that even he warns against that kind of thing. Anyway

24

see if you can prise out a bit more about that."

"If you wish, father, then I'll give it a try. Not sure I'll be much help to you though. And so what do you make of him?"

"I'm glad that he's not my son," I said, maybe a little unkindly. "But I think most of what he said was true. Only my feeling is that it's not the whole truth. I was struck by the way he used the word 'still in the library' when it happened. It was as if, for some reason, he should have left by then. And he referred to looking for 'things' and 'items' rather than books. It felt significant but I'm not sure why why. Anyway, you go off and I'll see you later with Osric."

So we had taken the first steps. But were they forwards or backwards? Towards clarity or confusion? Did John have all the answers or, maybe, none? I needed urgently to see the library and, even more so, see the body.

CHAPTER 5

'Ðir smylyng was ful symple'

I hoped that I was not jumping too readily to conclusions but after that first exchange with John I felt it very unlikely that he was responsible for Brother Peter's death. My modest experience in sorting out vendettas among the crusaders on the Prussian border had given me some insights into how killers conducted themselves. John was no natural killer and his confused response to my question about how Peter had died suggested strongly that he had not been actively involved in the murder. He didn't even seem to have thought about it. He was just mesmerised, it appeared, by Peter's deadness in the eyes.

So, yesterday's hue-and-cry was no evidence of guilt. But telling that to Father Eynesham, the cellarer, might not be easy. For a start he would be denied the merit of having captured the culprit. Added to which his authoritative judgement would be challenged. But above all it would leave the abbey with a crime still to be solved. For the time being, then, I would keep my own counsel. But I now needed to see the corpse for myself, examine the library and then establish what, if anything, I could glean from anyone else connected with Peter.

Walking across the Outer Court from the storehouse towards the abbey cloisters I heard my name called – clearly but not too loudly – by a woman. I turned and there, coming towards me at some speed, was Madame Eglentyne. We had briefly spoken the evening before and I had gathered that she was in charge of Wintney Priory, half a day's ride from Winchester. Like me she was staying in one of the abbey's guest rooms but hers was over the gateway from the Forecourt. She was young for an abbess I hazarded, aged about thirty-five, strikingly pretty and, as on the night before, dressed exquisitely although in a different habit.

"Good morning, abbess," I said. "How are you? Not too upset, I hope by this terrible death?"

"Oh I hardly slept at all," she said somewhat breathlessly. "I had so much turmoil in me I could hardly think of anything else."

"I am sorry to hear that," I replied as sympathetically as I could. But her tone puzzled me. Was she in fear of the murderer? Or was it another concern? Whatever the cause, though, she was an anxious woman.

"I wanted to speak to you about something I heard yesterday – but I didn't care to mention it last night in front of the others."

"Oh, why was that?"

"Well, as you will remember, Father Compton was not keen for us to discuss the matter around the dining table and Father Eynesham was so certain about what had happened I did not want to appear to contradict him."

Of course, she was correct.

"And also," she continued, "I didn't want to give too much of myself away – in that particular company."

"Quite, I entirely understand." I continued as smoothly as I could. "So what was it you heard?"

"As it happened, just by chance, I was over on that side of the cloisters at around the time these terrible events occurred. Obviously I was not aware that a death – a murder! - had taken place until later. But, at what might have been the critical moments, I was passing the library and I heard voices arguing, all seemingly angry and one of them, candidly, a bit drunk. I passed on, I did not want to be involved. But when I then heard about the death of Brother Peter it seemed to me that there might have been a connection. The voices were definitely coming from the library."

"Several voices, you say?"

"Yes, several. I could tell they were rowing with each other but the louder one, I now imagine, was Brother Peter's."

"And could one of the other voices have been young John's."

"I am absolutely certain that it was not," she said. "They were, shall we say, more brutal tones. And John has an educated accent. And the loudest sounded like an old man to me – so presumably Brother Peter."

"And you know this student, John, do you?"

"Yes, I am familiar with him. He is, I think, a well-known character around Winchester generally as well as here in Hyde Abbey."

"And you're regularly here, are you?"

"I visit Winchester frequently to St. Mary's convent, the cathedral and several other houses as well as this abbey in Hyde. I have contacts with them all. And John is also welcome at them from what I have seen. So I know him by sight and have also occasionally exchanged a few words with him – mostly about books."

"So he is in Winchester a lot as well as at Oxford?"

"It seems so, doesn't it? He's at that age, isn't he? But I just wanted you to know that I had heard arguing voices coming from the library and that John's voice was definitely not one of them."

I needed to think about it further but this reinforced my growing view that John was not involved. However, I was also intrigued by the Abbess's presence so deep in the monastery. Were there not rules against that? I asked.

"Dear Sir Matthew, you have been away for some time, haven't you?" she said changing her tone and seeming less anxious, maybe, now that she had delivered her evidence.

I agreed that I had been away for five years – and that England was much changed.

"Well, that is certainly true," she agreed. "And I have to admit to you that this abbey has become, maybe, a little more progressive over that time. It is something of an 'open house' and is well-known for it in Winchester. There is a view of several of the monks here – senior monks, I should add – that those old rules should be regarded as a thing of the past. And I must confess I am rather of that mind myself. Monks, nuns, priests alike, we all share in our zeal for the same thing – laity too, I suspect – and surely it is better that we join together to bring these great ambitions – for the church, I mean - to fruition. I know that, discreetly, I am welcome here. In fact, as a woman I am much welcomed here. So I frequently come down for theological

29

discussions and share my spiritual insights with my brothers in the Lord. And I don't think that any good Christian could seriously object to that. Do you?"

She had lowered her voice and I was having to lean in somewhat to hear what she was saying. She then flashed me a wonderful smile.

"It's no business of mine, Abbess Eglentyne," I responded feeling intrigued by her disclosures. "And if the authorities here are content then there's no more to be said."

"I suspect that not absolutely all of them would agree," corrected the abbess. "But the most significant ones certainly do. But there's no need to mention it to anyone. And indeed what I have told you about what I overheard is just for you alone. I felt I had to tell you. But I should prefer if you did not repeat it. Or at least not attributing it to me."

"Of course, understood," I said.

"Good, well no doubt I shall see you at dinner again this evening. And, just so there is no misunderstanding, I should add that although I am a frequent visitor and enjoy my visits I do not entirely endorse everything that happens here - or all the attitudes of the monks. They have still got a lot to learn when it comes to respect for their sisters in Christ in matters which are, shall we say, non-spiritual."

"By which you mean?" I asked, assuming she was implying some sexual dalliances. I was wrong.

"Well, to begin with, the rights of property and good management. As an abbess these matters concern me enormously. But we can talk more about that at some other time"

"Yes, indeed. But, before you go, I am right in thinking that from here you are intending to undertake pilgrimage – I mean after this visit?"

"Oh, yes, certainly," the Abbess replied with gusto. "And, in fact, I am bringing a number of priests associated with the convent with me as well as my assistant, Sister Avelina. They are so looking forward to it. It's such an opportunity for self-denial and prayer. And they appreciate and value that so much. In fact, Father Eynesham and I had planned this some time ago. We felt that in these very difficult times we should demonstrate the depth of our own faith by an arduous journey for the good of all. So certainly I am on pilgrimage – to London at least. And then maybe on to Canterbury too."

I had not heard of anyone going on pilgrimage to London before but I let that pass.

"And you, Sir Matthew?" she asked. "Why are you going to Canterbury?"

I demurred to answer. My feelings were too raw about both Matilda and my experiences abroad to want to share them with the abbess. "I'm sorry it would take too long to explain," I said apologetically. "I have a number of concerns in my life to sort out."

"Well, maybe I could help you," she said. "We could pray together."

"That's very kind of you indeed," I replied slightly uneasily. I certainly felt the need for prayer but probably best not with Madame Eglentyne. But I then quickly switched to one of the other questions on my mind.

"This Mistress Alison who was also with us last night. Do you know anything about her? She seems very charming – very lively."

The abbess's face changed, her smile disappearing and replaced by a hard line.

"Mistress Alison is, as you might say, lively for anything – and anyone, Sir Matthew, I should warn you. She has had several husbands already and I believe she would like to have several more before she meets her maker. She comes from Bath and I know she is always here in Winchester for the St. Giles fair – I understand that she is in trade, you see in the textiles business. But I also know – and keep this to yourself - that she has some doings with your neighbour, the Duke of Lancaster. She is of his allegiance, I think. And that tells you a lot about her – don't you think?"

This brought me up with a sudden stop. The Duke of Lancaster, John of Gaunt, had a hunting lodge not far from our manor in Somborne offering access to the New Forest. He was rarely resident but, nonetheless, there was a slight connection between us. And when Damian had gone warring two years earlier as a naive 18 year old it was as part of the Duke's recent inglorious campaign in France.

The Duke also had, it must be said, a reputation for amorousness. If Alison from Bath - a comely, outward-going woman - was connected to him personally, even many years back, it was almost certainly in one way particularly.

"Well thank you, dear abbess. It has all been very fascinating and useful too. And your secrets will be perfectly safe with me."

"Thank you, Sir Matthew." She smiled at me again. "I look forward to speaking with you further."

We bowed, each going our separate ways. Maybe she was going to a 'theological discussion'. I needed to see a dead body.

CHAPTER 6
'I pray to God his nekke mote to-breke'

Arriving at the Abbot's private office I was greeted by a slim, thin-faced monk of average height aged about twenty-five. He was obviously expecting me and gave a polite but cold welcome.

"I am very sorry, Sir Matthew, but Father Compton has been called away for the rest of the morning – he has had to go to the cathedral, I'm afraid. But he told me to be of service to you. My name is Thomas and I am his assistant in leading this monastic community for the time being."

I am hardly an expert on monastic management but I was surprised that an 'assistant' to the abbot, so manifestly young and inexperienced, should hold himself out as having such power.

"I entirely understand Brother Thomas," I said politely but with corresponding lack of warmth. "If I can see the abbot this afternoon then that would be perfectly satisfactory."

"I am sure that if there is anything you need from Father Compton – or indeed any decision required - I can provide that myself," he replied. "So how can I help?"

This sounded peculiar. I understood that Father Compton was merely in an interim role being but surely he would not be delegating decisions to such a child.

"If I may ask, Brother Thomas – how long have you been here at Hyde?" It was rather direct but I could not resist asking.

"How long, Sir Matthew? I am not sure why you should need to know that but, since you have asked, I have had the doubtful pleasure of being here in Hyde for just a few weeks. Since the previous abbot died."

I could not help but show my surprise.

"I am not a monk of this abbey," he continued. "I am from Saint Swithun's, the monastic community at the cathedral. I am sure that you are aware of its unique seniority. After the death of the somewhat inadequate Abbot Pechy, the Bishop and the

Prior saw that Hyde needed a little help, shall we say. So I was instructed to come across – for the time being – to give assistance. I think that they are seeing the benefits already."

He looked up almost daring me to disagree.

"That was most thoughtful of them I am sure," I replied.

"Are you now satisfied?" he asked acidly.

"Well, of course, absolutely – it sounds a splendid idea," I responded realising that this relationship was not getting off to a good start. But I was resolved not to be deflected from my main purpose.

"So, coming back to this sad affair with Brother Peter," I resumed. "I now really need to see his body – the corpse. Could you tell me where I will find it?"

"Is that really necessary, Sir Matthew? I mean it would be a very distressing experience for you to see Brother Peter. And, after all, he's dead and no doubt already resurrected in the Lord. His miserable life on this earth is over. He can now drink his fill at the Almighty's everlasting dining table. What more do you need to know?"

I sighed. If Brother Thomas was aiming to be helpful this was a peculiar way of doing it. For the sake of explaining the obvious, I described the necessity.

"If I am to investigate this murder – as Father Compton has requested – then I need to understand the cause of the death. Assuming that is, there has actually been a murder. Everyone has been leaping to the idea that Brother Peter was murdered. But that was purely Father Eynesham's interpretation. Maybe Brother Peter had simply had an accident, fallen and hit his head or had some internal collapse. Until I actually see his body I should reserve my judgement."

"If you don't mind me saying so, Sir Matthew, I rather think that you should respect the viewpoint I have just expressed that poor Brother Peter's body is not fit to be seen. For the time being."

z≈`Brother Thomas looked at me with irritated impatience.

"I think our understanding, Sir Matthew, is that he died because that little scholar boy killed him. Why, I do not know. But no doubt he had his own reasons."

I was now becoming quite exasperated.

"Well that's exactly what I am investigating, Brother Thomas - on the specific instructions of Father Compton whose assistant you claim to be. And I repeat, I cannot do that properly without seeing the body."

"Hmm, well we might need to wait for Father Compton to come back to agree to that I'm afraid, Sir Matthew."

"But I thought that the abbot asked you to help me!"

"I am helping you, Sir Matthew. As of this moment I don't think that you would like to see the body."

"I am sorry, Brother Thomas, but I must insist on this. This is for me to judge."

"No it's absolutely impossible now, I'm afraid. This afternoon maybe – but not now."

He sounded firm but I was fuming. Who was this little jumped up pip-squeak to stop me in my commission from the acting abbot? A commission which I was not keen to take up in the first place. This was the last thing I wanted to be involved in. It was only this newly-conceived sense of obligation or duty which was keeping me at it. But I could see that I would get nowhere with Brother Thomas.

"I am very unhappy about this, Brother Thomas. And I will not hesitate to make my views clear to Father Compton when he returns."

Brother Thomas shrugged his shoulders and did not look unduly concerned.

"Meanwhile, however," I continued in as cold but clear a tone as I could muster. "Can you tell me when the funeral is likely to be?"

"I think we are planning for Wednesday morning, Sir Matthew." That was two days hence. "I understand that you will have made your report to the abbot by Tuesday, that is tomorrow evening, so that seemed a reasonable time. It will, of course, be a large affair. All the community here naturally – and I think that we will have my fellow monks from the cathedral as well. And others, no doubt too, who wish to pay their respects."

"Just a moment. When you say 'my report' you mean?"

"I mean something in writing confirming that John Twyford was the person responsible and the motive was, one presumes, a possibly understandable reaction to an intimate and unwelcome approach by Brother Peter. Little boy Twyford can then be handed over to the secular authorities for whatever punishments they award in these circumstances. And all of us can then wash our hands of the entire messy affair."

I was taken aback by the way Brother Thomas trotted this out. It sounded like a framed-up account designed to answer any inconvenient questions and leave both the Oxford clerk John and Brother Peter – the suspect as well as the alleged victim - looking culpable.

But my instinct remained that John had not done it. And confirmed, in fact, by the evidence from Abbess Eglentyne about the age and accents of those involved in the fracas.

Nonetheless, I decided to withdraw but emphasised again that I would be back later in the afternoon to see the abbot.

"We'll be very pleased to see you – both of us will," said Brother Thomas with a dismissive, impudent smile.

"And meanwhile can I at least inspect the library?" I asked with as much civility as I could muster.

"I am sure that is perfectly in order, Sir Matthew," replied Brother Thomas but adding. "Unfortunately, as you may be aware, the abbey is temporarily without a librarian to show you round its rather limited treasures. I hope that won't be too much of a problem?"

CHAPTER 7
'Ther he is hurt'

I returned to our room hoping that Damian or Osric would be there so I could vent my frustration.

The pair of them almost jumped on me as I entered the door.

"Father, have you heard about the injuries?"

"What injuries?" I asked.

"The injuries to Brother Peter, father!"

"Well, from what John was saying this morning there was nothing obvious."

"That's not what we've heard," put in Osric.

"So what were these injuries then?" I asked, now very curious especially after being rebuffed by Brother Thomas from seeing the body.

"It seems he was attacked brutally in his private parts," said Damian with fascination. "Apparently there was blood everywhere – and he was no longer, shall we say, a complete man."

"So you got this from John did you – this morning? After I left you?"

"No, no – he didn't say a word about the injuries. All we talked about was Brother Peter – and that was interesting enough. No, I heard about the blood and everything when I went back to the kitchen later with the plate and flagon. It was the talk of the serving men. And they'd got it from a priest."

"And I heard it from one of the stablemen," said Osric. "Apparently they had heard it from a farmer."

"Word gets round fast," I said. "Why on earth would a priest and a farmer be privy to this? Because I didn't get very far at all. Father Compton had gone over to the Cathedral and his so-called assistant, Brother Thomas, refused to let me see the body. He claimed it would be too distressing for me – cheeky little devil. So I am really no wiser about any wounds."

"Well, it's the talk of all the people outside, I can assure you, father. 'Brother Peter had his privates cut off' that's what they're saying," said Damian. "Mind you, I suppose it could just be a stupid conspiracy story from a crazy priest. To frighten people. I mean. Isn't that what priests do?"

"Who knows!" I said with some exasperation. "I am just very vexed that I've not been allowed to see Brother Peter's corpse this morning. They've been very protective about it."

"Maybe this explains why," said Osric. "They've got something to hide – or maybe less to hide," he added with a grim laugh

"All I can says is that they're not doing it very successfully, are they?" I replied. "If the abbey is trying to stop me seeing the body, why is this priest going round with his gory tale?"

I paused to try to get my thinking straight.

"So tell me about this priest, Damian," I resumed. "You're sure he's a priest from outside the monastery – not a monk from the community here? I mean that would make more sense wouldn't it?"

"The people who told me said it was definitely a priest from outside the monastery," said Damian.

"So, how could he possibly know?"

"I asked around a bit," put in Osric, "and I tracked him down – well sort of. As Damian said, he's not a priest from this abbey. Like most of the people hanging around in the Forecourt he says he's a pilgrim. But he's a bit peculiar. For a start he doesn't look like a priest at all. He looked more like an ordinary working man. And he was wearing a pulled-down hood so you couldn't properly see his face and he had an odd kind of accent as well – I couldn't pin it down. Anyway, he says he comes from Chiseldon up beyond the Ridgeway. He could have gone direct to London. So why's he come here? Anyway, I then realised that I'd heard something about him - at least I think it was him – about a year ago. There was talk among some of the foresters who had come down from the Savernake area to our place. His parishioners love him, apparently a very devoted man. Bit unusual, in fact – wouldn't you say? I mean even these foresters were impressed – and they're not your religious types, are they?"

"You mean they thought he was honest?" I asked.

"Yes, they said he was sincere – for a priest. But he had a real reputation for being against the abbeys and monks. Said they were exploitative layabouts. And he was against the priests who go up to London to sing in the chantries and that kind of thing. He thinks they're too wealthy and too much out to line their own pockets. And he reckons they're all going to be damned. Or at least that's what these foresters were saying."

"Strong words. Priests damned for avarice - who'd have believed it!" I replied with mock shock. "But did you ask him how he knew about this mutilation?"

"I tried to but he was surrounded by a lot of people and jabbering away about all sorts," continued Osric. "But do you think he might have been just enjoying spreading the rumour because it made the abbey look bad? You know, because he hates the monasteries."

"It would certainly make the murder even more embarrassing for the abbey," I agreed. "And what about this farmer? Were you able to talk to him?"

"No – he was just an ordinary farmer, I think. I didn't see him. Maybe he'd spoken to the priest. In my view, lord, if we're interested in this rumour then I reckon that it's the priest behind it."

I turned this over in my mind. Were we interested in the significance of the rumour, I wondered? Certainly if Brother Peter's private parts had been mutilated then it might explain Brother Thomas's refusal to let me see the corpse while they tidied him up a bit.

"Well it's all very strange," I went on, "and it seems not to match John's account. But maybe he was too shocked to take it all in. We need to go back and talk this through with him. But, anyway, Damian what did you learn from John about Brother Peter?"

"Quite a lot really," said Damian with some satisfaction. "After John had something to eat and drink he calmed down and became quite forthcoming. Brother Peter, it seemed, was in a bit of a mess. He was aged about fifty and, as you heard, he was letting the library become chaotic. But it hadn't always been that way. When John came to the library as a boy about ten years ago it was well organised and Peter was strict - everything was in order. But over the last two or three years Peter was taking to the bottle and things started to get more and more out of hand. And what was starting to worry Peter most was that he suspected that, amidst all the chaos, books were starting to disappear. He was feeling guilty about it but seemed unable to stop it because he was drunk half the time."

"So he thought that books were being deliberately stolen?" I said. "Or were other people coming in to mess it up?"

"When I asked John about that he looked a bit shifty and wouldn't really answer. But what he did say was that some of the books and old manuscripts were very valuable and important. And whereas Peter had used to keep them neatly in a separated and secure place they were recently starting to get moved around and separated from each other. What sort of manuscripts could they be, do you think, father?"

"I know that this abbey goes back hundreds of years which is why they've got these kings buried here," was all I could say. "In the church. Ancient kings from a long time back. Maybe it's something to do with them."

"Kings? Really? I didn't know that," said Damian.

"I don't know much about it either," I had to confess. "It's all before King William's time. Those older kings ..."

"What, you mean King Arthur?" asked Damian excitedly. "They've got his round-table up at the Castle, haven't they? We need to go and see it! And I'd always wondered where King Arthur was buried."

"No, calm down, Damian. It's not King Arthur. It's a Saxon King. I think someone said it was King Alfred or King Athelstan or some old-fashioned name like that."

"It's a shame it's not King Arthur," said Damian like a petulant

40

child. "I love King Arthur! I love chivalry!"

"No it's definitely not King Arthur. But I don't think any-one is interested in these old kings any more. But maybe these manuscripts you talk about are linked to them."

"That William was a bad 'un for sure," broke in Osric. "All that forest area between your estate, sir, and the sea used to belong to the ordinary folk. Us Saxon folk who only speak English. But that William stole it – or gave it to his friends. Those Normans. And that's why the ordinary folk are getting very angry. There's a vengeance coming, I warn you, Lord."

I hadn't been prepared for this intervention from Osric. But maybe this growing anger among 'ordinary folk' was even more serious than I had appreciated. If someone like Osric is talking about it then it must be very widespread among the country people. Perhaps old grievances, passed on through the generations, were re-surfacing.

"Anyway, what we need to do now," I said in a tone which showed I wanted get back to business, "is to see John again and find out what he has to say about all this bloodiness. The mutilations. Then we must go to the library itself and get a feel for where it all happened. And after that I am determined that we must see the abbot – and see that corpse."

"Don't forget the other thing, father – you know, wandering hands," interrupted Damian, "As you guessed, John told me was that Brother Peter did have a bit of a reputation among the younger boys that, maybe he liked them a bit too much. A bit of petting, holding hands too tightly, that kind of thing. John himself had experienced a bit of it when he was a young lad before he moved across to the cathedral."

"That does tally, I have to admit, with what this Brother Thomas was saying. I should have mentioned that he – or maybe the cathedral - seems to have got it all sorted in their minds already. Peter was killed because he made a pass at John. That's the conclusion they want us to reach. Mind you, Father Compton said to us this morning that he did not think John was a murderer.

41

So it's all a bit of a muddle."

"John simply told me straight that Peter had this bit of a reputation," said Damian, "but not that anything really serious had ever happened, at least to him."

"So we need to talk to him about it again," I replied. "It's the kind of thing that is easy to suggest but actually might be just a cover for something else."

"You can't go too far wrong with lust as a motive, lord," said Osric. "I'm sure you and I know that."

I laughed grimly. Maybe he was right. Lust was always something you could rely on. Especially in a monastery.

CHAPTER 8
'A tale wol I telle'

When we re-entered the store-room John was back in the corner and asleep. I indicated to Osric to wake him up.

As he came to I spoke loudly to get his immediate attention – and maybe intimidate him a little.

"John, wake-up and listen to what I have to say."

He opened his eyes and glanced round nervously. Seeing Damian seemed to give him some reassurance.

"Now we're going to sit down and have a proper talk with you," I said as a way of taking command.

There was one stool which I sat on and Damian and Osric pulled together various bulging sacks and tried to make themselves comfortable.

"Right, John, I was pleased to speak to you earlier today and then you spoke to Damian here. We are starting to get a better sense of what happened yesterday in the library and to Brother Peter. That's been helpful."

I paused. He nodded.

"But I must tell you that we are not entirely convinced. I believe some of what you said – but not all of it."

I waited to allow that to sink in. Somehow he did not look too surprised.

"I should tell you that Damian and I have also been speaking to other people and getting their accounts. And so has Osric here. He's very good at hunting things down. So you might bear that in mind. Now before I ask you to say anything further I am going to give you a sense of what other people have been saying – particularly about you."

At this he looked distinctly nervous.

"One view, which is firmly held by some people, is that you undoubtedly murdered Peter. They don't suggest that it was planned but that, maybe, Brother Peter made an unwelcome proposition to you – maybe put his hand somewhere he shouldn't

43

and that, in response, you lashed out."

"No, that's not right. That's not right at all," shouted John. "Where do people get these ideas from?"

"There is also a suggestion," I continued, "that you used a knife on him and you cut him down there." I pointed to my genitals.

"Aagh! That's totally wrong," he asserted loudly. "How can people be saying these things? It's not what happened at all!" He was starting to lose control.

"Very well, there are other people I've spoken to who think that there was more than one person involved in the attack. They are not alleging that you were one of them but they think it is a strong possibility. And there's an idea that it could have been someone else who actually attacked Brother Peter while you looked on. Either way it means you were involved somehow. Now what have you got to say to that?"

"It's all completely wrong and nonsense!" he said very firmly and trying to regain his self-composure. "Why are all these people against me? I suppose they are just looking for a convenient scapegoat. And I'm an easy target. But I can see that you have already got your mind made up. What's the point of me going on?"

"The point is, John, that I want to get to the truth," I replied. "The position right now is that you say that you weren't involved in any way and just came across the body almost by accident. But there are other interpretations which suggest that although it was not you who actually committed the murder you were involved to some extent. So unless I get some more information I am going to have to say to Father Compton that on balance, having taken a number of views and thought about it myself, I consider that you were involved in the murder in some way – I can't be specific how - and that you should face the consequences. Of course what those consequences might be are not my responsibility."

I left him to think about this for a little time. He was now starting to look miserable but remained silent. He was clearly thinking over what his next step should be.

"So do you have anything else to say, John? If it helps you, I strongly suspect that there is another side to this story which you have not told us. And even though it might incriminate you somewhat it's better to tell us now rather than face something more serious later."

I could see that he was on the verge of unlocking. I just looked at him steadily.

"Alright, let me tell you the full story from my perspective," he sighed. "I don't understand it myself. But I can absolutely assure you that I was not involved in the murder and knew nothing about it."

"Well, carry on," I said.

"As you know, I am a student at Oxford but I come from Winchester and am well-known here in this abbey. As I told Damian, I knew Brother Peter well and I knew the library even better. I love books but books are expensive. Often at Oxford I could not find or afford books I really wanted or needed. That was one of the main reasons I came back here to read some of these books which were held in the library. But that wasn't really good enough – I needed the books full-time not just occasionally."

"And you say you could not afford to buy them. Your parents could not help?"

"I was adopted immediately after I was born – we were a poor family. My adopted parents aren't alive any more."

"I'm sorry to hear that," I said. "I know it's difficult if you don't know who your real parents are. So what did you do?" I asked - although I could already see the way John's story might be going.

"I started borrowing the books from the library here"

"With Brother Peter's permission?"

"Well, to begin with. This was a year or so ago. He said he would make a special exemption for me. But I had to give them back within a month. But to be honest as he became more chaotic and casual I stopped consulting him. Each time I visited I took a few books away with me and he didn't notice. And besides

45

no-one here was reading them! You don't have many scholars in this abbey any more I'm afraid."

"So you are saying that yesterday afternoon, you came to the library, started to remove some books and, for once, Brother Peter stopped you and something happened?"

"No, no, that wasn't it at all. If you just give me the time, I'll tell you."

He paused and collected himself.

"About three weeks ago someone I'd never met or even seen before approached me in an inn in Oxford. He was a middle-aged man who obviously knew my name and he offered to buy me a drink. I was a bit wary but I agreed. I could barely afford a drink myself anyway. So at first he seemed friendly and asked how I was enjoying Oxford. I was wondering where this was going and then he suddenly said. 'You've got quite a big collection of books in your room, haven't you? How can you afford those then?' And of course it was true, by then I had got quite a big collection of books – mainly from the library here at Hyde. But how he knew I'd no idea. And then he said to me 'You've been stealing them, haven't you? You've been stealing from that abbey in Winchester'."

"So someone else – maybe another student – had suspicions or had guessed and told him, do you think?" I asked.

"Yes, must have been. There are lots of other students coming and going where I live and quite a lot of them come from Winchester. They could easily have noticed and drawn their own conclusions. And then passed it on to someone."

"Beneficiaries like you, you mean, of the Bishop – Bishop William."

"Yes, that's right. That's why the Bishop wants his own new college. I suppose he wants to keep tabs on people."

"So someone, for whatever reason, had told this stranger about your collection of, shall we call them, borrowed books"

"That's right.

"And what happened next?

"He pointed out to me how embarrassing it would be for me if word got out that I was a book thief. It would end my career as a scholar. It would probably end my future doing anything in the church."

"So he'd got a hold over you?"

"That's right."

"And what were you expecting next?"

"Well that he was going to ask for something."

"Money?" I asked.

"Unlikely," John replied. "I've not got any. Or at least not much."

"Of course," I said. "So what?"

"He said that he simply had a small request to make – hardly anything at all and then this whole matter could be forgotten about."

"And what was it he wanted?"

"First, he asked me in a bit more detail about the library and how disorganised it was. He obviously had heard that the place was in a mess. I said that, although it was pretty chaotic now, I was so familiar with it that I pretty well knew where most things were - more or less. He then started to ask about the old charters. The really old ones – going back hundreds of years. I knew what he was talking about and he mentioned one in particular – I'm interested in that kind of thing."

"And what was this one?"

"It's the King Edgar charter - goes back over four hundred years. You've heard of King Edgar?" he looked up at me expectantly.

"Means nothing to me," I said candidly.

"Well, it's an important charter – it was given to the abbey when it was still in the centre of Winchester not where it is now in Hyde. This charter set the abbey up as an independent church and community and gave it lots of rights and properties. There'd been an attempt by the cathedral to take the abbey over but this charter gave it protection. Much of the property the

47

abbey owns goes back to it."

"And it was given by this king – Edgar, you say?"

"That's right," John replied. "So legally it could be enormously important."

"Even now?" I asked "And despite the fact that, as you just mentioned, the abbey has moved physically quite a long way since."

"Well that would be a matter for the lawyers wouldn't it?"

"I suppose so," I replied. "So he asked you if you knew this charter?"

"That's right."

"And whether you knew where it was in the library?"

"Exactly."

"And where was it?"

"Of course it should have been under lock and key. And a few years ago it would have been. But I think what had happened was that the last time old Abbot Pechy had consulted it – shortly before he died – nobody bothered. It had just been dumped down and then put away at the back of a shelf. And because I was always ferreting around I kind of came across it by accident – but I'd looked at it and just put it back. So I knew where it was."

"So what happened then?"

"This man, this stranger, said that he had a friend who was also interested in old manuscripts and that he didn't want to disturb Brother Peter over them. So the next time I was likely to be in the library could I just get them out for his friend?"

"And you were supposed to show it to his friend were you?"

"No, I was just to get it out and lay it on the main table covered up by a cloth – he gave me the cloth."

"And you agreed to all this did you?"

"I felt I had to. I really did not want to be denounced as a thief and what he was asking for seemed fairly harmless enough - trivial even."

"And so you agreed a time and a date?"

"He suggested it – yesterday afternoon during Sext when Brother Peter should have been in the abbey chapel."

"And were you then supposed to wait around?"

"Not at all. That was the curious thing about it. It was strict instruction. As soon as I had found the charter, and had put it on the table and covered it up I was then supposed to leave not only the library and the building but leave the abbey as well. In fact, leave Winchester. And not look back."

"And did you do that? Obviously not, by the look of it."

"That's right, I didn't"

"Why not?"

"Well, once I was there I wasn't going to waste the opportunity of getting one or two more books so, as I described to you, I went round to the other part of the library and quietly started having a sort through. When I heard footsteps coming into the main room I froze and stayed absolutely still. I then heard someone else coming in. After that I heard a kerfuffle of some sort and then, by the sound of it, people opening the door and leaving the library. When it seemed everyone had gone I came through and saw Brother Peter on the floor – dead.

"And could you see his injury?"

"I was too shocked to look and just wanted to get out of there. I just lifted him up and when I realised he was dead I made off as fast as I could. As I said before, I was worried that they might come back and do for me as well not least because I was not supposed to be there at all."

"And you'd put out this charter on the table under the cloth as instructed, had you?"

"Yes, just as they'd said."

"And could Brother Peter have noticed it do you think?"

"No, not at all – he was too drunk and just staggered off to his cubbyhole. Mind you I was a bit surprised to see him at that time. He was supposed to be in the chapel with the other monks then."

"And so you left the library and were seen by Father Eynesham and chased and so on."

"That's right – and it's all ended up with me being here with you."

49

"But Father Eynesham must have been very close at hand, mustn't he? I mean he must have gone into the library, seen the body of Brother Peter, turned to see you and given chase all within a few moments. Did you see him at all?"

"Yes, as I came out of the library I was aware of a monk approaching just some steps away – his hood was up and I didn't stop to see who it was - I just ran off in the other direction."

"So he could have just happened to be passing?"

"Yes, I suppose so."

"Even though he was supposed to be with the rest of the monks then in the church?"

"How do I know! You'd have to ask him. I suppose he should have been but Father Eynesham is the cellarer, he seems to do anything he wants, when he wants it. He's a law to himself."

John looked spent but he had got the story off his chest and appeared slightly easier for it. I waited for a few moments to let him recover.

"Of course, we also know that you're a bit of a law unto yourself, aren't you? You are a book thief. How do you feel about that?"

A further look of alarm crossed his face.

"Naturally I'm worried about it. But I've got rather bigger things on my mind right now, don't you think? Like being accused of murder."

He paused and looked at me in a way which was both beseeching and accusing.

"I mean that seems to be up to you now, doesn't it?" he continued. "My fate seems to be in your hands for some reason. I don't know who you are and now I've told you what really happened I don't know who else you might tell."

For a moment he made me feel uncomfortable. After all, I was no judge. I had no authority for this inquisition other than the temporary responsibility given to me by a monk who lacked the confidence to take decisions himself and who was only filling the job for a short time himself anyway.

50

"Look, John, I did not ask to do this. Father Compton asked me to do it because I have had some experience of the world – both good and bad. The details which you have told me I intend to keep to myself. Neither I nor Damian nor Osric here will reveal it to the church. So, to that extent, your secret is safe. All I have to do is pass a judgement as to whether or not I think Father Eynesham was right and that you are the murderer."

"And what do you think?"

I was not sure whether to answer this. Better to conceal my full thoughts for the time being.

"After we've been across to the library and I can see exactly what happened and where – and after I've seen Brother Peter's body – I shall let you know."

He nodded.

"Well thank you for all that," I said indicating that I had nothing further to ask. Any questions, Damian? Osric?"

Thankfully Osric then asked the obvious question. So obvious I had overlooked it.

"And what had happened to the charter, John?"

"Oh!" John almost jumped with surprise. "I don't know, I didn't look. I was just too upset and confused by everything else going on."

"So you didn't think about putting it back where you'd found it?" continued Osric.

"No, that was the last thing on my mind. And If I had thought about it I'd have thought it didn't matter. Brother Peter wasn't going to be looking for it was he?"

Osric seemed to accept that.

"Damian, anything?" My son shook his head.

"Right, John – thanks very much for all that. I need to think this over. You have to stay here locked up for the time being but I'll see you later on in the library so you can talk it through with me again in the place where it happened. Osric, go and get John another plate of food and flagon of beer. We really now must see this body."

CHAPTER 9
'Dave me excused if I speke amys'

I walked with Damian back towards the cloisters. I wanted to find out whether Father Compton had yet returned from the cathedral.

"What do you make of John now, Damian?" I asked.

"I'm inclined to think he's innocent - at least of the murder," said Damian.

"Good – that's my view too," I replied.

"But he's tricky character, don't you think?" said Damian.

"My instinct is the same. But in what way exactly?"

"Well, if we had met him before all this I imagine that we would have thought that he was entirely dedicated to his books and would never do anything sneaky or wrong. But there he was stealing books on a regular basis! And who's to know that he hasn't been selling them on to other students at Oxford. There's probably quite a lot of demand for those kind of books."

"I think that might be a bit hard," I said. "We've got no evidence for that. I feel sorry for him in many ways. He doesn't come from a rich family. Probably he's often wondering where he's going to get his next meal from."

"Exactly, that's what I am getting at. He'd probably feel justified in stealing and selling the books when he compares himself with other students from better-off families."

"You might be right, I suppose," I conceded reluctantly. "But I am not interested in pursuing that. If we lose focus on the murder then we'll end up going down all kinds of rabbit holes and the Lord only knows where it might lead."

"All right, father – I'll leave it...But I'm not sure I'd trust him with my purse."

"You might have a point but fortunately we are not being asked to do that."

Just at that moment I saw the Mistress Alison, my fellow diner from last night, standing in the archway which led to the

Forecourt where the crowd of itinerant pilgrims gathered before going into the main abbey church. She seemed to be talking to someone outside the gateway. I moved across a little way to get a better view.

"Look, Damian, that was the woman from Bath I was telling you about. I was sitting next to her at dinner last night," I said pointing towards her. She was gesticulating a bit wildly "Do you see her? I wonder who she's talking to?"

She moved aside slightly to reveal a rustic wearing a labourer's smock which was none too clean. He was hardly the kind of character, I imagined, who would be a familiar acquaintance of Mistress Alison – but that's what happens, I suppose, when you embark on the path of pilgrimage. You become entangled with a rag-tag assembly of people you would not normally meet.

"They look an odd couple, don't they," I said to Damian. "Maybe he's someone she met on the road coming across here. Or perhaps he's asking her for money."

"Looks to me more likely that he's getting a telling-off of some kind," said Damian. "Mind you she looks as if she's a fine -looking woman – or, at least had been in her time."

"Yes, well she's certainly well-travelled. She claims to have been to Jerusalem and everywhere in between. Due to her deep piety, she said. Anyway, let's get on."

Brother Thomas gave us his familiar cold smile as we entered Father Compton's rooms. I introduced Damian and he gave the merest nod.

"I am afraid that Father Compton is still not back from the cathedral, Sir Matthew. Can I suggest that you return after sext – I think that you will recall that I suggested that earlier?" he said pointedly.

"Do you have any idea why Father Compton is over at the cathedral?" I asked, more out of impatience than anything else.

"It is really not for me to speculate – let alone say," said Brother Thomas superciliously. "But following yesterday's events it would not be too surprising if the Prior wanted to be kept apprised of what was going on here – don't you think?" He paused and then added. "Think of it, we could all be murdered in our beds – guests included – couldn't we?"

"Oh, so it was the Prior he was seeing was it?"

Brother Thomas looked annoyed with himself at having inadvertently revealed so much. All he could bring himself to say, with precision, was, "Quite possibly."

"Well, do tell Father Compton that I am very anxious to speak with him and to see Brother Peter's corpse. And I will return after Sext."

"Indeed, you have said all that when you came earlier. Good bye."

He indicated the door.

"What was that all about?" exploded Damian once we had got down stairs.

"He was like that before," I explained. "Apparently he is not a monk from this community but was sent across from St. Swithun's at the cathedral to help out Father Compton."

"Implying what? That they didn't have confidence in the acting abbot?"

"I imagine so. Anyway let's go and collect John and take a look at the scene of the crime."

John had finished his bread and beer by the time we arrived and Osric was talking to him about forest life. John, it seemed was also from a forest family on his adoptive mother's side. They seemed to be forming some kind of bond.

"Right John," I explained. "The four of us are now going across to the library and you can show us exactly where everything happened."

Fortunately the humble brother in charge of the storeroom expressed no objections to us taking John away with us, 'Brother Thomas seems to have overlooked that one,' I thought to myself. But, for the sake of show, Osric held John in a firm grip as we walked back towards the cloisters.

Following our earlier experience I looked again across towards the gate to Forecourt. To my surprise Mistress Alison was still there, her back to us, and this time talking to two men – the rustic we had seen earlier and another man, slightly better dressed.

"There she is again," I said to Damian. "Mistress Alison from Bath."

Damian glanced across and so too did John. The movement attracted the attention of the second man who was looking in our direction and, almost automatically it seemed, he put up his hand to wave.

John noticed and immediately looked away. Was this embarrassment at being seen in custody? Or had he recognised the man – or maybe been recognised by him?

"Know them?" I asked John.

"No, no, not at all," replied John almost trying to hurry Osric on but in doing so prompting him to look across towards the gate.

"Oh look," said Osric. "There's the man I was telling you about – the one supposed to be the priest with the story of the mutilations. I'm surprised to see him still hanging around. I should have thought that he'd be on his way to Canterbury by now."

'Well you could say the same about us', I thought to myself. Like it or not were were all being detained in the abbey as if we were in some kind of lockdown against the pestilence.

"Well that's interesting," I said, "When I see Mistress Alison later I'll have to ask her about them. They seem a bit of a mystery couple, don't you think?"

The library door was shut but had not been locked so we – or indeed anyone else – could just walk straight in.

As John warned us the whole, large room seemed to be in a state of disorganisation and made worse in the immediate area by the door where a table had been knocked over and papers, books and manuscripts were scattered all over the floor. It was a sign of the lack of basic house-keeping, it seemed to me, that no-one had bothered to tidy-up after the death of Brother Peter. Still, it might provide us with some useful evidence.

I looked for any signs of blood on the floor but none was

to be seen. So if he had been stabbed in some way maybe it wasn't here.

"Was this the state of things when you fled after discovering the body yesterday?" I asked.

"Yes, I think so," replied John who by now was looking decidedly unsettled at being back here.

"Do you think anything has been moved?" I asked pointing at the room in general.

"How can I possibly tell?" said John almost defiantly. "You can see it's in a complete muddle – and it has been like this, more or less, for the past couple of years."

"And yet you knew and were able to find the charter?"

"Yes, well as I explained, it had been put on the back of a shelf and obviously not been moved. I only found them by chance but I knew where they had been left."

"You said 'them'," broke in Osric. "So was there more than one?"

"Did I? I didn't mean to. No, there was just one charter."

"And this library served as a scriptorium as well as a library, I suppose, John?" I asked.

"Yes, obviously the two functions were closely linked," he replied as if he was speaking to a naive novice.

"So tell me, John, who would normally be in here – apart from Brother Peter? Monks working on manuscripts, I suppose?"

"Look, Sir Matthew, you have to understand what has been going on here. Even in the ten years since I first came into the abbey there has been a marked decline. Then it was barely surviving as a place of learning – which was why I went to the cathedral instead. But of late it has become totally decayed. The library is very rich but is neglected. That was Brother Peter's fault but, really, it was all part of the same story across the abbey. This was not a good place to be."

"Huh, I see – it was as bad as that was it? " I said, trying to appear thoughtful but just feeling puzzled about what on earth had been going on.

"So, anyway, just show us exactly where you were and what you did here yesterday."

John talked us through once more the sequence of events. His arrival during sext, the library empty, and as usual everything in disarray and totally insecure. His removal of the Edgar charter – which he now started to refer to as the 'Golden charter' - from behind some other books on one of the high shelves and his positioning it on a writing stand in the middle of the room covered by a cloth. He then took us to the rear of the library, around a corner, where the chaos was even greater. High shelves packed with books.

"Damian, Osric – I want to check the acoustics. Go back to the writing stand and talk to each other in a slightly quieter voice than normal, a normal voice and then a loud arguing voice," I instructed them. "Also open and close the door."

Off they went. I could hear the sound of them speaking but could not distinguish exactly what was being said. Even at their loudest the sound was muffled by the books. With the door open noises from the Outer Court could be heard.

"Was that what it was like yesterday, John?"

"Yes, very similar," he replied.

So his story seemed to be standing up,

Then, to test out Madame Eglentyne's evidence, I asked them to do the same while I stood outside the library – first with the door open and then with the door shut. With the door shut I could hear nothing and even with the door open I could detect little more than a murmur. Did her account carry credibility? I was not sure. But why should she make it up?

"Right, let's go back and see whether we can find this manuscript."

John described what we should be looking for. The royal charter from King Edgar blazed with gold, he said, and at its centre was an image of the king himself, accompanied by St Peter and the Virgin Mary, presenting a golden book to God. And although it was called a charter it was more like a book containing many pages – indeed the very book in the illustration. "It's unmistakeable," he said.

But over the next hour or so, try though we might, closing and opening cupboards, pulling scores of books off the shelves, we could not find it.

"Is there anywhere obvious they might have put it, John?" I asked rather lamely.

"Look around you," he replied in a deadpan way. "If we can't find it I suppose the most likely explanation is that they have gone off with it. I had assumed that all they wanted to do was look at it. I hadn't imagined that they would actually steal it."

"But you have taken lots of books from here," said Damian.

"Yes, but that's because I want to read them – and then share what I've read with other people," said John in a self-righteous tone. "But what use could this charter be to them? I mean it's hundreds of years old. It's very beautiful but it's all dead history. What I am interested in is living ideas."

I did not want to get into a philosophical debate with him. But at the same time, in practical terms, I could see his point. Nonetheless there must have been some reason why these people wanted access to the charter.

"I am not sure what this is all about," I said after a short pause. "For whatever reason this document is important to them. And if they were to go to all this trouble to see it then I think it's most likely that they probably intended to take it with them. After all, it was quite thick from what you say. They would need time to read it."

"So do we think that they simply picked it up and walked off with it?" asked Damian.

"Well from what John has said there was some kind of deadly altercation with Brother Peter. But after that my guess is – as John has just said - they made haste to leave taking the charter with them. And that I think is what I am going to have to tell Father Compton."

"It will be interesting to see his reaction," said John. "My guess is that, given the state of things, he won't care very much. Still you can never quite tell with him. He's not very impressive as a man but he has got an eye for detail. Maybe he'll understand it."

"We'll see," I said. "Meanwhile, we have to determine what happens to you, John. Osric, remain here with John. We will come back shortly."

I beckoned to Damian to leave the library and we walked a little way along the cloisters.

"What do you think, Damian? What should we say to Father Compton about John?"

Damian looked uncomfortable.

"Look, father, you're the man with experience. I've got my views about John but I don't feel in a position to judge whether he's responsible for a murder."

"No, I understand. I mustn't put it on your shoulders. It's up to me. But when you say you've got your views on John, what do you mean?"

"Well sometimes I feel that he's a silly young man who's got himself into an embarrassing position and then was in the wrong place at the wrong time. And to be honest, in different circumstances, it could happen to me. I had a few scrapes in France I can tell you."

"I'd probably prefer not to hear," I replied. "But what else do you feel about him?"

"That he's not all that he seems."

"I know exactly what you mean," I said. "But you can't condemn a man for murder just because of that. And on balance I really don't think he was responsible for Peter's murder. I really don't."

"I have to agree," said Damian reassuringly. "I don't like him much but whatever my doubts about him I don't think he's a murderer."

"So, shall we just go and tell him that now and then go and give our decision – my decision - to Father Compton. He should be back from the cathedral by now. I really don't want this to drag on. Father Compton made it my responsibility so I am taking him at his word."

"Yes," said Damian, "but..."

"But what?"

"What about the books – the stolen books. You've got a confession out of him about those. Are you just going to let him get away with it."

"That wasn't part of my commission, Damian."

"Look, father, John's a self-confessed thief. I don't think we should let him completely get away with it. I mean I've done one or two things I'm embarrassed about but I'd never actually steal something. John's done that often."

Given enough time I would have explained to Damian that he had lived a life of privilege and he had no reason to steal. John was in different circumstances. But he had a point. I was so focussed on the murder that I had given scant thought to the thefts. But I also suspected that, on purely personal grounds of dislike, Damian did not want John to get off scot-free.

I paused. "Here's what I think we do," I said after a little while. "We'll require him to give an undertaking that over time he will gradually return all the books he's stolen. I'm not sure how we'll enforce it but we will come to some arrangement to ensure that he does."

"Easier said than done, I think. I'd prefer it, father, if we could require him to make a significant financial payment to the abbey now as gesture of good will."

"But he's got no money, has he?"

"I'm not so sure,"said Damian. "In the folds of that scholar's gown of his I saw what looked like a bulging purse. I noticed it when I was having that first conversation with him. When he was very shook up. But since then I've noticed that he's been covering it up. I think we need to see what's in that – and in that satchel of his as well. It looks pretty new and smart. Must have cost more than a few groats."

Reluctantly I agreed. Of course I respected Damian's desire

to thrash it all out. But it was just getting more complicated.

"Well then," I sighed. "We'll go back. We'll say that we have accepted his account of events in the library yesterday. And I will tell Father Compton that I think he is innocent. On my own authority I am going to let him go. I suppose I ought to consult Father Compton first but I can't bear the thought of him dithering over it. But I will tell John that he must make recompense for the stolen books and that starts with a donation to the abbey. To avoid any questions he can make it through you, Damian. Does that sound acceptable?"

"Agreed."

When we returned to the library Osric and John were in lively conversation. Osric was barely literate but they were sharing folk stories. Even so, as Damian and I approached them a look of nervousness crossed John's face.

"Right, John, I'll come straight to the point. Damian and I do not think that you were responsible for Brother Peter's death nor that you played any part in it. So I am going to pass that on later today to Father Compton and that should be the end of that matter."

"Thank you," he said with a slight smile and nod to both of us. "You've made the right decision. I was not involved in any way at all – but I thank you for it."

"However there is still the matter of the stolen books," I continued.

His face dropped somewhat.

"Although Father Compton is not aware of what you have been doing I do not think that Damian and I can just let it pass."

"So what are you doing to do? Tell the abbey?"

"Well, perhaps that is what we should do," I said. "But no, we are not. We have some sympathy for you as a poor scholar with a thirst for learning. But things cannot go on like this and so we must ask you to return those books which you have stolen. Not all at once but we ask that over the next couple of years you gradually return them. Will you agree to that?"

"Yes, alright" he said. "I will."

He did not sound very convincing so I moved quickly on to my next point.

"We are relying on your honesty to do that, John, but as a gesture of your sincerity we ask you now to make a contribution to the abbey funds."

"Well, how can I? – I don't have any money."

"Let's see about that shall we. I think you have a purse on you, yes?"

He did not respond.

"Osric, would you just check John's gown to see whether he has any money on him?"

It did not take more than a moment for Osric to lift a fat purse from an inner pocket.

"That looks a tidy sum," I said. "Shall we open it?"

Osric poured the contents on to a table. There was a large collection of pennies and a number of groats as well.

"So not so poor after all," I said. "Where did all this come from?"

"I told you, I do some teaching at Oxford. I've been doing a lot recently," he said resentfully.

"Well as a form of penance I want you to give three groats to Damian and he will make sure that the money goes to the abbey for its work with the poor. That way you will start to make amends but no one will know and there's no harm done. Is that acceptable to you?"

"Yes," he replied unenthusiastically, handing over the money to Damian.

"And just one final thing," added Damian. "Can we see inside your satchel."

The satchel, not very big, had been hanging inside his scholar's gown.

John looked decidedly unhappy at this.

"I don't want to open it," he said. "Why should I? You've decided I'm innocent. You're making me return the books and

63

pay a fine. Can't we just leave it at that."

"No, I really think we ought to see inside your satchel," said Damian, looking slightly awkward but firm nonetheless.

"Yes, John, please open it for us," I added.

Resentfully John twisted the satchel round and opened it up.

Inside it was a single piece of parchment, crammed full of writing.

At once Osric jumped on it.

"What's this, John? Is this the Golden Charter?"

John gave him a pitying look.

"Osric, I described the Golden Charter to you - it's beautifully decorated, there are images of a king, the Virgin, St. Peter and Christ on it. This is just a single page of handwriting."

"It might just be writing, John, but what does the writing say?" I asked. "Words can be valuable too. Give it to me."

I looked at it and frankly was no wiser. It was old writing and seemed to be a description of a piece of land in Latin with which I had only a passing acquaintance. But I wouldn't swear to it.

"Tell us, John. Is this piece of paper valuable?"

"Sir Matthew, I can assure you – as of now that parchment has no value whosoever. None."

"So why do you have it in your satchel?" Damian asked.

"I just like the look of it. I like old things."

Again for all John's deviousness I felt he was telling the truth. Or something that would pass for the truth. There were no reasonable grounds on which we could confiscate it. Besides, what would we do with it? He now had the moral advantage and I wanted just to bring the conversation to an end.

"Good, well that's everything, John," I said. "I am sorry that we've had to meet under these circumstances and that you have had to face this accusation. But I think it has been useful nonetheless in clearing up this matter of the books. You are now free to go and I will speak to Father Compton and Father Eynesham."

He nodded.

"And what will you do now?" I asked.

"I am going to London," he said. "I thought I would make pilgrimage. That was always my plan. I have friends here in Winchester who will lend me a horse. And after all that's happened since yesterday I need a change of scene."

"So we will meet again," I said.

"Very probably, I suppose. But for the time being, if you don't mind I will bid you good-bye."

"Yes, good-bye, John." Damian and Osric followed suit and there were token farewell nods all round as John left the room and then headed out into cloisters.

A short silence ensued while the three of us reflected on the events of the day.

"Oh, well I think that's all we could do," I said feeling somehow dissatisfied and not looking forward very much to telling Father Compton and others that I had let their prime suspect go for lack of evidence. Any evidence in fact. I felt that I had made the right decision but had achieved nothing in finding out who was responsible for the murder. But on further reflection I remembered that was not my problem. It was the abbey's.

"By the way, Damian, why did you want to look at his satchel?"

"Obvious, father, wasn't it? I thought it quite possible that he had actually stolen anther book yesterday even amidst all of the excitement. The satchel was the natural place to hide it. And when he looked so annoyed about it I thought we'd got him. But there we are – I was wrong."

"And it left him feeling in the right of course," I said. "We started off investigating one crime – mind you a very serious crime – and then we ended up dealing with something quite different. And I've still not got round to seeing the corpse – but it really doesn't make any difference now. As Brother Thomas pointed out to me, Brother Peter is dead. That's all that matters."

"But I should have liked to know whether the rumour was true about the mutilation," said Damian.

"It's not our problem any more," I said firmly. "I need now just to go and see Father Compton and bring it to an end. Damian, you come with me. Osric, we will see you back later in our room."

Leaving Osric to his own devices Damian and I headed off towards Father Compton's rooms. I was now feeling relieved that the whole thing was almost over and had been resolved. Needless to say, I could hardly have been more wrong.

CHAPTER 10

'For shortly this was his opinion'

"Welcome, Sir Matthew – and Damian," said Father Compton, smiling weakly, as we entered his room. "I know that you have been trying to see me. Brother Thomas mentioned that you have, as he put it, 'misjudged' my movements twice."

Brother Thomas, standing over by the window, gave a curt nod of acknowledgement. For my part, I was too irritated to speak.

"It has been a very demanding morning," continued Father Compton. "After yesterday's events Prior Hugh at the cathedral wanted to share his support with me and offer prayers for Brother Peter. So, as you will understand, I had to be there – I am sorry that it has inconvenienced you."

"It's no matter - I entirely understand," I replied trying to sound sympathetic.

"Now tell me, what have you have discovered? Do you consider that the wretched boy, John, was responsible for this terrible murder?"

"The answer to that Father Compton is 'No' I do not. Damian and I have spent a considerable time speaking in detail with John who is, I agree, a wretched boy in many respects. However, he has given us a full account of what happened yesterday. We've been to see the site of the murder. Both Damian and I have concluded that John was almost certainly not responsible for the murder. And, in the light of that, I took it on myself – based on the authority you gave me last night - to release him."

Father Compton's face looked surprised but relieved.

"Oh, well, well – that's an end to that then!" he said. "What, though, is Father Eynesham going to say, I wonder? He was so convinced of John's guilt. But you are saying that you are not persuaded by his account?"

"I wouldn't quite put it that way. I am simply saying that John gave a credible - and I believe honest - statement as to what happened yesterday. On the basis of that, both Damian and I consider that he has no case to answer. He was not involved in the murder – if indeed it was a murder – in any way. And as far as Father Eynesham is concerned, well, he saw what he saw saw for certain but, I believe, he simply jumped to a misinterpretation of what was happening. He drew the wrong conclusions. Understandable, maybe, in the heat of the moment but not reflecting the full facts."

"And those are?" asked Father Compton.

"John admits that, yes, he was in the library when the attack occurred but he was around the back in the stacks. He could not see what was happening by the door. He was consulting a book there when he heard noises in the main body of the library, voices and what sounded like a struggle. When he came to see what was going on he saw Brother Peter stretched out on the floor. John went to help, saw that Peter was dead and took panic and fled in case the culprits were still in the area. It was then that Father Eynesham saw him - and the rest you know."

"You say culprits?" broke in Brother Thomas who appeared to be irritated at our verdict.

"John says that he was only paying half attention but that he believed he heard two other voices in addition to Brother Peter's."

"And what were they saying," asked Brother Thomas.

"That, I am afraid, John was unable to hear."

"And you believe him?" asked Father Compton.

"Yes, I do - almost without a shadow of a doubt. I've known murderers, I'm afraid. John does not have that character. I grant you he is a bit odd. Rather irritating, in fact, as we have agreed. And I strongly got the impression that Father Eynesham found him exasperating. But he is no killer. And I have to add that there are one or two questions in my mind about how it came about that Father Eynesham himself appeared on the scene quite so quickly. After all, I imagine that he was supposed to be in church at sext at that time."

"You're not suggesting that he was involved in any way, I hope?" said Father Compton.

68

"No, I am not suggesting that, Father Compton," I said somewhat wearily. "I am merely indicating that it is sometimes very difficult to account for everything that has happened around an incident of this kind. All one can hope for is clarify the key actions. And in that respect I am quite certain that John, the Oxford scholar, is innocent."

"If that is firmly your view I must accept it and respect it," said Father Compton. "And although it was somewhat presumptuous of you to release him I grant that there was no point in further detaining him. I have no capacity or indeed appetite for further investigating him. But, to state the obvious, it leaves us with the problem that there is at least one – or maybe two - killers on the loose and we have no idea what their motive was or whether they might strike again."

"That is almost certainly true," I replied, "but I still do not have definitive evidence that Brother Peter was actually murdered. I have been denied the opportunity to see the body so I cannot be certain exactly what happened to the man."

A silence descended. Brother Thomas glared at me. I retained my composure. Then Father Compton, sensing that we were at an impasse, switched tone.

"Sir Matthew, have you and Damian had anything to eat?"

"No, not yet," I responded. "Our midday meal was rather postponed. And now that you mention it I must say I am feeling quite hungry and thirsty."

"And you, Damian?" Father Compton asked.

"Likewise," my son agreed.

"Well, Brother Thomas, would you be so good as to take Damian down to the kitchens and organise a suitable repast for him?"

Brother Thomas looked distinctly put out at having to go on such a humble errand.

"I am sure that Damian can find his own way," he said.

"No, please Brother, accompany him, show him the way and help him get fed – I've got a little something here for Sir

69

Matthew but sadly I lack Christ's ability to make it into a feast for two – let alone five thousand."

"Follow me then," Brother Thomas said gruffly and off they went with Damian looking particularly uncomfortable in the monk's company. And as the sound of their steps faded away Father Compton indicated that I should sit down and he drew up a chair close to me.

"Sir Matthew, I am very grateful for your efforts. Your conclusion is inconvenient in some ways but, in all honesty, I could not believe that young John was responsible. I was rather surprised in truth that Father Eynesham was so convinced immediately that he was to blame. But there we are! Now tell me again what was John doing there in the Library."

I had made up my mind not to betray the full story of what John had been up to but I was happy enough to give the bare facts.

"Apparently he calls in quite often when he's in Winchester to look at books he cannot find easily at Oxford," I explained smoothly.

"Yes, it is true that I have seen him from time to time wandering around. As a lad he was a very familiar figure here. But, as you have seen, we have so many people coming into the abbey grounds there's no way we can keep check on them all. Indeed we offer an open house to pilgrims who are free to visit both the chapel of St. Bartholomew and the main abbey church with all its glorious and miraculous relics. Sometimes I feel we are quite overrun. And our hospitality leaves us open to abuse."

"But that is mostly in the outer court isn't it it – not further in?"

"Yes, that's true but if you know your way round you can move from the church itself into the cloisters and once there you can go almost anywhere. And obviously John does know his way round. Anyway, you have decided that he is not guilty so that's an end to that matter and I am prepared to accept that conclusion even though Father Eynesham will, I am sure, be unhappy with it. He does like to go his own way and does not want to be crossed. But it leaves me with a major problem about

70

what to do next."

"Yes, it is difficult," I agreed but not sure that I had much to add.

"If you don't mind, Sir Matthew, I want to take you into my confidence and, I apologise for this, ask a further favour from you?" He looked up hopefully.

I repressed a groan. Father Compton was without resources and I could see that he needed support. I was going to find it impossible to refuse.

"Yes, by all means, go ahead," I replied as briskly and pleasantly as I could. "If there is anything further I can do to help you or the abbey I should, of course, be happy to oblige."

"That's very generous of you," he said appreciatively. "Now I need to be fairly quick while Brother Thomas is not with us. As you know he's not from this community. He's from the cathedral – helping me out. But they are rather different from us over there and naturally very close to the Bishop. Consequently, they do have a rather high opinion of themselves – and a correspondingly low opinion of us over here in Hyde."

"I had rather suspected that," I replied.

"So, as you have gathered, I was summoned this morning to go across to the cathedral."

"By the bishop?"

Father Compton laughed.

"The Bishop? William of Wykeham, former Lord Chancellor, Member of the royal council? Not very likely, I'm afraid, Sir Matthew. He's got far bigger matters to deal with. He's probably in London now in his grand palace in Southwark – attending to his geese and consorting with the young King Richard. No, as I mentioned, it was the Prior – Prior Hugh Basyng – he's the man who gets his hands dirty on matters here in Winchester. He's been in the job for almost 20 years and, although he's supposed to be independent of Bishop William, the reality is that he's hand in glove with him."

"And what did Prior Hugh want to talk about?"

"Not surprisingly, the murder."

"He heard about it very quickly."

"News travels very fast in Winchester – and especially between this abbey and the cathedral. I mentioned Brother Thomas..."

He frowned as he said this and let the thought hang. Anxious to clarify his meaning I asked him bluntly.

"A spy in the camp?"

"Brother Thomas is here to 'support' me, Sir Matthew. I'll leave it at that."

"And you've said yourself that you do need help," I prompted.

"I think that help given in good faith is certainly useful – but then there is the other kind of help which might, actually, be less than helpful to me but rather more beneficial to someone else."

"Father Compton you are starting to talk, if you don't mind me saying so, in riddles."

"I have probably said too much already so I will leave it there apart from making clear that the Cathedral is now an interested party in this scandal – of that I am sure." He looked at me as meaningfully as he could manage. "Nonetheless I am genuinely very grateful to you for your help in resolving John's situation. But, as we have agreed, it does leave us still with the question of who killed Brother Peter - and why? Although you seem to question the very idea that he was actually murdered."

"I am merely making the point that I have not seen the body so cannot be sure," I said slowly. "But, on the balance of probabilities, I think Brother Peter was indeed killed – but whether deliberately or not I cannot guess."

"Well, we may never know, I suppose. But, for better or worse, I am under acute pressure to come up with an answer to that question. It's not an easy one as you yourself concede. But I am almost at a loss as to what to do next. I am only the acting abbot, as you know, and, as I mentioned last night, I do not feel that I am suited to the post – even temporarily."

"But you must have been talented at something," I offered, trying to sound supportive. "After all, you were the prior."

"I am the only man in the abbey, Sir Matthew, who is confident in his arithmetic. That was why I was the prior here and why I had responsibility under Abbot Lechy for all the accounting. Ever since our foundation over four hundred years ago we have held estates and lands across the south of England. It meant that, at one time, we were a wealthy institution. It needed a lot of adding up of our finances. Not so any more, I'm afraid. We are owed money by our tenants and in some cases they have not payed what is due for years."

"Because?"

"Put simply, we are not the force we were. It all started, of course, with the pestilence. I had just started here as a novice when the terrible illness arrived from over the seas. Some say it was by way of Weymouth. No, it was Southampton. That is where we got in from. Straight down the Itchen to our front door. Of course it was! So it arrived here in Hyde very, very quickly."

I nodded.

"Father Eynesham joined as a boy, several years younger than me, at around the same time. It was a terrible, terrible experience. More than half the monks were killed by it as if by a voracious fiend. We have full records of those who died and when and how. And the pain they suffered. We have a carving of a devil on one of our corbels as a reminder. And as a new arrival I was completely confounded by the whole experience. But it also devastated our farms and estates. The peasants also died in large numbers, of course, and much of the land was just abandoned. So our income collapsed."

"Yes, it was horrible ." I agreed, "I was about ten at the time but we lived an isolated life and in some comfort. I was sheltered. We didn't see many deaths. Miraculous really."

"Maybe not so miraculous, Sir Matthew. The richer you were the more God favoured you. 'To those who have...' and all that. But anyway the abbey's fortunes were left devastated and the abbot at the time – Abbot Fifield - was forced to go to the cathedral and beg for support. They helped out, they kept us

73

going – but at a price. I might say a high price – a very high price."

"But aren't you all brothers together in Christ?"

"If only that were so… There has been rivalry between us and those at the Cathedral for hundreds of years going back to when the Saxon king, Alfred, was buried with us and not with them. And his son, King Edward, too – he was buried here. And the beloved Saint Grimbald. The Cathedral was jealous - and I am sure you have come across fraternal rivalry and how poisonous that can be. Even those who have been very close through shared misery can end up in venomous discord. But now the Cathedral monastery is the very big brother and we are the little brother and that is never a good place to be. So it's about money and status. We threw ourselves on their mercy during the pestilence. Yes, they supported us but since then they have used every opportunity they can to squeeze whatever possible out of us to the last degree. It's as if the Bishop didn't have enough income of his own!"

"I'd heard he was the richest bishop in the country."

"By a long way," said Father Compton.

"So why does he want to squeeze extra money from you?"

"Because although he has a lot coming in he also has a lot going out. And as an arithmetician I know where that leads. When he was Chancellor he subsidised the old King in his wars in France. Of course that bought him extra influence. And now, of course, he's got all these plans – first the college at Oxford, now the school he plans to build here in Winchester. It all costs money."

"So he wants to get his hands on some of yours?"

"That's pretty much the measure of it. And that's why they've planted the charming Brother Thomas here with me so that he can find out as much as possible about what goes on in Hyde. My predecessors would not have stood for it. But the death of our old abbot gave Prior Hugh the chance to start moving in. And now they want to take ever more control over us."

"And this murder has offered them an opportunity, has it?"

I asked.

"Well, take today for example. After Prior Hugh and I had prayed together – very briefly – for the repose of Peter's soul the Prior turned nasty very quickly. He said the murder was typical of what was going on at Hyde – disorder, crime, irreverent behaviour, women in the abbey. He went on at length listing all our failures. Quite how he knew every single detail of what has been going on here – and going back for years not just since Brother Thomas arrived – I don't know. But he concluded by saying that this murder was a test. Indeed, it was the final test of our capacity to remain independent and manage our own affairs. We had to find the culprit, convict him with suitable evidence and then hand him over to the civil authorities for punishment. Failure to do this by Easter would result in a formal investigation into the abbey which would lead to an inevitable conclusion."

"And that would be what exactly?"

"The suspension of my role and then the direct management of all our property and practices by the Prior on behalf of the bishop. They'd postpone indefinitely the election of a new abbot – or maybe just nominate someone who would be completely compliant. It's happened before. Many years back there was five years without an abbot. Anyway, I explained that we had a suspect and that I had asked you to investigate. The prior did not look too pleased by that. Especially when I told him who the suspect was. John was a child of the cathedral and it would not look good if he turned out to be the murderer. They've been paying for him to be at Oxford. So when I tell him tomorrow that you regard John as being innocent and entirely uninvolved he will be relieved twice over – on the one hand, no embarrassment for the cathedral and, on the other, a way of keeping pressure on me – on the abbey – to come up with the real culprit. Which is going to be difficult."

"Mmm, I see – so in some ways it would have been better for you if I had concluded John's guilt."

"Quite – but, of course, I would not have wanted that if he

75

were innocent. Which I think we both consider that he was."

"Indeed. But, if I read your thoughts correctly you now want – or, should I say, need - someone to continue to investigate how Brother Peter died."

"That's right," Father Compton replied. "Continue to investigate the death, identify the killer if there is one and then bring him – or, who knows, maybe her – to justice."

He waited for this to sink in.

"So will you do it – please?" he now asked outright. "We really need your help. The abbey needs your help. I need your help." And he offered me a piece of cheese as if that were sufficient payment for what I was letting myself in for.

CHAPTER 11
'Wepyns and Waylyns'

I hardly felt that I could reject Father Compton's request. But identifying the likely killer would be difficult enough let alone bringing him (or her) to justice. And asking me to do it for 'the Church' created a sour taste in my mouth. I had been fighting for the church – or allegedly so - with all its moral ambiguities for the past five years. I was not keen to re-enter that pit.

"Give me time to think about it. And I'll talk to Damian and Osric, Father Compton. Because, for certain, I will need their assistance as well."

"Of course, Sir Matthew. Think and, maybe more important, pray. Perhaps the three of you should pray together over it?"

"Yes, an excellent idea," I said, although the idea of Damian and Osric praying alongside me seemed a little unlikely. But, for myself, maybe I should. "I will let you know as soon as I can. Incidentally, will there be a guest dinner tonight?"

"We have a guest dinner at Hyde every night, Sir Matthew. And, of course, you are invited. It will be another muted affair, I'm afraid but the abbey cannot neglect its guests. And besides, I persuaded those who were there last evening to remain for two days specifically to accompany you to London. I'm obliged as much to them as to you."

"Very good. So I will think further about the investigation and let you know before dinner. But if I am going to continue I really need to see the body of Brother Peter – I should have done so this morning but, unfortunately, your Brother Thomas forbade it"

"Did he indeed?"

"Yes, I was severely put out, I must admit. I told him that I would complain to you. He did not look particularly concerned."

"No, well, he wouldn't – he knows that he has the support of the Prior over at the Cathedral for anything he does – or says – and that is good enough for him," said Father Compton with a look of irritation which expressed his lack of authority.

"So, I should be grateful if you would accompany me to the corpse, Father," I continued. "To put it bluntly, Thomas might not respect you but he could not, I imagine, actually stop you from examining the body."

"No, indeed – and why should he? And why did he stop you in the first place? Well, I expect he probably had his own reasons - or maybe somebody's else's"

"So I'll go now and collect Damian and Osric and I shall meet you shortly at the body – which is where exactly?" I asked.

"Peter's body is in the infirmary. It was taken there immediately Father Eynesham had returned to the library after apprehending John," explained Father Compton. "Two of the men loafing about in the Outer Court carried him down there apparently. He's been in the care of Brother Walter, our infirmarian, a very reliable man. One of the few we have here, I regret to say."

"And you've seen the corpse, have you"

"Actually no, I haven't seen it personally," said Father Compton looking slightly embarrassed. "I'm rather squeamish about that kind of thing."

"So you have no idea about what kind of wounds he suffered? I've been getting some rather mixed reports."

"No, I'm sorry I cannot help you on that."

"Oh, well – then we'll have to see for ourselves won't we?"

"Yes, indeed we will," said Father Compton resignedly.

There was one other matter which I felt I should put to Father Compton - the possible significance of the lost (or, more likely, stolen) 'Golden' charter of King Edgar. Presumably it had some part to play in Brother Peter's murder but I could not understand what that might be. The problem was that I did not want to explain the details that implicated John in its disappearance. But my instinct was that without understanding the value of the Golden Charter I was missing out on a major clue. So I tried a broader approach.

"Oh, just one other thing, Father Compton – when we were over at the library John was saying that some of those charters held in the library were interesting and maybe even important. Would that be so, do you think? They all sounded pretty ancient to me. What kind of importance might they have today?"

"Yes, well John really does know his way around our library!" Father Compton exclaimed. "I'm impressed that he's looked at those old pieces - but then he's a bookish lad. Mind you, they should all be locked away. That was one of Brother Peter's most important responsibilities – to keep them safe. Yes, John's right that some of those charters are important. Nobody much in the abbey takes any interest any more but I remember Abbot Lechy saying to me that one of them in particular was enormously valuable. This goes back to the tensions we had with the cathedral over our independence."

"So when was that then?" I asked.

"My understanding is that some time back the cathedral claimed that because we had moved physically from the centre of Winchester to here in Hyde we had lost our traditional rights and entitlements. In other words, we were a new institution starting from scratch. Abbot Lechy was able to refer to one particular charter – the very first one we had in fact – which clearly stated that those rights and properties belonged to the community and not the building and were to last in perpetuity. So it was very helpful in safeguarding our position. In fact, I'd say it was invaluable. Without it we might not have a leg to stand on when challenged by the cathedral - or indeed anyone else."

"And what was this charter called?"

"Oh, I can't remember that but it stood out. It was bright gold in hue and had a picture of the king who had presented it - Edgar, I think it was. This was all a long way back before you French came over. That's a good reminder for me. I ought to go and look at it and remind myself of the details."

At this point I felt I had to be a little more candid.

"I am sorry to say, Father Compton, that might prove difficult. When we were doing some tidying up in the Library with John he tried to find it. He couldn't. He thinks it might have been

79

stolen – presumably by the same people who murdered Peter."

There was a moment's pause.

"Ohhhhhhh!" rasped Father James. "NO, NO, NO, – without that charter we have let our drawbridge down – and who knows who might invade to ravish and destroy us! We MUST find it – we MUST get it back."

He was sounding truly desperate and suddenly some of the pieces began to fit together.

CHAPTER 12
'No lenʒer wolde he carie'

"Where have you been, Father?" asked Damian. "We've been waiting for you for an age! We thought that you might have actually decided to join the monastery."

"Well, who knows – I might yet," I replied, "but certainly not this one. Sit down the two of you – we have something to discuss."

They did as they were told. Our guest room - which would be perfectly adequate for one person - was feeling increasingly crowded. I was already longing to leave. I had put up with much worse conditions in both Prussia and in Africa but I was beginning to realise that mentally I was now more fragile than in those long off days. Being 'at home' was more stressful that I had imagined.

"I've had a long discussion with Father Compton and I have a much better understanding of the state of the monastery," I started. "I'll tell you more later but the key point is that it's being targetted by the Prior at the cathedral for a take-over."

"Is that a bad thing or a good thing, Lord?" asked Osric. "Whose side are we on?"

"Hmm, good question, Osric! In all honesty, I am in two minds about this. Maybe it would be better for the monastery to be better managed. On the other hand I don't like the idea of the powerful become even more powerful – especially at the expense of something smaller and vulnerable."

"I agree, Lord," said Osric with some feeling.

"But this murder has come at the worst possible time for Father Compton," I continued. "It gives another excuse for the cathedral to lean on him. And this morning the Prior gave him a warning. He either finds out who killed Brother Peter and sort out what happened – or face the consequences."

"And how does he feel about that?" asked Damian. "Pretty scared, I should imagine."

"More like rudderless, I would say. When I told him that

81

we were convinced that John was not our man he was pleased for John's sake but had no idea what to do next. Except, maybe the obvious.."

"Huh, I can see what's coming," said Damian who was starting to understand how the world worked. "Presumably he asked you to continue with the inquisition, father?"

"That's right."

"And have you agreed?"

"I couldn't do it on my own, even if I wanted to. I would need your assistance. What do you think?"

Both Damian and Osric looked uncertain how to reply.

"Damian, how do you feel?"

"Well, father, of course it is up to you but I rather fancy the challenge of it. I mean going on pilgrimage is very important and all that but trying to solve a puzzle like this would be, well, a bit more fun."

I did not think that was a particularly mature response from Damian. But I let it pass. He would learn in due course.

"Osric?"

"I agree with Master Damian here, Lord. It will stir things up a bit for us. And also I don't like to think of the murderer getting away with it. That Brother Peter. He was humble soul, I reckon. He did not deserve this. I want to see whoever did it, get caught. And if I can help do that then I am game for it."

"So in that case I'll tell Father Compton that we'll take it on. For myself I see it as a duty. And if I do nothing else with the rest of my life I can, at least, be dutiful."

"That sounds just," said Osric.

"And at last we have a clue – at least I think it's a clue," I added. "That Golden Charter which has disappeared – and which we think was stolen by the murderer – was extremely valuable."

"You mean in terms of money?" asked Osric.

"Yes, in a way, it is financial, I suppose," I replied. "But more importantly is its legal status. It was given by this king Egbert, in olden days and it established the independence of this abbey – by which I mean this community of monks - from the cathedral. If Father Compton and his fellow monks here in Hyde want to stay outside the total grip of Bishop William then they need to have that charter as proof of their rights."

"So that means we are now not looking just for the murderer but the charter as well," said Damian.

"That's it," I said. "I'm convinced the two go together. But for now let's concentrate on the body."

CHAPTER 13
'Riȝht so they han hym slain'

The infirmary lay in the outer court of the monastery, well away from the cloisters but facing across to the gateway so its comings and goings could easily be seen by loiterers. By now, a day after the murder, news of events in the monastery had spread far and wide and there was a growing crowd of gawpers drawn into the abbey's precincts by the scandal. Many no doubt were pilgrims visiting the abbey church as the first stopping-off point on the way to Canterbury. But there also seemed to be a variety of locals attracted by the sensational events. And on top of that there were some distinctly insalubrious characters looking, no doubt, for a thieving opportunity amongst the crowd.

The infirmary, a generous, clean and warm room with some side-chambers off the main hall, was almost empty. Just a couple of beds were occupied by the door but at the far end I could see Father Compton and two others standing by a screen which had been placed around one of the beds.

When the acting abbot turned to me his face was creased with distress. He nodded to me and added an acknowledgement for Damian and Osric. "Let me introduce you, Sir Matthew, to Brother Walter, our infirmarian and Dr Aloysious Nafis, our excellent medical advisor who comes in daily to deal with the more complicated cases."

They both bowed to us.

"I am not sure I have anything to add to what they might say to you," continued Father Compton. "So, if you don't mind I will leave you in their capable hands. I think poor Brother Peter's body speaks for itself. As you will see it is too, too terrible. And, Sir Matthew, I look forward to seeing you for supper – and to hear your decision as to whether or not you will continue to help us. Perhaps, having seen this, you will understand the depth of our need,"

"Father Compton, I can answer you on that point already.

I have spoken to Damian and Osric and we are all of one mind that we should continue our investigation into this awful matter. So the answer is 'Yes'. And we shall be grateful for your continued co-operation – and, of course, the other members of the community as well."

"Indeed, indeed – well that at least is good news. I am so very grateful to you."

And with that he departed leaving me, in effect, to take command of the situation.

Brother Walter was aged about fifty and had a neat, sensible appearance as if he were well used to looking after himself. The Doctor meanwhile was quite a lot younger than I had expected and with features rather like those I had seen in Africa. He could have been no more than thirty five and was wearing a distinctive red outfit slashed with bluish-grey and displaying an ostentatious gold chain.

"This is a very sad situation - Brother, Doctor – and as you have gathered, Father Compton has asked me to look into it," I explained.

"Of course, we understand and are grateful, I am sure," said Brother Walter sympathetically. "Brother Peter was a dear old friend. I am devastated by what has happened."

"Just look into it?" asked Doctor Nafis who gave the impression of being unnerved by the situation. "Surely it needs something rather more urgent than that!"

"Well, first we will look into it – and then we shall see what comes out of it," I said in a neutral tone.

"What comes out of it is going to be very unpleasant, I suggest," continued the Doctor. "Please follow me."

He led us around to the other side of the screen. There was Brother Peter stretched out in all his mortal frailty. He was under a thin blanket and, without a word, the Doctor whisked it off.

There is no need to go into detail. Brother Peter was an old, fat man. He would have been undignified in any death but was made infinitely worse by appearing naked with the mutilation of his private parts now on display.

"So this is what it comes to," I said. Corpses were not unfamiliar to me but the particular ugliness of Brother Peter was immediately grotesque and upsetting.

After a short period of observation I said. "Well, I think we have seen enough. Damian, Osric, anything more?"

They both shook their heads indicating they had seen all that was required.

"No, I think you need also to examine in some detail the neck," said Doctor Nafis pointing to dark, bruisings. "Although those wounds to the groin are striking it is more important, to observe the neck. It is broken. That was the cause of Brother Peter's death."

"And the wounds below?"

"They would have been painful but not fatal," explained the doctor. "In fact, I suspect not felt at all."

"So executed before or after death, do you think?"

He coughed. "I suspect afterwards – I doubt he would have felt anything."

The three of us bent over the damaged neck. It was clear that a considerable amount of force had been applied.

"Right, well that is very informative," I said in as matter-of-fact voice as I could manage. "Please cover Brother Peter up and then let us discuss what we have seen."

Brother Walter took us out from behind a screen and over to a table crowded with plates and jars of medicinal-looking aids.

"Do take a seat," he said indicating stools of various kinds around the table. "There's nothing to fear here," he said, pointing to what seemed to be a collection of magical effigies. "They are all Doctor Nafis's specialities."

"Well, thank you," I said not entirely reassured. "Now I'd just like to ask a few questions so I can be clear about the sequence of events yesterday. This might not be entirely material to our investigation – after all he was dead and the damage done by the time Brother Peter arrived here – but it just helps me to get the full picture of what was happening in the abbey. So when did you first see the body?"

"Me?" asked the doctor jumping in first. "Fairly briefly last evening. I believe that Brother Peter's body had been brought in some time earlier. Very shocking, of course. Very shocking indeed. Brother Walter told me what had happened and I just checked him over. But as Brother Walter has explained it was immediately obvious that he was dead. Nothing to be done. But I was already late for an appointment at St. Mary's, the convent. So I had to go almost immediately. I told Brother Walter that I would examine the body more carefully when I returned this morning. And that was when I noticed the mutilation."

"I see – and you Brother."

"I came back from the chapel after noon. There were a couple of men here with Brother Peter's body. They just dumped it down at the front by the door. All they said was that Brother Peter had been attacked – he was dead and that Father John, our cellarer, had instructed them to bring the body across."

"And who were these men exactly?"

"I don't know, I'd never seen them before. I think they were passers-by who had been hanging around in the almoner's hall and just been commandeered by Father Eynesham. It's the kind of thing he does."

"And Peter was definitely dead, was he?"

"Absolutely, there was no question about that," said Brother Walter. "I saw that at once. No breath, no life in him. No spirit in him. That was departed. I held his hands and felt his forehead. Already cold. I just felt very sad. He was a friend as well as a brother."

"And presumably there was a lot of blood everywhere?"

Brother Walter looked briefly puzzled.

"Oh. Because of the mutilation, you mean. Er, not that I noticed.."

"You don't sound too certain."

"Well Brother Peter was an old man and he always wore

very thick garments in addition to his habit. Rather more than St. Benedict's rule allows, I'm afraid. So I think they might have absorbed a lot of it. But I didn't look. As I said, he was dead. I would leave the detail to Doctor Nafis here."

"And you didn't notice?"

"No, all too upsetting. It was when I stripped him this morning after Doctor Nafis had examined him that I saw the mutilation."

"Ah well. But Brother Walter, why did not examine Brother Peter's corpse last night."

"Why should I? I do not deal with the dead. I deal with the living – or at least the living who are sick. I minister to them to keep them alive. After they have gone I have no truck with them – they live on but they are with Christ and he can care for them much better than I ever could."

"But you, Doctor Nafis – do you take an interest in the dead?"

The doctor bridled somewhat.

"Of course I take interest in a dead body, Sir Matthew – not least to ensure they are, in fact, dead. And sometimes you can learn more from a dead body than from a living one."

"And so did you look at Brother Peter's corpse – I mean, again, intimately?"

"If you mean did I look closely at him then the answer is Yes. But that was this morning."

"Why was that?"

"Well, as I said, I had no time last night while this morning I wanted to analyse more closely the nature of the force applied to Brother Peter's neck. And to look at any other effects. That was when the mutilation came to light"

"So, it would have needed a strong grip to kill him – and then an attack below with a knife afterwards? Is that what you are saying?"

"Not necessarily a strong grip. He might just have been pushed over and fallen heavily. Not everyone dies from a broken neck by any means. But some do. Brother Peter did. I was trying to work out why. Being so overweight did not help him I suspect.

But the force of it makes it look more than a trip-up. A push or even, I would suggest, a forceful attack."

"Of course – by one person or two?"

"One, I should have thought. Two would have been clumsy. However, if he had been just knocked over and then leapt on and was flailing about then a second person could have held him down. But with our limited evidence it is hard to tell."

"And what do you make of the mutilation? You say that would not have been necessary to accomplish the murder."

"Exactly – it was excessive."

"So why do you think it happened?"

"Ha, ha," said the good doctor. "That is a question! How can I get into the mind of such a person? I think he is ill."

"You mean physically ill?"

"No, I mean mostly mentally ill. Or at least obsessive in some way. It was done with a purpose."

"And when do you think it happened? At the same point as when Brother Peter's neck was broken?"

"I am not sure that I can answer that. We do not have enough knowledge yet as to the timing of injuries. But it looked as if it had been hacked at immediately after the neck was broken."

In what was already a grim atmosphere this added an extra chilling effect. Brother Walter was looking distinctly miserable and I could detect that Damian was undergoing unpleasant imaginings of his own about the experience of such an attack. Osric was looking on it more as if he were in the forest with a dead deer or fox.

"So, Sir Matthew, any more questions? I have other people to see – including Madame Eglentyne who is visiting from Wintney which is also under my care. I am travelling with her to Canterbury. I have never been on a pilgrimage before. I believe it is time I did."

"Ah, so you will then be of our party?"

"Probably so."

While we had been talking I had noticed on the table a number of medical books which I recognised from my time in Africa.

"These look interesting," I said. "Avicenna, Averroes – arab doctors aren't they. Yours, Brother Walter?"

"No. they belong to me, Sir Matthew," said Doctor Nafis quickly. "I have a lot of books scattered all over Winchester. I really need to bring them together at some point. But these ones are particularly important to me. I feel a strong affiliation to them."

"Well, I know from my time abroad that these doctors are very advanced," I said, remembering some rather peculiar moments under their care.

"You are right! Sir Matthew – I am glad that you appreciate that," said Doctor Nafis appearing to warm to me a little. "It's why I have their books here – these and others from over the seas. I'm afraid England still lags behind in some respects, Sir Matthew – apart from Oxford of course. John of Gaddesden's *Rosa Medicinae* – marvellous on urine in particular! Very useful indeed. I'm proud to say that I was at Gaddesden's college, Merton. Sadly he is no longer with us – but learning goes on." He paused for a moment. "Anyway, if you have no more need of me I must move. I have the pox to deal with at the cathedral. Sadly, no matter how our knowledge advances, the pox is always with us. So, Sir Matthew, I hope the Almighty may assist you with your investigations. And do remember that the person who did that," he pointed towards Brother Peter's private parts, "is not a well person."

Once Doctor Nafis had left the infirmary I felt Brother Walter relax noticeably.

"Has Doctor Nafis been attached to the abbey for long," I asked.

"About five years, I would say. He's very learned, read all the books, studied in Paris as well as Oxford, keeps himself up-to-date with all the latest thinking – and charges a lot of money for his services even to the abbey."

"But you can afford him?"

"Well that's a matter for Father Compton. But I wish I was earning as much as he does! But, of course, I have taken a vow of poverty," he said with a sour laugh. "Like many of the members of this community and those around it, Doctor Nafis grew up in Winchester from a young age. Although his parents, I believe, came from abroad as merchants to Southampton. But it means he's well-known and well-trusted. He is seen as a local man. And that's the important thing."

"And well-liked?" I asked somewhat riskily.

"That might be a different matter. But if you save someone's life – or appear to have saved their life – then they are bound to like you, aren't they?"

"If you don't mind me saying so, Brother Walter, you seemed slightly – shall I say – intimidated by the good Doctor."

"Well, you've seen for yourself; he's young, he's very learned and self-confident, he's had proper training and he knows so much more than I do – especially about the astrological aspects of medicine."

"And they are important are they?"

"Oh yes, very much so – that's the coming thing. He knows about the favourable stars and Natural Magic. That's the future for medicine Sir Matthew. And colours, of course too."

"Colours?" I asked somewhat sceptically.

"Yes, colours. That Doctor Gaddesden, you know, he cured the old King of the pox by wrapping him in red draperies. It worked, at least so they say. It's probably what Nafis is doing with this case at the cathedral right now. Anyway it's certainly why he always wears red."

"Ah yes, I noticed that."

"Sadly all I have to match him with is a collection of fading herbs." He pointed back towards the table. "But then I'm old-fashioned. But I still go out and buy them or pick them in our meadows. In fact I was out in town this morning at the market buying this pile." He pointed to the table.

"So you weren't actually here this morning?"

"Not all the time, no."

"So does that mean that Peter's corpse was not being safeguarded?"

"Oh, yes it was. The doctor was here this morning as he usually is. He came in and, as you heard, spent time with Brother Peter as well as our other invalids. But I am sure that, as he mentioned, he would have wanted to examine Peter carefully when he had the time to spare."

"But you don't?"

"Sir Matthew, as I said, I'm not going to be able to do much for poor, dead Peter – and certainly not with a handful of herbs. They are not going to bring him back from the dead. If he was near death, possibly. But not once he had died. He was not Lazarus and I am not Christ."

"No, you're right you can't bring him back from the dead. And really would Brother Peter want to be?" I asked reflectively. "My guess is that he wasn't a particularly happy man?"

Brother Walter sighed heavily.

"He was certainly getting old – no, he was old! I'd known him a long time. When he was younger he was dedicated – dedicated as a monk, dedicated as a scholar. But as things started to grow slack in the monastery he lost heart. He drank a bit more than he should. He was one of those monks who could regularly be seen in the taverns in town."

"But surely that was against the rules?"

"Absolutely, against all the rules. But discipline here has gone down hill, our numbers have grown smaller and demoralisation has set in. It was Peter's behaviour in town – and the reputation he attracted – which upset people so much. That and other things of course. And the numbers in our little school just collapsed."

"So when did that happen?"

"Well, it was Peter again. He was in charge of the school. It used to have a good reputation but that was before the Pestilence. And then when Peter took over the stories began to circulate about him."

"Which stories were those?"

"That he was too interested in the boys – I mean physically."

"Ah-ha, I see," I replied. "That familiar old story. How did you feel about that?"

"I am sure you've not got any illusions about monks, Sir Matthew. Good St. Benedict himself didn't. Anyway, whether justified or not, Brother Peter had that reputation. I don't know whether there were good grounds for it or not. But he and I just got on well together. We had the same outlook. However, I have to admit that recently things became quite disgraceful in the library. It was almost as if someone was deliberately creating chaos. It was about the same time as the stories circulated that outsiders were coming into the abbey at night and staying in the church until morning getting up to who knows what. And then there were the other rumours about women sneaking in. Not that I knew anything about that of course. It was just one thing after another. I can understand why people might want revenge."

"Revenge? So you think he might have been murdered as an act of revenge?"

"Well, let's just say there was an act of revenge in there somewhere – I suspect."

"Have you got any suspects in mind then, Brother Walter," asked Osric, a bit too directly for my taste.

There was a long pause.

"No, there's no-one I could name," he said eventually.

"Well, you have been very candid with us, Brother Walter especially under these very difficult circumstances," I said to bring our discussion to a close. "But if I might just ask you one last thing. You've described what's wrong with the abbey? What does it need to change?"

"New blood. It's stalemate at the moment about who'll be next abbot. I think it might have to get worse before it gets better. Meanwhile each of us must shift for ourselves."

New blood, I thought? So where exactly had Brother Peter's blood disappeared to?

CHAPTER 14

'She passed hem of Ypres and Gaunt'

We were pleased to escape the infirmary. Although it was well-organised thanks to Brother Walter's careful way of managing there was still a deep sense of death and moral squalor around it. When I returned from crusade I was expecting to come back to something better. My naivete hurt. The crusades in foreign lands – so innocently entered into on my part – had become deeply corrupting. My homecoming threatened to turn into the same.

"You go and cheer yourselves up," I said to Damian and Osric. "I better prepare myself for dinner."

I pushed away my gloomy thoughts not least because my eye was drawn once more to the gateway to the forecourt. Still to my surprise Mistress Alison, my well-upholstered friend from Bath, seemed to be in conversation with the two nondescript little men, both hooded, I had noticed earlier. Did she never go anywhere else? Or was it merely coincidence that I continually saw her there with that pair of unsavoury rogues? My curiosity was whetted. I left Damian and Osric went across to speak to her.

"Greetings, Lady Alison. My apologies for disturbing you. Am I going to have the pleasure of your company this evening?"

The two roughs seemed rather put out by my interruption, bowed their heads and looked away. But she turned towards me warmly.

"Oh, Sir Matthew – how very nice to see you," she said in her soft South West accent. "And how kind of you to address me as 'Lady' Alison. Of course I am a lady by nature but, sadly not by title – at least not yet. But do call me Mistress Alison. I do think that Mistress is such a nice word, don't you agree?"

"How could I possibly disagree, Mistress Alison? It's good to see you still here."

"But naturally. And I am looking forward to dinner this evening with Father Compton and his other charming guests – and particularly yourself."

She beamed. And while we were exchanging these little niceties the two men started whispering between themselves.

"Now Sir Matthew, you are planning to start for Canterbury tomorrow, aren't you?"

"Actually it's the day after tomorrow. If you remember Father Compton prevailed on me to look into this horrid murder and we agreed that I should have two days to do so."

"Oh yes, of course," she said. "I'm afraid that I have been too much wrapped up in my own affairs. And are you making progress on this, what you call, inquisition?"

"Well it's rather more complicated than the way Father Eynesham – you know, the cellarer – described it."

"Yes, indeed, I know Father Eynesham very well. This is not the first time I have passed through dear little Hyde Abbey although it is the first time I have had the privilege of being a guest here. Mind you, it does seem to be a doubtful privilege right now. What with this awful murder. Not quite what I was expecting, I must confess. But we pilgrims must endure vicissitudes must we not? But tell me, what have you learned so far?"

I hesitated for a moment. How much should I reveal at this point? "You will recall that Father Eynesham was convinced that this silly lad – John, the scholar from Oxford, was responsible. But I have concluded that was not the case." I said.

"Oh! Oh dear! So that means we still have a murderer running loose here in the abbey?"

At this point the two fellows seemed to decide that it was time to move on. They turned and wandered off towards a group of humble types who had gathered around a pipe player. I think they started to sing some dirge-like hymn. Meanwhile I focused back on what Alison had been saying and fashioned a response

"Yes, it might well mean that there is a danger still, I have to concede. But I am sure no threat to you Mistress Alison – this is all about the monks here in the monastery," I said trying to be more positive. "Moreover, it also means that this young man does not have a terrible crime on his conscience. And that must

96

be a good thing."

"If you say so, Sir Matthew. But for my part I should sleep rather more easily in my bed here if I did not fear that a blood-thirsty ruffian was about to descend on me."

"Well, I really don't think you have anything to fear, Mistress Alison. I suspect that the murderer – whoever he or, indeed, she might be – had very particular reasons for getting rid of Brother Peter at that time and in that place. I am confident that you have nothing to be frightened of at all. No more murders here, I am sure."

"If you feel confident that you will protect me, Sir Matthew, then of course I shall feel safe. Sadly I no longer have a husband to look after me."

"Oh, dear I am sorry to hear that, Mistress Alison," I said trying to appear sympathetic. "Has your husband died recently?"

"He is due to die shortly, I am afraid Sir Matthew."

"Oh that's very sad to hear. Are you going to Canterbury to ask for the good saint's intervention."

For a moment Mistress Alison's demeanour changed. She looked at me as if I were in a state of delusion.

"I really don't think there would be any point in that, Sir Matthew," she responded briskly. "None at all. After all, in the end they all die, don't they? Husbands, I mean. They come, they go. They arrive, they depart, sooner or later. Mostly sooner in my experience. And that is how the Good Lord has designed it. Who are we to complain?"

"Well wives too, I'm afraid, Mistress Alison. I am recently widowed and I am feeling it deeply."

Grief-stricken though I was I had shed no tears since first hearing the news of Matilda's death in Southampton. Yet now, talking about her to Mistress Alison, I felt ready to dissolve. And then, as Mistress Alison looked at me solicitously, I regained control and continued. "One of the reasons I was prepared to take on this inquisition was as a distraction as well as a duty."

"I am so sorry, Sir Matthew. I had no idea. I have to admit

97

my attitude towards marriage is rather more detached."

"You've been married more than once, I think?" I asked somewhat tentatively.

"You are correct, Sir Matthew. Five husbands, all dead. Well the fifth is on his way out now. Sadly the Almighty has not looked kindly on me – they all departed quite quickly after we were wed. I rather think it was his plan. A test. And me so young. But as the good book says, we know neither the day nor the hour. Fortunately they all left generous wills – even the youngest. Or at least he will do."

Not quite knowing how to respond to this rather unsettling revelation I switched the subject.

"If you don't mind me asking – those two men you were speaking to earlier – the ones who have just gone across to the group over there. They looked rather crude types. Acquaintances of yours? I can never get a proper sight of them. They keep their hoods well down."

"Oh, dear!" she hissed. "Frightful people. We met up by chance on the road from Andover yesterday. They too are intending to go to Canterbury. I was having a little bit of trouble with my mules and they helped me take them in hand."

"Your mules?"

"Yes, my mules – laden heavily I am glad to say with cloth for the continent. I have stabled them a little way out of town during my stay here. They do love my cloth across the sea in Ypres and Ghent – better quality, you see, than the local stuff."

"Well, I'm impressed," I replied, "But you were saying about those two odd-looking men."

"Yes they were helpful but unfortunately this seems to have given them the impression that I am in some way indebted to them and they can talk to me at will."

"And what do they talk to you about? Sheep? Wool? The weather?"

"Ah no, if only it were that simple. The rougher one is a common ploughman but the other one, is his brother and, would you believe it, he is a priest! They come from a dreadful little village – I know because I have ridden through it – called Chiseldon and all they do is complain about this new tax that the king has introduced. They say it is unfair. Of course it is not unfair – don't they know that there is a war on? – And that it has to be paid for?"

Chiseldon immediately rang a bell. Wasn't that the village that the priest and the farmer came from who had been spreading the story about Brother Peter's mutilation? And here they were making mischief about taxes. On both counts, I thought, I needed to keep my eye on them. Clearly there was trouble brewing – and not just about taxes.

"Yes, indeed, we must guard against dissent," I replied, "although I fear that this expensive war is not for winning, My son, Damian – you might have seen him with me – was with his Lordship, John of Lancaster, in France two years ago. He tells me it was shambles. Along with the rest of the army Damian had to come home with his tail between his legs. Unfortunately, I was away – otherwise I would have dissuaded him from going."

"But you are a knight, Sir Matthew – indeed a very gallant knight, the embodiment of chivalry from what I understand – surely you would want your son to follow in your footsteps?"

"Not in pursuing unwinnable wars, Mistress Alison, led by unwise, over-ambitious generals."

"You are surely not speaking of the Duke of Lancaster, Sir Matthew?"

"You may draw your own conclusions, Mistress Alison," I replied.

"Well I must tell you, Sir Matthew, that I have a high regard for the Duke of Lancaster. I knew him - in my own particular way – when I was a younger woman and I still remain attached to him. So I will not have a word said against the man."

"But you clearly did not marry him, Mistress Alice. He is, after all, still alive."

That might have been a rather impudent observation to a

99

woman I had barely met. But I had judged her mettle correctly.

"That is a very wicked thing to say, Sir Matthew!" and she burst out into a hearty laugh and continued giggling for some time. "If I could have married him, I should have done – and he would have remained alive. But, sadly, I was not quite at the right level of society for, shall we say, a more permanent relationship."

"Well if you don't mind me saying so, Mistress Alison, the Duke has a reputation for becoming, shall we say, very close to women of modest backgrounds."

"I am acquainted with the woman to whom you are referring, Sir Matthew. And I will have nothing bad said about her either. She is a friend. Well, a friendly acquaintance. And she has been poorly treated by the court."

This was, of course, Katherine Swynford to whom Mistress Alison was referring, the Duke's well-known lover and whose former husband was rumoured to have been poisoned on his orders. If she was on good terms with her then Mistress Alice had, perhaps, rather better connections than I had realised. So I needed to step carefully with Mistress Alison.

"Well, yes, I am sure that you have other things to deal with, Mistress Alison as indeed do I – so I look forward to seeing you this evening at dinner. Good afternoon."

She gave me a nod and walked away – although out of the corner of my eye I noticed her acknowledging the two roughs. Who were they exactly? And what were they doing? It was a question to dog me for weeks to come.

CHAPTER 15

'Into the blisse of heaven shul ye gon'

After Mistress Alison had walked off I stood for a little while outside the Gatehouse and observed the enormous mass of people coming and going into the abbey's great church. With its ancient royal tombs and, even more important, its mass of pilgrim-pleasing relics the abbey was still enormously popular despite what Father Compton had been saying. And everyone who visited hoped it would save them. But maybe this was part of its corruption.

I was reflecting on this along with my own hopes and prayers when Brother Michael, the porter, approached me. What had St. Benedict said about the porter in his Rule? "At the gate of the monastery a wise old man is to be posted, one capable of receiving a message and giving a reply and whose maturity guarantees that he will not wander around'. Yes, that summed up Michael perfectly, it seemed.

"Sir Matthew, what times eh?"

"Indeed, Michael, you're right – when I arrived yesterday I could scarcely have imagined that I would have found myself drawn into this awful mystery."

"So you're looking into it – trying to get to the bottom of it all, I understand. Father Eynesham told me. He said that you might be asking around, making enquiries."

"Yes, that's right. It's really Father Compton's responsibility but he feels that he cannot deal with it so he has asked me to try to work out what happened."

"And that young lad, John? I've known him for many a year. They were saying that he did it, like."

"Well let me reassure you on that point at least, Michael. He was not the one responsible, I'm sure of that."

"Well that's a relief at least. He might be a bit of a scallywag behind that show of shyness but not a bad lad, I was sure of that. So who do you think did do it, Sir Matthew?"

I breathed out heavily.

"Right now, I have no idea, Michael. But, you know, I reckon you might be able to help me."

"How's that Sir Matthew?"

"Well, whoever did it – and it might have been two people involved - must have been able to get access to the cloisters and then the library by way of coming through here - the Forecourt. Would you say that's right?"

"Yes, possibly," replied Michael cautiously. "Although you never know, they might have got into the cloister direct from the abbey church. Look at all those people going down there," – he pointed across the narrow Hyde Bourne stream towards the scores of people entering the abbey church's great west door. "Who knows what they're all up to once they get inside. It's large and very in places. But to get into the cloisters they'd have to get through the door from the altar which usually has a senior monk attending it. So it would be a bit difficult. Still it all depends on who you are, I suppose. And who you know."

It was a quiet insinuation but one I noted. It reminded me of the suggestion that security at the abbey was slack at best. Or at least had become so recently.

"So, just to be clear about what you are saying, Michael. It is possible to get from the abbey church into the cloisters but only with the permission – or collusion - of the senior monk on the door. Otherwise they would have had to come into the monastery through this very gate where we are now standing."

Again Michael agreed somewhat nervously, clearly understanding where this was going.

"Which means, if you don't mind me saying so Michael, they would have had to get past you."

I felt uncomfortable saying this. We had been acquainted for many years. Now, it almost seemed that I was accusing him of being complicit in the murder.

"Look here, Sir Matthew," he said heatedly. "I know nothing about this horrible thing."

"Calm down, Michael. Calm down. I am not suggesting that in any way. Certainly not accusing you of anything. I am just trying to understand how the murderers of Brother Peter got into the library."

"Well, if it was one of the monks who did it, then they'd not have a problem would they"

That took me aback.

"You think that's possible, Michael? Someone from the monastery itself?"

"Things have changed here, Sir Matthew, over the time you've been away. You must have seen that."

"If you're saying I shouldn't rule anyone out – that's a useful piece of advice, Michael. But for the time being I'd prefer to think it was an outsider who was responsible. After all, these are all brothers in Christ."

"Supposed to be," said Michael under his breath.

"I trust that they are," I said rather primly. "But, just help me here. I need to understand how outsiders – pilgrims, visitors - get through this gateway. You waved me and Damian and Osric through but you'd been told that I was coming. I'd sent a message ahead. But what about other people?"

Michael focused his mind.

"You can see for yourself, Sir Matthew, there's a rabble out there. They'd all love to get in here if they could. There's proper shelter, food, drink here. But we can't accommodate them all. Especially because a lot of them are chancers out on the road for fun. So, basically, my job is to keep them out. And let people like you in."

"Yes, Michael, but how do distinguish between them?"

"Well, Sir Matthew, there's a lot of them I already know – like you. Respectable folk. But others are strangers to me. And if they claim that they have been invited by Father Compton or Father Eynesham or Brother Walter or whoever then I have to allow them in – 'with a welcome' as good St Benedict says in his rule. I mean we've had people from Rome here – never seen them before but I'd be in trouble if I turned them away from the door if they said they'd be invited by the abbot or the cellarer. Or coming on behalf of the Pope – which happened once."

"And what if they are complete strangers but look like gentlefolk or maybe respectable clergy?"

"Then I have to make a judgement. But I see what you are getting at," he conceded reluctantly. "Maybe I did let in someone who I shouldn't. Or maybe they got through when I was attending to something else. I might be in charge, Sir Matthew, but I can't do this job on my own. You can see how busy it is sometimes. If I were to be distracted then someone could nip past."

In fact, I had noticed that while Michael and I were talking a younger man had stepped out from the Doorkeeper's shelter and had taken responsibility for vetting people coming through. As it happened, most had been turned away.

"So is that your assistant now, Michael?" I asked pointing towards the young man.

Michael turned round to look.

"Yes, that's right," he said. "Named Brother Timothy. He's alright I suppose but he's not one of ours. He's come across from the Cathedral. That Brother Thomas arranged it – you know the one helping Father Compton. He said it would be good to have someone on the gate with me who was familiar with the people from the cathedral and the priory since so many of them come across these days."

"Really? Why's that then?"

"Beats me, to be honest Sir Matthew. There's all sorts of people coming through given the nod by young Timothy. And it's not good for the abbey, I'm sure."

"Why, do you mean they're disruptive?"

"Who can tell?" Michael said. Then coming closer he almost whispered in my ear.

"These are strange times, Sir Matthew. More and more things are getting stolen, broken or turned over. We almost had a fire in the infirmary recently. And I think it's all because too many people are coming in - too many people we don't know. Brother Walter actually found one of those priory monks had stayed in his infirmary overnight – he was very upset about that. Very high standards has our Brother Walter. He's very particular about who he has in his ward. He allows no-one in without very good cause. But somehow people are getting into the monastery at night. It's as if someone is letting them in. But I've got no proof – so what can I do?"

"Well, I can see that's very unsatisfactory, Michael," I replied.

"It's more than 'unsatisfactory' as you put it, Sir Matthew - it's very worrying. I mean take those two layabouts Mistress Alison was chit-chatting to just now before you turned up. They tried to get in. I said I wasn't having it – not ignorant people dressed like that. But I know they've tried before. Maybe they've got through when I was looking the other way. Who can tell?"

"I think that one of them is a priest," I said.

"Yes, that's what he said he was, can you believe it?. Then Mistress Alison put in a word for them. She asked me if I would allow them in. 'They're such pious folk' she said. 'He's such a good, hard-working priest'. Now normally if a high class guest of the abbey asks for something like that, I agree. But I do have my limits – and those two – they looked like those Lollards to me. And if I let them in they'll be the devil to pay."

This stunned me. Lollards here in Winchester? Trying to enter the abbey? If so, they meant it no good. And what was Mistress Alison doing as their advocate? Why did she want them to be allowed into the abbey's inner areas in any case? Hadn't she just told me she had only met them by chance on the road.

"What makes you think they're Lollards, Michael. That's quite an accusation. It could get them into a lot of trouble. I mean they're very close to heresy. I came across some of their ilk coming across Germany and the Low Countries. The church was on to them like a shot."

"Well here it is different, Sir Matthew. Especially now that they've got that John of Gaunt supporting them. And some of the top nobs – like those Despensers over near your place. They think they can have the run of the church – and all they want to do is pull the whole thing down."

Again I felt that after five years away I was out of touch with matters in my own country. This was five years in which a new young king had come to the throne who was now largely under the thumb of his uncle, the Duke of Lancaster.

But could Duke John possibly be a Lollard-lover? Before I went away, he was famous for attacking the church and the power of the bishops. That surely could not mean though that he would back people like this pair of ne'er-do-wells, the so-called priest and his brother? And hadn't these two been complaining about this new tax for the war – a war with France which the Duke was anxious to prosecute. Somehow it didn't add up.

"So tell me, Michael, even though you've been turning these two away, do you think it is possible that they might have been able to get through the gateway over the past day or so?"

"Yes, all too possible, Sir Matthew. Young Timothy is not as selective as I am although he claims he knows a bad'un when he sees one. And it's even possible that this so-called priest might have been able to get in through the door by the altar in the chapel. He didn't fool me. But he might fool others."

"Yes, I can see that."

"And I have to be honest with you Sir Matthew," he said with a sigh, "I have a feeling that I might have seen them yesterday – around the time of the hue and cry over that lad, John. They could even have been the pair who carried Brother Peter across to the infirmary after his body was brought down from the library. How they got involved in that, I don't know. But I thought that I caught a glimpse of them from over here."

"Could you, indeed?"

"Yes, to be honest with you I'm pretty sure I did."

There were too many coincidences mounting up with this pair, I thought. I needed to pin them down. But I looked outside the gateway and they had wandered off into the crowd. They could be anywhere.

106

CHAPTER 16
'Wich sleves lonʒe and wyde'

I returned to our rooms to get ready for supper. Damian had just got back from a shopping trip to Winchester. He had a hint of alcohol about him and was wearing a new gown in what I understand was the fashionable new style - short but with absurdly large sleeves. He looked ridiculous. My son dressed like that! When I remonstrated with him about its impracticality the only thing he would say was that all the young blades were wearing them. My father would have ordered the shepherd to take a pair of sheers to them had I come home in such a garment. But there we are; fathers today are just too soft. Combined, in my case, with guilt about my long absence abroad. So I suppose I can only blame myself for his waywardness

Osric, by contrast, had spent his time as well as ever getting the measure of the latest gossip among the ordinary folk hanging around outside the abbey.

"You know, my lord, while we're caught up in this murder business there are bigger things happening in the world – things we don't hear about in Somborne."

"So what have you in mind, Osric?"

"There was a merchant I fell into conversation with outside the chapel, St. Bartholomew's. He was from Canterbury but he was on his way down to Southampton with a whole lot of goods he was taking across to Bordeaux. He normally goes the Harwich route apparently but was a bit nervous about passing through Essex right now. Lots of hold-ups on the road to the port."

"And why is that?" I asked.

"It's these new taxes again. The poxy poll tax. People over his way – the men of Kent - are getting really stoked up about them. He reckoned there'd be serious trouble soon enough if they tried to collect them by force."

"What do you mean by serious trouble, Osric?" I asked with an emphatic tone.

"I mean violence by lots of people my lord. Ordinary people – not you knights."

"When you say violence, Osric, I understand you to mean rebellion. Would that be fair? Be careful what you say. I want no talk of rebellion in our party."

"Well, I'm only telling you, lord, what this merchant was talking about. Maybe he was exaggerating. But my reading of it is that over there – you know closer towards London - they've got a lot more unemployed men coming back from the wars – old soldiers with a grievance and no jobs to go to."

"Yes, well I know what that looks like," I said, reminding myself that Osric, for all his physical strength, had never actually shot a bow in anger.

"They're not like the steady folk around our parts," Osric continued. "These kind of men think they've got nothing to lose – especially standing up to their own local Archbishop. They hate him, that's for sure. At least according to my merchant."

"Well he's probably got a point. Sudbury, as I understand it, is no William of Wykeham. When Wykeham was Lord Chancellor as well as the Bishop here he made a good job of both. But from what I hear Sudbury's only been Lord Chancellor for a year or so and is making a mess all round. It's a shame that the young king has to rely on people like him – it makes him look bad as well."

"Yes, that's what a lot of people were saying outside the abbey," said Osric. "The king is loved for himself and his father but he's badly advised and that gives the chance for trouble-makers to stir things up. And, Lord, do you know who the biggest trouble-makers are?"

"Tell me."

"It's the Lollards. They're the ones behind the scenes agitating people and getting them angry. And I reckon that explains this priest and ploughman or farmer or whatever he is going round with that story of the mutilation."

"Well, they were right, weren't they, about the mutilations. We all saw it."

"Yes, but why would you do that? Why would you go splashing that story everywhere? You might mention it to a friend but you wouldn't go round spreading it to all sorts - unless you had a reason."

"So what's your explanation, Osric?" asked Damian.

"It's because they're Lollards," he said again. "They don't like the monasteries and would do anything to hurt them. I am sure this so-called priest is one of them. I think there is a plan behind it. I think it all fits together."

He paused for a moment while we reflected on it.

"Now, I don't like this poll tax," he continued. "It's taking money from the poor to give to the rich. But if you tear down places like this abbey then it's the poor who will suffer. That's what these Lollards don't understand."

"I have to agree with you – up to a point," I said. "Like you I am suspicious of these two characters. I was talking about them to Mistress Alison earlier on – they'd be hanging out around her. But I am not going to be like the cellarer making wild accusations. If we are going to do this job for Father Compton, we're going to do it properly. We need evidence."

Osric sat brooding in silence for a while. Meanwhile, Damian had shut his eyes and seemed to be half asleep. Maybe dreaming of a girl – or another drink. Or probably both.

"Anyway, Lord," Osric resumed as if clearing his mind. "What I am saying is that this pilgrimage we're going on might lead us into a whole load of trouble."

"I appreciate that, Osric," I said. " But I've set my mind on it ."

"Well, I recall you saying, Lord, that you wanted to go on pilgrimage to get some peace. To leave violence behind you, that's what you said before we left. And now we may be heading straight into it. By the time we get to London the weather will be good and men will be up for a bit of fighting, you mark my word,"

"Yes, I know people are feeling disgruntled, Osric. You keep on telling me that. But that's what the English are like. They grumble but they don't take to the streets or the fields violently.

They're not like the French always thinking of revolution. There won't be any serious violence. Rest assured."

"And you know the French, don't you my lord?" Osric said in a way which I regarded as rather impertinent - but I let it pass. Yes, my family came over with the Conqueror and we know the French well. I grew up speaking the language. Osric and his forbears were old English. Most of his class were. But that did not mean I was any less English than he was.

"So are you saying that you don't want to continue the journey, Osric?" I asked. "I can't believe that you are saying you are afraid."

The latter I said as a bit of a challenge. It did not hit home. "No, lord, I am not afraid. I'll stick with you."

At this exchange Damian open his eyes and look around him.

"So, father, what do we do next?"

"Well, you and Osric best go down to the almoner's hall and get yourselves some supper - but not too much wine, I suggest, Damian. I'll be having dinner again with Father Compton and the other guests. I want to answer some questions which I should have asked last night if I'd had my wits about me."

"I'll tell you something straight away then that you really should know," said Damian sounding a bit smug.

"About what?"

"About who, you mean!" replied Damian sounding even more pleased with himself.

"So go ahead."

"I will. It's about John – the innocent John, Clerk of Oxenford and a Scholar."

"Tell us more." I said.

"He's a bastard!"

"He's a what?" I couldn't quite believe what I was hearing.

"He's a bastard!"

"You mean – literally"

"I mean probably in every way," replied Damian. "But certainly in the way that this parents were not wed when he was born and the father was never seen again after the night they did it."

110

"And where did you learn this?"

"The same little private tavern in the High Street that Osric and I entertained ourselves in last night."

"So it's just tavern talk," I said, not wanting to give it too much credibility.

"No, father, it's more than that. I know why you might be sceptical but it's more than that."

"So what the story?"

"The tavern is not far from St. Mary's - the Nunnaminster – the largest convent in town. They pick up stories there about what's in the various religious places round and about. The story is that twenty years ago – maybe a bit more – one of the local convents took in a girl from a good family from Netley way. She was not married but she was with child. She didn't say whether she had been raped or been let down by an unreliable lover. She didn't say anything but her parents, who were well connected, asked the nunnery to take her in. She produced the child - John. She then became a nun somewhere else and the baby was passed on to a poor but respectable family near Winchester. They're now dead."

"And what happened to the mother?"

"No-one was quite sure. She kind of disappeared. Who knows."

"And do we think this might have any bearing on the case?" I asked.

"The story was that John knew that he had been adopted and he probably had a grievance against both parents – but mostly the father. And who knows, maybe the father was a monk from this monastery. Wouldn't surprise me."

"Yes, I can see that," was all I could say.

CHAPTER 17
'Thus wole oure text'

I visited Father Compton in his private room before dinner to agree how much we should disclose to the guests about how the investigation was going. He invited me to sit down and I settled into an uncompromisingly hard chair with a stiff back.

"It's been a long day, Father Compton, and not without some results," I said trying sound positive. "So I just wanted to lay out to you where we've reached."

"Thank you," he said. "Please go ahead."

"First, as discussed, we have established to my satisfaction that John was not responsible for the murder of Brother Peter. Second, the cause of death was due to the breaking of his neck with considerable force - although, whether that was by his attacker or by his fall, I do not know."

"And this was what Doctor Nafis advised, was it?"

"Yes, that's right. Now, as to the mutilation of his private parts – why, when or by whom, remains a mystery. But at least the mutilation was definitely not the cause of death. It came afterwards. Maybe as a form of revenge or sign of contempt. But it was done to a corpse. So you might say it was immaterial."

"Not in the eyes of God, Sir Matthew," Father Compton responded sharply. "Remember that body will rise again of the day of judgement. And whoever did it is storing up severe trouble for themselves from a wrathful Christ. But also, more immediately, it suggests that there is a criminal with a mad menace running loose in the monastery. In some respects, you might say, it is worse than the broken neck."

"You mean because it suggests a kind of derangement?" I asked.

He said nothing but just gave a sad, thoughtful shrug.

"Now how much of this – if any – do you want conveyed to your guests this evening?" I asked. "I am sure that it is on their minds. And several of them have already spoken to me about it in parts."

A nervous look crossed his face.

"Well I am not sure what to say" he replied unhappily. "I know these are peculiar circumstances but I should have preferred that we glossed over this terrible incident as much as possible. Besides, what good would it do in sharing it with out guests or anyone else? I know that I have invited you to investigate – but I really wish the whole thing could be forgotten about by the wider community as quickly as possible."

I felt I needed to put some backbone into him to face up to what was happening now.

"I am sure that we would all prefer the murder not to have occurred, Father Compton. But – and I hesitate to remind you of this – the cathedral has required you to investigate. So the responsibility is down to you, I am afraid – but you have my assurance of support."

His face twisted further into discomfort. Having got my agreement to become involved earlier he now realised that this did not let him off the hook entirely. I drove the point home.

"And surely we cannot allow the culprits just to get away with it? Where's the justice in that?"

"Justice is mine, said the Lord.," he responded mechanically but then added. "So what do you want me to do?" he asked.

"I need to feel that I am fully backed up by your authority," I said. "In other words, that you trust me to undertake matters as I think best – and that includes dealing directly with the various interested parties. It will save time and, I would suggest, save you from unnecessary anxiety."

I allowed him time to take that in.

"Yes, I do understand," he said after a short pause. "Please continue."

"So far as this evening is concerned I am quite certain your guests will want to know what is happening not least because some of them are likely to be worried that the perpetrator has not yet been apprehended. They are shrewd people, I think. They won't appreciate the wool being pulled over their eyes. But also, from my point of view, I think that there is some benefit in actively involving them. After all, they may well have seen something - or maybe their attendants will have done so - which will offer us some clues. Indeed one of them has already volunteered some witness information."

"Who was that, might I ask?"

"The Abbess."

"Ah, the charming Madame Eglentyne who knows everybody but who is really known by no one," said Father Compton intriguingly.

"Yes, well, it was a slightly confusing observation she made I have to admit but sometimes even misleading information can help in an odd way," I said. "So I want to get their involvement if I can."

"You really think that they might help?"

"As guests they bring a different view on things. And remember they have had time just to sit and watch. Brother Michael explained to me that he tries to keep admission to the Forecourt on a tight rein but it is not easy. Now almost certainly our murderer – or murderers – will have come through that gate. So that means there is a good chance that they will have been noticed by one or more of the people here this evening."

"I see."

"And there is one specific thing I can add. We already have our suspicions about a pair of possible Lollards who have been seen around the Forecourt and the Outer Court quite a lot over the past two days. One of them might be a priest. And they seem to know Mistress Alison – or at least be acquainted with her."

"Lollards! Lollards!!" Father James exploded, his normal mild manner transformed into a state of outrage. "How dare they come to this church and this community and this place. And you say one of them is a priest? And they know that woman from Bath?"

"Yes, so it seems. The priest is possibly from a place called Chisledon, and so is his companion who appears to be ploughman. They are obviously very close and are invariably seen in each others company. But they look a very shifty couple. Also, they are the same people we reckon spread the story that Brother Peter had been mutilated. So it is conceivable that they are the ones behind much of what has been going on here over the last couple of days."

"Hmm! Very interesting that you should mention Chisledon," said Father Compton now calming down somewhat. "Before the pestilence the abbey used to have an estate at Chisledon. Most of it had to be sold off later although we still have a small-holding there. But the local people have a history of refusing to pay their tithes. It was what I was talking to you about earlier. When I was writing up the annual receipts for the monastery their entry was always a blank. We couldn't get anything out of them and when I went up their once, many years ago, I was bundled out with insults and pokes. One of the wretched villagers threw an old cauldron at me. Hit me on the head – very painful."

"And what happened?" I asked.

"Our abbot at the time - Abbot Walter - cracked down on them hard. Well he had to. And he was a strong man I can tell you, Sir Matthew. But, after him, we just gave up. We would not be in the state we are now if he were still around. That's why Walter, our infirmarian, has the name he does. Everyone admired him."

"Except, presumably, the people of Chisledon?" I enquired.

"You're right," conceded Father Compton. "I expect he was not particularly popular up there."

"So they might, conceivably, have some residue of hostility towards this abbey?"

"What, over thirty years later?"

"Perhaps it's history repeating itself," I suggested. "And some grudges last a long time. And maybe a loved one – a father or a mother – died of whatever happened way back when."

"If they didn't die then they would have probably died of the pestilence. They should count their blessings they did not die of that," said Father Compton with some bitterness. "I did

116

not mention it earlier but both my parents were victims. It was awful. And for some reason this murder is bringing it all back to me. For all my prayers to St. Joss I could not save them."

"I am very sorry to hear that Father Compton. So many lives ruined, so much suffering," I said trying to sound sympathetic - but I really wanted to move on. "So about these Lollards, it is only a possibility. But at the same time it does make sense. If Chisledon has a history of grievance against this abbey then it could explain a lot if Lollardy is rife up there – including even among the priests."

"Quite extraordinary!" continued Father Compton. "What do these people think they are doing? Envy and destruction – that's what it is all about! And to think of all that we do for the poor."

"Yes, you may be right," I said still wanting to keep him focused on finding the two men. "I mention it only because various people have spotted the pair of them and I would be interested if anyone else has seen them behaving in a suspicious way. So could you mention it to the community? Maybe tomorrow?"

"Yes, I will pass it on."

"But also encourage your monks to keep an eye out for anything at all which looks suspicious. I don't want to alarm you but I am starting to think there we've not seen the end of these disturbances."

"I understand, Sir Matthew and I suppose I have to agree with you. These questions must be put."

"Good, well I am glad that you support me on that," I continued feeling that a small victory had been won. "And just a word about my own affairs. I am still determined with Damian and Osric to undertake this pilgrimage to Canterbury, leaving the day after tomorrow. I feel that if I do not accomplish it now it might never happen. So you must allow me latitude in how I undertake this investigation. If necessary I will come back to Hyde afterwards."

"Yes, of course Sir Matthew. I shall just have to deal with the cathedral's endless interfering as best I may," he said with distaste.

"Maybe you could try to get Brother Thomas on your side rather more?"

"A lost cause, I'm afraid. I've tried that. It doesn't work. Brother Thomas is only on one person's side, I'm afraid – and that, I suspect is his own. And for the time being at least that means he only pays attention to one other authority – Prior Hugh."

"Yes, I can see that."

"But believe me, Sir Matthew. I am very grateful for any help you can offer. I worry for the future of this abbey. Without friends like you I fear we will be lost entirely."

This seemed a rather overstated accolade. I felt myself blush just very slightly. In my own mind I was still undecided whether the abbey was a force for good or not.

"In which case, then, Father Compton, let's go to feast on that. And may the abbey win more friends through your excellent wine."

"Well, at least wine is one thing that Father Eynesham really does know about," replied the acting abbot. "But how much that will count for him on the day of judgement I am not sure. He must hope that Saint Peter needs a really good cellarer."

CHAPTER 18

'De hadde the bord bigonne'

Father Compton and I entered the Abbot's Dining room to be greeted by a rather larger assembly than I had expected.

Along with last evening's guests there were also Brother Thomas and Doctor Nafis. And to my surprise Sergeant Henry and Roger Odiham, the Franklin, were still with us despite their assertion that they had urgent business in London.

A sense of impatient appetite was in the air and Father Eynesham indicated firmly to the acting abbot that it was time we were seated and fell to the business of eating. "Just the short 'grace', I think, Father Compton ," he said, "time being what it is."

I had been placed at Father Compton's right but was aware that Brother Thomas was sitting on his other side, no doubt to keep an ear cocked for what might be said between us. The acting abbot then surprised the company by delivering a 'grace' which included two extra verses which were scarcely calculated to give the guests the comfort they wanted.

> 'This night from peril thou me keep,
> My body's rest while that I take;
> And as long as mine eyen sleep,
> Mine heart in thy service wake.
> 'For fear of the fiend our foe,
> From foul dreams and fantasies
> Keep me this night, from sin also,
> In cleanness that I may uprise."

Anxious glances were being exchanged around the table before the 'Amen' told us that we could begin to eat. But not quite yet.

"Dear brothers and sisters in Christ," said Father Compton with as much authority as he could muster. "You are most welcome here again this evening. Sadly, we are still in the shade of yesterday's terrible events. So I am grateful to all of you, intent as you are on pilgrimage, for remaining here today. I know that some of you had intended to depart this morning. But I think we all owe it to Sir Matthew - who has so kindly put himself at our service in investigating Brother Peter's sad demise - to ensure that he has the benefit of your company here in the abbey and when you travel on to London.

"Now, I have asked Sir Matthew to speak to you before we begin…" At which point the cellarer gave a small groan of impatience. Embarrassed, Father Compton repeated himself . "Now I have asked Sir Matthew to speak to you briefly before we begin to eat so that he can put you in the picture about the progress he has made and where he might value your co-operation over the next couple of days. Sir Matthew, please speak."

"Thank you, Father Compton – and thank you ladies and lords for your kind attention," I began with a military briskness. "I don't intend to detain you for too long. Needless to say that when I arrived here yesterday afternoon I could never have anticipated how events would unfold. But I am a soldier and the first thing you learn in battle is to expect the unexpected – and certainly that is the story of today."

I paused briefly to see what response this might evoke. Madame Eglentyne for one, sitting immediately to my right, was certainly fully alert.

"As you will remember, there was a clear suspect for the murder of Brother Peter. It was the young Oxford scholar, John. I can tell you now that I have spoken to John at great length and we have inspected both the library where the terrible act took place and – with the assistance of Doctor Nafis here – examined poor Brother Peter's body. The result is that we are as certain as we can be that John was not involved in the murder. He was, so to speak, in the wrong place at the wrong time. That was partly his own fault it must be said…"

Madame Eglentyne raised her hand and asked, "In what way, Sir Matthew? You say that this was his own fault? Can you explain that?"

"Well I was just about to, Lady Eglentyne," I replied slightly curtly. "Simply put, John's long-standing relationship with the abbey and his personal relationship with Brother Peter meant that he came and went maybe a little too freely in the library. So he was there in a remote part of the room when the attack happened. But I am sure that in no way was he involved and nor did he actually see it – he was at some remove from the whole event. And indeed, dear Madame Prioress, I am grateful to you for your interesting comments earlier today in that respect."

At this everyone around the table looked with curiosity at Madame Eglentyne. I could see that they were wondering what I was referring to. I was not inclined to enlighten them – not least because I was still in two minds myself about what she had said.

"So does that mean the murderer is still out there?" asked the Franklin, pointing at the window looking on to the abbey church. "Presumably you have not caught him – or maybe her?"

"I'm afraid it probably does imply, Sir Roger, that the murderer – or maybe murderers – is still on the loose," I replied as matter-of-factly as I could.

"That makes me feel rather nervous, I must admit, Sir Matthew," the Franklin responded. "I rather wish we had gone straight up to London this morning after all," he said to his neighbour, the lawyer, who gave a consenting grunt in reply.

To my surprise Brother Thomas then cut in.

"Please be calm, Sir Roger. I am sure that you are perfectly safe here in Hyde."

"I hope you are right," said Sir Roger. "I always assumed this abbey was a safe place – but I fear that I might have been mistaken."

I felt I needed to give a little reassurance to my increasingly agitated fellow guests – a little, but not too much.

"Well, friends, please don't get concerned. It is quite possible - in fact more than likely - that whoever attacked Brother Peter has left the abbey's confines. After all, why would they remain?

Maybe they have even left Winchester. But, yes, it is notionally possible that they are still here and could be identified - maybe even by someone who is in this room now. That is why I shall be devoting tomorrow to speaking to as many people as I can – including those of you here this evening – to see if I can make some substantial progress before leaving for London. We will have these conversations in confidence, in private, so anything you say will be strictly between you and me. So I look forward to speaking with you later – and now I hope that you enjoy your supper. And, thank you once again Father Compton for hosting us so generously."

I sat down with my last remark having seemed to restore some degree of normality. People around the table started to converse with each other. I took a deep breath, let it flow out and began to relax.

"Might I ask you something, Sir Matthew?" said Lady Eglentyne.

"Of course."

"Having ruled out this little boy John, have you any serious suspects yet?"

"We do certainly have one or two people who are, shall we say, of special interest."

"And can you tell us who they are?"she asked.

"Well I can't give you any names. And besides they are only possible suspects. It's simply because that they have been seen in the vicinity quite often. They are not locals and they have been behaving in rather odd ways but I have no hard evidence against them – as yet."

"And are they likely to be known to any of us do you think?" the abbess continued.

"Well possibly – they may have been in conversation with one or two of the people here tonight," I said not wanting to give away my concerns about Mistress Alison and her acquaintances.

"But surely, Sir Matthew if you have suspects who are known, as you say to some of us, it makes better sense to share them with us now and then you can get our observations on these people – if we have seen them. Then, as you did with John, they can either be excluded or looked into more deeply."

"Those are very good points, Abbess Eglentyne. And I might well do that a little bit further on when I have accumulated more evidence – if it is available. But not for the time being. It is all a matter of timing – I do hope that you understand."

That seemed to placate the good nun and I was hoping for no more questions. I have to say though that since Madame Eglentyne had previously volunteered evidence of somewhat doubtful value I did not want to encourage her any further. However, the Sergeant, who had been listening to these remarks, raised his hand.

"Yes, Master Henry what would you like to say?" I said.

"Just a question, Sir Matthew. You think that there might be other possible suspects out there. As I mentioned last evening I am a lawyer although I normally steer away from crime. But I know from my criminal law colleagues there are rarely a number of suspects in cases of murder. You would have to be a monster to have so many enemies. And I am sure that Brother Peter was not that."

"Again I am not going to say anything about Brother Peter, Master Henry. But I will admit to you that I am still puzzling over the motive of the attack. Was it directed at Brother Peter personally or was it because of his role within the abbey. Was it a random attack for reasons we do not understand? Or was it targetted in some specific way? Or maybe it was, somehow, both. I don't know. But I think answering that question will be an important step forward. And for the time being I am open-minded."

"Well thank you, Sir Matthew," replied the lawyer who sounded not particularly impressed by my thinking. "I am sure that, like Father Compton, we are all grateful for your efforts."

I had been aware that Brother Thomas was listening to what I said with great attention. But it was Father Eynesham - clearly biding his time - who then came in like a slithering snake.

"As the person who actually found Brother Peter yesterday, Sir Matthew, I was wondering whether you might have been contemplating talking to me at some point?"

This was the conversation I had been nervous about. Father Eynesham probably felt that he had a point to prove. But I had resolved to be both polite and firm in dealing with him.

"Well, Father, I hesitate to correct you but strictly speaking it was young John who actually found Brother Peter, dead, yesterday. I think it was a slight misinterpretation on that point which caused all the confusion."

"I understand that you have reached your conclusion on John, Sir Matthew. I have my own views but I am not going to try to dissuade you. Frankly I am more than happy to let other people sort it all out. I merely reported what I saw and how I had understood it. If other people view it differently then I am not inclined to argue."

'What a great relief' I thought to myself. Maybe he cares less about this then I thought he did. Perhaps he just got caught up by the thrill of the chase after young John. And, once caught, he doesn't mind whether John is guilty or not.

"My more immediate concern," the cellarer continued, "is about the practicabilities for tomorrow if you want to speak to me further. Like others around the table I have postponed my departure for London until the day after tomorrow. But I have since made other important administrative arrangements for most of tomorrow outside of the abbey. Can you see me after vespers, I should have returned by then?"

"Yes, I am sure that would be fine," I replied easily. "Or maybe over the next day or two travelling up to London. I am very happy to make it at your convenience."

"In that case, Sir Matthew I suggest in London – at the Tabard."

"Agreed!" I said. And then turning to others around the table I announced, "So I should be most grateful if before you leave this evening we could agree times when I can see you all tomorrow – that is with the exception of Doctor Nafis, of course, whose time I very much appreciated this morning."

The Doctor gave me a nod of acknowledgement and half indicted that he wished to speak to me. But the moment was lost.

"Thank you," said Father Compton coming in quickly and wanting to close the discussion down before any more complications arose. "Now please enjoy your supper."

With that he turned promptly to his left and started talking to Brother Thomas – probably seeking reassurance that nothing untoward had surfaced. For my part, I turned once again to face Madame Eglentyne.

CHAPTER 19
'She leet no morsel from hir lippes falle'

"Dear Madame Eglentyne, I do hope that it has not put you out too much, having to stay an extra day here in Hyde?" I asked, searching her face for her mood.

"Not at all – I always find it spiritually enriching being here."

"That's good to hear," I replied. "Inspirational preachers are they, the monks? Or is it the divine office?"

"Neither," she replied sweetly.

"Oh what then?"

"Merely that they seem to do everything so curiously badly that I find it very encouraging about the performance of my own poor establishment. It raises my morale and confirms my own approach." She paused briefly and then smiled again, now apparently more relaxed than when we had spoken earlier.

"Anyway, thank you for our little conversation this morning – your account of what you heard yesterday was very helpful," I continued. "As I mentioned, I've spoken to John and have ruled him out from being involved in the murder."

"And what did you make of the boy, Sir Matthew? As a man of some experience I imagine that you must be a very good judge of character." Her tone, as usual, was nuanced with ambiguity.

"Well, that's kind of you to say so, Madame Eglentyne. I wouldn't particularly make that claim for myself. But I think I can recognise when people are telling the truth – at least by and large. Anyway, let's turn to happier things - tell me a little bit more about yourself. I can't quite place your accent - where are you from originally?"

"You sound as if you are interrogating me, Sir Matthew – to get to the truth," she laughed. "Now I am sure that is not your real intention because if it were then I should have to do the same to you. And maybe you would not entirely like that."

This cut me, I must confess, coming as it did with no

warning. I wondered what she was aiming at. I had plenty of faults and failings on my conscience but what might she have heard? Already, however, she had moved on.

"Originally, as you put it, I came from not too far away from here - down towards the sea a little."

"Ah, yes, a fine abbey there too."

"Indeed it is - so for reasons which I won't bore you with, Sir Matthew, I felt I had a vocation and through a family recommendation I joined a convent near London. But, as you might say, my roots drew me back to this area and – by the grace of Our Lady - I am now the Prioress of Wintney Priory."

"And that's a very fine institution too," I said.

"Do you know it then?"

"Well, of course, I have travelled past it on numerous occasions. I've not actually been inside or visited but it's on the London Road beyond Basyng, am I not right?"

"You are indeed – how very observant of you! But we are a poor place, abused and cheated by all and sundry so we have to work very hard to maintain high standards. Which is what we do. As it happens though, we have some properties here in Winchester near the High Street and also, by good fortune, two mills on the Itchen. So I have to come down from time to time to ensure that things are being managed properly. The same miller operates both - and he's a rather strange man, I must admit. Quite a handful."

"Yes, I can imagine," I replied. "Millers can be – how can I put it politely...?"

"Lying, devious cheats with a bottomless capacity for mischief and duplicity is how I put it politely," said the abbess briskly.

"Oh, I see that despite your calling you are still a woman of the world, Madame Eglentyne."

"I am not sure whether that is intended as a compliment or a disparagement, Sir Matthew, but I would have to disagree with you. I am not a 'woman of the world' as you put it – I am a 'woman of my world' and that's the way I like it."

"And how safe is your world then, Madame Eglentyne? I'm impressed that you come regularly down to Winchester. Isn't it rather dangerous travelling on these roads – especially at the moment? Surely you don't come on your own?"

"On that point you're quite right, Sir Matthew. I would be a very misguided woman to travel by myself – especially as I do tend to bring one or two jewels of minor value with me," she said pointing to a little golden broach she was wearing. "But, we have several priests attached to the convent and so I am normally accompanied by at least one of them."

"So they are with you on this occasion?"

"Yes, indeed. It is young Father Gregory, named after the Pope of blessed memory. He is a very earnest young man. Unfortunately Father Compton does not consider Gregory – who is something of a favourite of mine I will admit - to be important enough to dine in this select company. Sad but there we are. Gregory is truly an angel and, in truth, he is a very spiritual young man. He would much prefer to be on his knees than indulging in fine wines. Indeed, I am sure that he is at his prayers as we speak."

"Well, given your high standards, Madame Eglentyne it must be very reassuring to find a priest in whom you can have such trust."

"Oh, believe me, it is, Sir Matthew."

I was quite prepared for the sake of good manners to continue our conversation about nuns' priests and the relationships which might arise between them for the rest of the evening – and beyond if need be – but Madame Eglentyne insisted on coming back to the wretched boy John.

"Now tell me, what made you so sure that this John was innocent? In my spiritual reflections I often debate with myself about sin and guilt on the one hand and innocence and virtue on the other and how one can discriminate between them. Sometimes it is so difficult, the lines can become so blurred don't they? Did you come to the conclusion that John was innocent because you discerned his virtue?"

"This is a bit deep for me, I'm afraid, Madame Eglentyne," I admitted. "I'm a simple soldier and I just believed his story – it seemed to make sense. Although he is an irritating young man – and not totally honest, I suspect – nonetheless a kind of innocence came through. He was convincing in the way he told his account."

"And I am glad that you saw that, Sir Matthew. Yet Father Eynesham, whom I trust implicitly, seemed so certain of his guilt."

"Well I suspect that Father Eynesham rather enjoyed being so emphatic in his view," I replied. "He is a bit ostentatious, I would suggest. He likes to make a strong impression. He just acted on instinct. And probably both of us know that pure instinct is not always the best guide. It needs to be accompanied by thought and reflection."

"You are so right, Sir Matthew. Instinct too often leads one astray. Maybe that was young John's problem too."

I was now finding it tedious to return to the topic of John and his guilt or innocence. Right now I wanted to think of something else. I also wanted to enjoy my food. But she persisted.

"So did John actually see the killer, Sir Matthew?"

"No he did not. He said he didn't."

"So he saw nothing?"

"That's right, not until afterwards when he saw the corpse, And then – understandably, I think – he took fright and ran."

"By the sound of it then he was not able to give you any description?" Madame Eglentyne asked for confirmation.

"No, no description."

"But what could he hear them saying?"

"Nothing he could hear specifically – but there were raised voices – which does rather chime with your account – in some respects," I added slightly mischievously.

"Well that's all very interesting, Sir Matthew. Are you any clearer on the motive?"

"Not really," I replied evasively."We are still thinking about it"

"Was it theft, do you think? Was there anything missing?"

"I can't really answer that quite yet I'm afraid Madame Eglentyne –but maybe tomorrow. And besides I am sure that there are other things you would like to discuss than this rather squalid murder."

"Of course, Sir Matthew. I understand. Now, I am so interested to hear about your son. I thought I saw him with you today, this morning, going across to the infirmary. He seemed a very fine young man. So tall and so good-looking."

"Well that's very kind of you. I must say it was quite a shock when I saw him at Southampton just a few weeks ago after I had been away for such a long time. He had grown so big and I realised that I had missed so many important years in his life."

"So did you feel, maybe slightly, that you had not really been a father to him?" asked the nun. "I mean a proper father?"

"I wouldn't put it quite in those terms," I said rather defensively. "But I did feel that I had not been quite the support I should have been. As you might have gathered, my wife had died just before I arrived back in England. So he had to deal with that on his own. It shook me up very much. Indeed Madame Eglentyne, it is one of the reasons we are undertaking this pilgrimage – to rebuild that relationship which I have neglected while away crusading. And all for what? I ask myself."

"Oh, poor Sir Matthew. Please don't think like that. You were serving the church. You were fighting for Christ. Think how much credit you were building up in heaven. Do not acquire gold on earth but treasure in the next life."

"Well that's one way of looking at it, Madame Eglentine. Indeed that's how I used to look at it myself. That's what I said to my dear wife when I departed. But I think she could see through it. I was looking for adventure. And also, if truth be told, some gold on earth as well. My little estate near Ashley is not richly endowed."

131

"Nonetheless, I find it all quite fascinating, Sir Matthew. Your adventures, as you mention them, must have been so..."

She was looking for the right words. I supplied them.

"Bloody - and awful. But I really don't want to discuss it, Madame Eglentyne, I'm afraid. My intention now is to forget about the past insofar as I can and make good the time I have wasted."

At last she got the message. She nodded in acknowledgement of what I had said and changed tack.

"I am sure that your efforts are much appreciated by the abbey here, Sir Matthew. Father Compton here is, well, you know..."

She lowered her voice and gave me a meaningful look.

"Not cut out to be an abbot," I offered, confident that Father Compton could not hear us against the clatter of dishes and rising levels of conversation.

"Exactly," she replied. "Now I, of course, am just a mere woman but I think I could tell Father Compton a thing or two about how to run an abbey."

"In that case, tell me more about your own convent, Madame Eglentyne."

"I am very happy to do so," she said firmly, almost as if the whole conversation had been building up to this. "Wintney Priory is doing well despite being poor. We make the very best of what we have got. Whereas other institutions – and Hyde Abbey here is a prime example – are still suffering from the affect of the pestilence we have transformed Wintney into a thriving and, I might say, happy place of worship. It is now thirty years since the pestilence. We cannot keep using that as an explanation for poverty and backwardness."

"But there is a lot of poverty about, isn't there?" I ventured. "That's why there is so much unrest among the ordinary folk."

"That is down to trouble-makers – I am sure you have heard of the Lollards going around stirring up discontent?"

"Yes, I have heard a little about them," I agreed.

132

"But, much more important is a lack of leadership. Of course Winchester is lucky in its Bishop. Look at what he has done at Oxford? Look at what he is planning here in Winchester with his new school? It's a great shame that he is no longer Lord Chancellor. The young king would be in much better hands with William in charge. And I am sure his new school will train up young men to govern the kingdom in years to come."

"It may well," I replied. "But these things you are talking about though – schools and colleges and so forth. They cost money. Where is the money to come from?" I asked.

She gave me an impatient look.

"It is simple. You remove the means of making money from those who are incompetent - and give them to people who can manage properly. There are too many old men – bumbling old men – getting in the way."

"So what is your recipe for good management, then Madame Eglentyne?"

"Detail, attention to detail. That is one of the reasons I am here in Winchester now. Too easily the rights of convents are disregarded, Sir Matthew. I had to crack down today on that thieving miller of mine. But our rights have even abused by abbots and bishops from the past who thought they could walk all over us weak women. But I tell you, Sir Matthew, by Saint Loy I will not permit that to happen to Wintney. I will have the law on my side."

"Well you obviously have your work cut out, Madame Eglentyne," I responded, slightly overwhelmed by this onslaught. "I am surprised that you have the time to go on pilgrimage."

"It is a matter of piety, Sir Matthew. I have been to Canterbury once before when I was young and was guided into a better way. Now that I am a little older I feel that I should go again. And before we leave Southwark I intend to see Bishop William himself at his palace. If you want change you must go straight to the top. And William of Wykeham is in London."

Our conversation moved on to other things and in a break

between courses I excused myself and said I had to agree a schedule to see the other guests on the following day.

"Do you need anything further from me?" she asked. "Rest assured I am anxious to be of any possible assistance to you."

And that was when we heard the shouting and violent banging on the door.

CHAPTER 20
'Deere cometh my mortal enemy'

Bang! Bang! Bang!

"Father Compton! Father Eynesham! May I come in?" came a high-pitched, frightened voice.

"Yes, enter!" bellowed Father Eynesham.

A junior monk almost tumbled inside. "My deepest apologies Father Compton, Father Eynesham, guests of the abbey," he blurted out as the buzz of conversation started to lull. "But something terrible has happened."

"Come! What?" said Father Eynesham sharply.

"It's Brother Walter!"

"What's happened to him," said Brother Thomas.

"I'm afraid he's dead – murdered for sure."

The shock and anxiety rippled like a wave around the room. My own attempts to reassure the guests of their safety earlier in the evening now seemed threadbare. The Franklin and Brother Thomas stood up as if in utter disbelief followed by Father Compton who tried to quieten the commotion by inviting Father Eynesham to say an immediate prayer for the soul of the departed Walter.

We bowed our heads and followed the words, crossing ourselves afterwards but maybe not able to concentrate. Even I felt stunned – or maybe I more than the others. What in hell was going on?

After a chorus of 'Amens' Father Compton announced that he would remain with the guests – to provide comfort and solace - and then instructed the young monk to take Father Eynesham and Brother Thomas to see the corpse. Almost as an afterthought Father Compton turned to me, "Sir Matthew, maybe you should join them. I believe that you also have an interest in dead bodies."

Led by the young monk carrying a candle we made our way downstairs into the cloisters, over the bridge across the stream and into the Outer Close. There was no conversation between us.

Instead we focused on the light ahead in the lobby of the infirmary where a pair of monks were standing. Nods of sombre greeting were exchanged and we were then shown by an elderly monk into one of the back rooms, cut off from the main body of the infirmary.

"Where's Brother Walter?" barked the bristling Brother Thomas as soon as we entered.

"There brother," replied the elderly monk pointing to the floor behind a table covered high with all kinds of pots and containers.

It was a gory sight. The prone, bloody and lifeless body. Even without examining him closely it was obvious he had suffered a fatal wound to the neck. And, appallingly, the same mutilation to the groin as Brother Peter.

"Who found him?" asked Father Eynesham. "You, Brother Adam?" he asked.

"Yes, it was me," came the solemn reply. "Walter did not appear at compline. In fact he had not been seen since this morning and so we came across to see whether he was dealing with a particularly unwell pilgrim. This was what presented itself." He pointed again at Walter's body.

"Have you moved him at all?" I asked.

"Just pulled his legs together – straighten him out to make him somehow more dignified."

"Shall we go into the infirmary and find out of anyone heard or saw anything," I suggested.

The infirmary was deadly quiet, lit by just a single candle in the centre of the room. There were heavy sounds of snoring from one bed while two others emitted light, sleepy, groaning. And coughing. I was reluctant to wake them up – or even approach them - without knowing their illness.

"I think we should leave this until the morning," I said. The others did not demur.

"Brother Adam could you arrange to place Brother Walter on to the bed in his sleeping cell and cover him over," said Father Eynesham. "And would you then remain here overnight?"

"Certainly, Father," said Brother Adam grimly. "And if they come for me too then I shall be happy to join my friend in Paradise."

"I certainly hope it won't come to that," I could not resist saying although as soon as it was out of my mouth I felt that I had no cause for being so confident. One murder looks like an aberration but two is the start of a sequence.

"I think we must go back to the guests and Father Compton," said Brother Thomas. "We must tell them discreetly what has happened – I shall do that – and then we must agree what to do next." He paused before adding. "Of course I shall have to make an immediate report tomorrow to the Prior. I am sure that he will have views."

On our way back to the Inner Court Brother Thomas suggested to Father Eynesham that he should make some general comments about Brother Walter and what a loss he was. He would then follow up about the actual circumstances of the death.

Father Eynesham seemed to show no discomfort in being told what to do by this mere brother from the cathedral. And again I reflected on the question of who was really in authority in this abbey.

Once back in the abbot's dining room Father Eynesham whispered a few brief words in private to Father Compton and then turned to the guests at large.

"As you have heard, dear friends, my brother in Christ dear Brother Walter died this evening," he said easing into an impromptu eulogy. It was so smooth it almost sounded as if it had been pre-prepared. But then Father Eynesham was a polished operator – almost as polished as his shiny bald head and bright eyes which seem to shine even brighter now that he was the centre of everyone's attention.

"It is a deep, deep loss to this abbey of whose community he has been a much loved member for at least three decades. Indeed Brother Walter was one of the first monks whom I met when I arrived as a naive novice and he helped me steer the right course at the start of my vocation. But Brother Walter's loss is more than to the abbey itself. As those who know the abbey well will be aware, Brother Walter has been in charge of our infirmary for many years and both monks and pilgrims and local laity have all enjoyed the benefit of his skills and Christian devotion. Added to the deeply painful loss of Brother Peter this leaves us wondering how we can survive as an independent community. For this we must pray over the weeks and months ahead. Meanwhile, we must think about the funeral rites. I must confer with Father Compton," he nodded in the acting abbot's direction, "but it might be best that we have a joint funeral on the day after tomorrow for our two dear departed brethren, separated from us as they are but united now in the Lord."

Father Eynesham then said a further short – maybe, I thought, too short – prayer for Brother Walter and handed over to Brother Thomas.

"Thank you, thank you, Father Eynsham – a very moving and beautiful appreciation, if I might say so, of dear Brother Walter. I have been with the community here in Hyde for a short time so I cannot claim a close knowledge of Brother Walter but I had heard wonderful things about him and especially his works in the infirmary. As of this moment that is where, appropriately enough, his body lies having gone to his maker with whom even now, I hope, he is rejoicing in Paradise. No need for an infirmary any more. But his arrival there is premature. I will not speculate on the circumstances but, having just witnessed his body, I have to suspect that it was not a natural death. This would be horrible and deeply distressing at any time but coming in the wake of Brother Peter's death it will raise questions about how the abbey is being managed."

At this point he paused and looked across at Father Compton who seemed to shrivel with embarrassment. Brother Thomas resumed.

"That does not mean in any way, Father Compton, that there are any questions over your curacy here in recent months. It is much appreciated that you stepped in to fill a vacuum. Nonetheless I am duty-bound tomorrow morning to go to the cathedral to report on developments to the Prior. What he might then recommend to the Bishop, I do not know. But we will then have to see how this is then taken forward. In the meantime though I will understand that some of you will be feeling uneasy about your personal security. As you know, Sir Matthew here has been asked to investigate the circumstances surrounding Brother Peter's death. We will now have to consider how best to deal with this latest development. But rest assured all will be done to ensure the safety of everyone in this room. God bless you all."

Whether anyone around the table was reassured was difficult to discern. But along with anxieties about their own safety I sensed that the guests had noted how deeply and publicly Father Compton had just been humiliated. Brother Thomas had not wasted a moment in using Walter's death as another stick with which to beat the acting abbot.

Nonetheless, as soon as Brother Thomas stopped speaking Father Compton came across to me with a more steely look on his face than I had ever seen before. As the saying goes, even a worm will turn.

"Sir Matthew, given the circumstances and the likely connection between the two deaths would you be prepared to now include the death of Brother Walter in your enquiries?" he asked quickly.

Before I had a chance to reply Brother Thomas had arrived and broke in. "I think that Sir Matthew might be already doing too much for us, Father Compton. This, 'amplification' in violence takes us into a different place. I think we need to reflect and consult before asking Sir Matthew to become further involved."

I was not entirely surprised. It had occurred to me as we had walked back from the infirmary that the second death could prompt Brother Thomas and his controllers in the cathedral to dismiss me so that they could take this mounting problem under their own direct jurisdiction.

"No, I insist," said Father Compton now showing unprecedented independence. "For the time being at least I have the powers of the abbot of this monastery and I want Sir Matthew de Somborne to widen his investigation. Sir Matthew will you do it?"

My immediate reaction was to decline – not least because Brother Thomas, for his own reasons, clearly wanted to get rid of me. Added to which the prospect of taking on an additional burden – just when I was hoping to be free of the abbey and its problems – felt almost too much to bear. But the look on Father Compton's face was so pathetically brave that I could not bring myself to say 'No.'

Moreover this second death and similar mutilation suggested strongly that the murderer – or murderers – was still here in the abbey. There was a real risk to the lives of the people around me – including Madame Eglentyne and Mistress Alison. It would be unconscionable to walk away if they were in danger.

"Well, of course, I should be willing to undertake whatever the abbey would require," I said firmly. "Indeed, I have to say that two murders in so short a time in this relatively small community does suggest something..."

"Large and peculiarly evil which requires a wider approach than you, Sir Matthew, can fight against," filled in Brother Thomas. "I strongly suggest that we bring in Prior Hugh at this point, Father Compton."

Nothing could have hardened Father Compton's resolve further than this suggestion. He knew all too well the abbey was vulnerable but he would resist as far as possible any direct involvement from the cathedral. Turning to me he said, "Sir Matthew, you agreed to give me two days of your time. Will you at least continue through until the end of tomorrow?"

"Yes Father Compton, I will. I cannot promise you any results but I will do my very best until this time tomorrow."

"Well, thank you," said Father Compton smiling ruefully. "It's the least I can do for my friends. To find them justice."

Brother Thomas remained silent, quietly fuming. And then we separated, each of us going our separate ways – troubled and anxious - to bed.

CHAPTER 21

'How longe tyme wol you rekene and caste'

I made my way back to our guest room. By now it was getting very late. I was aching for rest not least as the memory of Brother Walter's mutilated body resurged in my imagination and I wanted some relief.

News of the latest murder had already reached Damian and Osric. Some of the abbey's lay servants had been in the Forecourt when Brother Adam had discovered the corpse and they had come to stare. So by the time that Osric and Damian had returned through the main gateway it was being widely discussed.

"Is it true then that they'd taken a knife to him in the same way – down there?" Damian pointed to his groin.

"Yes, I'm afraid so. It was grim to see. I'm not quite sure I've got over it yet. There were some token prayers for poor Brother Walter and plenty of shock of course but maybe not much compassion. At least not from Father Eynesham and Brother Thomas."

"But can we assume it was done by the same person?" said Osric, rising eagerly to the new challenge.

"I imagine that's likely but I'm not sure I'd jump to that conclusion too soon," I replied, forcing myself to see it as a puzzle rather than the tragic death of an ageing man. "It might be a copy-cat. Or it might be an accomplice."

"So does that mean we've now got two murders to investigate?" asked Damian.

"We have, yes," I said, "but it's an odd situation. After we'd been shown across to see the corpse Father Compton asked me, predictably I suppose, to investigate this murder as well. I felt I had to agree. But the little toad, Brother Thomas, didn't like it one bit. He said that it all ought to be handed over to the Prior at the cathedral monastery for them to investigate. He seemed to imply that they would do a better job of it from there. Father Compton, though, put his foot down. He was adamant about it. Surprisingly out of character, I thought. And so that's how we will spend tomorrow. Digging up what we can find – if anything - as to what's behind all this."

"So what do you expect?" asked Damian.

"I really do not know," I said wearily. "Extremely unlikely we'll find the murderer in the limited time we've got before leaving for Canterbury. But maybe we can at least make some headway in understanding why the murders have taken place."

"Well, who can you speak to?" asked Osric. "I know you've been talking to the high-ups. But as you said yourself, often it's the little people who have the real clue to what's going on. They see without being seen themselves."

"I agree," I said. "There must be someone out there in the monastery or among the numerous guests who has a suspicion or picked up a clue or seen something. It could be one of the junior monks, or one of the less important visitors like this priest, Gregory, who accompanies Madame Eglentyne - or maybe some of the servants."

"Yes, we should definitely be speaking more to them," said Osric. "I'm surprised they've got so many here."

"Yes, more servants than monks, that's for sure. Only we've got to be realistic. I suspect that tomorrow is all the time we've got," I explained. "Brother Thomas was seething and he'll be off to the cathedral first thing in the morning. So I am expecting an intervention. But we'll deal with that when it happens."

"And you, lord, have you not got any more ideas yourself?" asked Osric.

"Osric, I have to say I am feeling very tired. And right now I feel I don't have any clues."

Osric and Damian both looked disappointed – as if I could not be bothered to try.

"Oh, all right then," I sighed wearily, feeling my age and ailments. "There are some basic questions we need to work on. And that's what we can focus on tomorrow."

"And what are they, Father?"

"Oh really, Damian, Do we have to discuss it now?"

"Yes, father definitely – you might have forgotten them by to-morrow morning! And Osric and I can think about them overnight."

"So be it then," I had to agree. "To begin with the obvious points. Two older monks murdered – roughly of the same age, and they knew each other well, I am sure. Is that important or just coincidence?"

"Good start," said Damian. "Maybe they both knew something or were involved in something together. Who knows, it might go back years."

"That's possible. Next question. Does the explanation for the murders lie within the abbey or is it connected to something outside it? After all, this monastery is a place of pilgrimage. It has people pouring through it all the time. Peter and Walter might have been involved with someone or something, dangerous or bad, but unconnected with the church. After all both of them had regular contact with people outside."

"You mean people who were sick or using the library?" said Osric.

"That's right – so one or both of them might be caught up in something nasty away from the abbey entirely. Or maybe they both knew something they shouldn't and they had to be shut up."

"But who by?"

"Well, just as an example," I said. "I can't get out of my mind the two men – strangers apparently to the abbey – who carried Brother Peter across from the library to the infirmary. And who did they hand him over to? It was Brother Walter. At its simplest these characters have had direct contact with both the victims. Maybe they said something incriminating which Walter heard and therefore he had to be silenced. Yet these two seem to have had no direct involvement with the abbey more generally – at least as far as we know."

Osric and Damian nodded as if they were starting to take it all in and re-arrange it for themselves.

"But I am also interested in this country bumpkin so-called

143

priest and his friend, the ploughman who Mistress Alison was talking to and had apparently met on the road from Bath. Are these the same two as those who carried the body? If so, then that could be significant – especially if they turn out to be Lollards who, as we know, hate the monasteries and would do anything to embarrass them. So maybe these two couples are actually one and the same pair?"

"Yes, that's a possibility I suppose," said Damian.

"Yes," I agreed. "But it's no more than that. Although there is a kind of logic to it. I want to look at all the possible explanations – and then see if there is any evidence to support them."

"And what about the mutilations – the ugly mutilations?" asked Osric."To be honest with you, lord, my idea is that's the key to it all. It's either a very big insult to the two of them. Or maybe it's some kind of revenge. But I reckon it tells us a lot about what's in the murderer's mind. I mean it's some kind of perversion, isn't it? For me, that's definitely the thing that binds the two murders together."

"That's a fair way of looking at it, Osric – and you might be a right," I said. "That is what they have most obviously in common. But it might be intended to send us off in the wrong direction. Especially if the second murder had no direct link to the first but the mutilation was designed to throw us off the scent and make a false connection with the first."

"Yes, it's complicated," said Damian. "You'd have made a good assassin yourself, father – the way you think it all through."

That stopped me in my tracks as my mind turned back to my endeavours in Belmarye in Africa. Moments of fear, excitement and shame all melded together. And also an evil thrill as I sent my principal rival to his death. Was that an irredeemable mortal sin?

I tried to block that thought re-surfacing. Yet at the same time it was a nice moment to get a compliment from my son. Before I had a moment to dwell on that, however, I was brought back to the immediate challenge by Osric.

"But also we shouldn't forget, Lord. what our young scholar

144

John was saying about this charter. After all, that's where the story starts doesn't it? Where does that come in – if at all?" said Osric.

"Well, yes and no," I said – summing up my own uncertainty. "Assuming that everything little Jonny said was true, the plan was they this mysterious person – or persons – would come into the library when Peter was not there. In other words they wanted to avoid him – they didn't want to kill him. But who knows, maybe they did want to. Or maybe they just felt they needed to. Or wanted to."

"Oh, father, it's just getting more and more complicated," said Damian. "It just feels like we're going backwards and confusing ourselves."

"Well, that's what we've got to do, Damian. Map out all the possibilities and then try to find a pattern in it. The problem is there might be several patterns. So then we test out the evidence, put it on the map and see where it points. But I think the real problem is that we don't have enough evidence."

"That's why I'd still like to know what the significance of that old manuscript was," insisted Osric loudly.

"Don't get too excited, Osric," I warned. "But you're right. As Father Compton said, it's got legal importance. And he is very keen to get it back. But was that the motive for stealing it? I think it's more likely because of its historic interest. Maybe it's one of the Oxford colleges which wants it for their library – after all, John was tapped up in Oxford, wasn't he?. The charter goes back to some long-forgotten king, Edgar. Perhaps it's this new college in Oxford which wants it. They would probably love to have something that ancient for their new library. But what we do know is that it was exceptional because it was highly decorated in gold. Gold and lots of it as I understand it."

"Well that's the answer isn't it!" burst out Osric who now seemed to be flitting from one idea to another rather desperately. "Whoever was after it wanted it because of the gold. Scrape all that off and, by the sound of it, you've got a nice sum of money for the easiest robbery in England."

"You could be right," I had to concede. "It might just be as simple as that. But if those Lollards are involved then the motive would more likely be to expose the monastery as a place of wealth and privilege piling up gold in their library rather than using it to feed the poor and needy."

"But if this pair of so-called Lollards really are behind it – if they exist at all," broke in Damian, "how would they have known about young Johnny in Oxford and all of that?"

"All too easily, I think," I replied. "Apparently the ring-leader of these Lollards actually teaches at the university – at Oxford - name of Wickland or Wycliffe or something similar. He's completely against the monasteries and I am sure that he would want to damage Winchester with its big cathedral and several abbeys. He could easily have come across young Jonny."

"Wait though!" said Damian urgently. "Maybe, you've got it there. We don't think John was responsible for the murder but maybe he was involved in helping these Lollards. Perhaps he is a Lollard himself and he was the one who came up with the idea of handing over the manuscript to this other couple. You know what these students are like. Always wanting to tear things down. There's probably some grudge going back hundreds of years they want to put right."

"Hmm, that's perfectly possible too," I said. "He is certainly a troubled young man who probably thought too much about things and had a grievance against the rich and the powerful. Do we know what happened to him, by the way? Didn't he say something about going on pilgrimage. I thought that was odd in itself."

"Yes, I agree. Why isn't he going back to Oxford?" said Damian. "You'd have thought that he would want to get back there sharpish."

"Well I don't think they have very long terms at these universities and if all he wants to do is read, well, he can do that pretty well anywhere, I suppose," I said, being not very sure myself how universities were supposed to work. "Anyway, I think we've discussed enough for this evening. Let's sleep on it and tomorrow morning we'll decide how to divide things up between us. Today has been a very long day – and tomorrow might be even more so."

CHAPTER 22
'Lat us heere a messe and
so we dyne'

It was a grim night of tossing and turning as I alternated violent nightmares with periods of wakefulness populated by dreadful memories of failures and horrors. Even events which seemed happy at the time were distorted by my mangled brain into images of shame.

"Damian, I have not slept well – I have to tell you," I said as I hauled myself wearily out of bed the following morning and looked across to my son, full of youth and brimming with hope. "All that conversation we had last night meant that I had not dealt with the sight of Brother Walter. It was horrible."

"But father, I thought you had said that after all those years of fighting nothing could affect you."

"Yes, that's what I thought. That's how I felt. But it now seems I've changed. It's my age I suppose - or being here in England, at home with you. When it's on your own doorstep you can't escape it. I'm feeling it's stifling me. But if this is my cross then I must bear it."

Damian was as solicitous as a twenty year old boy, eager for adventure, could be with a man twice his age and desperately looking for tranquillity.

"Well, father, from what you say this could be the end of it today. We'll go off quietly to Canterbury and you can live peacefully thereafter."

"But without your mother."

"Yes, father – but you were without mother for the past five years."

It was meant kindly, I think, but the implied reproach was unavoidable.

"So after we've had something to eat I think I need to go across again and take a look at Brother Walter's corpse," I said as briskly as I could. "I don't relish it but it has to be done. I could not take it all in last night. And then we can have a hunt round the infirmary in case there is anything of interest to be seen."

By now Osric had joined us.

"Damian, you will come with me – and Osric, I would like you to go and talk to Michael again at the gate. Play the innocent a bit. Ask him again about the so-called priest and the ploughman. I know he's seen them hanging around in the Forecourt, he told me – but how much did they get into the Outer Court? Who did they speak to, that sort of thing."

"Yes, lord, I understand."

"And also try to get some more general gossip out of him – about what's going on in the monastery and anything he knows about Peter and Walter. Just see what you can find out."

"And after that"

"Yes, just keep and eye on the comings and goings. I'm particularly interested in anything odd that you might see about the guests from last night. I'm aiming to have a talk with the lawyer and his friend the Franklin at some stage. I haven't really had a chance to speak to them properly yet."

"They're not local, are they Lord?"

"No, you're right. Osric. The Franklin's from beyond from Basyng – and the lawyer is from London."

"Which probably means he's done it, Lord."

"What, the murder, Osric?"

"Yes, the murder, lord. These Londoners, you can't trust them. They come down here to the country and they think we're fools – especially the lawyers."

I had to concede that Osric had a point - but maybe not quite enough evidence to convict in a court of law. Could you be condemned just because you came from London? Yes, probably – at least in the court of popular opinion.

"Well, all the more reason to keep an eye on him Osric," I said, half smiling. "And also keep your eye on the ladies – Madame Alison and Prioress Eglentyne. I've got no suspicion of them as such – I can't imagine them murdering anyone and in any case

148

they were at table with me last night. But I don't have a clear idea of their hangers-on and servants. The Prioress certainly has a priest with her and, I think, another nun as well. She laid great stress on the priest's piety and how much time he was spending in the abbey church - and that makes me suspicious immediately. If you can, try to identify him and see what he's up to."

"Yes, I'll mention him to Michael – he might have seen him."

"And just one important thing about Michael," I said. "I've been acquainted with him for a long time and it was gratifying when he gave me a warm welcome especially given that I've been away for so long. But after I spoke to him yesterday I realised that I can't say I really know him. And it occurred to me in the middle of the night, when I couldn't sleep, that as someone who sees everything and controls who comes and goes, he would be a perfect accomplice for someone who meant the abbey no good. Just bear that in mind when you are talking to him. If I were trying to make trouble for the abbey he's the first person I'd try to get on my side."

"So basically, lord, you are saying 'Don't trust anyone.'"

"Sadly I think that is so," I sighed. "This abbey is deceptive. Sound and secure on the outside, it is fragile within. And that fragility is infectious – it means everyone is looking out for themselves – even the guests. My main worry is that even we might not be immune."

I looked at the other two who seemed puzzled and disturbed by my words. "Come on," I said, "Let's arm ourselves against that risk by going to mass and then having a good breakfast."

CHAPTER 23

'To speke of phisik and surgerye'

Following a short mass in St. Bartholomew's, the abbey's lay chapel, we were offered only a modest breakfast in the almoner's hall – in contrast, I suspected to what was provided in the abbot's lodgings. But, in any case, I realised that we needed to make every moment count today.

"Keep alert and we'll you see you later," I said to Osric as he went off towards Brother Michael's lodge at the gate leaving Damian and me to head to the infirmary.

Brother Adam was waiting for us at the door. He looked even more fatigued than I felt.

"I'm glad you've come, Sir Matthew. Doctor Nafis, the physician, is here. He's in a terrible state. Of course he is horrified – I think he had a high regard for Brother Walter. He's been raging. He says he wants some explanation of what's going on here."

"Well so would I," I replied slightly tersely. "But I am not sure that I can assist him. Where is he now then?"

"He's in the back, in the quiet room with Brother Walter's body. We put Brother Walter in there this morning alongside Brother Peter."

Damian and I walked down the middle aisle of the infirmary. The small number of sick and infirm were either sleeping or too preoccupied with their own condition to show much interest in us.

Doctor Nafis was sitting at the table which was covered by strange-looking remedies. He looked very shaken. What I assumed was the corpse of Brother Walter lay under a cloth on another table. Alongside him was Brother Peter who was now starting to smell somewhat. It was good that the funeral would be the following day.

"Dreadful! Dreadful isn't it, Sir Matthew. Absolutely dreadful. I don't know what the world – or at least this abbey – is coming to. Brother Walter was such a conscientious man."

"And you've got no idea of why this might have happened

151

Doctor Nafis?"

"I've had a few thoughts, obviously but..." he trailed away. Clearly he was not quite willing to share his thoughts with me yet.

Aiming to nudge him along I suggested.

"Do you think in any way it might be linked to the death of Brother Peter."

"And what makes you think that?"

"Well it's a natural assumption don't you think?" I said. "Two murders in as many days and both attacking the same parts of the body – and both on elderly men."

"Have you looked at Brother Walter?"

"Yes, I saw him last night."

"I mean really looked – I mean closely."

"Well no, not very closely," I replied, although feeling that I had certainly been close enough. "It was dark but I saw sufficient to understand what had happened."

"So did you think the mutilations were the same?"

"More or less, as far as I could see. Brother Thomas was anxious for us to return to the abbot's dining room and report on what had happened."

"Well, again, the groin attack was done after death," explained the doctor. "But just so you know, whereas the mutilation on Brother Peter was rather crude - wild as well as violent - the attack on Brother Walter was done with much more finesse. I don't think they were done by the same person. And certainly not in the same way."

"Well, that is very interesting," I said trying to appear calm and distanced about it. "It had always been in my mind that there might be two people involved."

"I think you're right but whether they were two people together or independently, who knows," he said.

"So can I be clear, Doctor. In the case of Brother Peter you said death was due to a broken neck – with the mutilation as a kind of extra."

"That's right. And in the case of Brother Walter his throat

152

slit. That was what killed him. So his mutilation was also, as you so delicately put it, an 'extra'."

At that point Damian asked whether he could view the body. Doctor Nafis raised the cloth and indicated the wounds to the neck and the groin. Such was my new state of mind that I could barely bear to glance at them. Damian, however, studied them intently. "Gruesome, truly gruesome," he said softly after a period of silence. "Yet, as you say doctor, also very neat."

The initiative swung back to me.

"So again - this mutilation - it was something vindictive, an afterthought," I suggested.

"I don't know whether it was an afterthought but it certainly came afterwards," said Nafis. "But it's all quite awful. I feel deeply sorry for Brother Walter but I also feel sorry for the person who did it. What must he or she be feeling now? The guilt, it must be terrible."

"Or maybe satisfaction, "I said. "We don't know. But why do you say she? That hadn't occurred to me."

"Well, as I said – the attack has been delivered with a certain finesse – a woman could be responsible."

"Actually doing it?"

"Involved in some way," he said.

"But I didn't think that women were allowed to come into the monastery?"

"But Sir Matthew, you've seen for yourself that they do. I understand that there were even two women dining with you and the other guests last night."

"That's true."

"But more than that, there are women coming into this monastery all the time. Some for perfectly reputable reasons – like your fellow guests last night, I presume – but others for not so reputable reasons. It's the talk of the town."

"How do you mean?"

"Well, when I say talk of the town, Sir Matthew, I mean the talk of the other monasteries and convents. These are the institutions I specialise in working with. As well as coming here in the morning and evening I also go to Nunnaminster daily and the cathedral monastery twice a day. And once a week I go up to Wintney Priory."

"Which is where Madame Eglentyne is the Prioress?"

"Exactly. And, frankly, Hyde is notorious for its goings-on. There are some nuns with loose morals who like coming in here – and some of the townswomen as well. Its all down to the slack discipline this monastery has fallen into recently."

"But what might have any of this to do with Brother Walter's death?"

"Look, I am not making any accusations. But the thing about Walter - and he was a dedicated and caring man in many respects – is that he did have a soft spot for the ladies and being based here in the infirmary - well, he could do pretty much what he wanted."

"So you're suggesting that some disappointed or aggrieved woman was responsible for this?"

"Who knows – but it was the first thing that entered my mind when I saw what had happened to him. Inspired maybe by what happened to Brother Peter. I think that might be the connection between them."

"You think that a woman might have attacked Peter as well?"

"Oh no – I don't think he had any female entanglements at all. Quite the opposite, in fact, from what I hear. Not that I knew him well. It was just hearsay."

I was starting to feel that I was getting nowhere. Doctor Nafis, Brother Thomas and anyone else I might speak to would each have their own wild theories about what had happened based on their personal prejudices about the monastery. I needed more facts and less speculation.

"So, that's been useful Doctor. I'll bear that in mind. Meanwhile can you just tell me, when did you last see Brother Walter alive?"

"It was yesterday morning, when I came to do my rounds as

154

usual. I'd come from the cathedral monastery and it doesn't take long to walk across here. I checked up on them – not that there are many here right now. I discussed a couple of the patients with Walter and agreed some new treatments. And that was pretty much it. I did call in very briefly in the evening but didn't see him. I assumed that he was at compline."

"Did you come into any of these back rooms?"

"I'm not sure I did. I was only intending to make a very quick visit in case anything urgent had turned up. It all seemed quiet."

"Presumably he attended all the daily services?"

"In principle, yes. But that depended on having one of the lay servants on hand here to keep an eye on things."

"And was there someone here last night?"

"Ah-ha, that's the other thing. Our usual servant has been unwell for a couple of days and so we had agreed that Father Gregory, Madame Eglentyne's personal priest – who has been with her here – would kindly step in. He hadn't arrived when I left but I assumed he would be arriving shortly."

"And presumably you haven't seen Father Gregory since?"

"No, I went straight home, back to my house in Winnal – just outside town on the other side of the river. And had no further contact until arriving this morning."

"And what do you think of this Father Gregory. I've not met him myself but Madame Eglentyne said he is very pious."

"Yes very pious indeed. Or, like you, so I am told by Madame Eglentyne."

"Well, he wasn't here last night when we heard about the murder and came across to see what had happened. Do you think he could have been involved in any way?"

"Extremely unlikely I should have thought," said the doctor. "Deeply devout by all accounts."

"Anyway, I need to speak to him as soon as possible."

"Indeed – but I should add one other thing. When I was walking back across the Outer Court I noted a couple of fellows skulking in the shadows by the gate. I could not see them very clearly but I had feeling that I'd seen them before when I came in yesterday morning to examine Brother Peter's poor body. There were still a few people coming and going but they were just waiting there and trying not to draw attention to themselves. But oddly enough that was what drew my eye to them."

"But it was two men was it – not a man and a woman."

"Definitely two men."

"Thank you. Doctor. Very useful. To be honest, I do not know how much longer I will be pursuing this. But no doubt I will see you tomorrow at Brother Peter's and, now, Walter's funerals?"

"Indeed – and then I will be accompanying you and several others I believe to London and then on to Canterbury. Despite these tragedies I am determined to go. It has been a long winter, hemmed in and I need some re-invigoration. Even more so after these past couple of days."

"Of course – I have to confess that I share your feelings. So I will see you tomorrow then."

"And that will be the end of the story, will it?" he asked somewhat anxiously.

"It might be for Damian and me," I said. "My impression is that they won't want me around for much longer. But for the abbey I think it's only just beginning."

CHAPTER 24
'Of his complexioun he was sangwyn'

I had arranged to see Sergeant Henry and his friend, Roger Odiham, the Franklin at mid-morning. However, the news that Father Gabriel was supposed to have overseen the infirmary on the previous evening compelled me to seek out the nun's priest immediately. I knew that Madame Eglentyne and Sister Avelina, her young assistant, together with Father Gabriel were staying in the abbey's other guest-house by the gateway so we made our way across there at pace.

The three of them were just emerging as we approached.

"Good morning, Sir Matthew," Madame Eglentyne said in a bright voice. "How are you getting on this morning with your inquisition? I am still in a state of shock about last night's terrible news. We all are, aren't we?" she said turning to her two companions whom she introduced to me. The nun nodded politely with a kind of knowing smile but Father Gabriel, who seemed remarkably young, was immediately effusive.

"I am overwhelmed by it, Sir Matthew. I had got to know Brother Walter a little over the past couple of days. He was very dedicated to his patients. It's horrible what has happened to him."

Father Gregory came across as sincere and sympathetic. Combined with his good looks I could understand how he would have have commended himself to the refined Madame Eglentyne.

"I gather Father Gabriel that you had kindly agreed to stand in for Brother Walter last night when he went to compline."

"Oh really – who told you that?" he said in a surprised voice.

"I've just been speaking to Doctor Nafis. He said that after he had done his rounds of the infirmary yesterday Brother Walter told him that you would be coming that evening so that he could attend divine office in the abbey church. Apparently the usual servant was not available."

"No, I think he must have misunderstood. I was at compline myself last night. I noticed that Walter wasn't there."

"Oh, well, that's odd – so there must have been some misunderstanding."

"I don't know why there should have been. I certainly did go across earlier in the morning to see whether I could be of any help to Brother Walter and he did mention that his usual servant was himself away sick. I think I might have made some general observation about being happy to help out. But we had not specifically agreed anything about compline. I thought he had found someone else. And I do so enjoy compline!"

"Oh well, that must have been it then – a simple misunderstanding."

"Mind you, a tragic misunderstanding – that's what makes me even more upset," said Father Gregory. "If I had been there then presumably Brother Walter would not have been killed."

"Or maybe," I said, to see the reaction, "you would have been killed as well?"

At this suggestion Father Gregory appeared to blanch and wither, shocked into silence. He did not look like a killer.

"I am sorry to have upset you, Father Gregory," I said quickly. "It is just that the problem with these murders is that we don't know the motives. It might well be that both Brother Peter and Brother Walter were personally targetted. Or it might just be that they had the misfortune to be in the wrong place at the wrong time. We just don't know."

"Oh, it is just all too terrible to think about" announced Madame Eglentyne firmly indicating she wanted to end the discussion. "And that is really all we have to say about it. You must excuse us, Sir Matthew. We are walking in to Winchester to purchase one or two last things for the departure tomorrow. After the funerals, of course."

"Well, I shall be joining you on the journey," I said.

"How delightful! I hoped that you would be!" Madame Eglentyne replied, pleased to have moved away from the turgid matter of the murders. "Now because we are leaving later than planned our intention is to stay tomorrow evening back at my own dear Wintney Priory. It's just a short way off the road to London, as you know. So if you and your party would like to journey with us we should be honoured to welcome you as our guests."

"That would be a pleasure," I replied without really considering the implications. After all it was likely to be much nicer than an inn in Guildford. "We'd like that wouldn't we, Damian?"

"Yes, absolutely!" he responded in an uncharacteristically gushing way having been silent and reserved – almost shy – hitherto. While also, I thought, casting admiring looks at Sister Avelina.

"So we are agreed," announced Madame Eglentyne. "We will travel to London together and you will stay tomorrow in Wintney. Excellent!."

And away they went.

I began to puzzle over how it was that Madame Eglentyne appeared so calm in the face of these murders. Of course, she had expressed anxiety in the right way but it seemed somehow a mere gesture as if, in reality, it did not affect her or her people at all. Maybe she assumed that as visitors that they were not at risk. Or maybe she somehow knew they were not at risk. Could that be right?

But time was moving on and I needed to speak to the lawyer and the Franklin. I had agreed to meet them in the almoner's hall which fronted on to the Outer Court and had less of the stifling atmosphere than the rest of the monastery at this time of day.

They were already seated on the far side of the large room apparently talking to two other, rather badly-dressed men whose faces I could not see. The Sergeant waved at us to come over and join him while at the same time saying something to his companions. At this the two men stood up and moved away rapidly before I could see their features.

"I don't mean to break up your conversation, Sergeant," I said waving in the direction of the two disappearing backs.

"No, no, don't worry in the least," he replied. "They were

just two pilgrims. Ordinary folk but so excited about the journey ahead. They said that they had never been to London before and wanted us to tell them all about it. But then I would need a whole day – a week in fact to do that, wouldn't I? London! Where does one stop?" He laughed urbanely. "Please, do sit down."

"Do you mind if Damian joins us?"

Not in the least. He smiled genially at Damian. "It will be a pleasure to get to know your son better."

Damian returned the smile and sat between me and Sir Roger Odiham. I turned to Sergeant Henry.

"You're a Londoner yourself, are you not?" I asked.

"Well, in fact I am from around these parts originally – Waltham actually. But I went to the Temple and then to St. Paul's many years ago to make my fortune. I didn't quite do that, sadly, but I do make a living."

"But you've obviously kept some local connections?"

"Well, we both have, haven't we Roger? Sir Roger comes from near Basyng."

Sir Roger nodded. He seemed at first glance, you might say, the silent type. But he was certainly no shrinking violet. Although he had said nothing very much at the abbot's dining table – just the odd nod – his bulk and his long white beard conveyed authority.

"Now you probably don't know, Sir Matthew – given that you have been away – Sir Roger here is a Member of Parliament, a burgess, and has been a Justice of the Peace. So he divides his time between being down in the shire and up at Westminster."

"Oh well, I am impressed," I felt I had to say.

"You don't have to be, Sir Matthew," responded the Franklin in a polite but confident and rasping voice. "There's nothing much to it. But one does need to keep an eye on things. Quietly I mean. As events over the last few days have demonstrated, wouldn't you say?"

I began to appreciate that maybe there was more to Roger Oldham than had initially met my eye. Sitting across the table

160

from me at the dining table on the previous two evenings he had said little but was probably taking it all - 'keeping an eye on things' as he put it.

"Well, that is exactly what I wanted to talk to you about," I continued. "You both know the abbey well, I imagine, so I was hoping that you might hazard some insights into what's behind these murders."

"Just to be clear, Sir Matthew," came another quick reply from Sir Roger. "I've been aware of this abbey for many years but I've never got to know it well as far as its personalities or politics were concerned. In fact, this is the first time I have spent any time here – isn't that so, Sergeant Henry?" He glanced across at his friend for confirmation who nodded his agreement. "And the stay was not supposed to be as long as this anyway. My relationships in Winchester have all been with the cathedral and the bishop. They're the real powers in these parts you know. But Henry here has done work for the abbey in the past. He's in a much better position to give a useful opinion than I am."

"Thank you for your confidence Sir Roger," laughed the lawyer. "But, Sir Matthew I doubt if I know much more than you do – or at least what you have picked up in the past couple of days. Nonetheless I will be candid with you and say that my impression in recent years is that this abbey is not a happy place. And do you want to know why?"

"Please go ahead – it might shed some light on recent events."

Sergeant Henry then enumerated what was by now becoming a familiar liturgy of failures in Hyde.

The number of the abbey's monks had dwindled; their quality was often poor; their education was inadequate; there was little discipline or leadership from the top and the opportunities the abbey might have had – such as founding a school to make good the losses of the great pestilence - had been wasted. Instead, Bishop William had taken the initiative and was building his own new school just outside the walls to complement his new college at Oxford. Sadly the brains would drain away from the city.

"And when you have a growing state of disorder, as you have here in Hyde, Sir Matthew," Sergeant Henry droned on, "that lends itself to an atmosphere of violence. These two murders - they might not even be connected. There is just a growing anxiety here of …..shall we say, that anything might happen, anything bad, I mean."

"That's a sobering account, indeed, Sergeant Henry," I replied. "And this is based on your direct knowledge of the abbey, is it? – although you did say a moment or two ago that you knew it no more than I did?"

"This, Sir Matthew, is based on common knowledge. When I visit my other clients in Winchester they all talk and say the same thing about this place, this community."

"So you think it is the state of decay in the Abbey which is responsible for the deaths?"

"No, no, we cannot excuse individual crimes on the grounds of institutional failings," he replied quickly. "I am a lawyer and I believe in justice. But that's the background to it. You can bring some poor serving girl to trial for these murders, convict her and execute her because she has no benefit of clergy but that doesn't get the bottom of what is really going on – or rather going wrong."

This comment certainly woke me up.

"Why do you mention a serving girl, Sergeant Henry? Is that what you've heard?"

"That's the rumour running round, Sir Matthew. I'm surprised that you've not come across it yourself."

"And where's the evidence for this? The witnesses?" I asked.

"The evidence and the witnesses are self-evident in the rumour, I would suggest, Sir Matthew," said Sir Roger breaking in.

"So what needs to be done – I mean to the abbey?" I asked, keen to hear the solution.

"The place needs to have its wings cropped," said Sir Roger sharply.

"In what way cropped?" I replied, by now very interested in

162

this Member of Parliament's views.

"Well, it's clear. Despite what my friend Sergeant Henry has described as a failing establishment the abbey is still wealthy. Everyone knows that. And it could be wealthier. Does it use its wealth well? I do not think so. Could someone else do a better job with this wealth – especially given the state of the country now? I think the answer to that is 'Certainly'. But all of that does nothing, I must admit, to explain specifically these – distasteful – murders."

"You paint a bleak picture," I felt forced to say - although reflecting that what I had just heard sounded like a political statement which he had pitched frequently. "But, if you don't mind, going back to this suggestion of a serving wench being involved. Have either of you actually seen or heard anything in the past couple of days which might have raised your suspicions of that being the case? Or, indeed, seen any other people behaving strangely."

The Sergeant suppressed a short laugh but then shook his head.

"I'm sorry," the Franklin said, "but it could be said that everything here looks odd and strange and corrupted – at least to some eyes."

That sounded dangerous talk and in some countries I knew it would have brought the church's Inquisition ferreting around very quickly. But, with his connections, maybe the Franklin was not afraid of that. Anyway, I made one last effort.

"So what about out there?" I pointed into the Forecourt. "To be candid with you, I've not heard anything about a serving wench but I do keep hearing stories about a rough priest and a ploughman. Does it ring any bells?"

Again both men shook their heads in professed ignorance.

"Ah, well – so be it." I sighed.

"Anything that you want to ask, Damian?" I said to my son.

CHAPTER 25
'Ðow miʒhty and ʒreet a lord he is'

Would Damian have the temerity to take on these two much older and experienced men-of-the world? That was the challenge I had put to him. Some might think it quite impudent for a youth to be questioning men of such distinction. If he had remained silent I would have understood. But to my pleasure he rose to the occasion.

"Well if you don't mind me asking, gentlemen" Damian said with assurance."What have you been doing in the monastery? Why are you here now?"

It was all about tone. He might be embarrassed with a young woman but he was quietly bold with mature men. Spoken with any aggression the questions would have soured things immediately. I was prepared to risk that. But instead, Damian spoke with such innocent curiosity that they seemed charmed.

"Ah well, that's simple to answer," said Sergeant Henry. "I have two or three little cases on locally – complications of land sales, land ownership that kind of thing for clients I've known for some years. So I took the opportunity of staying at Hyde for whom I've done work in the past. They are always quite hospitable – when they are not murdering people that is! And Sir Roger here was interested in joining me from Basyng for a couple of days. Winchester is always lovely to see. But what we hadn't bargained for was being caught here for the extra day."

"It was good of you to stay," I said. Damian nodded his agreement

"Well, it would have been churlish to refuse," said the Franklin. "But if you are finished talking about these horrible murders can I mention something else, Sir Matthew. Or rather, ask you a question?"

"By all means," I replied.

"What are your own plans? I mean after you complete this pilgrimage. You are a man of action. You have returned in triumph from crusade. And I think that we can all appreciate that you are a man of discernment. But what happens next in your life?"

The Franklin, in his worldliness, had hit the very heart of my own secret anxieties.

"As you may have gathered, Sir Roger – I returned home to find my dear wife had died," I replied. "Everything I had planned for the future in those years abroad just came to a halt. Of course, it has been a great joy to me to rebuild my link with Damian here. But he is ready to make his own way in the world. I cannot keep him in Somborne and Ashley for ever. So, in short, I do not know what to do with myself. I will ponder the question and pray on it for the next few days. And by the time I arrive at Canterbury I trust the good Lord will have given me an answer."

"Well, you have my sympathy, Sir Matthew. And I am very sorry to hear about your wife. But let me mention something else which chimes in with what you have just said. And, Damian, it might well be of interest to you too. After all you went with the Duke of Lancaster to France recently, did you not? I think that someone mentioned that to me."

"I did, sir, yes. Not entirely a successful experience but certainly interesting. At least I got away from it with my life."

Damian burst into a laugh. The other two joined in. I remained silent.

"And do you now want to make your career – your way in the world as your father was saying – as a soldier, a knight?"

"I do, indeed, sir. That is what I have always dreamed of – like my father here." He gave me a playful nudge in the ribs.

"Well, that's encouraging," said the Franklin, warming to his theme. "So let me explain. As you have gathered I am in Parliament and shall we say, I am familiar with the circle around the Duke of Lancaster. He is a very fine man, a great man I think, and in these troubled times he may well be the only man capable of holding England together. He embodies everything we could look for in nobility – he is, you might say, a new Arthur."

He paused for effect.

166

"I am sure all that might well be true, Sir Roger," I said feeling slightly irritated at the reference to the popular hero. "But what has it to do with us? Damian and me?"

"Give me time, Sir Matthew. Give me time. With his great ambition for England, the Duke of Lancaster is looking for good men. Men of respectable birth and education, wedded to chivalry. He needs young men as knights – brave men like you, Damian - and he needs men of experience, older men, wiser men - like you, Sir Matthew – to step forward to undertake various offices in government and in administration to serve this country with, it must be said, attractive annuities attached."

He waited for a reaction from me. I gave him none. But I could see that Damian was already hooked.

"So I think you can see the way my thoughts are running, Sir Matthew? And you Damian. I have heard from your comrades in France last year that you made a good impression. I am sure the Duke would be delighted for you to be with him on a more permanent basis as part of his retinue."

"I am flattered – that's very kind of you," piped up Damian. "I was lucky to be with such a gallant group of lads. Apart from the odd scare we enjoyed ourselves enormously."

'And so it begins' I thought. It starts with high jinx and it ends in shallow graves.

"Well from what I heard they were delighted you were with them," the Franklin continued. "But that was just a temporary excursion for the Duke. He is now planning for the future. And I am sure that you too, Sir Matthew, would have an immense amount to offer – and would be rewarded accordingly."

"Could you be a little more explicit?" I asked continuing to feel alarmed about the reference to Arthur, who was of course the ancient king. The Duke of Lancaster was no more than the king's uncle but were his aspirations rising higher? "I've been away a long time," I continued. "The old King was still on the throne when I left and I don't feel that I have yet fully understood the new set-up with a young king and a Duke who, by the sound of it, has ideas of his own."

"Let me reassure you on that point," said the Franklin passing his hand through his long white beard. "The Duke loves his nephew, our young King Richard. I am sure you know that he was devoted to the King's father, his brother – he was desperately upset when he died so young. So much promise left unfulfilled. But the country needs strong government – and it needs it now. And it needs it throughout the country – not just in London. Indeed, London might become a bit of a problem. But here in the south it's just a matter of light touch – but a touch is needed. Someone like yourself with your talents and experience, with your standing in society here in the shire – that would have much to recommend itself to the Duke. And, as I say, I think it would be much to your advantage as well."

Against all my better instincts I could not but feel myself becoming intrigued. Maybe it was the need to have something to look forward to. Or maybe hold on to.

"And what, if I might ask Sir Roger, is your authority to say this – indeed to offer such positions?" I asked.

"I think that things are coming to the boil, Sir Matthew. I feel it in the air. I hear what is happening around the country – especially further east over towards Kent and Essex. But to answer your question directly. Yes, I am close to the Duke. Many of our recent Members of Parliament are – although some take another view. So I am privy to his plans. I know the kind of people whom he likes to have around him – the kind of people he can rely on with an indenture of service - beneficial to both sides, as I say. I am confident that he would favour you."

"And where is he now exactly, the Duke?" I asked, really just playing for time.

"Ah, that's the thing. The urgent defence of the realm means that he will shortly be off north to deal with the Scots. He will not be coming south for some time, I fear. But I am in regular correspondence with him and I would be happy to put forward your name and that of Damian for preferment. I understand your need to grieve for your wife and to determine what next to do with your life. But here is an offer that I think you should take seriously."

For the sake of courtesy I expressed gracious thanks and indicated that I would, indeed, think about it. But in truth I was in no state to make that kind of decision immediately or, maybe, for some time. Could it be just what I required? Almost certainly it would suit Damian well. But I felt that I needed to be more specific about what the Duke's so-called 'plans' and intentions were for England.

"I know that it is a lot to take in – especially everything else you are dealing with, Sir Matthew," put in Sergeant Henry, "but I am sure that you can have further conversation with Sir Roger, maybe in more detail, on the road to London."

"Exactly," emphasised the Franklin.

"Yes, that might be useful," I parried.

"Oh, and one other thing," said Sergeant Henry. "I wouldn't worry too much about these unfortunate – very unfortunate – murders. They'll take care of themselves, I think. Or the church authorities will take care of them in due course. Two monks – one elderly and sadly a drunk, the other an infirmarium who was very vulnerable to catching diseases. They are now happily ensconced in Paradise with the Lord. I don't think we need to worry too much about how they got there. And on that note we will now leave you, I think, to go about our remaining business."

I thanked them for their time and said that I would reflect on what they had said. They nodded in acknowledgement, got up and left. Damian stood up to wave them off. The Franklin turned and gave him a warm smile.

"So what do you make of that then?" I asked Damian,

"Well, father, I was hoping that you could explain it to me. But, for myself, I have to say I am interested. Very interested. Once this pilgrimage is over I don't think I can just go back home and idle my time away. I am 20 years old. This is when I need to start building a reputation. And to have a proper position connected to the Duke of Lancaster would, I think, be an ideal place to do it."

His enthusiasm was understandable. But I was wary of over-mighty subjects - even those who might be close relatives of the ruler – and their ambitions. If they were to fall they might pull down all their followers with them.

"Yes, I understand your ambitions, Damian. My problem is that I am not sure that I trust old John of Gaunt. Many people don't. He is wealthy and, as I understand it, he has a lot of support and many retainers throughout the country. But he also has lots of enemies. And if he has ambitions to be king – which I suspect he might - then that would be trouble."

"But he is loyal to his nephew, isn't he? That's what Sir Roger said. He emphasised it."

"I certainly hope so. And as to the offer to me - I need time to think it over. Quite a lot of time, I think. And I didn't like the way they were patronising me over the murder investigation. I can't pretend to be enjoying it. But I do have a commitment to seeking out the truth. So let's get back to focusing on that. We need to find Osric and see whether he has dug up anything worthwhile. Ducal retinues can wait!"

CHAPTER 26

'Wich worthy wommen of the toun'

We were about to enter our lodgings when Brother Thomas called from the other side of the Outer Court.

"Sir Matthew! Just a word please."

Damian and I turned back and walked over to him.

"As I promised I would, Sir Matthew, I went across to the cathedral earlier this morning," he explained in his clipped way. "I brought them up-to-date with the latest developments. And they would like to see you this afternoon for an urgent discussion."

"And when you say 'they', who do you mean? Bishop William?"

"Oh no, no, no. See Bishop William?! That would be quite something. No, it's Prior Hugh of the monastic abbey you'll be seeing – but remember, he has the full authority of the Bishop. So what he says, goes. I'll see you after Sext. I'll be at the front gate. I'll take you across to the cathedral. Please don't be late. I don't want to inconvenience the Prior."

"Can I bring Damian with me?"

"No. Just you. We don't need to see your underling."

He turned on his heel and walked away.

"Not too surprising I suppose. 'Inconvenience the Prior'! What about inconveniencing me?" I fumed. "And as for 'underling'!"

"Don't worry, father," said Damian coolly. "I think we'll be able to deal with that later. Let's go and find Osric."

Approaching our room I could hear two voices coming from inside. One was definitely female. The other was Osric. The door was locked. I knocked – hard.

"Osric, it's Sir Matthew, here. With Damian. Would you let us in?"

There was a brief silence. "Yes, coming Lord – I'll be straight with you."

"Osric, I know you have someone in there with you so don't play any silly games."

The bolt squeaked across, the door then opened. Osric was

standing there accompanied by a young, attractive woman.

"I think you had better leave young lady," I said. "Osric and I have things to discuss."

"Well that's exactly what we've been doing," she said and marched out briskly, totally unabashed by her discovery.

"I don't like having strangers coming into our rooms, Osric," I said once she had disappeared. "If you wanted to have a cosy chat with that young woman it should have been elsewhere."

"Just wait to hear what I have to tell you, lord. You'll understand why we were here. And it wasn't what you think – well, not entirely."

Osric then gave an account of his morning. And very fruitful it was too.

"After I left you, Lord, I went straight across to Michael on the gate. He's quite used to me by now but he wasn't his usual self. I presumed it was because of Walter's murder. All the lower monks and abbey servants are pretty shook up about it. Peter being murdered was kind of in character. But Walter was a different story. Anyway, I started to ask a few questions but Michael clammed up. I don't know whether that was because he had been warned off by Father Eynesham or Brother Thomas but there also seemed to be some tension between him and his young assistant Timothy."

"Well, Timothy's like Brother Thomas, isn't he?" I said. "Basically a spy in the camp. I can imagine that there might be suspicion between them."

"Well, whatever it was, Michael was not saying anything – or even being faintly friendly. The only thing he did acknowledge was that this mysterious couple of villains – you know the so-called priest and the ploughman, the possible Lollards - had been seen again over the past day but this time they were dressed completely differently. In fact, if it hadn't been for the scar that the priest had on his neck Michael said he wouldn't even have been sure it was him. And, again they were talking with Mistress Alison. But aside from that he wouldn't say a thing."

"And how were they dressed then? This mysterious duo"

""Well dressed, much better. Quite respectable – Michael said they looked a bit like soldiers off-duty. And he hinted that one or two people had mentioned they were the ones behind the death of Walter."

"Did he offer any evidence or motive for that?"

"No, just said a couple of times that they were a suspicious couple. And that they had asked him where the infirmary was. And after that Timothy came over and he stopped speaking completely."

"Well if they had been the two men who took Peter to the infirmary then they would have already known where the infirmary was, wouldn't they?" said Damian. "So that rather kills that idea, doesn't it father?"

I had to agree. "But how come they were much better dressed?" I asked.

"No idea," said Osric. "It's all very confusing."

"Anyway, what did you do then?" Damian said.

"I thought I would have a wander round in the forecourt, just to see what might be going on. What with Easter coming up the crowds are starting to grow, mostly people going into the abbey church to see the relics there – you know, Saint Jos - and some folk going into the chapel just inside the front gate. And quite a few idlers. So as I was making my way towards the chapel I was approached by that girl you just saw. Mildrede her name is – or claims to be anyway."

"And does she make her living here then?" Damian asked bluntly.

"You could say that. She tried to start up a conversation – and I was quite happy to oblige. Nice girl and, I thought, she would have been keeping her eye on what was going on round the abbey for the past few days."

"And what did she have to say, Osric? I mean of relevance to us" I asked, trying to hurry him up.

"So, two things. First, Mildrede said that for all of Brother

Michael's honest appearance he is a flaky character. It was really confirming what you has said this morning, Lord. You might have been acquainted with Michael for a long time but you didn't really know him. It turns out that he was easily bribable to let people into the Outer Court."

"Meaning that if you slipped him a penny he'd let you in?" said Damian.

"You've got it. Now Mildrede had two or three friends, shall we say, among the monks. So to reach them for their cosy chats she had to pay, Michael. And she's not the only one doing this by any means as I understand."

"Well, well," I said. "I had a suspicion that he was a bit too good to be true."

"Your instinct was right, Lord. But I didn't want to take what Mildrede said just at face value. I said that I was not entirely convinced. She said, 'Well, I'll prove it, love – give me a penny.' So I did and saw it with my own eyes. She was very discreet about it, as was Michael – they've obviously worked out a handover method. But she went through the gateway easy as anything. I then followed and said we better come up here."

"Alright, Osric. Well done - that was smart of you. But where do these young ladies then go to meet their 'friends'?" I asked. "All the monks sleep in the same big dormitory, don't they?"

"And that's the second thing he said. Just think about it, Lord, for a moment. Where do you think there might be spare beds. And some of them quite private."

"Of course!" said Damian instantly. "The infirmary."

"That's right. The infirmary," confirmed Osric.

"But that must have also involved Walter then didn't it?"

"I'm afraid so. Rather seems as if they had a nice little business going on between them."

"So, Michael got his fee for allowing the girls in," I said, "And then, presumably Walter got his cut from what the girls were paid by his fellow monks. And maybe other people as well – posing as unwell pilgrims"

174

"You've got the idea, Lord. Either that or he was paid 'in kind' by the girls," said Osric.

"Well, I had already got the impression that he was keen on the ladies," I said, starting to think it through. "But where does this leave us with regard to his murder? I mean we had assumed that it was all connected to Brother Peter. But maybe there is something else going on here."

We sat in silence, the three of us pondering this possibility.

"And remember what Michael said. He was pointing the finger at this odd couple – the priest and the ploughman. Do we take that seriously?" asked Osric.

"Yes, this odd couple that we still cannot identify," I said irritably.

"Well, you also have to ask whether Michael was reliable in any way, don't you?" said Damian. "Is he hand in glove with this strange pair?"

"And then what is their relationship with this Mistress Alison?" said Osric.

"Especially as she has had five husbands already apparently," I chipped in. "She told me the first evening we were here. And she referred to it in this odd kind of way. I think most of them were elderly when they got married – and they didn't last long afterwards."

"So, father, you think she might be involved in the murder of Walter? After all, if she has a record of doing away with elderly men it would all fit, wouldn't it?"

"I suppose it would," I said. "But I think our imaginations might be running away with themselves. It's just that the doctor suggested that a woman might have been involved in the death because of the way the mutilation had been inflicted. But, no, I think we need to calm down a bit – or at least I do. And, Osric, something else. I've got a meeting this afternoon with the prior over at the cathedral. Brother Thomas told me this morning."

"What for, do you think, Lord?"

"My instinct is that they are going to tell us to stop investigating. But we'll see. And just so you know because it might affect you as well, I've also had an offer of high office from the Duke of Lancaster's agents – the Franklin and the Sergeant. It sounded an attractive prospect. But it also sounded as if they didn't want me to continue with the case either."

"So you'll be an important lord - but all of this, what we've been doing for the last few days, will have been a waste of time," said Osric sourly.

"No, I want to get to the bottom of this," I replied.

"In that case you owe me three pennies," he said.

CHAPTER 27
'Al the venym of this cursed dede'

I was to meet Brother Thomas outside the monastery's main gate on the London Road. I had arrived at the agreed time and stood to one side observing the various pilgrims as they trickled in and out. What a multitude they were and so diverse in class and profession. And tripping along on a road which went back to the Romans. For a moment I enjoyed a shining vision of all of us jogging along merrily united in the love of God.

But that did not last long.

I realised that Brother Thomas was now significantly late and it crystallised how much I disliked him and his tight arrogance. For a young man who had done nothing with his life except enjoy the benefits of a limited education, his arid self-assurance was infuriating. Moreover, it was being nurtured by the pliability of Father Compton and Father Eynesham who had been intimidated into accommodating this young and calculating puppy as he served his apprenticeship in duplicity. My only comfort was that Hyde was perhaps too easy a testing ground for later life. He would face tougher challenges elsewhere. Just see him trying to deal with the Dominicans in Oxford, I thought maliciously.

I repented quickly of this sinfulness – I was offending gravely 'in thought' ('word' and 'deed' had yet to come). So I determined to be polite and conduct myself in a gentil way both to him and the Prior. And when he arrived I restrained my irritation that there was no apology for his tardiness. Instead, he merely gave me a curt instruction to follow him as we set off down the road towards the City's mighty north gate with its chapel of St. Mary above.

I was expecting to walk the full distance to the cathedral in silence. That would have suited me perfectly well. So I was surprised that once we had passed through the gate into the city he fell into step with me. "Do you mind if I ask how well you know Winchester, Sir Matthew? Aside from your recent crusading I understand that you have spent most of your life in Somborne and thereabouts?"

"Yes I was born on the family's small estate near Somborne and regard it as my home but Winchester has always been important to me," I replied. "I am fortunate that my family has held land in this area going back to the days of the Conqueror."

"Yet you have also spent a lot of time away – as a soldier, I mean?"

"That's true," I replied. "Much of my service before the crusades was in the service of the king – Edward, that is – and even more with his son, the good Black Prince, mostly in France."

"So when was your first battle?" he asked rather crudely. "Being a man dedicated to peace myself, I've often wondered what it must be like to engage in fighting and possibly even kill another human being and send them to face divine justice - perhaps prematurely. What was that like? "

Notwithstanding my antipathy towards Brother Thomas he had flattered me with his interest and I could not resist telling the story.

"I was aged about twenty – the same age as my son, Damian is now. That's when I first encountered real combat," I explained. "I was young and did not reflect on the deeper implications of what I was doing. That came much later. Instead I was drunk on violence and the delight of survival. But it wasn't so much a battle as a siege – the siege of Rouvray in France. But, I have to admit, it was an inglorious start to my career as a soldier. With one or two others I stupidly strayed away from the main army and was captured by the French. I had followed a very silly young man whom I assumed knew where he was going. I could not have been more wrong – it was the arrogance of youth. We were captured and spent several months, not too uncomfortably, in a French prison until ransomed – generously I must say – by the king. But at least I came to the king's attention that way!"

"And what about the attention of other important people in the area? The Despencers for example, do you know them?"

So this was where this questioning was leading. The Despencers were grand and well-connected aristocrats also with property in the Somborne area. They were far more significant than my own middling stock and in recent times they had been calamitously close to royalty. It did not surprise me that young Thomas, in his calculating way, wanted to find out more about them.

"Well I am sure you know, Brother Thomas, the Despencers have land everywhere. But you are right, they do have substantial property close to mine near Somborne."

"Defensive works on the Winchester to Salisbury road, isn't it?" he said, looking for confirmation. "Ashley castle?"

"You obviously know all about it," I replied coolly. "But I am hardly acquainted with them at all. It's like the Duke of Lancaster and his hunting lodge which is also near me. I never see them. They have much more exciting things to do than occupy themselves in a remote part of Hampshire. But why do you ask?"

"I have my own reasons, Sir Matthew, I am sure you understand. But I could not but think of the Despencers when I saw what had happened to poor Walter and Peter. So shocking!"

"Oh really? Why in heaven did that make you think of the Despencers?" I asked, completely at a loss as to what the connection might possibly be.

"Well I am sure you are aware that Hugh Despencer, the younger one, was the earl of Winchester and like his son was executed for his turpitude "

"Yes, I am aware of that but I understand the family fortunes have recovered since," I said trying to maintain a companionable voice.

"But no-one can forget," continued Brother Thomas disregarding my remark, "that he was executed for his evil ways and above all for his unnatural relationship with the King."

He looked at me inquiringly. I said nothing. What he said was, of course, true and widely known. The relationship between Edward the Second – father of the late king – and the young Hugh Despencer, Earl of Winchester was notorious.

179

"The result was that he came to a particularly brutal and humiliating end to his life, didn't he, Sir Matthew?" Brother Thomas persisted.

Again he looked at me almost accusingly. Again I remained silent. What on earth was he suggesting?

"And this is my point, Sir Matthew. His private parts were cut off and he was mutilated in much the same way as Brother Peter and Brother Walter, weren't they."

He had pressed on too far and I had to respond.

"That might well be so, Brother Thomas, but I do not follow your line of thought. And it was all many years ago. A long time even before I was born."

"My line of thought, Sir Matthew, is simply this. That while we do not know who was responsible for mutilating my fellow monks in that way, it is more than likely that he had Hugh Despenser in mind as he did so. And who is more likely to have taken part than someone who has long-standing connections to the Earl of Winchester and is deeply familiar with the story of the Despencers?"

It took me a moment or two to appreciate that he was insinuating that I was involved, in some extraordinary way, in the mutilation. The preposterousness of the suggestion beggared belief.

But I also realised that in the absence of other suspects it would not be too difficult for Brother Thomas to float this absurd suggestion into the tide of gossip and speculation which must now be flowing around the abbey and its guests. The more far-fetched the notion the more it would be relished.

"Look, Brother Thomas, I don't know what you are playing at..." I barked challengingly, all sense of gentilness on my part having evaporated.

But Brother Thomas had timed his incendiary commentary well. We had now arrived at the Cathedral's priory door.

180

CHAPTER 28
'In our chapitre praye we day and nyght'

Ignoring anything I might have wanted to say about his impertinence Brother Thomas instructed me to sit on a stool in the lobby of the Prior's Hall while he sought out his *padrone*.

After some time, Prior Hugh arrived. A large, powerfully-built man of roughly my own age he appeared as formidable a cleric as I had ever met, oozing the self-assurance of someone who knew his way around both church and the state beyond. And as Prior of the monastery attached to Winchester Cathedral he had his eye, no doubt, on further elevation.

Ushering me into his generous-sized room, we took seats by a window overlooking the Inner Close in the heart of the monastery attached to the south side of the cathedral. Brother Thomas remained as a discreet, simpering presence just inside the door.

"Sir Matthew, I am so grateful that you could spare time to come across to our little cathedral," said the prior deploying a line which he had used, no doubt, many times before. "Brother Thomas has told me much about you and, in any case, your reputation was known here from several years back. I was very upset to hear about the loss of your wife. It must be a very bleak time for you. I will pray for her and, indeed, for you too. Had you not been staying with our much-loved cousins at Hyde for these past few days we should have been pleased to entertain you ourselves."

"That is very generous of you Prior Hugh," I replied, prepared to play the game of excessive politeness as my irritation with Brother Thomas began to subside. "I will remember that for next time I intend to stay in Winchester."

He smiled weakly but went on quickly.

"Now, I will come directly to the point. We are very worried here about what is happening at Hyde – much though we hold it in high regard. One murder is bad enough but two in quick succession is, quite frankly, intolerable. Not only have terrible, mortal sins been committed and lives, sadly, lost but word will spread very fast that Winchester – or at least the places of pilgrimage in this city – are not safe. The damage which it is already doing, collaterally, to our beloved shrine of St. Swithun is incalculable. And that will be very bad indeed for everyone in ways which, I am sure, I need not enumerate."

I nodded.

"Now as you know, Hyde is an independent house. We are all Benedictines and Hyde is in charge of its own affairs."

He made the latter point with great emphasis before adding. "But only to a certain degree."

"There comes a moment when Bishop William – or his representative given that the Bishop himself is so busy on other matters in London - must intervene to correct the community if matters are going badly. And make no mistake things are going badly at Hyde Abbey right now. It needs all the assistance it can get. Which is one of the reasons that my much-loved Brother Thomas," he smiled across to the imp-like figure hovering by the door, "is kindly giving extra support to Father Compton. Of course, the sooner that the abbey has its own permanent abbot the better. But, as of now, the time is not propitious for the most appropriate candidate to emerge."

He paused again to allow me to absorb all this. I thought his reference to the times being 'not propitious' a little strange but my instinct was to allow him to proceed and get to the purpose of our meeting.

"Here at the cathedral – and in this context I am speaking on behalf of the Bishop - we have seen discipline deteriorating at Hyde for some time now. And let me tell you that we don't like it. Indeed we had become quite alarmed. But, these murders, I need hardly tell you, risk bringing matters to something of a crisis. It was incumbent on Father Compton to deal with it. But he appears not to be doing so. Now I do not want to chastise

182

him. He is after all only the acting abbot. But the responsibility lies firmly on his shoulders. And rather than dealing with it himself - as he should have done - he has turned to you. I can understand why he might have been tempted to do so. You are, I know, an experienced man of the world. And of course we hold you in the highest respect. You have also been – and I do not mean this in a hostile way – a man of violence – a man of blood. From what I hear you know about murder and savagery. Of course, it was all to advance the interests of Mother Church so it redounds to your credit. But we are not dealing here with pagans over the seas. This is taking place within the family of Christ – it needs to be handled by a churchman. To make myself clear as the Bishop himself would say, it is quite inappropriate for a layman such as yourself - unconnected to the abbey in any formal way - to be involved."

Again, he paused. I said nothing.

"I trust that you understand what I am saying?" he asked.

"I take it that are you asking me to stop providing help to Father Compton?" I said, baldly stating the obvious. "You want him to be left to deal with it on his own – even if the task is manifestly beyond him?"

"That is exactly right, Sir Matthew. That is exactly what we want you to do. Of course, we understand that you have the best interests of the Church - and Hyde in particular - at heart. But I must insist that you now desist. Father Compton is being informed of our decision that he is to undertake any further inquiries himself, closely assisted by Brother Thomas here and that both of them will now be accountable to me for their progress."

I glanced across at Brother Thomas who was clearly relishing every moment of this.

"Moreover, if Father Compton requires any advice on points of law then he has the benefit of being able to draw on the services of Sergeant Henry who is well-known to us and acts as our own advisor on certain legal affairs both here in Winchester and in the courts in London."

Yes, indeed, that is convenient, I thought – not least when the Sergeant himself had clearly indicated to me that solving the murders should not be seen as a major concern. And moreover, he had, by his own admission, little knowledge of criminal matters. However, I realised there was no point in highlighting this to Prior Hugh who, meanwhile, had been reciting further legalistic platitudes – until he moved suddenly on to the matter of the Despencers.

"Also, Sir Matthew, it has come to our attention that it might be perceived that you have a conflict of interest in this case given certain similarities with the dreadful Despencer executions."

"What on earth do you mean, Prior Hugh?" I almost growled.

"Do not upset yourself Sir Matthew. We are not accusing you of anything. It is just that Bishop William's predecessor, Bishop Adam of blessed memory, was responsible for the accusations against the Despencers. It is still a sensitive matter in this cathedral. So it is our view that any connection with the Despencer family carries with it dangers. Indeed, I shall be astonished if Thomas, the present Earl, does not follow his predecessors to execution in due course."

On that point I have to concede the Prior displayed great foresight. But any suggestion that I had any connection with the Despencers was quite absurd, a trumped up attempt to impugn me – in the worst traditions of Bishop Adam himself.

"So you think that I am tarred with the same brush as the Despencers, do you?" I asked.

"No, no," the prior responded. "It is all a matter of perceptions – no more. But there may be suggestions of a vendetta - or revenge. So we cannot be too careful."

This was, of course, all complete nonsense. But whoever had dreamed it up clearly thought that it would provide a convenient way of creating a fog of confusion to any onlookers and a way of sowing doubts and muddle – as well as embarrassing me. I let it go.

"So I should be grateful if you would accept our thanks,"

184

said the Prior by way of rounding things up. "And now feel free to focus on your own spiritual journey and the well-being of your family. Yes, I think it is in everyone's interests that you should do that."

At last he stopped and gave me a vicious smile. I was not surprised by this turn-of-events. There were plenty of good reasons why the cathedral monastery should involve itself in this investigation but it looked very much as if they were aiming to close it down rather than open it up. But I was hardly in a position to argue.

"Of course, Prior Hugh," I replied in due course. "I am bound to be governed by your decision. Presumably though you will have no objection to me passing on to Father Compton and the good Sergeant one or two pieces of information which might be of assistance to them?"

"Not in the least, Sir Matthew. Any insights from you will, I am sure be welcome. What I must ensure though is that Hyde Abbey should take full responsibility for what has happened – or indeed what might happen in the future. There can be no room for shifting responsibility elsewhere any longer. Which is why, as I mentioned, it is in everybody's interest – including particularly your own – that you should withdraw from any further investigation. I am sure that you would not want your own reputation to be further tarnished by any continuing involvement in this affair."

I nodded and shrugged my shoulders and was about to leave – there seemed to be nothing more to add - when he said.

"I am glad that we should understand each other, Sir Matthew. To be absolutely candid and not for repeating, I feared that you might have been deceived and misled by the rather scheming monks of Hyde. They have always had delusions about their own importance based on the accident that they might have one or two ancient kings buried before their altar. Kings so far back in time, it must be said, that our present kingdom did not even exist then. And relics – they have spent vast amounts of money buying bogus relics to boost their modest reputation. Of course, authentic relics are supremely important for the faithful – but when they are as fraudulent as most of Hyde's are, they deceive the credulous and abuse the devout. They are living off their history. But that is not acceptable any more. Bishop William will not have the church undermined in that way. It simply feeds the attacks of the enemies of Mother Church - I am sure that you will support us in that view?"

I gave a slight nod and walked slowly to the door.

"A useful conversation, I trust, Sir Matthew?" said Brother Thomas as he saw me out.

"I was delighted to meet the Prior," I replied with as much decorum as I could muster. "I now know where I stand."

I hurried down the stairs regretting that I could not think of a more cutting remark. But there would be time for that later.

CHAPTER 29

'An it is al another then it semeth'

"So, father, what happened?" asked Damian somewhat impatiently. "Did that the monstrous Bishop William gobble you up and spit you out!"

"Had I met the actual Bishop maybe he would have done," I said with a grim laugh. "After all, if anyone is the dark power behind all this, I presume it must be him. Maybe he could tell us what the devil is going on here. But no. I did not meet the Bishop – just Prior Hugh. Mind you he is pretty formidable in himself."

I then gave Damian and Osric a full account of what had happened. In their different ways they accepted that we had been discharged – Osric because he had been forewarned by me of its likelihood and Damian because he was looking forward to a new future as one of the Duke of Lancaster's retainers. Tracking down murderers was of diminishing interest.

"And what about you, Lord?" asked Osric. "Are you content to let go? After all it has little or nothing to do with us. Just three days ago we knew almost none of these people."

I had to agree with him. And yet, having started on the quest, I could not walk away that easily. But I also had to be realistic about the constraints. And although it was cowardly, I acknowledged the point about not wanting to have my reputation besmirched if only because of the repercussions for Damian.

"I shall speak to Father Compton this evening to share our conclusions so far and that will be the end of it," I said. However, I was not being entirely candid. While I had agreed that I would not pursue the murders there had been no mention of the loss of the Golden Charter. That had either been forgotten about or overlooked. I would raise it with Father Compton before dinner. If he gave his blessing to me to continue that investigation then I would do so with a clear conscience.

Feeling the need for some quiet contemplation I left Osric

and Damian and went down to the abbey church. I knew that the monks accessed it by way of the cloisters but was not sure that I would be admitted that way. With a service imminent I could see some of the monks making their way in by the side door. As I approached, however, Brother Adam intervened. "I am very sorry, Sir Matthew, only community members are permitted to enter the church this way. It leads directly into the choir. Would you kindly go in by the main entrance."

"I am so sorry, Brother Adam. I wasn't sure what the rule was. And this applies to all guests does it?"

"Yes, indeed, Sir Matthew. We may not be as strict as we should about some things but I try to be vigilant on this point. Nobody apart from members of the community is allowed to enter - or leave - the church by this door. And above all that applies around the times of the holy offices."

"And a very good rules it sounds too," I replied supportively. "Just as a matter of curiosity, though, were you here on the door a couple of days ago – in the afternoon?"

"You mean the day of Brother Peter's murder? Yes, indeed I was."

"Did anyone leave then – I mean during the service?"

"Let me think, now. Of course, Brother Peter left. He mentioned that he wasn't feeling very well. He was, I must admit, staggering rather. And, sadly that was the last time I saw him alive."

"Anyone else?"

"Now I think about it, Father Eynesham also left shortly after Brother Peter. He said that he had an urgent meeting with a dealer about a horse which he was buying for the abbey. 'Unavoidable clash' he said. Personally, I didn't think that was a very good excuse for leaving the church in the middle if a service. A few years ago, it would have been unimaginable – but what could I say? That's what Father Eynesham is like. He's well-known for it."

"Well, he's a genial man, isn't he?" I replied.

"Indeed, he is," said Brother Adam somewhat sententiously.

"And what, you then saw him go off into the forecourt, did you?"

"Oddly enough he seemed to be hanging around on the other side of the cloisters. But then I had to go into church myself – so I didn't see what he did next."

"So he could have gone into the library?"

"It's possible I suppose – and he must have done at some point, mustn't he – because that's where he saw young John."

"Yes, you're quite right," I said. "So either he didn't go and see a dealer about a horse – or maybe that was just an excuse and, for some reason, he went to the library instead of returning to the church."

All the time we had been speaking monks had been gradually entering the church and receiving acknowledgements from Brother Adam.

"Oh, here's Father Compton coming," he said. "Once he's in, I need to close the door."

"Of course, I said – no Father Eynesham?"

"No, not by the look of it," Brother Adam replied. "But not too much of a surprise there on a day like this. Lovely afternoon for a ride. He'll be on one of his 'special visits to the poor of the parish' no doubt."

I turned to Father Compton as he was about to squeeze between us.

"Father, I don't want to hold you up now – but can I see you before supper this evening? As you may know I have been asked to cease any investigation into the murders"

"Yes, indeed, Sir Matthew. I had heard as much," he replied with a strong hint of fatigue. "Come to my room and we will speak."

CHAPTER 30
'Til that the soule out of the body crepeth'

I made my way out of the cloister, across the Outer Court and towards the gateway. I could see Brother Michael and his assistant, Brother Timothy, with their backs to me. Still absorbing what Osric had told me earlier about Michael I did not want to get into conversation with either of them. I merely slipped past them and, gave a brief wave. Turning right I walked down the hill towards the main entrance to the abbey church.

It was a relief in some ways to feel that I was free of the responsibility of solving these crimes. If I wished, I could just forget about them entirely and concentrate on my own concerns. And my intention now was to be swallowed up in the monks' prayers and chanting of Nones.

The abbey church at Hyde is remarkably long and dark and designed so that pilgrims can process around the various altars festooned as they were with a variety of relics and a multitude of candles to illuminate the gloom. It was this which made Hyde Abbey such an attraction, so close as it was to Winchester with its own magnificent shrine to Saint Swithun. Of the authenticity of the remains of St Swithun there could be no doubt whatsoever. Hyde Abbey's relics, however – as Prior Hugh had made clear - were less reliable. The head of Saint Valentine, for example, which had been donated by a Viking Queen apparently – well, really? And what about the bones of Saint Josse, a French saint whose remains apparently had been brought across the sea several centuries earlier. This was the pride and joy of Hyde. But was this credible?

So as the monks began to chant from psalm 118

'It is better to take refuge in the Lord
*   than to trust in humans.*
It is better to take refuge in the Lord
*   than to trust in princes'*

My thoughts turned to questions of trust. Who was trust-worthy and why? The pilgrims at Hyde believed in these relics not least because it gave them a direct, physical link with sanctity and, thereafter, divinity. It inspired their faith. Meanwhile the authority of the abbot and the weight of the building in which they were housed reinforced hope in their efficacy. So naturally as a pilgrim you would want to give credibility to these accounts. And once they were established in the popular consciousness it would take a brave radical to challenge them. And that might prove highly risky - as the Lollards were starting to see.

As I mulled over these matters, I began to see my own pre-occupations in context. Going back to the start of this horrible investigation, had I believed what I had wanted to believe? Did I trust my own intuition over the innocence of John the student rather more than I should? Did I compare John's position to that of my son Damian and thereby give him too much of the benefit of the doubt?

Oh well, I said to myself at last, it was too late now to reconsider – thank St. Josse at least for that.

The service over, the monks filed out. I decided to remain for a little longer to compose my thoughts. And still the pilgrims shuffled from altar to altar around the perimeter of the church.

After some time, however, Brother Adam rang a bell and began to make an announcement.

"Dear brothers and sisters in Christ the abbey church will be closing soon. Would you please leave. We are preparing for a funeral service tomorrow morning. We need to get ready. Please leave by the main door."

It took him some time. Many people were reluctant to go. They had come a long way to see these relics. They would not leave without paying their respects. Brother Adam explained they would be welcome back the following afternoon. I started to move towards the door but Brother Adam came across and said that I could remain if I wished. The shrouded bodies of Brothers Peter and Walter would be brought in soon. There would be a short service and then they would remain in the church overnight. Monks would be with them at all times.

I thanked him and moved into a remote corner. It seemed appropriate somehow to be there. I still had a feeling of responsibility towards them and now felt guilty that at times over the past two days I had resented been asked to investigate their deaths.

Two sets of four monks carried the corpses, placing them on biers before the High Altar. Seeing the two simple shroud-covered bundles I felt an enhanced determination to do what I could – however informally or behind the scenes – to ensure that they had justice.

Father Compton accompanied by Brother Thomas then led the prayers. It was a quiet and dignified service. Tomorrow, the actual requiem mass, would be a much larger affair.

Within the quiet of the church and observing the rituals I was able to focus my mind on what I should say later to Father Compton. Ineffective though he might be, he still represented the abbey and could give me some authority for continuing to investigate – not the deaths themselves, of course, but the disappearance of the Golden Charter. And that, I believed, was still the thread which had to be followed to uncover the truth of what had really happened in the library. And, who knows, maybe to the death of Walter as well.

I moved towards the main door immediately the service was over, the air rich with incense. I did not want to get caught up with Father Compton or Brother Thomas at this point.

By now it was dusk and the church was getting very dark indeed although still illuminated in parts by torches and candles. As I passed the side chapel closest to the entrance, I thought I heard some slight movement – a rat maybe? It seemed to be coming from behind the altar upon which rested a magnificent reliquary chest finely displayed and illustrated with images of St. Peter, the Virgin and the saint whose bones, I presumed, lay within. Perhaps I should have investigated that shuffling noise. But by now my thoughts were elsewhere.

193

CHAPTER 31
'For gold in physic is a cordial'

When I arrived at Father Compton's private rooms ahead of supper I heard a couple of voices within. They seemed to be in disagreement. Not shouting although each was firm. Undeterred, I knocked. I needed Father Compton to give his blessing to my continued search for the Golden Charter and this would be the last opportunity to see him privately before we left for London the following morning.

I knocked harder. The voices went silent and then Father Compton opened.

"Oh, yes, Sir Matthew – it's you. Good to see you. Do come in."

"Yes, I am sorry to disturb you, Father Compton, but as I mentioned I need to speak to you before supper. It's quite important."

"Certainly," he said, almost sounding relieved and opening the door wider. "Sergeant Henry is just leaving."

If I was surprised that it was the Sergeant arguing with Father James then I should not have been. No doubt they had been tussling over how to take forward the murder investigation. Father Compton signalled to the Sergeant that he should depart.

"Well, I shall see you later, Father Compton – we do need to spend time on this," the Sergeant said. "And I look forward to seeing you later, Sir Matthew."

I nodded to him in as friendly a manner as I could muster. Following my discussion with him and the Franklin earlier in the day prudence dictated that I should keep on pleasant terms with them both.

But with door closed behind me I felt I could ask a provocative question of Father Compton.

"Wearing you down is he – the Sergeant?" I asked in a quiet voice.

"Not so much wearing me down, Sir Matthew, as hammering me to pieces. Anyway I imagine that I know what you are here to talk about. I have been given my full instructions from the Prior courtesy of Brother Thomas and now the Sergeant. Being instructed on what to do by someone who is barely a novice! This is what it has come to! And by a lawyer who descends from London as if he were the voice of God! It stretches my patience to breaking point, I can tell you Sir Matthew. But what can I do?"

"You mean, you have to just do as you are told?"

"That's right, we are fast approaching that point. I am barely clinging on. But it only shows how low this abbey has fallen.

Two hundred years ago we were one of the greatest abbeys in the land. Our abbot moved among the mighty. My predecessor Abbot Aston, one hundred and fifty years ago, was a witness to the signing of Magna Carta. But we have been the victim of envy and jealousy for decades. They may be fellow Benedictines at the cathedral but they are no brothers of ours!"

By now, Father Compton was almost shouting with a passion driven by impotence.

"You have all my sympathy, Father Compton. I can see how deeply offensive and disrespectful it is."

"Indeed. Indeed."

Silence descended as he gradually regained his composure.

"Anyway, what is it you wanted to say to me?" he asked. "I know that you have been told by the Prior to cease your investigation. But maybe it does not make much difference. You want to go to Canterbury with your son. You have other things on your mind. So all I can do is to thank you for the time you have spent on this over the past two days."

"Well, I cannot say it has entirely been a pleasure, Father Compton, but it was the least I could do under the circumstances. And, aside from dismissing the allegations against young John, I do not feel I achieved much. I have been left with several possible motives for both murders – and several possible suspects. Including unknown suspects. It may well be that the murderers came from outside this place and, frankly, could never be discovered."

"So at least I can report that to the Prior – and that will give him and everyone else a good excuse for quietly dropping the whole thing while still making my abbey look corrupt and ineffective. They will like that," he said bitterly.

I nodded sympathetically while Father Compton glowered.

"So tomorrow you will attend the funerals, Sir Matthew? And that will be the end of it?"

"Yes, certainly we will come to the funerals – but, maybe, that is not quite the end of it," I said. "With all the attention, understandably on the murders we have rather overlooked one thing - the disappearance of the Golden Charter."

"Yes, that's right, I agree," said Father Compton with a kind of resigned determination. "One of our most important and valuable treasures. As we discussed before, its loss would be very serious. Especially in current circumstances. Of course, most people have entirely forgotten about it - but not everyone. Someone out there realises its importance."

"As well as you" I said coaxingly.

"Absolutely, it's very much on my mind."

"So you would like it back?"

"Very much so. I realise that the abbey is in a very difficult state. But if I were to hand over the responsibility of this office to my successor having lost the Golden Charter as well as having experienced these other calamities then I am not sure my conscience could bear it."

By this time Father Compton was looking thoroughly miserable. My heart went out to the man.

"So would I have your commission to continue the search for it?" I asked. "You don't have to tell Brother Thomas about it – or the Sergeant. Do they even know that it's been lost?"

"Curiously enough that was one of the things the Sergeant was asking about just now. As I said, most people have forgotten about our Charter from King Edgar - but by no means everyone. I am sure that the Prior is aware of its significance and the Sergeant was trying to establish whether I had it. In fact, that was what we were talking about when you arrived. And to be honest with you, I was being evasive. I said I had other things on my mind right now but insisted that it was held securely. But he was demanding to see it."

197

"So, by the sound of it, he fully understands its importance?" I said.

"Well, either him or more likely the cathedral," said Father Compton. "It was my experience while looking after the abbey's accounts that even the smallest detail - which one might assume had been disregarded - would always have been noted and remembered by the person most affected by it. Or indeed a lawyer. That's why I am aware of the immense significance of the Golden Charter. And I had mistakenly assumed that Brother Peter, even in his latter days, would have had it under impregnable security. Sadly I was wrong. So, to answer your point I am most anxious to retrieve it. But really what chance is there of finding it? Any more than finding the murderers?"

"Slightly better, I think," I said affecting greater confidence than I actually felt. "Because whoever has it will want to do something with it. Which means it is likely to be passed on or sold or exploited somehow soon. And that will give us our chance."

"And do you have any suspicions as to who might be responsible or where they might be?"

"Only a matter of probability, Father Compton. Of course, there is a chance that it's someone unknown who has already departed the area. Maybe even destroyed it after scraping off the gold. That's why I worry a lot about these two odd individuals who might – or might not – be the acquaintances of Mistress Alison. But apart from that I believe it's either a member of the community or one of the guests or their servants. And that's why our journey to London, starting tomorrow, is so important."

"In that case, Sir Matthew, rest assured that you have my blessing – and my prayers. May St. Josse aid you! Or, maybe even better, St Loy – the patron saint of goldsmiths. If anyone can help you find the Golden Charter then it should be him."

CHAPTER 32
'You love I besτ, aŋd shal, aŋd ooτheR ŋooŋ.'

"So I've won the support of Father Compton," I explained to Damian and Osric. "Our mission now is to find the Golden Charter – and also, I would suggest, the rogues who stole it."

"It's not as interesting as murder though, is it?" said Damian in a petulant voice.

"Look, I'm sorry, Damian, I know it's been a strange two or three days for you – penned in here with not a lot to do except the odd bit of shopping and drinking and buying outrageous new clothes. It's almost as if the pestilence has been raging. But by tomorrow afternoon we'll be on our way to London and in a couple of days plenty of new things will start to happen. So just get through tonight and then we'll all feel much better. What do you think, Osric?"

"I agree, Lord. I'll take Damian out on the town tonight and we'll have a good time - again."

"Sounds an excellent idea. You must be sick of seeing the inside of that almoner's hall – and the tavern."

"We certainly are, Lord," said Osric laughing. "No, in fairness we've discovered a pair of good places – good ale, not too expensive. We shall be fine."

"Excellent – I am glad to hear it," I said feeling, as so often, that Osric was doing a better job as a father to Damian than I was. "And when you are out and about still keep your eyes open. What I am curious to know is where young John – our talented scholar – has got to. It would be very interesting if you came across him. Anyway, anything more that you can pick up about him – or anyone else for that matter – please do."

"And what are you up to, father? Another fine dinner with all those creepy monks?"

"Hmm – you might well put it that way. This is the third night we'll be eating together and the charm is starting to pall.

Mind you, something extraordinary seems to happen every time – so we'll see what occurs tonight. But, like you, I'll be happy to be on our way and tomorrow evening we shall be enjoying the delights of Wintney Priory."

At this Damian blushed briefly but rapidly pulled himself together.

"Right," said Damian. "I'm ready to go. I'll see you shortly Osric by the Forecourt Gate." And off he went.

"Thank you, Osric," I said.

"For what, Lord?

"For looking after him. One way or another I owe you a big debt."

"It's nothing, Lord, but thank you for saying it, He's a nice, good lad. He just needs to get going properly in life. And he was badly knocked by his mama's death. You don't know the half of it, Lord. That's why this prospect of getting in with the Duke of Lancaster has unsettled him a bit. He really wants to do it. But he's worried that you might not go along with it."

"Ah, well – I'm not too surprised."

"Also, Lord you should be aware that…"

"What, Osric?"

"He's fallen in love."

"What!" I exclaimed. I shouldn't have been surprised – he was the right age. Rather older in fact than I was when I had my first dalliances and, as I recalled, sowed my first oats.

"So who's he in love with?"

"This is where it gets a bit tricky," Osric hesitated.

"Spit it out Osric."

"He's fallen in love with a nun."

"Oh, dear!" I said, my heart plummeting. "So how's that happened?"

"It's that pretty young nun with Madame Eglentyne. They've fallen into conversation several times over by the lay chapel. I've been watching them – seen them together."

"You mean by the main gate?"

200

"That's the one. With all the people coming and going it's very easy there to just blend in. He can't get enough of her. And by the sound of it she can't get enough of him either. Odd being a nun, I thought."

"Well I'm not sure that all nuns are necessarily strangers to love, Osric. But let's not mention that to anyone. So what's Damian planning to do? Elope with her? It wouldn't be the first time to happen."

"He's in a complete daze, right now. I think they both are. I've said all the usual things about not being carried away and that there are plenty of other trout in the Itchen. Yes, he says, 'Old Trout' – and they're not for him. But no, he insists this is the love of his life."

"And what do you make of her, Osric?"

"Oh, she's a bright lass and no mistake. If you don't mind me saying so, Lord, probably brighter than our Damian. That's why she's Madame Eglentyne's personal assistant."

"So, I suppose that we'll have to hope that he gets to London and finds someone else and that this all fades away," I said. "And sooner rather than later."

"Yes, but we're staying tomorrow night at Wintney Priory, aren't we Lord, so there's going to be plenty of opportunity for them to see each other there."

"Oh, my heavens! Of course! How stupid!"

I was worried. Maybe more worried than was reasonable or that I could say or explain to Osric.

"Lord, don't worry about it," said Osric reassuringly. "You go off and have your dinner – and we'll see you in the morning. After all, we've got two funerals to look forward to!"

He nodded and was gone.

Rather gratefully I shifted my attention to those funerals. It would be interesting to see who was in the congregation. Neither of the monks were particularly elevated. Maybe there would be just the Hyde community and a few others such as ourselves.

My understanding was that immediately after the requiem mass the corpses would go straight into the ground in the cemeteries which were adjacent to the abbey church itself. Not a great deal of ceremony – but enough. It would be ironic if the murderer or murderers were to be in the congregation. But that was no longer my direct concern. My sole interest now was in the Golden Charter. And in that respect the number of suspects was narrowing.

CHAPTER 33
'An al was conscience and tendre herte'

The familiar, expectant faces were to be seen around the abbot's table but this evening the numbers were swollen by the presence of Prior Hugh. Was this the first step towards the cathedral imposing its authority on Hyde Abbey before absorbing it fully?

I was relieved, for once, not to be placed next to Father Compton. Instead he was hedged in by the Prior on one side and Brother Thomas on the other. By contrast I found myself between the two ladies, Mistress Alison and Madame Eglentyne, each of whom welcomed me whilst ignoring each other.

Immediately after Father Compton had said grace the Prior rose.

"Thank you, Acting Abbot, for inviting me to Hyde this evening," he began in his charmingly silky but authoritative voice. "It is always a pleasure to be a guest in this venerable if somewhat troubled institution. And I regard myself this evening as being here both in my own right and as representing Bishop William who asked me to pass on blessings to you all."

He paused to look around the whole table to ensure that the generosity of this benediction had been appreciated. It had.

"Now, I am sure that I can offer thanks on behalf of my fellow guests to you, Father Eynesham – as cellarer - for providing this generous hospitality during what is, we all understand, a very difficult time for the abbey.

"Tomorrow morning we will be together in the abbey church for the distressing funerals of your much loved brothers, Peter and…" he looked to Brother Thomas for a prompt, "yes, Walter. Highly valued and much loved members of this community. Exemplary monks, devout and diligent to the end. I am not going to say anything further about the circumstances of their deaths other than to reassure you all that everything is in hand to ensure justice is realised for them both.

"Now, Father Compton has told me that most of you here this evening will be leaving for London tomorrow and then on to Canterbury to the shrine of Saint Thomas of blessed memory. I envy you this beautiful opportunity but, sadly, duty compels me to remain in Winchester. And, indeed the same applies to Father Compton. However I am glad to say that Father Eynesham will be accompanying you and I hope that you will take advantage of the monastery's offer to stay overnight in London at the Tabard Inn, one of Hyde's many properties – perhaps, one might say, too many properties for an abbey of this size."

He turned to Father Eynesham.

"Remind me, when did the abbot acquire it?" he asked rather coldly.

"About seventy years ago, I believe, Prior," came the reply, slightly uncertainly. "A wise investment, I think."

"A wise investment indeed – for the abbots and their friends but possibly not for the wider community," the Prior responded sourly. "Anyway, dear fellow guests I won't hold you back from your repast any longer other than to say that I think these recent sad events have brought the communities of Hyde and the cathedral closer together – for mutual advantage. And the more of that the better, I think. Now, let's enjoy our meal and each other's company in the presence of the Almighty."

Following this self-serving little homily I would have happily departed. But that would have been both rude and a mistake. So I resolved instead to concentrate, instead, on my neighbours and their affairs.

"Mistress Alison, are you looking forward to our ride to London," I said in as loud a voice as I could reasonably manage having realised, by now, that she was slightly hard of hearing.

"I am looking forward to it very much," she said. "The weather is turning nicely and the road to London is easy. But then I am much travelled. I enjoy it – whether for business or pleasure."

"Or indeed for the good of your soul," I commented wryly. "On pilgrimage, I mean."

"My soul? I do not worry about my soul, Sir Matthew. I have confidence in my Saviour and I know my place in the church is secure. After all, look at me seated here this evening!"

"But you are going on pilgrimage for the good of your soul, surely Mistress Alison?" I said again slightly teasingly.

"Of course, I imagine so," she said flatly. "And after Canterbury I will be taking ship to the continent."

"Oh, really? Another shrine?"

"No, Sir Matthew. One shrine a year is enough for me, I think. No, I am going for commerce. As you know, I think, I have a textiles business. That is why in London I must meet some weavers – Flemish weavers as it happens. I shall then be taking samples of my workshop to Boulogne and then onwards."

"Oh, well I am impressed," I said. "These are still dangerous times for us English venturing over to the other side of the Channel."

"This annoying war with France goes on and on but it does not stop the enterprising, Sir Matthew, and it does not stop trade – one way or another," said Mistress Alison firmly. "So no hold-ups at the ports, please. A point I was also making to the dear Duke of Lancaster the last time I saw him. As a soldier you might not understand this but to ensure the future of my business – and those I employ – I want friendly relations with France and elsewhere. So when I am in Canterbury I will ask the holy saint to bless me with a good crossing and good business - as well as good health to preserve me from the pestilence. Oh, and for good profits too – one should never forget those."

I know little about business and have even less interest but I felt I had been scolded. And, maybe, fairly. So with a smile I turned my attention to Madame Eglentyne who was daintily wiping her lips after the first course.

"I have just been talking to Mistress Alison here about her business, Madame Eglentyne. What about you? Are you happy with what you have seen in Winchester – your mills? Have they been working satisfactorily?"

"Thank you for remembering, Sir Matthew," she replied in that sweet voice with its underlying edge. "The mills are working well – but maybe not so much the miller himself whom I have just had to sack. Just one little deception too far I am afraid."

"Oh, heavens," I replied. "Was that difficult for you? An uncomfortable conversation, I imagine."

"Not in the least," she replied briskly. "We caught him red-handed – or maybe I should say flour-handed. Sister Avelina set up a clever little ruse. He fell for it completely. I am pleased to see the back of him. But we do have a slight problem now of recruiting a new miller."

"Of course."

"But I have more than that on my mind, I am afraid. Events here in this abbey concern me. You have seen for yourself how things are. That creates instability not just for this house but for others like my own dear priory. I do not want to bore you with my affairs but do you know we are being taken to court for maintenance of the road outside our property in the High Street here in Winchester? That's the other thing that I have been dealing with over the past two days. Has the Council got nothing better to do with its time, one wonders, than persecuting poor women over potholes?"

"Oh, so you have more property in Winchester than just the mills?"

"We do – and it is a heavy responsibility for a poor priory. And we are very much on the breadline by comparison with our neighbours. Look at Nunnaminster here in Winchester. Look at Romsey! Look at Wherwell! All of them overflowing with wealth and patronage. But no-one loves little Wintney. And, as I might have said before, they think they can bully us because we are women."

"Oh, I am very sorry to hear that Madame Eglentyne. It must be very vexing for you – and you a woman of such spirit. Do you have a lawyer to advise you?"

"We do – he's a tenant of ours here in the town. But I am not sure he's very capable – or influential. We need someone more sophisticated – better connected – to get things done. Someone like Sergeant Henry here this evening, for example. He seems like a vigorous man."

"Have you asked him?"

"I have mentioned it to him just now – and will speak more on the road over the next few days. My friend Father Eynesham here is also giving me advice." She paused. "But on a happier note – you will be staying with us in Wintney tomorrow, won't you? I do hope so."

"Yes, that would be very kind of you - if you can accommodate the three of us – as you know I have my son, Damian, and servant yeoman with me. I would not want to take advantage of your hospitality especially, as you were saying, the Priory is not especially well-off."

She laughed.

"We can always make an exception for special guests, Sir Matthew. So do not worry yourself about that. And besides it would be such a pleasure to welcome your son! I must say I have heard quite a lot about him. My companion, Sister Avelina seems quite taken with him!"

For a moment I was uncertain what to say.

"You mean as a pious believer, I suppose?" I said without much plausibility.

"Well, I am sure he is, Sir Matthew. But more, I was thinking – or so Avelina tells me – as a redoubtable and energetic young man." Her emphasis on the final word was firm and hard.

"But surely you don't approve of anything – romantic, shall we say?"

She gave me a smile and a long knowing look. She then pointed to the motto on her golden broach '*Amor Vincit Omnia*'.

"Let's say no more about it," she whispered. And sipped her wine delicately.

CHAPTER 34
'Dave a soper at oure cost'

And so the dinner wore on. Gradually there was increasing merriment and again I was aware of the contrast between the grim bloody murders which had taken place and the apparent indifference of the guests. But tomorrow, I supposed, they would all be away pursuing their own interests forgetful of what they had left behind.

So as my neighbours turned and talked to each other, I started puzzling over the connections across and around the room. Were there alliances or rivalries, friendships or hostilities which I had not discerned? Well, maybe the next few days would reveal them.

"What, lost in your thoughts, Sir Matthew? Past battles and ancient conquests in more exotic places that this old abbey, I warrant?"

It was Sir Roger Odiham, slapping me on the back. I looked up at him.

"Nothing so exciting, Sir Roger," I said quickly contriving a response. "Just rather mundane thoughts about how my estate would fare while I am away. As my son Damian is with me it will be in the hands of my tenants."

"You are right to be concerned, Sir Matthew. From what I am hearing the peasantry are getting ideas very much above their station. It's like a fever starting to spread and as the weather warms up we gentry are likely to face a strong challenge. And along with us the King's Government too. And that must be faced with iron."

"You really think it will become that serious, do you, dear Master Roger?" put in Mistress Alison who had turned at the sound of the Franklin's penetrating voice.

"I do, dear madam, I do. And now you and I really need to catch up – it's been some time. And I've something for you," said the Franklin, reaching into his pocket and presenting her with some strange looking tokens. "As a collector of things foreign I thought these might be of interest to you."

He had given her what looked like a pair of copper amulets, the size of coins with square holes in them and strange decoration.

"What on earth are they?" she asked.

"I've no idea but a shipman from the south-west gave them to me as payment for a little favour I had done him. He'd picked them up in Spain. Quite amusing, don't you think? I'm sure you'll find some use for them on your travels. Who knows they might even be valuable."

"And I have something for you in return," she replied, pulling out from her red robes a small but fine piece of pottery, blue and white and of exotic looking design. She handed it to him. "Well, we are a pair, aren't we!" he said laughingly. "As ever, thinking along the same lines."

I had not seen the Franklin and Mistress Alison speak together before so I was interested and intrigued that they seemed to be on terms of such close cordiality. "A tribute to our travels," I heard her say. And then I realised, of course, that they were both adherents, in their different ways, to John of Gaunt, Duke of Lancaster.

After reciprocal admiration of the gifts they returned to the matter of the peasants' discontent.

"We had rumbles about this new tax – the poll tax – in Bath, Master Roger. I wrote to the Duke about it, just to keep him informed. He sent a kind response but his attention is elsewhere."

"You're right there, Mistress Alison. Getting ready to deal with the damned Scots! Why are they always ready to stab us in the back I simply don't understand. Were he to be here down south I think the Duke would get a grip on the situation as it unfolds over the Summer. But this current Lord Chancellor – Sudbury – is worse than useless. And to think that he is Archbishop of Canterbury as well! Why even William of Wykeham – bad though he was and still is, I might say – would be doing a better job."

"You should not criticise the Bishop of Winchester," interjected sharply Madame Eglentyne. "He is an excellent man in

210

every respect. But he is no longer in charge of matters and as a result everything is in disorder. Yet he will come back – mark my words on that. But in the meantime my concern is what will happen to the courts in London."

"You think they'll be affected?" I asked. "By this agitating among the lower orders."

"You don't know or see what I do, Sir Matthew," she replied. "Wintney is almost in Surrey and there's no question about the scale of the discontent in that county – it's discontent with the king and with the law. These peasants do not know the law. They do not care about it. They want it overthrown. But the law – properly applied - is the only way we can protect our rights! I realised that a long time ago. But if these peasants become organised then they will march on London and overthrow the courts. And that will be the end of everything. King, the courts, the law – maybe even the church. Everything will be lost."

I found it hard to credit all she was saying. Surely this was alarmist nonsense. 'The end of everything'? I doubted it very much.

"Well, I sympathise with your concerns Madame Eglentyne," I said soothingly. "But I cannot believe that there will be a revolt against the King. Yes, people might get very upset - but this is England. If things do start to get out of hand, as you suggest, then the king, young though he is, need only appear and all will calm down. Just you see. So long as he is loyal to his own country the people will love him."

"I hope you are right, Sir Matthew. But I am not convinced of it," she continued.

"Please, Lady Eglentyne, enough of these dark worries," I said trying to lift the mood. "We have the pleasure of a ride to London ahead of us. Let us be content with that."

"And yet before we leave, Sir Matthew, we have these grim, sad funerals. Don't forget that."

"Indeed, of course, Lady Eglentyne, I have not forgotten it – believe you me. And what about you Mistress Alison?" I asked, turning to the businesswoman of Bath. "Will you be in church tomorrow for the brothers' service?"

"That would be my intention, Sir Matthew, because I do so love a good funeral," she replied enthusiastically. "After all, I have seen four husbands away into their pits – and I expect my fifth is not long for this world. So normally the answer would be 'Yes' – bringing back happy memories, so to speak. But on this occasion probably not. I did not know these men and the circumstances are too – shall we say - disturbing. Besides which, I do not ride quickly and I have a long way to go. We aim to be off early."

Who was this 'We' I wondered. Well, time would tell.

"But will you take up the offer of the Tabard Inn?"

"I think probably so. It would be rude to ignore it. But I know this Tabard Inn – I've stayed there before. It is very conveniently placed. But it is imperfect in some respects. I will leave it at that."

"How so?"

"You will see for yourself but I think it attracts the dregs. But, of course, each to their own. When I first get to London I shall be going to the Savoy."

"The Savoy?" I asked like a country bumpkin away from the capital for many years.

"Yes, you must know it belongs to the Duke of Lancaster. The finest palace in London! I know that I will always get a warm welcome there from the steward. It's so large that they can entertain all the Duke's many friends. I believe that Roger" - she pointed at the Franklin – "might be lodging there also for a night or two when he returns from Canterbury. Like me, he has his business to attend to. And from what I gather you may be thinking of joining us yourself – as a special friend, that is, of the Duke?"

'A special friend of the Duke' - is that what I was possibly lining myself up to be? How quickly gossip gets round!

"Of course I am a great admirer of my Lord of Ghent, Mistress Alison," I replied as diplomatically as I could. "Who could not be aware of his great worth? But a little premature, I think, to

212

say that I was yet one of his special friends. Certainly one or two things have been suggested to me – and for my son too. And one must think about the future. But I am still fresh in returning to England and facing the reality of having lost a dear, dear wife. I need time to think and reflect. I am sure you understand."

"Oh yes, Sir Matthew!" Mistress Alison exclaimed with what sounded like genuine feeling. "Excuse me please, I had forgotten the loss of your wife. Maybe what I said about the despatch of my own, several and various, husbands struck an unfortunate chord with you. But of course our conditions are very different. You were clearly in love with your wife while I was ..." She left a vacant space for me to interpret as I preferred.

"Remember Mistress Alison," I had to respond. "I had been away from my wife for five years. I do not want to portray myself as a dedicated, self-sacrificing saint. It was Matilda, my wife, who was the patient Griselda. And that is what I must now live with."

"I understand," Sir Matthew, "I do indeed. One disposes of the things one should love and pursues, instead, the shinier trinkets. But time heals, I assure you,"

"I trust you are right, Mistress Alison. And so does sleep – which is where I am now heading. I wish you 'Goodnight' and I look forward to seeing you on the road tomorrow."

CHAPTER 35
'A good felawe to have his concubin'

Tomorrow was likely to be a long day but that had not deterred Damian and Osric. They had returned to the abbey from another lively evening in Winchester's taverns and were full of their adventures.

"Guess who we saw, father! You'll never guess!"

Confronted by such a challenge I surrendered immediately. "No idea? The Pope?"

"Don't be ridiculous, father! We saw John of course!"

"Which John?" I replied weakly, my mind not working for fatigue.

"Little John the scholar, the clerk of Oxenford, the man formerly regarded as the prime suspect," replied Damian, mockingly and enjoying squeezing every drop of humour from his announcement. "After all, didn't you ask us to look for him!"

"Yes I'm sorry, I did – I'm just tired" I had to concede. "So where were you?"

"More importantly, father – where was he?"

"Yes, alright. So where was he?"

"I saw him first, Lord," muscled in Osric. "He was coming out of a brothel. It's well-known to the city folk – and to the monks at the cathedral of course." He laughed uproariously. "Anyway, it's in a little street just outside the city – Gynge Lane. Beyond the South Gate."

"And what were you doing there?"

"We weren't actually in the brothel, father – honest," said Damian, putting on a special voice to make it sound as innocent as possible. "You wouldn't catch me in one of those places – not now. But there's a tavern at the top of the lane on the main road from Southampton. We'd been there earlier and we were walking down to the Kingsgate. And there he was, coming out of the brothel and having a cosy little chat with one of the girls."

"She was saying 'See you again soon, Johnny' - and he said

something like ' 'You certainly will Ethelfleda, after I get back from Canterbury.' Then she said, 'And thanks for the lovely big tip!' And gave him an enormous kiss."

"And you watched all this did you?"

"Yes, Lord, from across the lane."

"And then, father as he began to move away he saw us and looked very embarrassed. So I thought it would be a good chance to get some more information out of him."

"And how did he respond?"

"I was a bit heavy with him, Lord, to be honest," said Osric. "But in a nice way. I said something like he owed us one – given that you had declared him innocent. And the least he could do was buy us a drink or two. Especially as he seemed to have some money on him."

"And so we almost dragged him," continued Damian, "up the lane and back into the tavern and Osric told the barkeeper that the drinks were on Little John. He didn't look happy about it – but he never said that he couldn't pay. Anyway, after a little while he relaxed a bit – once he realised that we weren't actually going to rob him or beat him up."

"And did he say what he had been doing?"

"Yes, he told us the whole story. After you'd let him go he disappeared out of the monastery and came across town. And since then he had been staying, as he put it, with someone 'connected with the cathedral'. He seemed to have been having a high old time enjoying himself but was still intent on going on pilgrimage, leaving Winchester tomorrow."

"So were you able to get a bit more out of him about this 'someone connected to the cathedral'. Was it the Prior or someone like that?"

"He was a bit cagey about it and we didn't press him too hard but towards the end, after he'd had a few drinks – and frankly he had more than we did – he kind of wound up by saying, 'So, I need to get back to the doctor's – he'll be wondering where I've got to'."

"Well, well, well," I had to burst out. "That is interesting. If it's our Doctor Nafis that would make sense. He is connected to the cathedral but also to the cathedral monastery and St. Mary's convent and to Hyde abbey. In fact to all of them. So he's been hosting our Oxford scholar! Well, well, well!"

I paused for a moment to consider whether that was surprising or not. I suppose I would have expected John to be staying in a guest house at the cathedral but maybe he had become friendly with the doctor at some point. They could discuss Gilbertin and Gaddesen together. After all Gaddesden was a Merton man, I think I had heard say. I was musing on this when Damian broke into my thoughts with another great howl of laughter.

"Now Madame Eglentyne – she's a one!"

"What on earth do you mean, Damian?"

"So, father, I have a bit of a confession to make – Osric knows about it so I can tell you about it in front of him."

"Alright," I said a bit uncomfortably. "Is it that you were, in fact, also a customer at the brothel this evening."

This brought further howls of laughter from Damian.

"No, no, no. I told you, nothing like that at all. In fact quite the opposite. Its just I have been seeing quite a lot of Madame Eglentyne's little nun. Avelina's the name. She's very sweet." He paused. "Are you shocked?"

"Actually I am not," I was able to reply. "As I said I was sitting next to Madame Eglentyne at supper and she had obviously heard quite a lot about you from this young woman – who is, I need hardly remind you, a nun. My impression was that romance runs riot up at Wintney Priory."

"I definitely think it does, father. According to Avelina it wasn't so long ago that the previous Bishop had to intervene directly at Wintney because there was so much partying going on with all sorts of people turning up for a good time. Lady Eglentyne has toned that all down – but only in as much as people outside no longer know what's been going on. It's all much more discreet. But the biggest thing is this..."

"Ah, ha? Go on."

Damian drew himself up as if to make a big announcement.

"Avelina is very loyal to Eglentyne but she is a bit of a gossip and she let slip that she thought that when she was younger – I mean much younger around 15 or so Eglentyne had had a baby. It was a big scandal at the time not least because she came from an important family – but of course it was hushed up. She was a novice up at Wherwell Abbey – you know about ten miles north of here - and something pretty terrible happened. Anyway she got pregnant but was kept on at one of the convents until the baby was born. The baby was then adopted and Eglentyne was packed off up to London to Stratford. And then about a decade later she returned down here - but not to Wherwell where she would have been too well known - but to Wintney. And then, pretty quickly because of her connections, she became Abbess. Amazing, isn't it?"

I was briefly lost for words but then managed to ask.

"And what happened to the baby? Do you think she kept in contact?"

"Well, that's the big question, isn't it?"

CHAPTER 36
'In a glas he hadde pigges bones'

Damian and Osric's revelations about John and Madame Eglentyne raised too many questions for me to have an easy night. Combined with anticipation of the forthcoming funerals I endured hideous dreams reliving horrors from the past. But as my soldiering career had taught me, running away rarely did more than postpone the day of judgement. I had to persevere and make the best of what was before me.

None of which had prepared me, however, for what happened next.

The three of us were just about to eat breakfast when there came a huge thumping at our door. Surely not another murder I thought?

"Sir Matthew! Sir Matthew!! Wake up please. We need you urgently – now."

Outside the door was Father Eynesham, He looked in an almost deranged state. The normally suave appearance was totally dishevelled, his eyes were absurdly staring.

"What on earth is the matter, Father? A death?"

"No. Yes, Quick, Come."

He almost dragged me out of the room and down the stairs. Whatever had happened. it struck me as curious that once again it was Father Eynesham who appeared to have discovered it.

"Father Eynesham, please compose yourself a little and tell me what's the matter," I said as he tugged me across the Outer Court. "I'll be better able to assist if I understand what is going on."

"It's the relics – it's the relics!" he almost shouted as he took me into the cloisters towards the entrance reserved for the monks and then into the abbey church. "The relics of the saint!"

"What's happened to them?" I asked, having an image of them piled into a vast heap and pummelled to pieces by marauding Lollards.

"You'll see, you'll see."

Entering the church I caught a glimpse of the two covered corpses placed decorously on the ground before the altar waiting patiently for their interment. Were their spirits still in attendance or had they already departed for the next world, I wondered.

Father Eynesham, however did not pause for a moment to cast a glance at them. Instead he hurried me into the north aisle where I could see a small group of monks – including Father Compton and Brother Adam - crowding around the altar which was dedicated to Saint Josse. Some were kneeling, others murmuring prayers but most just looked numb.

Father Compton turned to look as Father Eynesham pushed me into the centre of the little assembly. "Oh, Sir Matthew!" he said. "Who can possibly have done this?" He pointed.

There at the foot of the altar was the smashed reliquarium which had contained St. Josse's relics. The large sacred box, big enough to accommodate the length of a leg, was beautifully decorated in gold foil and red paint and covered with images of the saint. But the lid had been stove in and the contents looted. Probably not having been opened for well over a century the internal wood was rotting. It was a sorry mess.

That, however, was only part of the story. Lying behind the altar was the body of Father Gregory, Madam Eglentyne's cleric.

I gasped when I saw him. "Oh, dear – poor Father Gregory! Is he dead?"

"Fortunately, no," said Father Eynesham who had now calmed down somewhat. "But I think he's been badly beaten about the head and he seems unconscious. We need to get him across to the infirmary - Doctor Nafis can examine him when he comes in later."

"Perhaps we should move him straight away," I suggested. "At least we can make him more comfortable than he is now."

"We wanted you to see to it - but I'll deal with it from here on," said Father Eynesham and he moved away, summoning assistance from two figures hidden in the shadows whom I assumed to be abbey servants.

"Poor Father Gregory – I do hope that he will recover well," said Father Compton with some feeling.

"So what was he doing in the church do you think" I asked.

"He had very kindly agreed to stand vigil with the two Brothers overnight. As you know, he was very pious and already he had made a close bond with our monks. Normally a couple of our own community would do it but because so many are aged and infirm that was not possible this time."

"So he was by himself?"

"I am afraid he was," said Father Compton. "And then I presume he was attacked – overwhelmed rather – by the heretics who wanted to destroy the reliquary. No doubt they had not expected to encounter anyone when they entered the church intent on their misdeeds. Let alone anyone as brave and dedicated as Father Gregory."

Silence fell as we all reflected on what had happened. But after a pause Father Compton came to life realising that it was his responsibility to get a grip on the situation.

"My dear brothers in Christ," he said to the monks surrounding him as if starting a sermon. "This terrible act is almost too much to bear – but like a cross we must endure it. Unfortunately now is not the time to express all our feelings about this hellish act. Our first concern must continue to be the requiems for our departed brethren. They must go ahead as planned and we must prepare to welcome our guests from the cathedral and its monastery."

At this there was some whispering of the Brothers between themselves but they seemed to accept its necessity.

"So now, please, can we collect together these scarred remains and clear the area around the altar?" continued Father Compton. "For the time being I suggest we can lodge them in the storeroom across the court. And then we must get on with our preparations. We will have to convene after the service is over and our guests have departed to consider what we do next."

"Father Compton is right," said Father Eynesham who had

221

rejoined the group having despatched Father Gregory's still-unconscious body. "But can I ask you all – and that includes you too Sir Matthew – to say nothing whatsoever about this. Nothing that you have seen here should be revealed to anyone at all outside our community. Is that understood? And just to ensure confidentiality we shall put a screen in front of the altar. No-one should see this beyond ourselves."

"But Father Eynesham," objected Brother Adam. "Our guests will notice it – so will the pilgrims who come in later today – they will all see that Saint Josse is not here. They will ask about it. What are we supposed to say to those who need the saint's help?"

"Say nothing!" instructed Father Eynesham. "If compelled you can acknowledge that the reliquary has been removed temporarily for restoration – which is true. Say, it will be returned at some point in the not-too-distant future. But preferably say nothing. There really is no need to say anything. God works in mysterious ways and all is for the best. Just say that."

Father Compton looked intimidated by this but kept silent. I looked around for Brother Thomas. This scene of desolation would have been a delight for him no doubt. "Brother Thomas not here?" I asked Father Compton.

"No – I think he spent last night back at the cathedral," replied the acting abbot. "He normally does. But no doubt he will have a lot to say about this when he does eventually arrive. I feel that I will have to tell him – and, of course, it will then get back to the Cathedral no matter how much we try to hush it up."

"Right," continued Father Eynesham, now self-assured and fully restored to his normal self. "Let's get this all cleared up and cleared away as soon as possible."

Then taking me by the arm he walked me down to the main door at the west end.

"I am sorry to have involved you in on this, Sir Matthew," he said in a tone which was in marked contrast to when he first arrived at our door. "It's such a terrible thing to have happened so my thoughts naturally turned to you. But I hope that I can rely on you not to speak to anyone about it – not even your son or servant. I suggest that you say there had been an accident to an altar but it had now been resolved. We need to pray and to meditate on this before we decide what to do next."

"But what will you say to Madame Eglentyne?" I asked. "She will want to know about Father Gregory."

"Don't worry about that, Sir Matthew. I know Madame Eglentyne well. I will reassure her. So I now look forward to seeing you a little later on this morning."

And with that he ushered me out of the abbey church and into the cloisters.

CHAPTER 37
'The wordes moote be cosin to the dede'

Walking back to our quarters I felt distinctly uncomfortable. The capitals in the cloisters displayed all sorts of mythical beasts and I was starting to feel trapped and vulnerable in their wild wood. Who were the frightening predators out to entangle me? And why had Father Eynesham decided to involve me in this latest crime especially when the Cathedral had dismissed me from the investigation of the murders?

Inevitably the question arose; might there be a link between the St. Josse theft and the two murders? Or was it just part of the wider campaign to embarrass and hurt the abbey? And how did the theft of the Golden Charter – which was now my only official inquisition - fit into the bigger picture? Assuming, that is, there was one.

I pondered all of this as I walked across the Outer Court. And if I thought there was a connection then surely I could not conceal it from Damian and Osric?

I paused and overlooked the stream which ran directly thorough the abbey's grounds and under the principal guest house. The water arrived, flowing clean from further up the Itchen valley but by the time it exited the abbey grounds on its way to the sea it was full of the monastery's refuse and ordure. There must be something symbolic in that, I supposed - but it would probably take an Oxford scholar to riddle it out.

Putting that to one side I rolled my mind back through the events of this morning. The dramatic banging on the door, the desperate account of what had happened, being hauled across to see the scene of the crime – and Father Gregory being left to lie on the cold floor purely so I could see him there, as an exhibit for evidence.

My growing feeling was that I had been set up.

By giving me full access to the event but then morally binding me into not talking about it I was, in effect, being corralled into silence. The abbey was proofing itself against me finding out about it later and then asking awkward questions.

On that basis I felt justified to disregard the agreement to silence I had been induced to make. The pressure applied to me was not done in good faith. So I would take Osric and Damian into my confidence. If Father Eynesham could play tricky then so could I.

Arriving back in our room I gave a quick account of what I had just seen.

"Was he looking bloody, Lord?" asked Osric. "You say that he had been badly attacked."

I paused to remember.

"I did not see him too well, Osric. Maybe I should have gone closer to inspect. Someone simply said he had been beaten and was unconscious. And, when I looked, there he was lying behind the altar. But it was not well lit and I could not really see him properly."

"So we don't know for sure?" Osric persevered. "But you believe he's not dead?"

I realised that we had got to the point where we had stopped believing anything we were told – or even seen with our own eyes. And Osric was the most suspicious of us all.

"So you are suggesting what exactly, Osric? That Gregory was just pretending? Or that he was actually dead?"

"It could be either," he replied bluntly. "All I am saying, Lord, is that we do not necessarily take it for truth just because it seems so."

"Well, I have to agree with you on that point. Nonetheless there is no question that the reliquary had been smashed and bust open. And the bones were gone."

"Assuming that is, they were ever there in the first place," put in Damian, making his own contribution to the shared sense of distrust.

I had to laugh at that point. What if the monastery had been perpetrating a fraud for years and there was actually nothing in the box? And how would the thieves have felt when they came to open it and the bones had disappeared? Had a miracle occurred and was the tomb left empty?

"What are you smiling at, Father?" Damian challenged. "It's a serious question."

"I know, Damian. That's why I'm laughing," I responded. "But I think we have to draw a line somewhere. We might be in danger of driving ourselves mad if we cannot believe anything at all. My understanding is that St Josse's relics have been in the care of this community for over three hundred years."

"And where did they come from before?" asked Osric.

"France, I believe. Northern France."

"And you would believe the French wouldn't you?" said Osric in his edgy, challenging way.

"The story is that they were brought to Winchester for safety, Osric – to stop the Vikings destroying them." I responded in a reasonable voice. "But, as you know, I am not an expert. Mistress Alison was talking about St. Josse at table the other night. But more important right now is that I am supposed not to have told you any of this. Having taken me into their confidence Father Eynesham effectively bound me to silence."

"So why have you told us?" asked Damian, sounding a little shocked.

"Because, Damian, I have a bigger responsibility and obligation for truth to you and Osric than I do to Father Eynesham – or indeed this abbey. And I think there might be some connection between what happened this morning and what else has been going on."

"What do you mean?" asked Damian. "What with the murders? Or just the general decay of the place?"

"I am not sure," I had to admit. "My instinct is that somehow all these crimes are connected. But I cannot explain how. I am asking you, though, not to say anything about it. That's not for the sake of the abbey but for our sake. You and Osric should know about this theft. But, for the time being, let's keep it between ourselves."

"Agreed, lord," said Osric reassuringly.

"Alright, father, I won't say anything."

"Not even to this young nun, Avelina?"

"No, not even to this young woman, Avelina," replied Damian with some irritation.

I was definitely starting to feel the strain of having to deal with endless small challenges from my son and my favourite servant. Some time soon we needed to have a break from each other.

"But assuming there were bones there in the box, father," Damian continued after a little while. "What would be the point of their theft."

"Well, there's no question they'd be wanted by someone who would probably pay a nice price for them," I said. "The thieves probably couldn't do much with them in England but they certainly could abroad – in France for example. After all that's where they originated. But maybe even in Italy, in Rome."

I looked at Osric for a snide response. There was none.

"Just think of all the money these pardoners make by selling old bones," I continued. "A complete set of St. Josse would probably attract a fortune from some French or Flemish monastery. So look out for pardoners! But really I don't want to get too drawn into this. For now let's just put it to the back of our minds – at least until after the funerals."

CHAPTER 38
'ϜΟΚϾΗ ϢΕ ΚΙΔΕΝ'

Probably the less said about the requiem rites for Brothers Peter and Walter the better. You can tell a lot about the character of a community when it is faced by a tragedy. I had come to understand this on crusade. The pressure of calamity either fragments or bonds depending on the prevailing spirit. The church was almost full with clerics from across Winchester but not with love. So despite all the sanctimonious gestures there was little sense of unity. Instead there was rivalry and suspicion.

After the mass the two coffins were borne out for burial in the monks' graveyard adjacent to the church where they had the simplest of graves alongside scores of their brethren who had died over the past two and a half centuries.

We stayed until the very end out of respect for the service but we were eager to get away as soon as was decent. I had seen Madame Eglentyne and expressed concern for Father Gregory. "Yes, it was very upsetting for him – but I think he will recover well," she said. "He's more robust than you might think. He's remaining behind here for a day or two but I am sure that he will be back with us in fine fettle before too long."

"So he's regained consciousness then has he?" I asked.

"Was he ever unconscious?" she replied. "I hadn't noticed."

I restrained any sign of surprise. I was eager to depart and get on the road.

There had been some talk among the various pilgrims, now free of their obligations to the abbey, to ride as a single party. "Perhaps you could all tell stories to each other?" suggested Father Compton limply, a proposal which was received indifferently. It was clear that the various groups wanted to travel at their own pace and stay at separate inns on the way. But there was a general agreement that we would all reassemble at the Tabard on the day after next.

I said a slightly awkward good-bye to Father Compton who

indicated that he hoped to see me again soon when I returned to Hampshire. I wished him success as he pursued further inquiries into the deaths and offered again my commiserations about the theft of the Saint Josse relics.

"The murders I can live with," he admitted. "We live in a wicked world and we are stalked by Satan every waking moment. But our refuge and strength in this abbey lies in our faith – and particularly our faith in our relics. They are what give us hope when the world seeks to destroy us. How we will now cope without St. Josse and, indeed, the Golden Charter at the heart of our community I cannot imagine."

He looked as if he was about to crumble. All I could do was clutch his shoulder as a gesture of support. But I then walked away.

"At least we can offer you and your son and your servant a comfortable night for this evening," confirmed Madame Eglentyne as we mounted our horses.

Our riding party now amounted to five. Madame Eglentyne and her nun, Avelina, together with Damian, Osric and me. Out of the corner of my eye I had already noticed Damian and the young nun making moon faces at each other but I was determined not to become involved in any way. That situation could best work itself out without any intervention from me. If anyone ought to intervene it should be Madame Eglentyne.

Just as we were about to set off, however, she looked across at me and said, "Oh by the way Sir Matthew, I do hope you won't mind if that young scallywag, John, rides with us? I saw him yesterday and he said he was feeling rather lost and still upset about the accusation he had faced, He didn't think that he could make the journey to Canterbury on his own. He looked like a little mouse. I felt so sorry for him that I said he was perfectly welcome to travel with us. I trust that will be acceptable to you?"

Once again I felt I had been caught off-guard. Especially after the revelations from last evening, I did not relish any further contact with John, the Oxford clerk. Ever. But what could I say?

"Of course, Madame Eglentyne. How very kind and thoughtful

of you! I am not sure how enthusiastic John will be to see me again but if he needs company on the road then who am I to deny him?" I then turned to Osric and Damian. "Did you hear that boys? Young John the scholar will be riding with us."

Together the two of them raised their eyebrows – but then smirks crossed both their faces. I could not contemplate any amusing conversation with John - but maybe they could.

"He's not here now is he?" I said to Madame Eglentyne looking around the assembled crowd of mounted riders leaving the abbey's Forecourt for the London road beyond.

"No, he's meeting us a little way out at St. Swithun's church in Headbourne Worthy," she replied. "Apparently that's where he's been staying for the past couple of days."

That couldn't be right, surely. Wasn't he supposed to be staying with Doctor Nafis in Winnal which was across the river and some way from Headbourne Worthy? And I wondered once more where exactly the Doctor fitted into all this.

As it happened, I had noticed that Nafis had left as quickly as possible after the church service to join with the lawyer and the Franklin in setting off for London. Three professional men together. What would they be discussing? I wondered.

I had wanted to say goodbye to Michael on the gate before we departed but he was nowhere to be seen. I had adjusted my view of him after hearing about his racket with the girls and Walter but I could not hold it too much against him. It was now part of a familiar pattern. "I've not seen him since last night," said Timothy, the sour-faced assistant gate-keeper as I enquired on the way out.

"Well, give him my greetings, please, when he turns up." Sour-face nodded. "Tell him that Sir Matthew de Somborne looks forward to seeing him again."

And then we were out on the road and heading off for London. We followed the river along the valley with downland stretching out ahead of us and water-meadows to our right. The weather was warming up. The countryside was looking joyous.

231

There were some flowers starting to bloom. Bluebells were on their way. Birds were singing. London and Canterbury and the joys of southern England lay ahead. For the first time in many weeks I started to feel pleased to be alive.

But that wasn't going to last long.

CHAPTER 39
'My Lady Prioresse, and ye, Sire Clerk'

We rode in silence the short distance to Saint Swithun's Church in Headbourne Worthy, perhaps reflecting on the journey to come and enjoying the promise of a lovely April morning. Some way ahead of us at a distance on the rolling, up-and-down road I could see Mistress Alison on her ambling horse and, as she approached the church, three horsemen appeared out of the roadside trees. Although I was too far away to see exactly what happened they all seemed to acknowledge her and she paused briefly to talk with them. Then she set off again accompanied by two of them who had her laden mule train in tow. The third man got off his horse and waited.

As we approached I realised, of course, that it was John.

I allowed Madame Eglentyne and Sister Avelina to ride on. As far as possible I wanted to avoid any exchanges with the young man.

"Good morning, my boy!" shouted Madame Eglentyne in an uncharacteristically raucous voice. He waved back and nodded also with some familiarity to Avelina. They spoke briefly together and then John mounted his horse and regained the road. Avelina remained alongside.

John had not acknowledged us and so Damian, Osric and I allowed them to get a little ahead before we resumed.

"I am really not sure I made the right decision in agreeing to travel with Madame Eglentyne and her party," I said. "Staying tonight at Wintney takes us somewhat out of our way and I had no idea that John was going to be tagging along with us. What do you think Damian?"

"Well, father, I have to be honest with you. I had been thinking that it would be rather nice to see some more of Sister Avelina but, look, she's almost cosying up with that John already, I hope its not going to be like that all the way to London."

"Don't get too jealous, young man," said Osric laughing. "I can't imagine that little pipsqueak has much appeal for the ladies."

"Well, you can never tell," I had to say. "Some women have

curious tastes in men. Anyway, Damian, I hesitate to say this but remember she is a nun – there are limits to what the two of you can do."

Immediately I had said it I reproached myself. Hardly any time had passed since I had determined not to involve myself in Damian's love life in any way.

"Oh, father, please don't give me that," he said trying to sound like a man of the world. "I can look after my own affairs." Of course he was right. I should keep my mouth shut. Instead I focused my attention on John.

"Osric, at some point today could you rebuild your link with John and find out why he's going to Canterbury. It didn't make much sense to me."

"Yes, I'll try, lord, but I suspect that he's a clever little twister and he'll have some devious explanation," Osric responded. "After all he is an Oxford man He's deceptive by nature. I thought that straight away when we were talking with him about the murder of Brother Peter."

"But you seemed to be getting on so well with him."

"It was all an act, Lord. Him with me and me with him. He's not stupid and I'm not either. Talking about the Forest and its stories and ways was just a means of weighing each other up."

"You mean you think he was lying – and I was fooled by him?"

"No, lord, not that. You had your instinct about him and the murder and you know a lot more about murders than I do. But I think that he was telling his story in the best way possible – only selecting what he wanted us to know. So I'm not sure I'll get much out of him by way of the truth – anyway, no more than he wants to tell us."

"Yes, you're probably right, Osric. In fact, I don't know why I'm worrying about it. He can do what he wants as far as I'm concerned just so long as he doesn't get under my feet."

And so we rode on. After a while Damian moved up and joined Avelina on the other side from John and she graciously turned towards him. I couldn't hear what they were talking about and did not want to. But from what I could see John did not not seem particularly put out by Damian's arrival.

However, seeing Madame Eglentyne on her own I felt I should join her. The route to London by way of Wintney took us first through Basyng and for the sake of conversation I asked her what was happening there.

"I go there rarely," she confessed. "We Cistercians have the misfortune to live in far away places. They did it deliberately, you see. When they built our convents they planted us away from distracting towns. Of course as the prioress I have the privilege of some travel. If I didn't, dear Sir Matthew, I think I would be driven mad with boredom. But fortunately I do." She turned and gave me one of her bright smiles.

"But the priory is comfortable enough, I understand?"

"It is – we make it so. Just about. On very restricted means we do our very best. As you shall see. But that is why we must ensure that we are not being cheated out of what is ours by right."

"Well, I am very much looking forward to seeing it," I said thinking ahead to the evening. "And you have a number of priests with you in the community I understand – in addition to poor Father Gregory."

"Indeed we have three priests. Alas, we poor women are apparently incapable of saying holy mass for ourselves so we need men to say it for us. Not that I do not like men, Sir Matthew. On the contrary but, after all, Christ did say when three are gathered together in his name then he is with us. He didn't say it had to include a man, did he? But that is why I like doing things in threes."

That smile again.

"So tell me some more about Father Gregory. By the sound of it he is not in as bad shape as I had assumed"

"Of course, it was a very upsetting for him, Sir Matthew, there is no question of that. But he did not tell me too much about what happened – he was being too brave. You see he is so pious and that was why he insisted in staying in the abbey church all night to keep company, so to speak, with those dear dead brothers. He has been a kind of martyr. Of course he did have good St. Josse looking after him."

"But St. Josse has disappeared!" I said puzzled.

"Yes, so they say. But then who can tell? I am sure that he is still there in spirit" she replied in her typically opaque way. "Anyway I am glad to say that although Father Gregory was very badly hurt he is, as I mentioned, going to be quite alright. I have been praying for him. And that always seems to work miracles in my experience. And of course, Doctor Nafis saw him this morning as well so I am sure that between us all we will have Father Gregory back up very soon and on the way to London."

"And I gather that the good doctor visits you regularly? I mean at Wintney."

"Yes, indeed, he did," the abbess said with, for the first time, a slightly less enthusiastic tone in her voice. "In the past I was always delighted to welcome Doctor Nafis. He used to come regularly, every week. But now, maybe, I am not so sure."

"What, you mean he is too busy?"

"Yes, you could put it that way – on the various things he does," she replied slightly hesitantly but then changed tack. "Yes, on second thoughts, that's a very good way of putting it. That's exactly what he is. Too busy."

A change, it seemed, had taken place in their relationship but I was perplexed as to what it might be.

"So do you have much illness among your nuns? I hope not." I said.

"I am glad to say, virtually never. Our infirmary only has one bed – although, that said, it has been regularly occupied."

We jogged on talking about nothing very much until Basyng appeared with the church of Saint Michael welcoming us from far off.

"Shall we halt for a little something to eat, Madame Eglentyne?"

"Yes, that would be a good idea, Sir Matthew. I suggest we stop at the Mote Hall. Maybe you men could then go to a tavern and get us a little food and drink. Some people think that life in Basyng is rather dull but that's not always so. As I think we might see."

CHAPTER 40
'Of vitaille and of oother purveiaunce'

What can we say about Basyng? It had neither a corporation nor a common seal but just fields full of sheep with a wool market to match. And, important though these might be, they held little interest for me. But I was not looking for excitement. Just a quiet lunch before resuming a tranquil journey through the gentle countryside.

Having dismounted I despatched Damian and John into the Ram's Head for some sustenance. Sister Avelina rejoined Madame Eglentyne and finding some clear ground outside the Hospital of St John the Baptist we sat down to wait. Meanwhile Osric was looking after the horses.

For a little time I enjoyed the growing warmth of the sun and it was refreshing after those claustrophobic days in the abbey to be out in the open.

"But, seriously, can anything interesting ever come out of Basyng?" I asked Madame Eglentyne teasingly.

"Prior Hugh comes from Basyng," she replied immediately. "Did he not mention it?"

"Maybe he prefers to keep it quiet," I said.

"Worth remembering," she said.

"But why?"

"You never know," she said. "He could be the next Bishop of Winchester for all we know. It's always useful to be aware of that kind of thing. It might prove useful."

Personally I very much doubted this but after a while reflecting on Madame Eglentyne's appetite for amassing endless detail about people I became aware of my empty stomach. "I'll go in and see what they are up to," I said.

As I entered the tavern there was a blast of alarm. The scholar, John, was sprawled on the floor holding his hands up as if to protect himself while the squire, Damian was having to be held back by a couple of men as he struggled to attack him with a knife.

"Damian! Stop it! Stop it! What on earth are you doing. Put that knife down at once!" I shouted.

Reluctantly, Damian dropped his arms and the knife to the ground. The restraining men loosened their grip. "I'm his father," I said with some embarrassment to the two men who, I saw with a glance, looked familiar somehow.

"What on earth has been going on, Damian! Apologise to these men. And to John. And then get outside."

He did as he was told. I turned to John and felt that I had to give him the benefit of the doubt – again – even though he made me feel distinctly irritated.

"John, I don't know what's been happening here. But you look like the victim. Get yourself a drink and some food for Madame Eglentyne and Sister Avelina and I'll see you later on. And here's some money for your pains."

I gave him four groats thinking that would keep him happy for a little while. "And buy a drink for these men as well." I said indicating the couple who had restrained my son.

Outside, Damian was looking abashed and ashamed. He was standing with Osric by the horses and seemed keen to get away. Madame Eglentyne and Avelina were looking on with some astonishment. I went up to them.

"I am very sorry ladies but there seems to have been some altercation between Damian and John in there. I've no idea why but I mean to find out. But for the time being I think we should go our separate ways."

"Oh dear! I am so sorry to hear that," said Madame Eglentyne. "But look, I don't want this to spoil our journey. I am sure it's just boyish horseplay that got out of hand. You ride on, we'll follow shortly. Let everyone calm down. We'll see you this evening in Wintney."

In the absence of any other plan I agreed that I at least would be at the Priory that evening. About Damian and Osric I was not so sure. Indeed, by this stage I was in a quiet fury with Damian.

Whatever had happened he should not have lost control like that.

I instructed the two of them to mount up and simply announced, "We're going." They followed although Osric complained quietly that he had been looking forward to a drink. "Later," I said sharply.

As we road down the little High Street I was so full of annoyance I almost overlooked Mistress Alison. But there she was as large as life, in her big red hat and a flowing mantle standing by her horse outside the Mote Hall. And, more to the point she seemed to be now in the company of the two men who had intervened in the fight.

I was hardly in the mood to speak to her and exchange pleasantries but felt that I could not just ride by and ignore her.

"Hello, Mistress Alison – we meet again and so soon!" I called across to her without stopping my horse.

"Hello, Sir Matthew. How nice to see you! I'm just doing some business – buying some samples for Bruges. It's the local wool here – absolutely marvellous!"

"Well, that's very good," I said trying to put some jolliness into my voice. "We'll see you again soon enough I'm sure."

We rode on. I was relieved that she did not speak further. A little way down the road, I looked back. She was now instructing the two men to load up a pair of mules with what looked like some heavy folded bundles. And John now seemed to be talking to them as well probably chewing over the assault he had just suffered.

"Did you take a note, lord, of those two men?" asked Osric.

"Yes, I did."

"I could be wrong but they looked to be the pair who were going round saying that they were the priest and the ploughman back in the abbey. But they were looking much better dressed this time. It was hard to recognise them at first."

"What the ones who were making the claim about the mutilation of Brother Peter?"

"Yes, that's right. That couple. They seem to pop up every-

239

where don't they. By the looks of things they were with Mistress Alison too."

"I suppose that's not too surprising," I said. "She told me some story about how they had helped her out of a problem coming across from Bath – and maybe she just needs a bit of muscle, I mean for all these bundles of wool she is carrying. Seems to increase by the day."

"Yes, maybe so, Lord. But I'm planning to keep my eyes peeled for them," said Osric bravely. "You never know."

'You never know?' I could hardly disagree with that. Clearly I could not just drift off into my own thoughts and flee the world. I needed to keep my wits about me. And in any case I wanted to get Damian's account of what had happened in the tavern.

"So, tell me Damian, what was it all about?"

"I'm sorry, father. I really am. It must have looked terrible."

"It did."

"So. We went into the tavern and had to wait a bit to be served."

"Yes, I'd guessed that."

"Anyway although John and I had been riding together we'd not really spoken to each other at all. Both of us just spoke to Avelina. They seemed to know each other already but I could not understand why. So now it was a bit difficult - especially because of how he and I had met outside the brothel."

"Understandably," I said.

"But then in the tavern he started at me almost immediately. 'Be careful with Avelina,' he said. 'She's not interested in you in any way. All she wants to do is find out is what your father's up to'. Why would she want to do that? I asked. 'Because she's just that sort of girl. She wants to be able to tell the prioress what's going on. And the prioress wants to know everything.' How do you know? I asked. 'Just take it from me, I do. In any case, if you want to impress her don't bother with all that soldiering stuff you were going on about. That won't open up her heart to you – or anything else for that matter.' He said I needed to quote poetry at her, love poems and then he mentioned some Italian or Greek or something. 'Do you know any of those?' he asked. Well of course I didn't. 'In that case' he said, 'just forget it – you not her type at all'. And then he added he was just trying to be helpful – but he said it in such a patronising way. So I then said to him, 'So if I'm not her type who is? I suppose you are?' 'I am actually', he said. And that's when I lost it. I went for him."

"What with that knife?" I asked with some amazement "I didn't think you had a knife like that. It looks rather common."

"No, I started to punch him. He was the one who got out the knife, waving it around to frighten me. But I just knocked it out of his hand – easy. I picked it up and moved towards him and that's when those two men jumped in."

"And they're the same two we've just seen with Mistress Alison?"

"Possibly, I didn't really notice."

"And had they acknowledged John in any way, before they got involved?"

"Not that I saw."

"And then I came along."

"Exactly."

"And where was he carrying this knife? I'd not noticed it."

"Came out from deep in the pockets of that student gown of his. They're petty capacious you know."

"Alright, Damian – well it's not quite as bad as I thought – I mean from your perspective. Even so, I can't say I'm pleased. But I can understand why it happened. He was obviously being very provoking but you were the one who resorted to violence first. It was a good job that nothing worse came of it."

"Yes, I realise that – I'm sorry, father. And I wonder now what he'll be saying to Avelina. They'll probably be having a good laugh about it."

"That is possible I suppose," I conceded. "But tell me – had Avelina been asking questions about me – or about what we'd been doing?"

"Er, yes, father, now I think about it – she had."

"What you mean everything connected with the murders and what the Prior has said to me and so on?"

"I'm afraid so, yes. But lots of other things as well. Where you'd been on crusade. What happens at home in Somborne. How things were with mother. All sorts."

"And how do you feel about her now."

"I still like her very much, father. I just do. Sorry."

"Hmmm," I replied. Osric, who had been listening in, rolled his eyes. Damian's love life was getting off to a bad start. 'Like father, like son' was all I could think.

CHAPTER 41
'And preestes thre'

I now had to decide what we were going to do that evening. I tried to weigh up the significance of Madame Eglentyne being so curious about my affairs. Was it just reasonable curiosity from a woman in authority who wanted to be aware of what was going on? But, then why did she need to know 'everything' as John had put it? And using Avelina as a spy to get the information. That was what I really did not like. Damian was a bright, brave, charming lad but still naive in many ways. I didn't want him treated like a fool.

I made up my mind.

"Damian! Osric! I'm sorry but I don't think it's wise for you to stay overnight at Wintney this evening. After what I've heard about the fight and Avelina's prying curiosity I think it would be asking for trouble – and certainly embarrassing whatever happens. So I want to create a bit of space between us and the Prioress. You two, I think, better ride on to Guildford. It's a bit of a distance but you should be able to make it before it gets too dark."

"But you'll still go to Wintney, will you lord?" asked Osric.

"Yes, I think I must. At least one of us should be there as agreed and it ought to be me. It would be too rude to Madame Eglentyne not to. And besides I'd like to know what she's up to, what her game is. If she's got one that is."

"I suppose that's best," agreed Damian reluctantly. "If that little stuck-up student needled me again I don't quite know what I might do."

"That's sensible, Damian," I said, "but let me tell you now that if you want to become part of the Duke of Lancaster's household you are going to have to learn self-control and become more cunning. More circumspect. Sometimes you have to ignore provocation. They'll be plenty of rivalries among his knights. It will be a den of conspiracy and deception. Steer clear of taking offence too easily. Time for revenge will come but do it in your own careful way and not just when you are driven by passion."

"So where should we stay, lord, in Guildford?" asked Osric who was more concerned with his own immediate future than Damian's long-term career progress. As we travelled further from his native woodland I could tell that he was starting to feel uncomfortable. Only the lost St. Josse could guess what he would make of London.

"Go to The Angel in the High Street," I replied. "I'll meet you there as early as possible tomorrow morning."

I handed over some coins to both of them – enough for a generous bed and board for the night - and we continued on the road. "We better quicken up," I said, "you've got a long way to go."

There was little further conversation between us until we reached Wintney and the road which would then take them to Crondall and on to Guildford.

"Keep your wits about you, both of you," I said. "And it wouldn't surprise me in the least if you were to come across some of our fellow pilgrims tonight. Try and enjoy yourselves but don't give too much away. And say nothing about the Golden Charter."

And off they went. It was an odd feeling. Although I would be seeing them on the morrow I had got used to them being with me. Despite the little irritations of having them around me day-after-day I had relished the chance of catching up on all those lost years. And soon enough, I was sure, Damian would be leaving me again more permanently.

Distracting myself from these morose thoughts I made my way from the main road up to the priory. I had decided to wait outside until Madame Eglentyne and her companions arrived so found a convenient patch of turf and settled down.

Almost involuntarily my mind wandered back to the murders. Away from Hyde the events of the past three days seemed almost incredible. Were these crimes of passion or careful deliberation? Who had benefited? And how were they connected, if indeed they were? And was it just coincidence that they occurred while I was there?

It was also becoming clearer to me that the disappearance of the Golden Charter must be somehow connected to the rights of the abbey and its status. The suggestion that the document was stolen purely for its gold leaf seemed far-fetched. No, this must be about the status of the abbey being either claimed or resisted. The place had few friends of influence and greedy looks were being cast over its wealth. That had to be the key. And there were plenty of people who had cause to want to cut the abbey down to size and enjoy its fruits.

I was turning over the implications of this when a finely-dressed priest on a sturdy horse turned off the road and began to approach the priory. "Greetings!" he called out. "Are you waiting for Madame Eglentyne?"

"I am indeed," I said, standing up.

"Thought you might be – you look her type," the priest said with a slight smile on his face. "And you are?"

"Sir Matthew de Somborne," I replied. "I met Madame Eglentyne at Hyde Abbey in Winchester a couple of days ago. I'm on pilgrimage and she very kindly invited me to stay overnight here on my way to London."

"Well, she's very generous in that way," replied the priest, the smile on his very handsome face increasing rather wider. "And, of course, she is starting on pilgrimage tomorrow. As I am also. We're all going on pilgrimage!" he laughed. "What fun we're going to have!"

"And you, sir priest, are? If you don't mind me asking?"

"Not in the least," he replied briskly. "I am John Lydezorde, rector of Elvetham, just over there." He pointed to a village on the near horizon. "And I have the privilege of being the confessor to the prioress and nuns here in Wintney. I've been here six months or so."

"Appointed by Madame Eglentyne herself then?" I asked.

"Oh, no. Not at all. I owe my appointment to Bishop Wykeham himself. And, as you know, you can't get much higher than that. Well, of course, you could but I wouldn't want to." He laughed.

"Meaning what?" I asked, having no idea what he was talking about.

"Well, I would not like to be in the shoes of the Archbishop of Canterbury right now – would you? I am very happy being a humble little cleric who knows his place serving a charming prioress in this little backwater."

"But you are going to Canterbury nonetheless," I said.

"Well, that's the plan," he said in a more serious tone of voice. "But whether we will get there is, perhaps, a matter for conjecture."

"Why is there a problem with the road – the road from London to Canterbury?"

He looked at me as if I were a complete fool. And somehow standing there in my stained and smudged tunic I began to feel one despite being described by Father Lydezorde as Madame Eglentyne's 'type'.

"Obviously the news does not travel much to – Somborne, did you say? So here's how it is. Things are now getting quite serious down in Kent. Not, Sir Matthew, the roads but the people. The tax collectors are having a very difficult time and the people are having it harder. Plus there are the usual rabble-rousers – people spreading misleading reports – going round lying just to cause confusion. It stirs the ordinary folk to fury. They are being misled and I wouldn't be surprised if they are storming the Tower by the end of the Summer. Breaking in, sitting on thrones, stealing the symbols of state, hunting down the king's ministers and turning over offices. Oh yes, I can see it all now."

All of this he described with relish – as if he found it amusing.

"So if things start to get serious by the time we get to London I am just going to reverse my horse and return home. But I've told the Prioress that I would come with her that far – and I keep my promises. And I plan to enjoy it as much as I possibly can."

So, another, cynical and self-serving cleric I thought to myself. But that did not mean I dismissed his account of what might lie ahead.

"And where does the Archbishop of Canterbury come in to this?" I asked.

"Well, people want to hate someone, don't they – and the Archbishop, God bless him, is the unlucky man whom almost everyone hates right now. I wouldn't be in his shoes for all the old bones in Hyde Abbey."

"And what about Bishop William then? Don't people hate him too. After all, isn't he the richest man in England?"

"You do not get that rich without also being very clever," said Lydezorde. "And my friend and patron Bishop Wykeham is clever enough not to be caught out. But he is in London too. In his lovely palace by the river – probably enjoying every moment of this knowing that when the world turns again he'll be back in the centre of power. Just mark my words."

I took all this in and suddenly the events in Hyde – even the murders – seemed rather trivial. If the country was on the edge of major revolt where would that put Damian and me?

"So how was your stay in Hyde – Hyde Abbey, home of long lost and forgotten kings. Eventful?" he asked in his voice which was charming but carried with it an undercurrent of mild contempt.

"Well, where can I start?" I said feeling it was now my turn to show off some up-to-date news. "Tragically there were two murders just before we left. You could scarcely credit it but two of the brothers were attacked and killed – very unpleasant and almost incomprehensible. And other odd things going on. Stolen relics. Strange people coming in and out of the abbey..."

"Sounds like a shocking catalogue of evil," he said completing my sentence in a matter-of-fact voice. "Yes, I heard about all that."

"And did you hear that poor Father Gregory had been attacked too – that's why he won't be back here this evening with the prioress."

"Yes, I'd heard that something nasty had happened to the pretty boy – but I am sure that he'll get over it very quickly. He's up for anything that young man."

"Well you are very well informed, Father," I said feeling a little shocked by his dismissive tone of Father Gregory's injuries. And where did he get his information from? My surprise was clearly evident on my face,

"When you live on this road, Sir Matthew, with all the traffic up to London, news arrives very swiftly. I know what happens at Hyde Abbey. With all the comings and goings of people – pilgrims, merchants, lawyers, priests like me – we hear it as fast here in Wintney as people do in Winchester itself. Maybe sometimes faster. That is, if you make the effort to find out. So, for example, I knew you were coming. I am just slightly surprised that you seem to be by yourself. I was under the impression that you would be accompanied by your son and an attendant."

"Well, that was the plan," I agreed. "But it did not quite work out that way. Damian, my son, and Osric, our yeoman, have gone on to Guildford."

"Oh, well that is disappointing," he said, for the first time in our conversation sounding sincere. "But I am sure there will be other opportunities to meet them. But ah, what do I see? Here comes the good Prioress with the lovely Avelina – and there's John."

I turned and about one hundred paces away the three of them were about to turn off the road.

"You know, John, the student?" I asked.

For a moment he looked uncertain what to say but quickly recovered.

"Hmm, yes he's been here once or twice before, I believe. Probably on his way to somewhere even more exciting than Wintney like Cambridge – you know what these students are like..."

He turned his horse round and trotted off to meet them. I could see exchanged greetings and then some hurried words of

248

discussion. I prepared myself to welcome them. However, before I had a chance to say a word Madame Eglentyne cooed out to me

"Hello, dear Sir Matthew – so glad to see that you have found your way here but I am sad that your charming son is not with you! We were all looking forward to getting to know him better – weren't we, Avelina?"

"We were indeed, Madame. I am very sorry that dear, kind Damian is not here." She looked at me intently and smiled so very sweetly that I almost felt in danger of falling for her myself..

"It's most regrettable that the little altercation between the two boys has spoiled our plans," Madame Eglentyne continued, "and I have spoken to John about it – haven't I John?"

He bowed his head and looked admonished.

"But what's done is done so let's forget about it for now. Let's all go inside and get comfortable – you've met our kind and understanding confessor, Rector Lydezorde haven't you? Oh the secrets he must hold!"

"Yes, indeed, I was very pleased to meet him," I said nodding in his direction.

"And we have so much more to confess since he arrived, don't we Avelina?"

Avelina turned to me and smiled again knowingly. If I am not careful this could become very dangerous, I thought.

CHAPTER 42

'So be thy stronge champion this day'

By comparison with Hyde Abbey, Wintney Priory was a modest establishment. I believe there were no more than ten nuns there and everything in the public areas looked threadbare. The chapel was unadorned aside from a small statue of the virgin and child and the cloister was bare of any ornamentation.

My guest chamber was adequate but no more than that. So I prepared myself for a penny-pinching supper and was thankful I was only staying for the one night. I reflected enviously on what Damian and Osric were probably getting up to this evening in Guildford accompanied by solid fare and strong beer.

When I arrived in Madame Eglentyne's private rooms, however, it was a different matter. Everything here was elegant and well-upholstered. There were bright hangings on the walls and plentiful candles. It was pleasingly warm and Rector Lydezorde, John and Sister Avelina were already there relaxedly having a drink. I was offered a glass of very good wine - 'A good vintage from Bordeaux' said the Rector - by a little serving nun who then scuttled about for the rest of the evening, waiting on a well-spread table and doing as she was told.

When the prioress entered she was barely recognisable. Gone was her nun's habit and instead she was wearing the fashionable dress of a woman of the court. And, contrary to her Rule, under a light veil she had kept her luxuriant hair still untouched by any grey. With a juddering shock my vague memories from two decades ago crystallised. This was not the first time that I had seen Madame Eglentyne displaying her seductive power.

The food was excellent – easily surpassing anything we had enjoyed in Hyde over the past couple of days. Tender lamb and delicious fine white bread together with plenty of fruit and sweet-meats – it was by any standard a feast. Meanwhile a pair of little dogs to whom the prioress was obviously devoted yapped away throughout the meal to everyone's suppressed irritation – apart

251

from the prioress herself who rejoiced in pretending to scold them.

The conversation was mostly restricted to local ecclesiastical matters and discussions of the activities of the surrounding gentry. To my relief no-one seemed to feel the need to dig over the recent events in Winchester. But as the last of the plates was removed from the table Madame Eglentyne looked at me and said in a very deliberate voice. "Now tell me, Sir Matthew, what are your plans for our short stay in London? Are you taking up this offer of the Tabard or will you go straight on to Canterbury? How much of a hurry are you in?"

"Well I am not really sure, at the moment, Madame Eglentyne. Yes, I am intending that Damian, Osric and I should stay at the Tabard. It could hardly be more convenient. But I would like Damian to explore London a little – see Westminster Hall, the abbey, St. Paul's and so on. Had I not been away this past five years I should certainly have taken him to London by now. So here's the opportunity to catch up on those things I failed to do had I been a better father."

"So you admit that you have not been a good father, do you Sir Matthew?"

"To my shame Madame Eglentyne I have not been as attentive to my son as I should have liked – nor indeed to my dear, dead wife."

Madame Eglentyne gave a sigh implicit with condemnation. Trying to retrieve my reputation somewhat I said rather lamely."I would not say that I have been a bad father or husband – I never set out intentionally to harm, pain, offend or upset Matilda or Damian, But my attention was often elsewhere. That is why I am trying to make amends now."

"I am sure that is most commendable of you," she replied in a raw cutting way. This was not the charming prioress of the previous evenings. But suddenly she shifted tone again.

"So, returning to London, Sir Matthew. It is possible then that you might have a little time free?"

"Yes, it could be so," I said in a confused way not wanting to alert her to my plans regarding the search for the Golden Charter but also troubled by my growing suspicion of our past connection.

"Good, well let me explain," she continued her voice now back to her normal light but firm timbre. "I have business to do in London – as I had business to do in Winchester. I have told you before we are a poor, out-of-the-way Priory, down-pressed in every way - as you can see for yourself this evening. And now is the time we must assert our rights and regain what has been stolen from us. So while I am in London I need to go to the palace of the bishop ...

"You mean the Bishop of Winchester? In Southwark?"

"That's right. And not only there but also, as you mention, possibly to the courts in Westminster Hall as well. We shall have to consider. But over the next few days I have a lot to do. I have a number of people to see. I have a number of people to persuade."

She paused to allow me to take all this in.

"Now, coming to London with me will be Avelina, of course, and Rector Lydezorde and dear Father Gregory assuming, that is, he has recovered and catches up with us – as I am sure he will."

"That sounds a fine tally of supporters."

"Up to a point," she said. "But it becomes complicated. I don't want to discuss with you now all that we want to achieve. But I certainly feel that we have a powerful and persuasive case. And we are even better armed, I think, than when we went to Winchester last week. But sometimes it takes more than a good legal argument to achieve justice. And that is where I thought you – and maybe your son as well – might be of some assistance."

"What in the courts?" I said rather defensively. "I am not sure that I am qualified for that."

"No, not so much in the courts, Sir Matthew. It's more a matter of moral support. Look, I'll come direct to the point. We are dealing with powerful men – a bishop, a prior of the Cathedral, maybe a duke. And a lot of self-serving sycophants around them. Personally I am not frightened by any of them. We have good arguments – legal arguments and we will, I am sure, have legal proofs too. But I know how the world works. If I go in with Avelina to argue my case they will be polite but I will not convince them. Even if Rector Lydezorde or Gregory were to come with me I am not sure that I would be able to secure any justice. We need a person of some substance and title – a warrior in the world - to be alongside us. Someone who would slightly intimidate them."

"If you don't mind me saying so, Lady Eglentyne, you are a strong personality. I am not sure you need any help from me."

"I'll take that as a compliment, Sir Matthew, but I'm afraid that without a champion of your substance beside me I don't think I will be taken entirely seriously. It is unfair, it is unequal, it is unchristian. But it is the harsh truth of the time. It might be different in the future but for now I have to be realistic and play them at their own game. We have to show that we mean business and will not be intimidated into silence. And, in any case, I think that you owe it to me to offer help in this case."

This surprised me for I could not see what she was referring to - but it would have been ungracious to challenge her over the claim.

"So you want me to be what you called a 'warrior' do you?" I asked. "I am still not sure that I understand."

"You are correct, Sir Matthew. I want you to stand with us and demonstrate some bravery. After all, I gather that you might well be joining the Duke of Lancaster's household shortly. He is the force in the land right now. I think that having you on our side might well tip the case in our favour when it comes to exercising our lawful rights – especially as you have not joined the Duke quite yet. It means that you can still be seen as a well-connected but an independent figure. Of course, you will need a new set of clothes and get out of that absurdly dirty tunic – but that can be arranged."

"So you have been speaking with the Franklin about me have you?" I asked with irritation at the thought of her poking her fine nose into my affairs.

"I overheard your conversation at the abbot's table. You were not keeping it very secret."

I was unhappy to hear this. I had given little further thought to the Franklin's invitation. I really did not want half the county to be speculating about my future.

"Of course I am sympathetic to you, Madame Eglentyne. And if you feel that the priory has been cheated then you have my support."

"So in that case, you will assist us," she firmly.

Once again, I felt, I was being manoeuvred into an un-looked-for responsibility. As at Hyde the presumption seemed to be that, as a former crusader, I was available for taking on any righteous cause. But, once more, how could I decline? After all, it would be ungentlemanly to do so.

"Well, yes, I am happy to do what I can," I said with some resignation.

"Excellent! Excellent! So we shall talk again – in detail – at the Tabard on the day after tomorrow. I shall know more by then – just a little more but of crucial significance. So let's drink to that."

And drink to it we did. All five of us. Everyone else seemed to know what was going on. But what was I letting myself in for?

CHAPTER 43
'Wel ouȝhte I of swich murmur taken hede'

I left early the following morning for Guildford feeling that I'd had my fill of Madame Eglentyne and her bevy of attendants. I needed some time and space on my own before meeting up with them again in London.

So as I departed Wintney I suppressed the apprehension that once in Southwark I would be constantly at Madame Eglentyne's beck and call. I resolved that I would attend her, as agreed, at the Bishop's Palace and Westminster but nothing further.

Instead, I was curious to see what London was like after all these years away. My last visit was in the dying days of the old King when his administration was racked by controversy and under the influence of the king's mistress. Now it was in the hands of a stripling younger than Damian and steered by an unpopular Archbishop. Would that be any better?

The ride across the gently rolling flatlands to Guildford was good for my spirits. It also gave me an opportunity to return to the continuing puzzle of the stolen Golden Charter.

All my instincts were that the mystery could be unlocked over the next few days in London. This was based – as I had to admit - on the merest of intuitions. My notion was that because the charter had been given by the Saxon King, Edgar, then any dispute about it would have to go back to the King's courts – otherwise new interpretations could not be enforced.

Added to which King Edgar had been working hand in glove with the Bishop of Winchester at the time – whose successor was now also in London. So if the charter was to be called in evidence in any way then it would be in the courts of the capital.

Peculiarly it was the absence of Damian which gave me the peace and quiet to think this all through. But how I would miss him when he was gone! The lad was bursting with energy, good spirits and, no doubt, lust. But he now needed to build on that base to enter the wider world without me to inhibit him.

I was jolted out of these paternal reflections as I entered the village of Ash and saw for myself for the first time directly the brewing storm of revolt that Osric and Rector Lydezorde had described.

A small group of officials was outside the church and had clearly been trying to herd together the whole of the little community. As I rode up I heard shouting between a rather paunchy, well-dressed man and a miserably thin woman. "Where's your husband," he kept on saying. "I know he's around somewhere. Hiding in that cart is he?"

With obvious bitterness she replied, "I told you, he died before Christmas. He's with Christ and safe from devils like yourselves. Have you no conscience bullying a woman old enough to be your mother? You just want to tax us, don't you? Tax us until we all die. And who are you going to tax then? Start taxing the friars and the monks, that's what I say."

This was greeted with claps and whoops by the surrounding villagers, presumably her neighbours. The officials made some sort of scoffing reply which I could not hear but tension was clearly mounting on both sides. And as other members of the crowd became drawn into the row, pushing and shoving the officers with some vigour, I foresaw it tipping into violence. While I had some sympathy for the impoverished woman I feared that if her anger led to injury to the officers then there would be severe consequences before too long.

Deciding this was one fight I should probably avoid I kicked my horse into a trot to move quickly down the road. But it had been an unnerving experience. If emotions could be raised so high in this tiny village among people who were normally resigned to their lot. then what was it going to be like in the larger towns – let alone London itself?

Arriving in prosperous Guildford, however, it all seemed busily normal. Maybe the resentment against these new taxes was confined to the rural poor? Putting my concerns aside I made my way to the Angel Inn in the High Street, a place I used to know well.

Inevitably it was all changed. The landlord showed no sign of recognising me and maybe even looked askance at my less-than-fashionable, tarnished and stained garb. But I persevered and he acknowledged that yes, Damian and Osric had been guests overnight and that he believed that they were even now in the stables attending to their horses.

"Hello, father – welcome to the Angel!" shouted Damian warmly as I entered the barn. "How was your journey?"

"Good," I said, "apart from a minor disturbance which I saw at Ash but I'll tell you about it later. And you?"

"Very good – wasn't it, Osric?"

"It was very good indeed, lord," Osric replied giving a big smile. They had clearly been having a high old time in my absence.

"Soon after we separated from you, father, we caught up with with the lawyer, the Franklin and the doctor. They were very welcoming and we had an enjoyable journey from then on. They were telling stories and joking and the road passed very quickly. Then, when we got here, they were very kind. The landlord was a bit reluctant to let us all stay – the inn is very full - but the Franklin pulled his rank and got us a room and then entertained us royally until late last night."

"Oh, well I'm very glad to hear that. And are they still here?"

"I wouldn't be surprised if the Franklin was still eating," said Damian. "He's a terrific gourmet. I've never known anyone who knew so much about food and how it should be cooked and what sauces went with which meats. It was extraordinary – he actually went into the kitchen at one point and showed one of the cooks how to make a sauce - more 'zesty' as he put it."

"I suspect that he would not be very interested in my views on food then," I said. "Even on the highest tables I tended to go for the plainest choice. Better for my digestion, I thought."

"Don't worry, father - they were eager to meet up with you again and said that they would delay their departure until you arrived. So we're going to be a nice little party on the road to Southwark."

I wasn't sure whether to be flattered or suspicious of their enthusiasm to see me. For Sir Roger in particular it might just be another opportunity to persuade me to throw my lot in with the Duke of Lancaster. But maybe I could pick the brains of the lawyer on matters connected with the lost charter. And as for the doctor, well I was sure that there was plenty I could learn from him.

But I could hardly have guessed just how revealing it would be.

CHAPTER 44
'And forth we riden'

We set off in pairs from the Angel and I made sure that I was alongside the doctor.

"I understand that you were generous to Damian last evening, Doctor Nafis – it's much appreciated."

"Well, it was more Sir Roger than me, Sir Matthew. Personally I am rather careful about what I eat…and what I pay for."

"Likewise," I responded.

Doctor Nafis smiled and continued. "But Roger, appears to be a born *bon viveur*. And he likes sharing - and your son and your servant seemed happy to enjoy his hospitality. They were appreciative guests. But Damian's a very capable young man, Sir Matthew, you can be proud of him – although I gained the impression that he had missed you whilst you were away for, what was it, five years?"

"I am afraid it was, Doctor," I said apologetically. "Five years which I now look back on with regret. Which is why I am now trying to make it up to him, helping him to make something of himself in the world. He's capable but he needs further opportunities."

"The opportunity of war, you mean?"

It was a good question. How many fathers have despatched their sons to the battlefield in expectation of a glorious victory and have witnessed their entombment instead.

"Have you ever fought yourself, Doctor?" I asked.

"No, not in the sense of being a warrior although, as you mighty have guessed, my parents come from Africa and I have spent some time there studying. That was when I observed violence at first hand. But only a little and that was more than enough for me. As the wise man says, no man living in times of peace can imagine war."

"Yes, I suspect that's true. But even then, until you have killed your first enemy, face-to-face, it all seems rather unreal."

He looked at me strangely but also with a kind of reluctant respect. That embarrassed me. I had not intended to talk of war or warfare. But I was intrigued by the doctor. He saw people in distress and observed death no doubt every week.

"How do you cope with seeing pain in others, Doctor?" I asked.

"In what sense?"

"I mean your patients."

"I ignore the pain, Sir Matthew. I only look for the cure."

"But how do you cope with corpses, sometimes bloody I am sure?" I felt compelled to ask. "I was used to seeing them on the battlefield and had no remorse. But now I am older I think I am finding it more difficult. I realised that when I saw the bodies of Peter and Walter. I was surprised how shocking I found them. Much more than I had expected."

"When the spirit has departed the body I lose interest entirely, Sir Matthew. That is a matter for priests and those who read the bible. We are told that they will rise again – but that is the work of someone else." He pointed up to heaven, "It's not my responsibility."

"Nonetheless, if you don't mind me asking Doctor Nafis, have you had any further thoughts about the death of Brother Walter? Any ideas of who might be behind it. I ask purely out of personal curiosity."

"That is now a matter for Father Compton, Sir Matthew. I have no further thoughts on the matter."

He seemed to want to close down the subject but there was one point I had to clear up.

"Just one final question, though, and I am sorry to bring it up. The fact that there was so little blood around those mutilations. Walter and Peter alike. Did that strike you as odd? Could it have meant that they were actually inflicted quite a long time after death?"

Doctor Nafis paused, obviously wanting to change the subject. "Who can tell, Sir Matthew. There is still so much about the body we do not know or, more important, understand. We need more discoveries – that's all I can say. But, of course, there are limits to what we as physicians are allowed to investigate. Sadly."

I nodded and we jogged on for a little in silence. The he turned to me.

"Sir Matthew, now let me ask you some questions."

"Certainly – go ahead."

"I understand that you stayed last night at Wintney. Were you well-entertained by Madame Eglentyne?"

"Hmm, it was certainly excellent hospitality – maybe a little better than I expected when I first arrived. I was a little surprised by how ..." I searched for the right word,"modest Wintney is."

"Well, maybe there is a little more wealth there than you might have seen, Sir Matthew. The lovely Prioress is quite good at concealing what she does not want the world to see."

"You know her well, then, I imagine? You pay weekly visits don't you?"

"I did."

"You mean they've stopped?"

"I am afraid so. No one is indispensable and Madame Eglentyne has decided that she wants someone else to attend on her – and her community,"

"So are you disappointed?"

"A doctor is always disappointed to lose a patient, Sir Matthew in whatever the circumstances."

"Do you know why she's changing to someone else? I imagine that you were exceptionally valuable to her – especially coming up to such a rather out-of-the way place?"

"It's a rather painful subject and delicate, Sir Matthew. All I can say is that some people get bored. They want something new or different. But tell me, last evening, was the Rector Lydezorde there – at dinner with you?"

"Yes, he was actually. He seemed pleasant enough. He obviously has a good relationship with the prioress – as a confessor, I mean."

There was no response so, tactlessly, I returned to the matter of the Doctor's breach with Madame Eglentyne.

"And this dismissal – it just happened recently did it?" I asked a little too insistently and immediately realised my mistake.

"Yes," he said coldly. "I told you – I do not want to talk about it."

And then he kicked his horse on so as to join Damian and Osric riding a little way ahead. Damian turned towards him and

263

immediately, it seemed, they fell into more merry chat.

Maybe I had something to learn from my son, I reflected. My intention was always to be respectful and make people feel comfortable but too often I seemed to produce the opposite effect. Having set off this morning with a light heart I was now feeling out-of-sorts with everything. How could I have been so insensitive in pursuing my inquiries?

For some time I rode on mulling over my failures and errors. Behind me I could hear Sergeant Henry and Sir Roger chatting away earnestly. I could not quite hear what they were talking about but every now and then the Franklin seemed to say with special emphasis 'The Duke thinks this……The Duke said that ..' and then, most powerfully 'The Duke's plans are…." But I never caught the detail of anything.

As we approached Leatherhead, however, they spurred their horses on and caught up with me.

"We were much impressed by Damian last night, Sir Matthew," said the Franklin. "He's a fine young man-in-the-making – and I can see a fine soldier too. So I hope that you have given some further thought to my offer on behalf of the Duke of Lancaster, I am sure that the Duke would be delighted to have the de Somborne family as part of his extended family."

"Again, I am grateful for the kind offer, Sir Roger," I replied with as much patience as I could muster. "And I have to admit that Damian is very interested. He was very grateful and impressed by your friendship last night. But I think we need to complete this pilgrimage before we make any decision. I do hope that is not a problem?"

"Of course, it is not a problem, Sir Matthew. But I have to say that it is an inconvenience. Tensions are mounting, I think, by the day. John of Gaunt, Duke of Lancaster is one of the few rocks of stability in the kingdom. He needs to know who his friends are. And he will be very generous to those friends. But those who are not his friends – those who have other allegiances, shall we say - might find that they are friendless at a time when that is a dangerous status to hold."

264

I realised now that I was in a serious conversation with someone I should not want to offend. But why could they not allow me go peacefully down my own way? Was John of Gaunt becoming so desperate to secure his position against his nephew that he had to turn even to people like me?

"When you say 'other allegiances' Sir Roger I am not quite sure who you mean. Are you referring to France or Scotland?" I asked.

"Not France or Scotland, Sir Roger," was the laughing response. "No something much more insidious – the enemy within who is working away to undermine the kingdom for their own power and enrichment."

"Who have you in mind exactly?" I asked in a tone that implied I thought that this was a somewhat far-fetched assertion.

"The church, Sir Matthew, the church. These bishops – you must see that. I mean look at the Bishop of Winchester – wealth beyond compare and now intending to put more even more of its money – by which I mean your money and my money - into schools and colleges. Meanwhile gentlemen like you and hundreds of others across the land are getting poorer every day and facing higher demands from the riff-raff of the peasantry. It cannot be allowed to continue. You must see that."

"So what does the Duke want to do?"

"The Duke wants to rein them in, these ambitious bishops, trim their wings – above all, make them pay their way. Stop these self-regarding clerics from milking the rest of the country. Stop them telling the rest of us what to do while they take their commands from Rome. Let them continue with their prayers by all means. But take back control of the land and return it to the people who gave it to them in the first place. People like your ancestors, for example. I am sure that your great-great grandfather, generations back, gave many hydes of land to Mottisfont, Romsey or Wherwell. It's time they handed it back! And then let royal power be exercised by royalty and nobility, the people born to rule – not by jumped up little nobodies from nowhere like Wykeham and Sudbury. They are the ones responsible for the mess we are in now."

Sergeant Henry had been listening to all this but with no apparent indication of either support or dissent. I assumed that, given his friendship with the Franklin, he had heard it all before.

"So Sergeant Henry, if I might ask, where do you stand on this? After all, are you not acting for the church"

"Dear Sir Matthew, I am a lawyer. You must know that I cannot talk about my clients' affairs. I act for my clients but I act according to the law. If the law changes then I will act according to that."

"But you have your own views, surely?"

"Indeed, Sir Matthew, I have my own views and for that reason I keep them to myself. I might be acting for a bishop today – but tomorrow I might be acting against them. Either way it is not personal. I leave politics to the politicians like good Sir Roger here. Meanwhile I stick to the firm ground of the law."

"Well that sounds a very balanced approach, Sergeant Henry," I said. "I would hope that I too could also occupy such, shall we say, neutral ground."

"I'm afraid your life cannot be as easy as that, Sir Matthew," said the Franklin with some passion. "You're not a lawyer – you're a great man in your little part of Hampshire. You could join me in Parliament. You should be a knight of the shire. People want to look up to people like you and see leadership on behalf of the Duke in that great stretch of country between Winchester and Salisbury. Do you want to abandon your friends and neighbours and leave them all to be ground underfoot by Wykeham? How could your conscience allow you to do that – to stand aside and see the place be squeezed dry by their greed when there is an alternative?"

He stopped. He had said his piece. His long white beard was starting to ooze spittle. "Anyway, that's enough. But think on't, Sir Matthew. Talk to your son. And we'll speak again in London."

He jabbed the flanks of his horse into a trot and joined the advance party with Osric, Damian and the doctor. So there were now two people I had seemingly offended or frustrated. How would I get on with the lawyer?

CHAPTER 45

'In Southwark, at this gentil hostelrye'

"I wouldn't get too concerned about my friend Roger," said the Sergeant reassuringly. "He's very passionate. He deeply believes what he says, he's a great admirer of the Duke. He probably does believe in his heart of hearts that Gaunt should be king. But, he's getting a little bit carried away. Anyway, Gaunt would not go that far. He does not want to usurp his brother's son's crown. But this year, I think, will be difficult. And then things will get back to normal. At least for the time being. The one I would look out for is young Bolingbroke. I wonder where he will be twenty years hence?"

"You mean the Duke's son?"

"Yes, that's the one. But by the time he's old enough to strike you and I, my friend, we'll be too old to care. Not least because we will probably be dead."

"Hmm," I said non-committally.

"What I did want to speak to you about though, Sir Matthew, was these two sordid little murders."

"You're supposed to be advising the Prior and Father Compton on them aren't you?"

"I am indeed. But as you probably appreciated there is little likelihood of identifying the culprits. The Prior, the monks, they want to make a gesture but, really, it will come to nothing. Who really knows what was going on there – I mean behind the scenes? Between you and me they are an odd lot, these monks at Hyde. You've probably noticed that yourself. Anyway, I had agreed that I would meet Father Eynesham, our cellarer friend, at the Tabard to discuss it. He's been nominated as the go-between and he'll give his account in due course to the abbey and the prior. But I want to give him something to report back on. Which is difficult because frankly, I've got nothing to say. So I am cheating I'm afraid – but then good lawyers do. I just wanted to know whether you have had any further thoughts which I might pass on."

I laughed to myself at this request. What a game the whole thing was. All I could offer was my own confused guess-work.

"No new insights, I'm afraid, Sergeant. But if I were still involved I would be trying to find out about those two low-life characters. They were the ones supposed to be a priest and a ploughman – although that didn't seem very likely to me. They kept on popping up all the time. They even seemed to be in Basyng yesterday with Mistress Alison. But they are a puzzle – sometimes they are dressed one way, sometimes another so that I am still not sure whether there are two of them or four of them! Maybe you should speak to Mistress Alison about them when we get to London. Aside from that I've nothing to suggest."

"Yes, I think I know the couple you mean. Odd certainly. Anyway, I'll mention it to Eynesham. It won't be the first time a murder's happened there which has gone unsolved. Nor, I suspect the last. The sooner that I can forget about it the better."

"So you're still going on to Canterbury are you?" I asked.

"Yes, in a couple of days – along with you I expect. But I've got to be in court tomorrow."

"Church business?" I asked.

"Yes, as it happens."

"But you'll be staying in the Tabard?"

"Yes, it's easier for a couple of days. Otherwise I have to travel out to Stratford."

"Oh Stratford-at-Bowe?"

"You know it?" he asked.

"I don't but I believe that Madame Eglentyne has a connection with it?"

"Yes, that's right. I know the convent there. Living in the area I do some work for them. And that's how I became involved in acting for Wintney. They recommended me to her. And, as you know, one thing leads to another. Father Gregory comes from there too. So sad about the way he was beaten up in the abbey. Shocking behaviour, don't you think?"

I had to agree although I was still not sure quite how badly he had actually suffered. But who was I to deny his pain?

By now we were getting a sense that London was looming up ahead of us. The roads were getting busier and people seemed to have a greater sense of urgency. There were also more gentry to be seen. But along with that there were further scenes of growing alarm and anger about the new taxes. Ordinary folk, instead of being at work, were gathering in groups and there was shouting about the evils of the people around the king. Again and again I heard chants of ' Sudbury Sucks' and 'Lock him Up'.

"Do you know where the Tabard actually is?" I asked. "I know it's on the Southwark side but I am not quite clear where exactly."

"It's perfectly situated for us pilgrims," explained the Serjeant, "It's just where this road arrives before going over London Bridge – and that's also where the road to Canterbury begins."

"Until recently I hadn't realised that the abbot of Hyde had such a place," I said.

"Yes, not many people do. It's a peculiar arrangement. I was told that the abbot at the time - more than a lifetime ago – had ambitions to keep up with the Bishop whose palace is just down the river. Anyway, there's a nice mansion at the back of the site away from the road and that's where the abbot stays when he's in London. And at the front, on the roadside, there's the inn. It's quite spacious and food's good, I understand - although actually I've never stayed there. It will be a first time for me too."

We trotted on and eventually arrived in the midst of Southwark in all its dissolute squalor. It might boast an abbot's mansion and a Bishop's Palace but all the roguery from London seemed to have drifted down there. Most prominent was a gang of shameless friars who seemed to have taken up with a handful of Winchester Geese plying their trade outside the Tabard itself. For all I knew maybe these friars were offering similar services to those who had exotic sexual interests. Mixed in with them were the odds and ends of clerical hangers-on, the pardoners, the summoners plus the odd radical priest shouting the odds about corruption in the church. They were all as bad as each other. Everyone it seemed was out to dupe or steal from everyone else, and mostly in the name of the Almighty.

"If I had known that it was going to be like this I would not have agreed to stay here," I said to the Sergeant.

"Well, I've passed through the area many times and it's pretty much what I am used to," he said. "It's all down to the Bishop of course. This is his manor and William Wykeham loves being able to take a cut of everything that goes on here. Meanwhile, he sits in that palace of his and cultivates this image of purity through his links with Oxford and talking about the importance of good manners and learning. But that's the way the world is Sir Matthew. You must have seen it yourself."

"Yes, but it's different when it's your own country – and more to the point, as you say, my own Bishop who is in charge of it all," I said in a rather bad tempered way. "Anyway, let's go in."

Whatever the squalor outside on the street, The Tabard was a different world entirely. The rooms and stables were wide and there were a couple of decent, upstanding men on the door to keep out the beggars and the drunkards. And then a kind of comfortable peace descended as we moved into the main reception room.

Master Roger took the lead and was given a warm greeting by the landlord, a man named Harry Bailey. They hugged each other like old friends, clapping each other on the back and exchanging fond greetings. I then heard Bailey say that Father Eynesham had arrived earlier and warned him that there would be a big party from Winchester. So guest rooms had been reserved in advance for a few of us in the abbot's mansion which lay across on the other side of a large lawn from the inn itself. It was a wise move because with good weather the pilgrimage season was now under way and plenty of people of all types were arriving. Meanwhile, Father Eynesham had retired to his room in the abbot's mansion leaving invitations for us to join him for supper

At this point I rejoined Damian and Osric with whom I had not spoken since we had left Guildford. They were in a little world of their own, quite different from mine. Damian had obviously been given the full treatment by Master Roger and was keener than ever to accept the offer of signing on with the Duke of Lancaster. I did not disagree but batted it away saying we would decide after we had got to Canterbury. I then switched the subject to advise him that Lady Eglentyne and her party would probably arrive before the end of the afternoon and that it would be a good idea to steer clear of them. "Probably better for you and Osric to sample the delights of Southwark," I suggested - albeit against my better instincts.

"Here's something that might be of interest to you, lord," said Osric before they went out. "The doctor opened up to me a bit – it was after he'd been talking to you. He was digging to find out whether you had found out anything new about Brother Walter's death. He seemed to think that you might have learned something from your stay at Wintney. He wasn't precise about anything but he was definitely worried, I'd say."

"And he only spoke to you about it, is that right? Not Damian?"

"Yes, he seemed to be a bit more relaxed with me, lord to be honest. But he definitely seemed to be making some kind of connection between Brother Walter and Madame Eglentyne."

"Well, well, that's interesting," I said trying to puzzle over its possible significance. "Alright then off you two go. Don't get mugged, steer clear of cut-purses, don't get into any theological debates with scruffy looking priests – and try to avoid getting the clap," I said pointedly to Osric.

"It's not me you should be telling," he said defensively.

"I'm hoping this other one is still too much in love to go down that alley," I said patting Damian on the cheek.

I was just turning away to head towards the mansion when to my surprise Madame Eglentyne walked through the door accompanied by John and the Rector and with Sister Avelina a little behind. They had obviously made fast progress on the road and I gave them as friendly a welcoming wave as I could manage. "Come on, Damian," I said as I walked past him towards Madame Eglentyne. "Try and give them a greeting. You too Osric."

Madame Eglentyne acknowledged me with a polite smile but my eye was on John and how he reacted to Damian. It really would be too tedious if the two boys were going to be in a state of hostility for the whole time we were together. Somehow, I thought, we might have to keep them separate from each other.

But while Damian was trying to restrain a scowl John was remarkably, unaccountably, warm in his approach. He gave both Osric and me a salute and then turned to Damian.

"I am very sorry, Damian – I apologise for being so irritating. It was unconscionable what I said to you and I feel that I let us all down."

Not for the first time it was clear John was capable of turning on the charm when it suited him and, for whatever reason, he now wanted to build a bridge to Damian. I did not trust him for a moment but it would be slightly better than having the two lads growling at each other all the time.

Before I had a chance to say anything Madame Eglentyne stepped in and said, "I think that you two young men ought to go off for an evening by yourselves and get to know each other a bit better – and here are a couple of groats to lubricate your introduction to London."

I was relieved that Damian did not remain aloof to the invitation. An olive branch had been held out and, gratifyingly, he took it – I am not sure that I would have done the same at his age. So they agreed to meet up and go out in the early evening. But I still could not get the measure of John's transformed manner.

Meanwhile Sir Roger appeared and hailed everyone saying that he was delighted that all had arrived safely in London and carefully inviting selected people to have a drink with him. It was only by the end of the evening that I would understand why.

CHAPTER 46
'A manly man, to been an abbot able'

The six guest rooms in the Abbot's House were markedly more comfortable than the travellers' room in the Tabard Inn allocated to Damian and Osric. I should have felt guilty that the two of them were having to share a space of modest proportions while I had a generous bed and easy seating together with the view of the garden. But sometimes the devil cannot be resisted and I collapsed into gentle sleep stretching out luxuriously in anticipation of a good supper.

That said, I was under no illusions that tonight I had to bring to a head questions which had been troubling me throughout the journey from Winchester. If the theft of the charter - and the related mystery of the murders - were to be resolved then I had to start unmasking them now.

Above all I needed Father Eynesham to come out from behind his veneer of urbanity to be honest about what was happening in the monastery. As the senior monk present from Hyde he would be our host this evening and no doubt intent on turning on the charm. So after my refreshing sleep I made my way, earlier than invited, to the Abbot's private Dining Room in the hope that he might already be there.

My instinct was right. As cellarer he was sampling the wines and giving instructions to the lay servants in the kitchen. Although we had seen each other regularly over the last few days this was my first opportunity to speak to him in private since I had declared my opinion on John's innocence of Brother Peter's murder. He was polite but, unsurprisingly, cool.

"Father Eynesham, thank you so much for allowing me to stay here in the abbot's private quarters," I said, once the servants had departed. "It really is delightful having some peace and quiet and yet being so close to the City with all its excitement."

"Indeed, the property acquisition made by our predecessors all those years ago has certainly paid off," he agreed with his focus still on the wine.

"It just shows the importance of having abbots with good sense and foresight, I suppose – a bit of worldly wisdom too," I said.

"Well, you're certainly right there," he replied in between sips. "Do excuse me while I find exactly the right wine for this evening."

"Of course," I said. "Do take your time – I am glad to be the beneficiary of your skills and taste."

He grunted as as he gargled. After a little while though I could not hold back.

"So who will be the next abbot of Hyde, do you think?" I asked trying to sound as casual as possible. "Presumably it has to be resolved fairly soon?"

"Not for me to say, not at all," he responded having put down his glass and looked at me sharply. I noticed also that he had begun to colour very slightly.

"The reason I ask," I persevered, "is that it seems clear to me that Father Compton, for all his qualities, is not up to the job and, even more important, that he does not want it. I am sorry for being so frank with you but that's the way I see it."

"Yes, Sir Matthew – well, I suspect that Father Compton himself would rather agree with you."

"But, if you don't mind me saying so, Father Eynesham, I have a suspicion that you do want the job – but maybe not quite yet."

"What on earth makes you think that?" he asked, now blushing obviously.

"I think it would be apparent to anybody," I said baldly. "You are just biding your time."

Had I been too aggressive? Maybe. But rather than being offended he just seemed stumped for a reply. I had confronted him and unsettled him. Now, I thought, was the time to strike.

"I've got something else on my mind," I went on. "Sorry not to give you warning but can you tell me how it was that you arrived so quickly on the scene of Brother Peter's death. Some

274

observers might think it was almost as if you were expecting it – or even willing it?"

He could have dismissed the question entirely. It was no longer my business. I would have understood if he had instructed me to leave the dining room and never darken the doors of the Tabard ever again. But again he was silent. I had scored a hit. I could see him suffer a kind of internal collapse. He then sighed deeply as if wanting, finally, to get something off his chest. Maybe being away from the abbey gave him licence to be honest.

"No, Sir Matthew, I did not 'will it' as you put it. I didn't want poor Peter to be hurt at all – let alone be killed. That was the last thing I wanted. "

"But you wanted something?"

"Yes, indeed I did," he sighed. "But it all went terribly wrong."

"So do you want to tell me about it?" I asked as gently as I could. "Of course, you are under no obligation whatsoever to tell me. You have your own confessor."

It was the word confessor that finally got him. For all his bravado and breaching of the rules of St Benedict there was still, at root, a sense of responsibility to his faith.

"Yes, you're right," he replied with resignation. "I might as well tell you before I speak with my confessor – huh, it will help me get my story straight."

"Before God?"

"That, I rather think will be a matter for the Last Judgement."

"But you were involved in some way with the murder?" I resumed.

"Absolutely yes – and absolutely not," he said.

"You are not making sense, I am afraid. A simple explanation would probably be best – maybe even to God."

"Unfortunately, the simple explanation is not so simple, Sir Matthew. But as you have asked, here is the state of matters. As cellarer, as you know, I am responsible – among many other things – for dispensing wine to the brothers. The Rule of St. Benedict states clearly that half a pint a day of wine should be

275

sufficient for all – although the saint also says that 'Wine leads even wise men into infidelity.' But as cellarer I had some discretion and because I knew Brother Peter had a fondness for wine I often allowed him more than his usual quota. And on that particular day at lunch I allowed him a lot, lot more. Far more than I should have done."

"So was this out of generosity to him?" I asked, genuinely puzzled. "Surely the rule means you should restrict him?"

"Of course you are right but…Oh well! It might as well all come out now. After all, a dreadful death has resulted."

He composed himself before resuming

"For quite a long time now I have been breaking the rules in the monastery – this rule and many others."

"I see," I said, not entirely surprised. "But why?"

Again he heaved a sigh.

"Because…because… the Prior told me to."

"You mean Prior Hugh?"

"Yes, Prior Hugh at St. Swithun's at the cathedral."

"But why?" I asked again.

"Very simply because the Prior wanted Hyde Abbey to become a scene of scandal – not a very big scandal and certainly not murders – but enough disorder and laxity and rule breaking to justify the cathedral moving in and assuming control of everything – including, I have to say, its income."

"And that was why Brother Thomas was there alongside the acting abbot?"

"Ah yes, the delightful Brother Thomas! That was a first step. His job was to be the eyes and ears of Prior Hugh within the abbey. He was there to help undermine it but not so badly as the whole community would collapse – just badly enough to warrant it being taken over."

"And allocating Brother Peter more wine than he could handle was part of that plot?"

"It was a small part of the bigger picture, I am afraid. One cracked stone in a fractured mosaic. It meant that the library would become chaotic and then word would gradually creep out that this was typical of Hyde's failings. But there were plenty of other things as well. Such as Michael on the inner door being effectively the porter for a brothel. Did you discover that? It was all part of the same plan for gradually disgracing the place."

"And you were happy being part of that were you?" I said beginning to feel angry. "Betraying your own monastery – letting down your brothers. How could you justify that to yourself morally?"

"I wasn't happy about it," he said defensively. "But, yes, I went along with it because I knew that Hyde was broken and it needed something better – it had to be dissolved first before it could be restored comprehensively. And, in any case, it has been coming for the past thirty years."

"You mean since the pestilence?"

"Yes, it has never recovered. The men who died then were the cream – those who went out visiting and supporting the poor and the sick. I knew them. I respected them But once they were gone we never replaced their kind. It was mostly people like me – people out for an easy life of bed and board and a few luxuries to boot. So I realised deep in my conscience that Hyde, in its own interests, needed to be taken under the wing of the people over at the cathedral. And then allow the likes of me to gradually die out and be replaced by something better."

He sounded just about plausible. Lazy and self-serving but not outright evil. There were plenty of those about. But I also needed to be careful not to abrogate to myself some kind of moral authority. After all, given my history, who was I to judge?

"So these two murders will speed up what they had already planned," I said.

"No, no, Sir Matthew. There was no plan for any murders. That would be a terrible sin. I honestly have no idea who was responsible for the murders. You have to believe me on that. I really do not know. I cannot even imagine who might have done it."

"But maybe the conditions you created in the abbey led to these murders?"

"Yes, sadly, that might have been the case. But I am mystified how it has come to this."

"Nonetheless, presumably it gives the Cathedral or the Prior exactly the excuse they need to move in and take over – and put in a new abbot who will do their bidding?"

"That's it."

"So who will be the next abbot?" I asked. "You?"

"Yes, I think that is probably so," he said with a strange mix of resignation and satisfaction.

"So the understanding is that you will be appointed abbot - and allowed to enjoy your life of hunting and so on - but the real authority would rest with the Prior and other people at the cathedral. I suppose ultimately Bishop William."

"That's right. Father Compton probably appreciates that too. He's just waiting for the moment for it to happen. I'll be abbot by Christmas I reckon," he said, before adding wryly. "You must come back and enjoy our Christmas feast."

"Well, thanks for the offer – I'll think about it," I said trying to dampen the sarcasm in my voice. "But meanwhile do you want to have these murders solved?"

He hesitated for a moment. In the end he brought it out.

"Well, I cannot let the death of two of my brothers go neglected, can I?" he said. "The truth is, however, that while the prior has taken over the investigation I am not sure he is particularly concerned about producing a culprit. He would probably say that this kind of episode was to be expected after years of poor leadership at Hyde."

This was the cynicism I could no longer tolerate. I had seen enough of it among the Crusade commanders. I was not going to stand for it in my own homeland.

"Well, if the prior is not going to do anything serious about it then the moral responsibility comes back to me," I said forcibly. "So let's go back, what was special about that particular day?"

He gave another long sigh – a sigh from someone who was not normally given to so much soul-searching.

"As I explained, I knew that I had overdone it at lunch with Brother Peter. I had given him far too much to drink. In church I could see him swaying around, clearly very inebriated. And then suddenly he just disappeared – he just staggered off outside. I thought he might return but after a little time he hadn't come back and so I thought I should go out and see that he wasn't up to anything too dangerous."

"Such as what?"

"Burning the library down for a start. That would be a disaster too far."

"So what did you do?"

"I went into the cloisters - and then you know what happened next. A cowled figure coming very quickly out of the door and there was Peter on the floor – and my instinct at once was that he was dead."

"And why were you so sure that the cowled figure – John – was responsible?"

"It was a natural assumption, I think. Somebody running off like that in a panic. Furious to escape. I couldn't recognise him as John. But also I must admit I was feeling guilty. If I hadn't – deliberately – made Peter drunk he would not have left the church and probably not died as a result. So I was looking for someone to blame."

"And did you see anyone else in the area. On the stairs. Or just at the entrance to the cloisters?"

"I think I did see someone else – or rather two people. But I was focused on John so did not pay them much attention."

"Did you recognise them?"

"As I say, I was running and only focused on John's back. So, as I passed them, one was just a flash really but the other might have been in clerical dress. He was wearing some kind of long cloak. But I didn't have time to look."

"Father Gregory might it have been?" I offered. "Madame

Eglentyne's priest?"

"Yes, possibly, I suppose. Good looking young man. But then I did not see this man's face. And maybe a bit smaller than Father Gregory. But hard to tell."

"But you would recognise Father Gregory? People say he's very pious."

"Do they?" said Father Eynesham. "Well, it might have been him – but I could not swear to it. I was focused on the escaping figure of John. Oh, I think I hear our other guests coming."

He pulled himself together, resumed his normal beaming smile.

"Will you excuse me?" he said. "I think that I have already said more than enough already."

"But," he then added, "you can congratulate yourself – you would make a good father confessor."

CHAPTER 47
'To speke of phisik and of surgerye'

Father Eynesham's hospitality could not be faulted for its generosity. As he explained, when in London he tried to measure up to service in the Great Hall of the Bishop of Winchester's palace, half a mile away in the Liberty of the Clink.

"Of course, we do not compete on scale with the Bishop but we excel on quality," he declared as he finally poured the Bordeaux whose bouquet he had been enjoying earlier.

But the conversation was laboured. We were all tired from the journey and some of us had other important preoccupations. Madame Eglentyne had excused herself thereby making it an all-male event. Alongside me there was the doctor, the Franklin, the Sergeant and Father Eynesham himself, confined around the table trying to make lame conversation. After dining together for three nights in a row in Hyde the atmosphere was flat and stale. Fortunately the excellence of the dishes gave us something else to think about.

Towards the end of the meal there was a knock on the door and Harry Bailey appeared. He was very jovial and briefly lifted the mood across the room. He was introduced to us all and it soon appeared that there was more to him than met the eye. It turned out that he knew the Franklin very well because they had served in Parliament together a couple of years earlier. Strictly speaking, of course, he was an employee of the abbey and a servant of Father Eynesham. But that was not how it seemed. From an odd remark or two he seemed to have his finger on the pulse of everything political and ecclesiastical in London and elsewhere. He seemed to know everyone, high and low alike, regardless of station. He was the abbey's eyes and ears in the capital.

"I gather that you're going to be the new abbot then Father Eynesham," he suddenly announced. "How are you feeling about that then?"

Eynesham looked distinctly uncomfortable. "Oh really, Harry, where did you get that from? Nonsense I assure you."

"That's not what they saying down at the Bishop's palace I can assure you, my friend. But they are also saying you've got to get on top of these murders – the Bishop doesn't like it – he doesn't like it at all."

"My, how quickly word gets round!" said Eynesham, now very unhappy.

"Well, you can't keep quiet about a murder – just not possible," said Harry. "Anyway that was just a word of advice. So I won't disturb you any longer – and I hope you enjoy your supper gentlemen." And off he went.

A very embarrassed silence descended and soon the Franklin said it was time he was off to bed. The rest of us followed suit and after expressing our thanks to Father Eynesham we each made our way towards our respective destinations.

I had agreed that before turning in I would meet up with Osric and Damian over in the Tabard's main hall but my path took me a little way with Doctor Nafis.

With wine loosening our tongues I felt that this was going to be the last opportunity I would have for a candid conversation with him. Having upset him earlier by my over-intrusive questioning about his breach with Wintney Priory I knew that I was taking a risk. But I was especially anxious to get his view on those mutilations of the two monks. He had avoided comment earlier in the day And if he wouldn't speak to me now then so be it. I would have lost nothing by asking.

"A rather dull evening, doctor, don't you think notwithstanding the excellent table?" I said. "Mind you, it makes a change not to have a murder announced to break up a sociable occasion."

"I suppose so but, for myself, I must tell you Sir Matthew that I am not feeling particularly sociable at the moment."

"Well I noticed that you were a little quiet this evening. Tired from the journey, I expect? And I am so sorry if I upset you in any way earlier today."

"Not your fault. I am just feeling a little, how shall I put it, melancholy. Inadvertently you touched a sore spot. But it will pass – probably."

I assumed that he was referring to his dismissal from Wintney Priory. But by the sound of things this was more than just a professional disappointment – maybe something more personal?

He was, I reflected, an odd mix. He seemed to have lots of money and be very busy and devoted to his profession. But he also seemed troubled.

I shifted my attention back to the murders.

"Excuse me, Doctor, but I must ask you something. I know it's getting late and I am sorry to come back to it. But I cannot forget these mutilations – to the monks, I mean. I remember that when we looked at Brother Peter's private parts, you said that whoever had done it was a very sick person. What did you mean by that?"

"These are very good questions, Sir Matthew. But we can't talk about them here – in the open. Come into my room."

That's a good sign, I thought. At least he was prepared to countenance discussing them.

"So you didn't guess?" he said as soon as we had crossed the threshold. "I thought that you must have done. Guilty conscience I suppose."

"What do you mean, I didn't guess?" I asked.

"Who was responsible for the mutilations."

"No, how could I have guessed?" I said.

"I thought it would be obvious – although I tried to cover it up."

"I'm sorry, I don't follow," I replied by now feeling very confused.

"It was me," the doctor said very forcefully. "I did it. Couldn't you see that?"

This was the first time in these strange few days that I was really, horribly shocked – indeed appalled.

"You! What on earth were you doing? Were they dead at the time."

"What do you mean – were they dead?" he said sharply. "Of

283

course, they were dead! It explains why there was no blood. What do you think I am – a murderer? " He said with a mockingly bitter laugh.

"So why on earth did you do it?"

"Very simple, Sir Matthew. That's why I thought a man of wide experience such as yourself would have realised. If I had known that you were going to investigate the murders in such depth I wouldn't have done it."

"You give me more credit than I am due, "I said. "Please explain."

"I am a doctor and I think a progressive one," he said with some professional pride.

"But what about all that emphasis on astronomy?" I asked almost scathingly.

"Oh that's all just for show," he said dismissively. "Sometimes, Sir Matthew, you have to blind the patients with science – but not real science. The more elaborate and fraudulent the better for most patients is my experience."

"But you are concerned with medical truth as well?"

"Of course I am and, in particular, I am very interested in the work of Guy de Chaulliac – a French physician. Have you heard of him?"

I shook my head.

"Well you should," the doctor continued dryly. "Sadly he died just over ten years ago. But he was an inspired innovator. And he believes that all doctors should get to know the human body at first hand - from the inside. He has written a beautiful book – the *Chirurgia magna*. It encourages doctors to 'dissect' the human body to investigate how it works in precise detail. But, of course, it is not easy to find the right bodies. And I am a novice in these matters. Most doctors are on this side of La Manche. But elsewhere it is different."

"So that was why the Brother Peter was mauled so badly? You'd not done anything like that before."

"Yes, that's right."

284

"And Brother Walter was, shall we say, much neater."

"He was. I learn quickly. From slitting and nipping Brother Peter I learned how not to do it. I did a much better job with Brother Walter."

"But why did you suggest that it was linked to the murder?"

"Well, you know this kind of work is controversial. I became flustered. Some people do not like it. The church does not like it at all in England. And even though I have shared this with you I should be grateful if you did not reveal this conversation to anyone else. Anyone at all. It could be disastrous for me."

"So why are you telling me?"

"Because I now know you better than when we first met. I can see that you are an honourable and intelligent man. You will understand why I did it."

"But why did you start on their most private parts? It looks, if you don't mind me saying so, suspicious at the very least."

"Exactly because, Sir Matthew, they are the most private parts. They are the source of life. They are the source of the greatest pleasure. So, of course, I was drawn to them first. I am fascinated by the whole of the body but given a very limited opportunity I went to the most extraordinary place of all from whence emerges both life and poison. And, to be entirely honest with you, I had some direct personal interest as well. I must to admit to you I have problems down there myself. I am, as I said to you, sick in that respect. I wanted to find an explanation to find out why."

This was a rare kind of conversation and I did not know how to take it forward. There was a lot to absorb. But I had to push on while the doctor was in this state of honest candour.

"Do you mind if I ask whether this 'problem' links to Madame Eglentyne and perhaps why you are not as intimate with her as you had hoped to be?"

"It's the other way round, Sir Matthew. It is why she is no longer friendly with me. But it grieves me deeply that she will not be friendly with me any more. And that is all I am going to say on the matter. I am sure you will understand – you are a gentleman after all."

"Just one last question though? How did news of the 'dissection' as you call it leak out. It was all over the abbey forecourt by mid-morning."

"I know. That was extremely annoying. It was not my intention at all. It was that pair of roughnecks. They were the ones apparently who had brought Brother Peter up to the infirmary after he had been killed. Somehow they managed to get into the Outer Court and just barged straight in to 'see how he was managing' as they put it. Getting on? He was dead for the sake of allah! Fortunately I wasn't working on Brother Peter at the time. They just saw the results of my very poor skills."

"And had you told people – like Brother Thomas – for example that you were not to be disturbed while you were doing it?"

"Yes, I told Brother Thomas particularly that no-one was to be allowed into the infirmary that morning. He didn't query it. He just accepted it. I think he likes to take orders from people in authority. And then to pass them on with impunity."

"Ha! And so that was why I was forbidden to go anywhere near Brother Peter's body on that morning."

"I'm afraid so. But really did it make much difference? Brother Peter was dead."

"Yes, that's what Brother Thomas said," I replied rather tersely because, in spite of myself, I was now becoming irritated by the doctor's professional self-righteousness. "But in the same way as you felt the need to investigate the corpse, Doctor, so did I."

"Yes, I understand that now."

"And then, as I remember it, you tried to throw me off-course by suggesting that maybe a woman had mutilated Walter's body because it was more neatly done."

Recollection of this clearly embarrassed him.

"I apologise for that. It was not right. To be honest I was feeling rather guilty about what I had done and did not want to be discovered. So I admit I tried to send you in the wrong direction."

"And how are you feeling about it now?"

"Hmm! I have been thinking about it – a lot – but I'm not feeling ashamed at all. Yes, I had my own motives but if medicine is to advance then doctors need to be allowed to understand properly how the body works. But this is just the start. Although I realise that is not a popular view. Which is why, as I said, I would prefer you not to mention it elsewhere."

I reluctantly agreed. I was sure that Damian and Osric would ask about it at some point. But I would worry about that when it happened.

"And tell me, Sir Matthew, have you now discovered the answer to your question. Who did it? Who was responsible for these murders?"

"No, I have not," I had to admit.

"And neither have I to my question. So we are in the same position. And now I really am tired. So good night. And your God be with you."

He opened the door to let me leave. I gave him a nod but then relented and gave him a sympathetic smile. He seemed to appreciate it.

And, one by one it seemed, the mysteries were being revealed. But how much further would we get the following day?

CHAPTER 48
'O cursed synne of alle cursednesse'

Later than I had intended I walked across to the main hall of the Tabard. It was becoming dangerously full with scores of men and a scattering of women starting to howl for more beer and wine. Some were Londoners but judging by their accents there were plenty of people from the provinces. I even saw a man who looked like a sailor up from the west country.

The hostelry was well-known as the start point for Canterbury from London so most of the guests were pilgrims preparing for departure over the next day or two. But the riotous drinking and entertainment was illustration enough that this was a period of holiday rather than Holy Days. The revels before a period of sober revelation? Well, maybe.

Through the good offices of Master Bailey I had reserved a small room off the main hall to meet Damian and Osric. By now it was approaching midnight and needless to say Damian was late. But I chatted with Osric and as usual he had ventured wide that evening. But he also had some worrying news.

"You don't have to go too far from this Bankside, lord, and you soon run into people up from Kent – and I tell you they are now seething."

"You mean this poll tax?"

"That's right," he replied grimly. "There are merchants and delivery men coming up on the Canterbury Road saying that they've seen massive discontent down there. And people coming through from Essex say the same. They simply can't pay the taxes being imposed on them. Why the government doesn't understand that I do not understand. Added to which there are now rebel priests going round stirring up trouble."

"What, like that couple of roughnecks at Hyde?" I asked.

"Maybe lord – but we couldn't quite pin those two down could we?

I had to agree.

"So who are they attacking now, these mobs? The king, I suppose?"

"Not that I heard, lord. They are blaming it all on clerics and administrators – people who sit in offices and never get their hands dirty."

"And the lawyers?" I suggested.

"Yes, definitely the lawyers. And they've got muscle behind them as well these rebels. There are a lot of veteran soldiers roaming around coming back from France where they've had a rough time. They've got no jobs, they've got no money. And when they see their families worried sick about this tax you are getting a very nasty situation steaming up. There's some wild talk about a march on London to see the king. And the place we are heading for, Canterbury, is probably the biggest hotspot of all."

I took what Osric said very seriously. He wasn't the sort of man to be alarmed without good cause.

"So do we go on?" I wondered. We both sat in silence pondering it.

"A bit quiet in here, isn't it?" announced Damian loudly and laughing as he swung into the room and slid onto the bench next to me. "I don't know about you two but I've just had an extraordinary evening!"

"Well, you seem remarkably sober for it," I said, pleased to be escaping anxieties about possible revolution. "I thought that you and your new best friend would go out and get utterly dunked on those groats from Madame Eglentyne."

"That was exactly what John did," Damian replied. "But I think I have a stronger head than he has and then, once he started talking, I knew I had to stay sober to take it all in."

"Really. So what was he saying?" I asked.

"We went to this place near the Bishop's Palace in Winchester Walk. There were quite a lot of Hampshire folk there and it was a nice atmosphere. Anyway, it seemed to loosen John up and after he'd had a few drinks it was almost as if he wanted to unburden himself to me. He said one or two things about who

290

his real mother was which was all very interesting." Damian glanced up and gave me a strange look. "But then he moved on to what the Franklin had told him earlier this afternoon after he'd arrived here at the Tabard. It seems that Sir Roger took him off for a welcoming drink somewhere."

"Yes, I noticed that," I said, pleased not to be hearing more about John's family history. "It all looked a bit conspiratorial."

"So, once John and the Franklin got drinking and talking the whole story about exactly what happened in the library poured out."

He stopped and glanced around him just to check there were no eavesdroppers.

"Really?" I asked, very surprised. "So what's the Franklin got to do with it?"

"It turns out that the two people who went into the library to look at the charter were, would you believe, the Franklin himself and, amazingly, Father Gregory."

I grunted with only mild surprise. I had suspected that when the truth came out it would involve some combination of the people we had seen in the abbey that day. And Father Gregory had always seemed a bit of a dark horse. Osric though seemed indignant.

"The Franklin! Why's he involved? He's a member of the parliament isn't he! He shouldn't be going round stealing things – or murdering people."

"Good point," I said. "I'm not too surprised about Gregory though because this evening Father Eynesham told me that he might have seen Gregory hanging around the library at the time of the murder. But to have him in league with the Franklin is not what I'd have expected."

"Well I'm not surprised," said Damian sounding worldly wise. "He seems to have his finger in every possible pie so it was almost predictable that he would be involved somehow in this."

"So did they kill Brother Peter?" I asked, "Did the Franklin admit that to John?"

"That's where it gets confused," began Damian. "Obviously

John asked him about that and the Franklin's story was that it was only after Father Gregory had lifted the cloth and checked that it was the Golden Charter that Peter arrived on the scene. The Franklin thought that he had come out of the small tucked away office area - completely drunk and immediately furious that these two strangers were in his library meddling with things. The Franklin said he gave Peter a polite apology and then made a quick get-away leaving Father Gregory to deal with him – and, presumably, to collect the Golden Charter as well. So he denies any knowledge of what happened next. Which means, I suppose, that the only person who knows exactly what happened is Gregory."

"And why was the Franklin telling John all this?"

"The way John told it, I think, was to make him more complicit in what had happened – binding him more closely into them. Having entrapped him into finding the charter for them in the first place they now seem to regard him as part of their gang. And therefore available again in the future."

"And so why would they want to do that?" asked Osric.

"It's all part of building up this massive network of underground supporters for the House of Lancaster apparently," explained Damian. "The Franklin is Gaunt's agent and recruiting officer for Hampshire and he had recruited Gregory about six months ago. And having already got a hold on John over the book thefts they feel that he's bright enough – and you might say devious enough – to have on the payroll for the long-term."

"Yes, if you are thinking a decade ahead," I said, "then you would very much want people like John – who might be a top man at Oxford or even a Bishop by then – on your side."

"And that's what they were talking about today?" asked Osric.

"That's right. The Franklin decided to take John into his confidence and lay out everything that happened – and their plans."

"And what are they exactly?"

"So the point about this Golden Charter is that it was given to the abbey – back as it was 400 years ago – by this king, Edgar, to ensure that it had independence and plenty of property for ever into the future. Now the Franklin – on behalf of Gaunt – would love to get his hands on the abbey for that reason. He wants all the lands and the power that goes with it. He thinks it's wasted on the lazy lumps of monks as he puts it."

"But as you say, this was all given to the abbey hundreds of years ago by the king," I said. "It seems that there's a picture of this king – Edgar – on the charter."

"Yes, but that's the point, father. The Duke believes that the time has come for the king today to reclaim powers which he thinks have been stolen by the church. He wants this King Edgar's powers to be taken back by King Richard. That's why the Franklin wanted to get his hands on the charter so that some expert lawyer here in London can look at it in detail. Then he can see if there is any get-out clause which they can use to reclaim everything which was handed over – buildings, lands, rights and so on. So tomorrow the Franklin and the lawyer are going to the court at Westminster with the charter to get an expert opinion."

"Well they've taken pretty drastic action to do that, haven't they? I'd have thought a simple request would have been enough."

"That's the interesting bit. Something like that would have to be approved by Bishop William – and they knew that in no way would William of Wykeham be prepared to be helpful or co-operate at all on anything which had Gaunt's interests behind it. So they decided to take it into their own hands. What they hadn't bargained on, of course, was having a drunk old man trying to stop them."

"So it's all up to the court - or rather the lawyers - then?" I asked. "That should sort it out."

"Apparently not. And this is where the Franklin made a big mistake in talking to John."

"Because?"

"The Franklin is just out to get results, father. He'll use the law if he can to keep it above board. But if not then he'll find an alternative way."

"Which is?"

"If the lawyer looks at the charter tomorrow and decides that the abbey's got total legal rights which cannot be retracted or challenged then the answer is..." He paused giving me a moment or two to work it out.

"Of course! It's obvious," I said sourly. "Just destroy the charter, deface or lose it. Then there's no way the abbey can protect itself. That's what Father Compton was talking about."

"That's absolutely right," said Damian. "They're going to destroy it – they told John as much," said Damian. "And that's where they made their big mistake. They underestimated him."

"You mean, John?"

"Yes, John, father. Although he's a devious little bastard – literally – he genuinely does love these books and these old manuscripts and so on," explained Damian. "I mean, you and I have never seen this Golden Charter but apparently it's very beautiful for those who like that sort of thing. There are sixty pages of it. So John was really shocked that they were just planning to burn it or tear it up. He reckons that it's just a wonderful and important book in its own right. He couldn't understand how they could be so brutal. So he now wants to save it."

"But maybe he was saying all this while he was drunk," I put in trying to be realistic. "How's he going to feel when he sobers up?"

"Yes, but in *vino veritas*," said Damian displaying a knowledge of Latin I found strangely touching.

"So what does he intend to do?"

"He wants to get the charter back come-what-may – and he wants us to help him."

"Oh, does he," I said sighing just a little. I was keen to get the charter back myself but when could I get this brat out of my hair?

"Father, it's an adventure. And right now, that's all I am interested in. Having adventures. And I've come round to liking John a lot. He's quite a character once you get over his irritating manners. And he's not in love with Avelina or anything. He was just saying that to wind me up."

I laughed both admiring his youthful innocence and being irritated by where it might take him – and me.

"Damian, I need a rather better argument than that for doing anything with John involved."

"Be realistic, father. I think John's the best hope you've got of getting justice and redeeming yourself. Think about Father Gregory – think what he probably did to Brother Peter. Collaborating with John is the best way forward to sort it all out."

Yes, I thought to myself, Damian was probably right. Unless Peter had suffered some bizarre accident in his drunken fit then Gregory was the murderer whether by intent or by accident. And he needed to be held to account.

"So you – or maybe John – definitely think it was Gregory who was responsible for the death?"

"That's right, father. I think it has to be. John says that the Franklin is a canny man. Although he'd planned all this he disappeared immediately Peter appeared on the scene so that he could not be implicated in any violence – this was not going to be a joint enterprise. He wasn't going to hang around to see what might have happened so that he could not be a witness. Moreover he left the charter for Gregory to take – he didn't touch it and he's got no intention of doing so. He had Gregory alongside him to do the dirty bits."

"I see, so he is distancing himself from the theft and anything else which might be seen as a crime," I said, now grasping the implications of their arrangement. "He's got a perfect denial."

"That's right. And the Sergeant is doing the same. He's going to read the charter, comment on it, advise on it but do nothing which might expose him to accusations of theft or damage. Or indeed being involved in any way. And in any case they are relying on this top lawyer in London at Westminster to make a judgement about it."

"So that if anything goes wrong it all falls on Gregory," I said. "He's the buffer between the Franklin and justice – in the unlikely event that justice ever turns up. And are you saying that Gregory's the one who has actually got the charter now?"

"That's right – the Franklin and the Sergeant won't touch it under any circumstances. So Gregory is bringing the charter up from Winchester – and they are expecting to meet him here in the Tabard by mid-morning tomorrow and then Gregory and the Franklin will take it across to Westminster."

How any of this linked up with Gregory's night in the church overseeing the corpses and then being knocked out during the theft of St. Josse I could not make out. But that would have to wait.

"And they've got this senior lawyer lined up to examine it and judge the scope of the Charter and how much protection it offers to the abbey?" I said.

"Yes – and then either they will use it in the courts or consign it to the flames," confirmed John. "And they plan to move fast at a time when the abbey hasn't got a proper abbot to stand up for it."

There was a pause in the conversation broken by Osric saying.

"Well I think it's simple – we just knock Gregory over the head tomorrow, grab the charter and it's all done."

"It's a tempting prospect," I said.

"Presumably father, you'd like Gregory to face justice for the murder of Peter and get the charter back for the abbey."

"Yes, that's right. Of course. But saying it is simple enough, Damian. Actually doing it – and dealing with the consequences afterwards is much more complicated. For a start if you and I take a stand and obstruct the Franklin then any hope you might have of becoming one of the Duke of Lancaster's knights would be over. But, really, given what we know about how Gaunt operates, would you want to be a supporter of his anyway?

"I suppose not," said Damian with his voice trailing away.

I felt for the boy. He wanted to shine but to do so he needed a patron. Riding under Gaunt's flag would have been perfect – except for the moral price he would have to pay. And who knows, maybe some years hence he would be part of a rebellion to put Gaunt himself – or more likely his son – on the throne.

Did I want that for Damian?

"My advice, Damian, is to put that offer out of your head. The first thing you must do, if you want to serve chivalry as a knight, is to keep your conscience clean and your loyalties clear. Signing up with Gaunt is unlikely to let you do either."

I said no more. As the reality of the situation hit home Damian became subdued. In the excitement of his evening he seemed to have overlooked that pursuing the adventure of recovering the charter could not be reconciled with serving Gaunt and his career. "You're right," he finally said in a low voice.

"Don't worry," I replied. "Before too long other opportunities will arise. You can serve the king – he's maturing rapidly. He'll make his mark. But that's enough for this night. We'll be up early in the morning. We'll meet with John. And we'll see just he keen he really is to thwart the ambitions of the Franklin and the Duke of Lancaster."

CHAPTER 49
'Suffiseth hym hir youth and hir beautee'

I slept remarkably well. No doubt the comfort of the bed in the abbot's mansion helped – and also that for the first time in several days I did not have to share with Damian and Osric with all their movements and noises. But I also had a strong feeling that the stresses and problems of the past week were about to come to a climax and conclusion. While today would be difficult I hoped to have resolution by supper time.

Following an early breakfast in an empty abbot's dining room I crossed the garden to the Inn. Making my way through the main hall – surprisingly clean and fragrant after last night's scenes of excess - I knew that John's room was upstairs next to Damian and Osric's. I knocked on his door hoping that his head would not be too sore from his drinking episode last night. Now, more than ever, we needed a sensible and honest discussion of what was to be done.

"Who's there?" came the groggy response.

"It's Sir Matthew, John. I'm sorry to come so early but I think we need to talk."

"Oh, alright!" he replied slightly grudgingly. "You better come in."

He was sitting up in bed and not quite as dishevelled as I had expected. Not for the first time I was struck by a similarity to Damian in his look if not in his physique.

"Good morning, John. Are you feeling well enough to talk? I hear that you had quite a night of it last night."

"Yes it was an outing and a half," he said. "Damian and I had a lot to talk about."

"Yes, so I gather. He told me about it. Very illuminating."

"Did he tell you everything?" John asked.

"I assume so," I replied, "but how am I to know?"

I held his gaze for a few moments expecting him to respond

299

but he said nothing. I realised it was a challenge to me.

"You can assume that I heard the full story about what happened in the library," I said, "and that you feel strongly about the need to recover – indeed, save - the Golden Charter from being destroyed. I respect that – I respect that a lot. And I am also assuming that we are agreed that it was almost certainly Gregory who killed Peter?"

"Agreed on both points – at least that's what Sir Roger told me. More or less. Assuming that is that one believes him."

I did not debate the finer points of that reply – we did not have the time.

"And you want our help in trying to regain the charter?" I said.

"I do because I don't think I can do it on my own. And also because I think you, Sir Matthew, want to see some justice done. But getting justice is difficult."

"That's right," I agreed. "I have a commission from Father Compton to recover the charter. You want to save the charter because you see intrinsic value in it. So we have something in common. And we need a plan. Have you had any ideas?"

"I have one or two – but you're the soldier. I'd like to hear what you have to say first." Amazing, I thought, youth deferring to age. What had come over him?

"Well, John, as I understand it, Gregory now has the charter and he will be probably arriving with it here at the Tabard around mid-day to meet up with Roger. And the pair of them will then be going across to Westminster so that this expert lawyer – whoever it is - can examine its provisions. And presumably the Sergeant is involved as well."

"So I was told."

"Now my yeoman, Osric, suggested just knocking Gregory on the head and running off with it."

"Not a good idea," he said. "Not neat enough. It would leave us looking ugly. And once you start a fight you don't know where it might lead"

"That's right," I said. "So we need something a bit more subtle.

Ideally, maybe extracting the charter from Gregory without him even noticing – if that were possible."

"That would be ideal," agreed John. "But I want to add in a couple of extra angles which would make success a lot more interesting, shall we say. Although pulling it off might be rather more difficult."

"Pulling it off at all is going to be pretty difficult!" I said. "Let alone adding in anything else. But...."

I paused. This was not perfect timing but it was probably the best chance I had.

"Before we go into all the details, John, there's something else – something else important and different - which I feel we need to talk about. You and I. And we need to talk about it now. Is that alright?"

I could see his mood change. I had his total attention. It was almost as if he had known this moment was coming. But then, in truth, he had planned it.

"I think I know what you are aiming at," he said calmly. "In fact, I'd prefer it if I started. Are you alright with that?"

This was a surprise. "Go ahead," I said.

"You might have noticed that Madame Eglentyne knows me quite well."

"Yes, I had seen that. She knows you a lot better than I had expected."

"And that sometimes she shows what might almost be called a maternal care for me."

"Indeed – it looked something like that. But I didn't know what to make of it."

"And the reason for that, Sir Matthew, simply, is that she is my mother."

Again he gave me one of those bright challenging looks. And I felt almost relieved by this confirmation of what I had, maybe, sub-consciously suspected ever since Madame Eglentyne has cross-questioned me about John on the first evening we met. Her concern about his fate went beyond general interest.

301

The way she looked at him was almost passionately intimate, no matter how much she tried to disguise it. But it was also directed at me. I thought back to my feelings at seeing her hair at dinner in Wintney.

"So do you want to tell me the story" I asked. "Or do you want me to tell you what I think it is."

"Alright, if you want to - you tell me," he said.

"I think your mother gave birth to you when she was about fifteen. It was out of wedlock, obviously. And it was the result of a silly, misguided encounter with a young man, about five years older."

"That's right," John said.

"Both your mother and the young man were full of romantic ideas. They had both read and heard far too much of the stories of King Arthur's Court and the Round Table – and particularly of Guinevere's love for Lancelot. And they had seen King Arthur's table in Winchester and that made it feel even more exciting but right."

"I didn't know that." said John.

"So, over this very short time, your mother and the young man were deeply in love," I continued. "And then, at no notice whatsoever, he was summoned to go to war. For complicated reasons he did not even have the opportunity to say good-bye. And then everything changed."

"Yes, that's one way of putting it," said John.

"And so, after that I imagine, your mother had to go off to have the baby in a friendly nunnery – and then the baby was taken away and given to foster parents in some obscurity."

"That's right, you've got it, almost all of it, I'm impressed," said John in a bald way. "But with the addition that my mother did not forget about her baby son but kept in contact with the family – very discreetly. And when the couple died she then came back to the area to join the community at Wintney Priory, to be a support to him and see him from time to time."

"That was fortunate," I said.

"Well, fortunately she is an exceptionally able woman and very good at making the right connections," John said firmly. "And her reputation was such that she rapidly became head of the house. And although, of course, nothing could be said to anyone they began to see quite a lot of each other – mother and child. Which has been wonderful. But nonetheless the experience does leave scars. And when, many years later, the father then re-appears on the scene it is complicated. Or at least the person whom my mother suspects is the father - but has not seen since she was fifteen when she barely knew him at all – so she can't be absolutely sure."

No words came from me. I went across and gave him a big hug. At first John was unresponsive but the touch then worked and he squeezed me briefly in reply. And then we separated and we sat looking at each other for some time weighing up what happens next.

"I need to see Madame Eglentyne this morning," I said eventually. "And we will work at it gradually – the three of us. And somehow Damian must be part of this as well."

"Fine," he said. "That will be good. It will be strange being the older brother but it will be good. I felt that last night."

After that initial curious closeness a distance descended between us. It was uncomfortable but was broken by John.

"So coming back to the matter of the Golden Charter," he said. And I felt relief. Here was something practical we could focus on together without the uncomfortable mess of more soul searching.

"You've gathered from Damian that I do care – care deeply - about this charter," he continued. "I don't want to see such a beautiful work of art destroyed. But that does not mean I am particularly interested in its legal status nor, frankly, Hyde Abbey. In fact, I should warn you that where Hyde Abbey is concerned I do not regard myself as a friend especially because of what I saw of it when I was younger. So I want you to be aware of that."

"But you are not out to destroy it, are you?" I asked, now

wondering whether John was another member of Prior Hugh's plot.

"I want what's just, that's all," said John. "And to protect beautiful books and manuscripts."

"I suppose I can't argue with that," I said. "So, what other thoughts have you had about getting hold of the Charter."

"Right, so this is how I see it," John replied switching completely into a businesslike tone. "There is a very strong likelihood that Gregory will be carrying the Charter in a satchel – just like the one you saw me with and I've got here now." He pointed to the leather bag at the end of his bed. "I know that he's got one just like this and equally new because mother bought two – one for him and one for me. He has his with him all the time and as you may have noticed I do the same."

This was the first time I noted that he called the prioress 'Mother' - it was a brief but striking moment.

"So she treats him rather like a son," I said. "That must be difficult."

"I really don't want to talk about any of that now," he said curtly. "But, if she did, she certainly doesn't any more I can assure you of that. She's been disabused of Gregory's whole fraudulent pious act. Can we move on?"

"Yes, of course," I said, reminding myself that whatever my new relationship I must not forget his prickliness. Maybe now more than ever.

"Somehow then we have to do a swap of my satchel for his," continued John. "And we need to do it at a time and place that he won't think to check it. A place and a time with lots going on."

"Yes, well given that we don't know quite when he's arriving or exactly what their plans are, we're going to have to play it by ear, aren't we?" I said.

"That's right – not easy" he agreed.

At this point I went back to my own plan.

"If Damian is prepared to go along with this then, between the two of you, it might be possible. The Franklin is keen to recruit Damian as one of the Duke's young knights. If Damian can stick close to the Franklin from the time Gregory turns up then it might be possible to pull off some kind of deception with you involved as well."

"That sounds a good start," John agreed. "But, as I said, there are one or two things I need to add."

"What exactly?"

"It's important for me that it's not just a bag swap. After we've made the switch over then it's vital that my satchel must still be taken to the court and opened up and the contents seen by this expert lawyer. And we need to get his view of it. So I need to be there."

What was this all about? Why all the extras?

"John, this sounds very complicated. It is going to be difficult enough without adding anything else. Surely it's best just to get the satchel and run."

"That would be a missed opportunity," he said.

"Well if you say so but I'm not sure I understand it. What's going to be in your satchel?"

"I will have bulked it out so that it has the feel of the Golden Charter but the document that they actually open – thinking it is the Golden Charter – will be the one you saw when you searched me back at Hyde Abbey."

"And the significance of that is?"

"Alright," said John reluctantly as if he was doing me a great favour. "I am only telling you this now because of, shall we say, our new relationship. And because this is just as important for me as the Golden Charter. Actually, more so."

"Fine, I understand. Go ahead."

"Hyde Abbey is not the only one relying on ancient charters for its rights," John began. "The more modest charter in my satchel belonged many years ago to Wintney Priory."

"I see," I said but still not seeing where this was going.

"But it was stolen – probably about two hundred or more years ago when the country was in a state of anarchy."

"Who by?"

"A long dead abbot from Hyde when he wanted to 'acquire' – you might say – a rich tract of land adjacent to the Priory. He stole the charter, hid it away, and pulled the wool over everyone's eyes to claim the land for Hyde. These rich fields, he said, belonged to them because they had also been given to the abbey by King Edgar. But of course they hadn't."

"And he got away with it?" I asked.

"He did indeed – and he and his successors have got away with it ever since, earning a nice rich income to boot for more than one hundred years. So much so that almost everyone had forgotten about it."

"Except, presumably, the prioresses of Wintney."

"That's right - it's been a bone of contention for centuries, passed on from one generation to the next. But there was nothing they could do about it without the original charter. They were sure it was held by Hyde Abbey somewhere but did not know where. So they stopped making a fuss about it."

"And then you found it?"

"That's right. By pure chance when I was looking for the Golden Charter I stumbled across it. Ironic really, isn't it. It must have been taken out of the locked store by accident by Abbot Pechy the last time he looked at the Golden Charter. And then Brother Peter, in his negligence, overlooked putting it back. So there it was. I knew of its significance from what mother had told me and I grabbed it. But it now needs endorsement from an independent lawyer. And that's what I hope we're going to get later today. In fairness to Hyde Abbey they did not destroy it. They might have done but they didn't. Probably because they knew that it could come in useful at some point in the future. It was just Brother Peter's carelessness which allowed me to find it. So if nothing else, I have that to thank him for."

"Maybe we both do," I said.

CHAPTER 50
'What nedeth it to sermone of it more?'

After leaving John's room I needed a little time to digest everything we had discussed – from his parentage to the immediate challenge of pulling off this satchel-exchange. It was all far too much to absorb and work out my feelings.

I do not want to dwell here on my emotions but they were consistent with the state of my conscience since I had quit the crusade. Here was another sin – a grave and mortal sin of neglect beyond bearing - to add to the list.

But meanwhile I had agreed with John that he would alert Madame Eglentyne that I wanted to speak with her. He would then wake Damian and Osric and give them a short account of what we had agreed regarding Father Gregory. We would then all get together at mid-morning.

After a little time of wandering around the private garden attached to the abbot's mansion I steeled myself for the interview with my former youthful, albeit brief, lover.

"Oh, Sir Matthew – how charming to see you," she said in a voice devoid of emotion as I entered the room. "I could say, what a surprise. But John told me that you might call by."

"Madame Eglentyne, thank you for seeing me... I'm afraid I don't know where to begin."

"Then don't," she said. "You and I both know what happened then and what has happened since. I am not sure there is much else to discuss in that respect. We were very silly. I was very innocent. You were older but very careless. Or maybe you would see it as romantic. And one of us paid a very heavy penalty for that. But fortunately we both survived and, in different ways, have enjoyed successful lives – although maybe not quite the ones we had envisaged. And we are now bonded together – lightly, I should emphasise – by our shared interest in John. I do not want to say or discuss anything beyond that. Are we agreed?"

"May I just say," I continued stumblingly, "that you are still very beautiful."

"That is kind of you," she said coldly, "but you will understand if I cannot return the compliment."

We looked at each other for a little while in silence. In due course she resumed.

"What we can usefully do, however, is consider how to deal with Father Gregory."

"Yes - yes certainly," I agreed both impressed and disappointed by her no-nonsense approach.

"I will admit that I made a mistake with Father Gregory. It was a very bad mistake but one I have a habit of making, misjudging young men," she said. "As you probably know our Franklin friend, Sir Roger Odiham, lives not too far from the priory and I saw him very occasionally. About six months ago I was in need of a further priest for the priory. He heard about this and he suggested Gregory. I was in something of a rush and he was a personable young man and so we took him on. But I had accepted him on trust – something I should not have done. As I now painfully realise."

"But just a few days ago you were saying how devout he was."

"Yes, well he was very convincing and I was very misled. As these last days at Hyde have revealed. But I was planning to have a confrontation with him when he rejoined us from Winchester after his injury in the church. Place before him some uncomfortable truths."

"So can you tell me what you have discovered?" I asked.

"Yes, I can but hardly know where to start. It seems that he is a fraud, a liar, a manipulative trickster – and, I fear, a murderer. That seems evident from what John learned from Sir Roger. He was not very complimentary about him, I gather. But he regarded him as a useful tool."

"And that was why the Franklin recommended him?" I asked. "He was nicely malleable?"

"Yes, that and because, as you have realised, the Lancaster

faction is placing its men everywhere they can to get a little bit of power and influence - even in our little priory. As you know, they have been trying to get their claws into John – and your Damian. Rector Lydezorde saw it in due course and warned me about him but I gave Gregory the benefit of the doubt. He came from a respectable family and appeared loyal."

"So what happened in Hyde?"

"Sister Avelina, my charming little assistant who speaks to everybody, gathered from Michael, the porter, that Gregory had latched on to Brother Walter's extra-curricular activities with the ladies of the town. He made an arrangement with Walter to enjoy the company of one of them – something which I gather that a number of Hyde monks do regularly. When he went to pay Walter he was amazed to see how much money the brother had amassed and greed overtook him – he wanted it. And he attacked Walter to get it."

"And how did Michael know this?"

"Well, Gregory told him apparently. But he didn't expect Michael to gossip about it to bright little Avelina."

"So what happened?"

"From what Michael told Avelina, Walter refused to hand over the money to Gregory who then cut him with a knife and just walked off with the monk's money bag. Gregory probably expected that Walter would be unable to complain since what he was doing was quite illegal. But of course Walter died from the wound anyway – and was then subjected by the doctor to that vile mutilation."

She shook her head in disgust.

"So you knew about that?"

"I certainly did," she replied. "At one stage the doctor and I were friends – but no longer."

"And then what happened?"

"Sister Avelina found the money bag when she went to Gregory's quarters before the funerals to check up on him after his assault in the church. He was still unconscious – or pretended to be - and simply hadn't bothered to conceal the bag properly. Michael had given her a description of the purse and it matched exactly. The money had all gone, of course, but the purse was there."

"And Michael knew the purse, presumably because he saw it every time he crossed over to get a pay-out from Walter," I said trying to keep up. "But he wasn't going to tell the authorities because that would then incriminate him in Walter's dirty little business.

"I imagine so."

"And do you think that Gregory was also party to the theft of the St. Josse relics?"

"I don't know – but it would not surprise me," she said.

"And who do you think was behind that?"

"I have no evidence but I do have my suspicions."

"Who?" I asked impatient now.

"I said, I have no evidence. If I have evidence then I will tell the appropriate authorities. However, I do not think that you fall into that category."

Put in my place but now reeling from all these disclosures I decided to turn back to the pressing problem of how to secure the Golden Charter.

"So do you think that Gregory knows that you have now seen through him?"

"I doubt it. Sister Avelina just left the money bag where it was. He has no reason to think that he has been caught out. Indeed, without the quick wit of Avelina he would not have been. Although I must say my suspicions had been growing. He just seemed too good to be true. His devoutness was becoming, frankly, unbelievable."

"But you did not confront him? Because you still found him charming?"

She did not respond. So I continued thinking through how events might work out.

"If Gregory has not realised that he is under suspicion then

310

presumably he and the Franklin have worked out some explanation as to why they need to go across to Westminster together especially as Gregory has only just arrived. It will sound a bit odd, I suppose but I expect they think it will satisfy you.

"I am used to being underestimated." she said.

"Now John has proposed a switch of their identical satchels before Gregory departs with the Franklin to Westminster. Of course that depends on Gregory actually having the Charter in the satchel in the first place. It is possible but not guaranteed. So maybe once he arrives you insist – absolutely insist – that John inspects him. Say that he's been studying some physick at Oxford and knows what to check up on. Say that you will only let him go once you're reassured that he has recovered from his wounds and bruises. And then when he's taking off his clothes Damian can do the switch. Would that work do you think?"

"Possibly. And, remember also, John will have to insist that he wants to accompany them to see this lawyer in Westminster," continued Lady Eglentyne, "so that when our stolen charter is revealed John can get the lawyer's view of it. It's the only way we can get the opinion of a top, independent authority."

"That could be a bit tricky," I said and my anxieties seeped back about trying to do too much. Keeping things simple is normally best in my experience. This extra dimension might ruin the whole plan.

"I think John told you about the other charter - our charter – and how important it is, didn't he?"

"He did – but you might have told me about it earlier."

"Well, it's a matter of trust isn't it, Sir Matthew?" she responded pointedly.

"So do you think I should be present at all?" I asked in a fit of pique.

"On further reflection, having come up with this plan, I don't think your presence will be necessary, Sir Matthew – but it would be good if Damian could be there to whisk the Golden Charter away once we had hold of it."

I bridled at the view that my involvement would not be required – but Damian's would!

"Of course, I will do as much - or as little - as is helpful, Madame Eglentyne."

I then turned and walked away feeling much irritated and discontented. She might be the mother of my newly-discovered son and he might be a clever little imp, but let them get on with it. The plan was too complicated, I was now sure. It wouldn't work. They would make a mess of it. And I was glad that I was not part of it.

CHAPTER 51

'God be with you, where you go or ryde!'

With a plan now agreed between them Madame Eglentyne, Sister Avelina and the two boys busied themselves fine-tuning the arrangements. Rector Lydezorde, I noted, seemed to have absented himself entirely having found, no doubt, better things to do elsewhere in London.

Osric and I felt completely unwanted so we indulged ourselves drinking morosely in the Tabard's snug bar while still casting an occasional eye towards the front door for Father Gregory's arrival.

Mid-day and then lunchtime came and went with no sign of him. Madame Eglentyne and Avelina retired to the Abbot's mansion and Damian was delegated to stay on watch while John would alert them as soon as Gregory arrived.

And so the early afternoon wore on. I was also aware that the Franklin had not appeared all day. Should I go across to the mansion and check his whereabouts? No, that might give the game away.

And then Harry Bailey appeared as hale and hearty as ever. "Good afternoon, Sir Matthew I hope you are enjoying your stay in London. Have you yet sampled the delights of the Bishop's Soke?"

"Thank you, Harry, yes it's all very satisfactory," I said in as genial a tone as I could muster. "I think I am a bit too old for some of those Southwark delights unfortunately but I am certainly enjoying my bed in the Abbot's mansion."

"Ah well," he said, "whatever might be happening in Hyde we do aim to maintain our standards here."

"Indeed. Tell me Harry have you seen your friend Roger this morning? There were a couple of things I wanted to talk to him about – slightly urgent."

"Ah, the good Franklin! He's a busy man Sir Matthew. Ambitious man. I saw him leaving from the back of the mansion not so long ago. We have a rear entrance, a bit concealed, it's a short-cut to the river and the bridge."

"Oh, right," I replied feeling a little stunned. "You don't happen to know where he was going by any chance?"

"Westminster, I think he said. Something to do with the courts?"

"That sounds quite possible," I said as calmly as I could. "I look forward to seeing you again later this evening."

"Excellent!" he said. "I'm expecting a full house for tonight – it should be a merry time for all."

I smiled but only to hide by anxiety.

So it seemed there was not going to be a meeting here at the Tabard. No rendez-vous between the Franklin and Father Gregory. Of course, once you thought about the arrangement, it made much more sense to go direct to the courts and meet Gregory there. I started to worry. Had John been deliberately fed a line by the Franklin to fool or distract him – and maybe us? Whatever the truth I had a strong and urgent instinct that we needed to get across to Westminster as soon as possible.

"Osric, come with me – we're going to Westminster now."

"Yes, lord. What about Damian?"

"Leave him here with John – just in case I've misjudged what's happening. But from what Harry has just said I am sure that Gregory has gone direct to meet the Franklin at the courts."

Being aware that time was now of the essence I was in two minds whether I should explain to John and Madame Eglentyne what I was doing. But that would waste time. I now wanted to get to Westminster as fast as possible and not get into complicated discussions. But at least I felt I should tell them that we were leaving.

I went into the Tabard's hall to where I had last seen John. He was not there but Avelina was, having returned to the inn. She was sitting patiently holding John's satchel. As calmly as possible I approached her.

314

"Avelina, could you tell John and Madame Eglentyne that Osric and I have had to go out. Good luck. We'll see you later on this evening."

She looked rather surprised but acknowledged me with a serious nod. Obviously the tension was getting to her as well. And then curiosity overwhelmed me.

"Could I just quickly look at the satchel?"

Without waiting for a response I reached out and withdrew it from her hands. She looked put out when I then opened it and saw within the single piece of parchment packed full with ancient writing wrapped around a block of other papers.

Entirely without any justification I pulled out the charter and announced.

"If you don't mind, Avelina, I'll have this – just for a short time."

"Give it back, Sir Matthew," she cried.

"I'm so sorry but I must have it – just for a while – besides, John says it is of no value whatsoever."

And then I dashed off – feeling guilty but also, for no good reason, convinced that I was carrying the trump card. Taking the back exit, Osric and I were swiftly out of the Tabard and heading for London Bridge.

Being the age I was I could not run as I did when aged twenty. But, as best we could, Osric and I pushed our way through the dense crowd and past the packed shops hanging over the Thames. Once on the north bank we turned west into Ropery. There was no scope for talk. We just huffed and dodged our way through a mass of Londoners. I was feeling hot, anxious and remembered that my youth, when I had first met Madame Eglentyne, was now a long time ago.

"Osric, you're in much better shape than I am. You go on. And I'll follow as fast as I can."

"But, lord, I don't know where we're going!"

"Just keep straight ahead. When you reach the city wall go out thorough Ludgate and follow the river. It takes you to

Westminster and the courts there. They should be obvious. Or ask someone. Then look out for the Franklin and for Gregory. Use your initiative. Keep an eye on them – and intervene if you think they are going to do something desperate."

"Like what, lord?"

"Like tearing up the manuscript."

For a man who was usually self-assured in his own way Osric looked distinctly nervous. He would be alone in the hostile city.

"Off you go," I said. "Be quick! I'll follow on as fast as I can,"

He ran off looking very much like countryman come to town. I suddenly lost confidence and felt that I had probably done the wrong thing. But at least if I had miscalculated John and the rest of them were still at the Tabard and they might still be able to pull off the satchel switch.

I now hastened along as best I could. While still an able horseman I realised that walking had become almost a lost art. My legs were soon aching and and my bunions were almost unbearable.

The worry also increased that maybe Westminster was not the Franklin's destination. Maybe he had deliberately told both John and Harry Bailey that in order to mislead. Possibly he had fed John a lengthy rigmarole to send him off in the wrong direction. But if he was not going to Westminster then where would he go?

Of course! The Savoy Palace, John of Gaunt's lavish residence on the Strand. As one of the Duke's men that would be a natural place to do business. How I might gain entry there I had no idea. But with Osric covering off Westminster it would be a better use of my time to try my luck there – and besides it was a lot closer.

By this time I was a little way down Flete Street having crossed the Flete stream. This had flooded with the April rains so it was unpleasant to push my way through the water which now seeped into my boots.

Squelching along I was wondering how both Osric and John and Damian were doing. Maybe it was already all over and my efforts were all for nothing.

The end of Flete Street was starting to loom and I recognised that I was approaching the Temple. With a terrible judder I realised that my latest brilliant intuition of the Savoy Palace was probably completely wrong. If the Franklin was going to have a consultation with a lawyer then it would be much more likely to be here in the Temple than in the courts of Westminster or at the Savoy Palace. What a fool I was!

So rather than continuing on westwards I swung off Flete Street down Temple Lane and towards Temple Church. And with a mix of walking and almost skipping I thrust my way through pockets of advocates standing chatting in the narrow lane. Why couldn't they move, get out of the way, instead of straddling the public highway? All I could do was utter a small prayer to St. Josse to steer me in the right direction – after all he was the patron saint of pilgrims.

The good saint did not let me down. To my amazement and joy there, standing outside the main door of the fine Temple church, was the Franklin accompanied by three other men. I stopped and stood back to see what would happen.

They were in deep conversation. The Franklin was being deferential to a larger, younger man who seemed to carry great authority. Despite his relative youth he was presumably the expert lawyer whose counsel they needed. The two other men still had their backs to me. One I guessed was the Sergeant and as he turned his head slightly this was confirmed. The fourth I imagined had to be Gregory but even from behind his profile did not look quite right. He was certainly carrying a large bag which he now started to open. But this was no satchel of the type that John had.

"Can I help you at all? You seem to be rather lost."

The firm voice with a pronounced London accent broke into my concentration on the Franklin and his friends.

With some irritation I turned to see who it was. "You seem to be taking an interest in Master William Gascoigne over there." he gestured towards the impressive young man. "May I enquire why? Are you a client of his?"

Caught a little off balance all I could reply was. "I may well be – I will be talking to him shortly."

"I see," he replied rather suspiciously. "We do have to be careful of strangers here, you see. We do have a lot of mad people trying to talk to our lawyers."

Feeling a mite offended I went on the attack. "And who might you be?" I asked in my most polite but firmest tone.

"I am the manciple here to this Inn," he responded, now vigorously, "and I take it on myself to ensure we do not have any disreputable types or deadbeats wandering at will around the precincts."

As he said this he made a slight gesture towards my admittedly tarnished tunic. But at this point my attention was drawn back to the book - which I imagined to be the Golden Charter – being passed across to this Master Gascoigne and which he began to study intently, making comments every now and again.

To get rid of this manciple I turned to him and said, "My name is Sir Matthew de Somborne and I have come a long way from Hampshire with great urgency to see Master Gascoigne about a very important matter concerning my friend, the Duke of Lancaster, and his hunting lodge which neighbours my own estate. I am afraid that I really must not be disturbed."

The mention of the name of the Duke of Lancaster combined with my adoption of a highly arrogant tone had an impact. He looked at me for a moment longer. The cockney was briefly intimidated by the country gent with the look of a soldier. Then he nodded his head and walked away.

I turned back immediately to see what was happening with the Golden Charter.

The four of them had not moved but the face of the Franklin suggested that he was not hearing good news. The Sergeant's features, which I could now see in detail, remained immobile. The fourth man, now definitely looking slimmer and smaller than Gregory, still had his back to me.

As the minutes wore on it was clear that the Franklin had not received the verdict he wanted. His face had drooped and was sour. He exchanged one of two observations with the Sergeant who expressed sympathetic looks but said little. The lawyer, Gascoigne, was bringing things to an end. He offered the document to the Franklin. He, like the Sergeant, declined to accept it pointing instead to the fourth man.

This, I thought, was my moment to strike. I walked smartly across and with as much confidence as I could muster I commanded, "Gentlemen, I am sorry to disturb your meeting but I must insist that you give that document to me so that I can return it to the acting abbot of Hyde Abbey. He has asked me to do so and I am sure that you will have no reasonable objection! I am acting under his authority."

The fourth man turned round.

It was Brother Thomas.

But of course – he was the Judas! Suddenly it all fell into place. The Duke of Lancaster's influence was everywhere - even seducing those whose loyalty should have been unquestionably to William of Wykeham or Prior Hugh. But a snake in the grass like Brother Thomas would be more than happy to act for both sides if it was in his own interests. And as Father Compton had said, Thomas's only allegiance was to himself.

I seized the Golden Charter and adopted that warrior stance wanted by Madame Eglentyne with my hand clearly on my dagger. The two lawyers quickly indicated that they wished to remove themselves from this awkward transaction.

"Gentlemen, I think I will leave you to resolve this little interruption between yourselves," said Gascoigne.

"I think I better leave you as well," said the Sergeant. "I have another appointment to keep at St. Paul's."

"Certainly – but just before you go," I said to William Gascoigne. "would you kindly take a look at this document and give me your first impression."

He looked pained but accepted the parchment I had extracted

319

from John's satchel earlier.

After a few seconds he handed it back with mild boredom. "It's very straightforward," he said. "About two hundred years old. A man of whom I have never heard, Geoffrey FitzPeter, giving extensive land in Hampshire to a Cistercian convent in which I have no interest, Wintney Priory, in perpetuity. Only the usual conditions – endless, futile prayers for the sanctification of his no-doubt wretched soul. Still valid, of course. Is that what you want?"

And with that he turned very smartly on his heel and walked away briskly with the Sergeant in tow. I had no reason to detain them.

I turned to Brother Thomas. "It was you, wasn't it! You murdered poor drunk Peter when he surprised you and Sir Roger in the library. And then you probably did the same to Walter when he wouldn't hand over his ill-gotten gains from the prostitution racket. And to make things worse you very cleverly framed Gregory for it – the man least likely to have done it then became the most likely."

"And you," I said turning to the Franklin, "you're the one behind it all. Manipulating everything in sight, weaving people like Michael and Thomas and John and no doubt others into your web. Well, not any more you're not."

"I don't know that you are talking about," said the Franklin. "I haven't touched this document and I certainly know nothing about any murders. And you, Sir Matthew had better be prepared to face the wrath of the Duke of Lancaster."

Alongside him Brother Thomas was shaking. Guilt was all over his face.

"What should I do, Roger? What should I do?"

"Get out, boy – go, go, go," the Franklin hissed."Now!"

Thomas turned on his heels and sprinted off. I made a pathetic attempt to follow but with the two charters in my hand and aching legs and sore feet I was not going to catch him. And when I stopped and turned round Roger Odiham, the Franklin and Member of Parliament, had disappeared.

POST-SCRIPT

I trudged back painfully from the Temple to the South Bank.

I was pleased to have rescued the Golden Charter but frustrated that the murderous scoundrel Brother Thomas, whom I had disliked from the moment we met, had slipped through my fingers.

My best guess was that he would have scampered westwards to the Savoy Palace and had found a hole within for refuge. Little chance of prising him out from there. Or maybe he would just disappear entirely into the squalid back lanes of the City.

And as to the Franklin and the Sergeant, I could not see how they could be successfully prosecuted for any crime – especially with the might of John of Gaunt behind them. As the poet Langland proclaims,

"The baron, by scattering handfuls of bright gold coins, bore down most of the judgement and wisdom of Westminster Hall. For he need only trot up to a judge and tilt at his ear with a few words, like "Take this, my good man. And let the matter drop'- to unhorse all his honesty."

But at least I now knew what had happened even if I could see little scope for justice being secured. But the abbey would have regained its Golden Charter to guarantee its future. And the Prioress would have her charter too so she could regain the land stolen by Hyde Abbey. Enough to be satisfied with then.

Walking back very slowly dusk had fallen by the time I arrived at the Tabard. An increasing number of pilgrims were arriving and I could see that it would, indeed, be a full house this evening. If nothing else I was starting to look forward already to my comfortable bed.

Entering the Tabard I was greeted warmly by Mistress Alison who has been making her way only slowly from Basyng with her pack mules weighed down by bolts of cloth. "It's good to see you and a pleasure to be here at last," she declared in her friendly way. "What a journey I've had of it though," she declared, "so fortunate though that I've had the support of Luke and Piers over there – a bit rough but such nice men. They're brothers, you know. Luke's a priest and Piers a ploughman, they tell me. Or maybe it is the other way round. Anyway I must get on."

I glanced across. Were they the two roughnecks who kept on popping up everywhere in Hyde and elsewhere? I was too tired to pursue it.

Damian and Osric, John and Madame Eglentyne were nowhere to be seen. I felt bad about Osric. I hoped that he was not still waiting about in Westminster in the vain hope that the Franklin and Gregory would turn up.

Tired as I was I felt badly in need of a drink and I retired to the little snug bar off the main hall. "Had a good day, Sir Matthew?" asked Harry Bailey. Enjoyed the sights, I hope?"

I smiled wanly at him. "Yes, quite satisfactory," I said. "By the way, any sign of Sir Roger."

"No, not so far – but I'm sure he'll be back soon. We're going to have a big crowd in tonight. Pilgrim season really picking up now. Can I get you anything?"

"Yes, please – a large one."

"Righty-oh."

I collapsed onto the bench, clutching the two charters closely to my breast. I was feeling very much in need of some sleep and was actually about to doze off when I was shaken awake.

"Well look who we have here then, his lordship himself!"

It was Osric beaming at me – I had never seen him so forward and full of laughter in the face. And then I realised that behind him were all the others linked in glorious expectation.

"Osric! You're here! Excellent! I'm so pleased you've got back in one piece."

"And we're delighted to see you safe and sound too, Sir Matthew," said Madame Eglentyne solicitously. "We've been stuck here worrying about you for hours! But what about the charters?"

I was now coming to myself again.

"Well, I am delighted to say I've regained the Golden Charter. Look – it's here! I've got it back – it's a long story." I waved the

322

Golden Charter in the air and some of the other guests looked over to see what was going on. "And I've also still got this one," I said, holding up the single piece of parchment from John's satchel and the five of them started to clap and I felt embarrassed. "It's been confirmed by a top Temple lawyer as legitimate," I announced. "The land is yours!"

"Thank Saint Loy for that," cried Madame Eglentyne and tears sparkled in her eyes.

"But what about you, Osric? What happened at Westminster?" I asked.

"He's the real hero of the hour," announced Madame Eglentyne. "I've appointed him my next miller."

"He's my knight for today!" said Sister Avelina.

"He's our saviour," declared Damian.

"He's the best father I never had," shouted John.

There was laughing around the group. Obviously something huge had happened!

"Tell me, Osric! Quick!" I said.

"Well, lord, as you would have guessed, I had no luck at Westminster Hall. I've never seen such a bunch of rogues – the lawyers being the worst. Or maybe it was the judges. But it was all confusion. And so after a while I gave up. I started walking back the way I had come. Then just as I got to the start of Flete Street that little whipper-snapper, Brother Thomas of all people, suddenly ran out from a side passage into the road. It was as if he was on fire and full of fury, dashing through the crowd. And he crashed straight into me – BANG!"

Osric clapped his hands loudly.

"He recognised me in a flash and shouted something I cannot repeat in front of Madame Eglentyne. We tumbled on to the ground and he clearly seemed to think that I was actually there waiting for him on purpose – to arrest him! So that's when he tried to attack me with a knife – the same knife as he probably used to kill Walter. Well, this time he did it to the wrong person, I can assure you. It was very easy to disarm him and get him in an arm lock – and apply a bit of pressure. He was pathetic. He began to whimper. But after that I didn't know what to do. But there were a lot of witnesses, passers by and several of them said I should take him before a magistrate. They asked me where I was staying and when I said the Tabard they said 'Simple – take him back across the river and hand him over to the Clink'. They told me where it was – over the bridge and turn right – and that's what I did."

"And did he tell you anything about what had happened?" I asked.

"Tell me? Huh, as we marched along – him with his arm locked behind his back and me asking questions he spilled it all out. Every single detail of it. Murdering little bastard. He killed Peter and Walter alike. He admitted it – at least he did after a bit of heavy encouragement. Peter's death was a bit of an accident, he claimed. But Walter's was deliberate – he slashed him to steal his money bag. And then he dropped the empty bag in Gregory's room to suggest that he'd done it. And he gave the nod to his mate Michael to spread it around. He just poured it all out – guilty conscience, I suppose. Mind you, he was blaming everything on other people and I suspect that he's hoping his powerful friends will get him out of it somehow. Benefit of clergy and all that. But it will take some time, I hope. Let him rot there in the Clink."

"Well the Clink's not the nicest place in London, I can assure you Osric," said Madame Eglentyne, "But what I hate so much was how I was so misled over poor Father Gregory. They told me he was wicked and I believed them! But he really is as good as he appeared. I feel dreadful that I doubted him. But the way that evidence was planted in his room – that purse of Walter's – when he was feeling so ill and the allegations made against him were absolutely outrageous! I think that the Franklin wanted him at Wintney so he could have an agent to spy on us. But Gregory wouldn't co-operate – and that's when they turned against him."

"And Rector Lydezorde? You said he warned you against Gabriel."

"Hmm," snorted the abbess. "I'm going to have to think about

324

our rector. Maybe he's not quite what he seems either."

"Don't forget Madame Eglentyne," I said, "I've still got this for you!"

Madame Eglentyne's eyes lit up again.

"Oh, yes, that's all I need!" she exclaimed with some excitement.

"So you showed it to the lawyer?" she asked.

"I did indeed. A Mr William Gascoigne, a bit snooty but seemed to know his stuff."

"Gascoigne!" she said. "Well, they certainly knew to go to the top person. And what did he say?"

"All very straightforward, was his remark. The charter was given two hundred years ago by a Geoffrey FitzPeter to confirm the donation of extensive lands in perpetuity to the Cistercian convent of Wintney Priory. All you have to do is say some prayers for his soul."

"I think we might be able to manage that," she replied dryly. "But that's absolutely marvellous, marvellous. Thank you Sir Matthew - that makes up for so much! I might not be the purest prioress in Wintney's history but I am certainly one of its most righteous."

At that her son and my son started to cheer and Sister Avelina leaned over to give her a big kiss. Tears were now falling in abundance.

"So we got there in the end despite our cunning plan not working out," said Damian.

"Well, I'd been completely deceived by the blasted Franklin," said John. "He certainly told me a convincing story – and I believed every word of it. The meeting at the Tabard with Gregory, going to Westminster, meeting a lawyer there - the lot of it, all a web of lies."

"I think it was a kind of test, John," said Damian. "Don't blame yourself too much. But it's certainly a warning to me. I won't be listening to his blandishments again".

"And neither will I," said Madame Eglentyne. "So first thing tomorrow morning I will go along to the Bishop's palace and set things in motion with what we've now proved is my charter! And, if you remember Sir Matthew, you agreed at Wintney that you would accompany me and lend me your moral support."

"Indeed, I did Madame," recalling my evening in the priory which already seemed a lifetime away.

"So I can rely upon you – now and in the future, may I?" she asked with a very ambivalent look on her face.

"Madame Eglentyne, I can assure you of my undying support from now on," I replied.

"In that case," she said, "by this time next year we will have secured the land and, I intend, many, many years worth of compensation as well. We'll see how Father Eynesham likes that when he becomes abbot – which I assume he will soon. We'll stop his hunting across the meadows for a start. It's strictly forbidden anyway by St Benedict."

"And you always follow the rules don't you, Madame Eglentyne?"

I couldn't resist saying teasingly.

"I always follow the rules in my own convent, Sir Matthew, because I am the one who makes them."

We all started to laugh but our laughter was soon drowned out by a bellowing from the hall. It was Harry Bailey.

"Now, lordynges, trewely," he declared. *"Ye been to me right welcome, hertley; For by my trouthe, if that I shal not lye, I saw not this year so merry a company in this Inn as is now. You're off to Canterbury. Well, God speed. But I've just come up with an idea for some fun for you and it will cost you nothing..."*

He continued speaking but Damian pulled my sleeve and whispered in my ear. "Father, we still don't know who stole the bones of St. Josse."

"Tomorrow, Damian. That can wait until tomorrow."

THE END ...
..... but look out for the sequel 'Swear by the Saint'

CHARTER FOR MURDER –
THE HISTORICAL CONTEXT

GEOFFREY CHAUCER (1340s – 1400) is best known as the author of *The Canterbury Tales* although he also wrote many other poems. His primary career, however, was as a senior civil servant and diplomat having been a soldier in his early years. He became closely associated with John of Gaunt who, at the end of his life, married Chaucer's sister-in-law. It is likely that he started to put together his ideas for the Tales and the Pilgrims around 1380/81.

CRUSADING

By the mid-14th century the geographical reach of crusading had reached far beyond the Middle East. Chaucer makes clear that his **Gentil Knight** had fought from one end of the Mediterranean to another and also in north eastern Europe into Russia and Lithuania on behalf of the Teutonic Knights. There is also a suggestion that he might have acted, effectively, as a mercenary on behalf of Islamic rulers - so his crusader credentials are by no means uncompromised.

HYDE ABBEY was a Benedictine monastery which opened in 1110 on a site immediately beyond the north walls of the City of Winchester. It was the successor establishment to the **New Minster** which occupied a central location and had been commissioned by the Anglo-Saxon king, Edward the Elder, as a dynastic mausoleum and centre of learning. Alfred the Great and several of his descendants were buried there and all were translated to Hyde in 1110 along with a great library, a collection of famous relics and other treasures. (The original site of New Minster can be seen today immediately to the north of Winchester Cathedral).

Thanks to extensive royal patronage, New Minster was endowed with extensive landholding rights across central southern

England. Similarly, from the 10th century onwards, New Minster/ Hyde Abbey attracted donations of important relics including notably the skull of St. Valentine and the bones of St.Josse (or Judoc), a much revered Breton saint.

There were on-going tensions between Hyde Abbey and the nearby Winchester Cathedral, the seat of Bishop William of Wykeham, which had its own monastic traditions. By the late 14th century Hyde seems to have been in a state of organisational decline and underwent a series of critical 'visitations' by representatives of the Bishop which exposed deep breaches of the Rule of St. Benedict as well as general lax management. It is these reports which have inspired the depiction of the abbey in *Charter for Murder*.

WINTNEY PRIORY was established around 1150 and is believed to be the first Cistercian house for women in England. It was founded with the backing of local grandee Geoffrey FitzPeter and although it held property both in Winchester (a mill and land) and elsewhere it was never wealthy. The Prioress of Wintney was named on at least four occasions as being involved in court cases involving land holdings.

Although the Cistercians were notionally committed to a strict discipline Wintney became notorious for its laxity around the time of *Charter for Murder*. Its Prioress in the 1380s, Alice Fyshide, was regarded as 'unfit for office'. She provides the inspiration for Madame Eglentyne. (For more read the fascinating accounts in the excellent *Hampshire Convents (Phillimore) by Diana K. Coldicott*).

On July 22 1536 the priory was suppressed although by this time its reputation was much restored. In common with Hyde Abbey, most of the priory's buildings were soon demolished.

THE GOLDEN CHARTER OF KING EDGAR (reigned 959– 975) was given to **New Minster** in 966, probably on the orders of Bishop Æthelwold, in order to secure the independence and rights of its new monastic community. The charter is presented in the form of a book written entirely in gold. Its text, written in gold letters with over 60 pages, records King Edgar being prepared to protect the community of the New Minster from any threats or interference by other clergy. When New Minster was demolished in the early 12th century the charter was taken by the monks to their new home in Hyde. The Charter is now held in the British Library. See *https://www.bl.uk/collection-items/new-minster-charter#:*

THE TABARD was well-known as an inn for pilgrims departing London for Canterbury and hence its selection by Chaucer as the start point for his Prologue. It was acquired by the Abbot of Hyde in 1307 and remained in the abbey's possession until the dissolution of the monastery in the late 1530s. Harry Bailey, identified as the landlord by Chaucer in the Prologue was an historical figure and a well-known London character.

JOHN OF GAUNT, DUKE OF LANCASTER (1340 – 1399) is probably best known to the general public for his death scene in Shakespeare's *Richard II*. As the uncle of the king he had played a vital role in maintaining the stability of England when his nephew came to the throne aged just 10 in 1377. However, he was hugely ambitious and was hostile to the wealth of the church and saw it as a rival power to the state's authority. This led him to show sympathy for John Wycliffe and his Lollard followers until the Peasants' Revolt exposed them as radical opponents of the Establishment. His son, Bolingbroke, deposed Richard II and took the throne as Henry IV in 1399.

WILLIAM OF WYKEHAM (1320 - 1404) was Bishop of Winchester from 1366 and, intermittently, Chancellor of England. He founded New College, Oxford, and New College School in 1379, and established Winchester College in 1382. He was highly effective as an administrator but he faced great difficulties in funding the wars with France. Although initially friendly with

John of Gaunt the two men subsequently became enemies and rivals.

**For more on the historical context of the
Gentil Knight series go to the website**
The World of the Gentil Knight
www.gentilknight.co.uk